Praise for Lois Greiman

"Dangerously funny stuff."—Janet Evanovich

"Lois Greiman delivers."—Christina Dodd

"Greiman's writing is warm, witty, and gently wise."
—Betina Krahn

And for

UNZIPPED

"Fast and fun, with twists and turns that will
keep you guessing. Enjoy the ride!"
—Suzanne Enoch, *USA Today* bestselling
author of *Flirting with Danger*

"Amazingly good . . . Chrissy's internal thoughts are
hilarious, as are the situations she gets herself into. Plus,
the sexual tension between Chrissy and Rivera spices
things up but never detracts from the pacing. Greiman has
put out a winner that will hopefully become a series."
—*Romantic Times* (Top Pick!)

"Move over, Stephanie Plum and Bubbles Yablonsky, to
make way for Christina McMullen. . . . The chemistry
between the psychologist and the police lieutenant is so
hot that readers will see sparks fly off the pages."
—Best Reviews

Also by Lois Greiman

UNZIPPED

Unplugged

Lois Greiman

A DELL BOOK

UNPLUGGED
A Dell Book / March 2006

Published by Bantam Dell
A Division of Random House, Inc.
New York, New York

This is a work of fiction. Names, characters, places, and incidents
either are the product of the author's imagination or are used
fictitiously. Any resemblance to actual persons, living or dead,
events, or locales is entirely coincidental.

ISBN-13: 978-0-440-24263-5
ISBN-10: 0-440-24263-0

Printed in the United States of America
Published simultaneously in Canada

www.bantamdell.com

10 9 8

*To Caitlin Alexander, the only editor
who thinks I'm as funny as I think I am.
Thanks for everything you do.
You're the greatest.*

1

Matrimony and firefighting. They ain't for cowards.

—Pete McMullen,
shortly after his first divorce

You MARRIED?"

I hadn't known Larry Hunt thirty-five minutes before he popped the question. But the fact that he was scowling at me as if I were the devil's handmaiden suggested our relationship would never work. The fact that he was sitting beside his wife also posed a problem for our connubial bliss. Weighing all the signs, I guessed they'd been married for about twenty-four years.

But I'm not a psychic. I'm a psychologist. I used to be a cocktail waitress, which paid about the same and boasted a saner clientele, but it kept me on my feet too much.

Two weeks prior, Mrs. Hunt had called my clinic to

schedule a therapy session. My practice, L.A. Counseling, is located on the south side of Eagle Rock, only a few miles from Pasadena, but hell and gone from the glamour of New Year's morning's Rose Bowl Parade.

As a result of that call, Mr. Hunt now seemed to be wondering how the hell he had landed in some shrink's second-rate office, and had decided to fill his fifty minutes by probing into my personal life. But I suspected what he really wanted to know was not whether I was married, but what made me think I was qualified to counsel him and his heretofore silent wife.

"No, Mr. Hunt, I'm not married," I said.

"How come?"

If he hadn't been a client, I might have told him it was none of his damned business whether I was married, ever had been married, or ever intended to be married. Ergo, it was probably best that he *was* a client, since that particular answer might have seemed somewhat immature and just a tad defensive. Not that I secretly long for matrimony or anything, but if someone wants to lug salt downstairs to the water softener for me now and again, I won't spit in his eye. Even my thirty-seventh ex-boyfriend, Victor Dickenson, sometimes called "Vic the Dick" by those who knew him intimately, had been able to manage that much.

"Larry," Mrs. Hunt chided. She was a smallish woman with sandpaper-blond hair and a lilac pantsuit. Her stacked platform sandals were of a different generation than her clothing and made me wonder if she had a disapproving daughter who had taken it upon herself to update her mother's footwear. Her eyes were sort of bubblelike, reminding me of the guppies I'd had as a kid, and when she turned her gaze in my direction it was pretty obvious she'd been wondering about me herself.

It's not uncommon for clients to think a therapist has to be half a couple in order to know something about marriage. I soundly disagree. I've never been a lobster, but I know they taste best with a pound of melted butter and a spritz of lemon.

I didn't have a lot of information about the Hunts, but I knew from their client profiles that Kathy was forty-three, four years younger than her husband, who worked for a company called "Mann's Rent 'n' Go." They both sat on my comfy, cream-colored couch, but to say that they sat together would have been a wild flight of romantic fancy. Between Mrs. Hunt's polyester pantsuit and Mr. Hunt's stiff-backed personage, there was ample space to drive a MAC truck, flatbed trailer and all.

I gave them both my professional smile, the one that suggests I'm above being insulted by forays into my personal life and that I would not murder them in their sleep for doing so.

"You're an okay-looking woman," Mr. Hunt continued. "Got a good job. How come you're still single?"

I considered telling him that, despite past relationships with men like himself, I had managed to retain a few functioning brain cells. But that might have been considered unprofessional. It might also have been untrue.

"How long have you two been married?" I asked, turning his question aside with the stunning ingenuity only a licensed psychoanalyst could have managed. It was five o'clock on a Friday evening, and I hadn't had a cigarette for five days and nineteen hours. I'd counted on my way to work that morning.

"Twenty-two years," said Mrs. Hunt. She didn't sound thrilled with the number. Maybe she'd been doing a little math on her way to work, too. "This May."

"Twenty-two years," I repeated, and whistled with admiration while chiding myself for overguessing. It was her pastel ensemble that threw me. "You must be doing something right, then. And you've never had any sort of therapy before today?"

"No." They answered in unison. By their expressions, I had to guess it was one of the few things they still did in tandem.

"Is that because you didn't feel you needed help or because—"

"I don't believe in this crap," Mr. Hunt interrupted.

I turned toward him, brilliantly even-tempered, which shows how mature I've become. Five years ago I would have taken offense. Twenty years ago I would have called him a wart-faced turd head and given him a wedgie. "Why ever are you here, then, Mr. Hunt?" I asked, my dulcet tone a soft meld of curiosity and caring.

"Kathy says she won't . . ." He paused. "She wanted me to come with her."

So ol' Kat was withholding sex. Uh-huh.

"Well," I said, "as I'm sure you're aware, you don't have to tell me anything you're uncomfortable with."

I glanced from one to the other again. Mr. Hunt beetled his brows. Mrs. Hunt pursed her lips. They didn't really look like they'd be comfortable with much. Maybe a non-committal, how-was-your-day kind of exchange—if no prolonged eye contact was required.

I cleared my throat. I hadn't gotten much of a bead on the Hunts yet. But the law of averages would suggest that he wanted more sex and she wanted, well, maybe a nice facial and a one-way ticket to Tahiti. She looked tired. She also looked stressed enough to blow her lacquered curls right off her head.

My current forms don't ask whether or not my clients have kids, but in the Hunts' case, written confirmation was about as necessary as soft drinks at a bachelorette party. She had that old-woman-who-lives-in-the-shoe look about her. They'd probably spawned a good dozen of the little buggers.

"And of course," I continued, "everything hinges on your own specific goals."

"Goals?" asked Mr. Hunt, and rather suspiciously. As though I were trying to trick him into mental health and conjugal happiness.

"Yes." I swiveled my chair a little and crossed my legs. I was wearing a ginger-hued sleeveless sheath and matching jacket by Chanel. Buying clothes secondhand at a little consignment shop on Sunset Boulevard, I'm able to dress marginally better than your average L.A. panhandler and can still afford my flax-colored sling-back sandals for $12.95. The shoes matched the ensemble's piping and did good things to the muscles in my lower legs. I looked fantastic. Who needs a husband when you're wearing Chanel and look fantastic? "What are you hoping to accomplish with these sessions?" I asked.

Mr. Hunt stared at me with a mixture of irritation and absolute stupefaction. I turned toward Kathy, hoping for a bit more acumen.

"What is *your* main purpose for coming here, Mrs. Hunt?"

"I just . . ." She scowled and shrugged. I got the feeling she might have had quite a bit of practice at both. "I thought it couldn't hurt."

Ahhh. A ringing endorsement. Someday I'll have that embroidered and framed above my desk.

"So you're not entirely content with your current relationship." It was a guess, but judging by the anger that rolled off them like toxic fumes, I felt pretty confident about it.

"Well . . ." She throttled the strap of her beige handbag. It was the approximate size of my front door. "No one's completely happy, I suppose."

I gave her an encouraging smile and turned to her husband. "And what about you, Mr. Hunt? Is there anything you'd like to see changed in your marriage?"

"Things are okay," he said, but he was still glaring at me.

I gave him my "Aha" smile, as if I knew something he didn't. Maybe I did, but chances were, he didn't care where my house key was hidden or how to wax his bikini line without screaming out four-letter expletives.

"So you're here just to make your wife happy," I said. It was a charitable way of saying I knew she'd dragged him in kicking and screaming. Nine times out of ten, that's how it works. Men tend to think everything's hunky-dory so long as the little woman hasn't put a slug between his eyes within the past seventy-two hours. "It was extremely considerate of you to agree to come, then. Is he always so considerate, Kathy?" I asked, and turned toward the little woman.

The change was instantaneous and marked. Her lips flattened into an almost indiscernible line and her eyes narrowed. For a second I wondered if she'd brought a handgun with her. God knows, her purse was big enough to house a cannon and the man o' war that carried it. Ol' Larry might want to sleep with one eye open.

"He leaves used Kleenexes in the family room," she said. Her tone was cranked tight, her knuckles white against her mammoth satchel—as if she'd caught Larry sans pants with the woman in charge of weed whacker rentals.

To the uninitiated, Kathy's statement might seem like a strange opening gambit, but I'd been around long enough to realize it's not the sordid affairs that most often end a marriage. It's the toothpaste left in the sink. *Psychology Today* says, *"The human psyche is a complex and fragile phenomenon."* Personally, I think people are just funky as hell.

"I have a sinus problem," Larry said, apparently by way of defense.

"So you can't put your Kleenex in the wastebasket?" His wife's tone had risen to drill sergeant decibel. I glanced from one to the other like a Wimbledon spectator.

"You leave the orange juice out every damned morning. You don't see me making a federal case of it."

"That's because you don't give a crap!" she countered. "I could leave dog doo-doo on the counter and you'd just march off to work like everything was sunshine and roses."

"I don't know what the hell you're talking about," he

said, his voice rising. "I've been bringing home paychecks twice a month for twenty-two years. You think I'd do that if I didn't care? You think I give a damn how many floor grinders Mann's rents out per week?"

"Yeah, I do," she said, cheeks red and eyes popping. "I think you care more about floor grinders than you do about me."

The room fell into abrupt silence. I refrained from grinning like a euphoric orangutan. The first half an hour had been the conversational equivalent of pabulum. But this... this was something I could sink my teeth into.

Fifteen minutes later I was ushering the Hunts out the front door. They still looked less than ecstatic, but they had agreed to try a couple of suggestions. He would pick up after himself on a regular basis and she would make him breakfast on Tuesdays and Sundays.

I waved congenially, then turned with a sigh and slumped into one of the two chairs that faced the reception desk. My receptionist was behind it. Her name is Elaine Butterfield. We'd bonded in fifth grade, agreeing that boys were stupid and stinky. In general terms, I still think they're stupid. But sometimes they smell pretty good.

"Want to pick up some Chinese?" I asked.

Elaine stuffed a file in the cabinet and didn't turn toward me. "Can't," she said. "I have an audition tomorrow morning."

Elaine is an actress. Unfortunately, she can't act.

"So you're not going to eat?"

"Chinese makes my face puffy."

Elaine's face has never been puffy in her life. At ten she'd been pudgy and buck-toothed; at thirty-two she's gorgeous enough to make me hate my parents and every fat-thighed antecedent who had ever peed in my gene pool.

"What are you auditioning for?" I hadn't heard a single hideous line in several days, which isn't like my Laney. Usually she spews them around the office like pot smoke at a Mick Jagger concert.

"It's just a little part in a soap."

"A soap opera?" I asked, managing to shuffle straighter in my chair. "You love soap operas. They're steady work."

"Yeah, well . . ." She shrugged and stuffed another file. "I probably won't get the part."

"Laney?" I tried to see her face, but she kept it turned away. "Is something wrong?"

"No." She was fiddling through the V's. The only file left out was Angela Grapier's. Elaine has an IQ that would make Einstein look like a shaken-infant victim. I was pretty sure she knew Angie's name came before "Vigoren."

I stood up. "What's wrong?"

"Nothing. I'm just tired."

"You don't get tired."

"Do too."

"Laney," I said, rounding the desk and touching her shoulder. She turned toward me like a scolded puppy.

"It's Jeen."

I blinked, unable to believe my eyes. Her face *was* puffy. And her nose, flawlessly shaped and perfectly pored, was red. "What?" I said.

"It's . . ." She shook her head. "Nothing. Don't worry about it. I just—"

"Jeen?" I parroted, but then the truth dawned. For a few weeks now, she'd been dating a myopic little geek named

Solberg, to whom I'd had the bad manners to introduce her. It had been patently cruel on my part, but I'd been in a bit of a bind. Some people call him J.D. I could only assume his real name was Jeen, since Elaine isn't vindictive enough to think of such a nasty nomenclature on her own. Unfortunately, the same obviously couldn't be said of his parents. He was short, balding, and irritating, but he had a cushy job at a place called NeoTech, and a really kick-ass car. "What about him?" I asked.

She shrugged, but her eyes were still puppy-dog sad.

"What about him?" I asked again, and suddenly I was imagining the worst. "He didn't . . . Oh God, Laney! He didn't touch you, did he?"

She didn't answer.

Anger exploded like firecrackers in my head. Some people think I have a bit of a temper. My brother Michael used to call me Crazy Chrissy. But he'd earned every purple nurple I ever gave him. "Damn that nerdy little troll!" I cursed. "I warned him not to—"

"No." Elaine shook her head, scowling. "That's not the problem, Mac."

I winced. Dear God, did that mean Solberg had touched her? Did that mean she'd liked it? Did that mean the world was crumbling beneath my very . . .

"Damn it, Laney," I said, quiet now with awful dread. "He didn't hit you, did he?"

"Of course not." She lifted her bottle-green gaze forlornly to mine. If I weren't a raging heterosexual I would have begged her to marry me on the spot.

I relaxed a little. "Then what's the problem?"

"He just . . ." She shrugged again. "He hasn't called me, that's all."

I waited for the bad news. She wasn't forthcoming. "And?"

She gave me a disapproving glance as she shoved the Grapier file somewhere in the XYZ group.

"I haven't heard from him much since he left for Las Vegas."

"Oh, yeah," I said. I remembered her telling me about NeoTech's esteemed presence at a big-ass technology convention. J.D. was supposed to be some kind of geekmaster there. I should have been paying more attention, but I'd been trying to deal with a few issues of my own. My septic system, for instance. It had been installed sometime before the Miocene Epoch and kept threatening to spill its venom down the hall and into my antiquated kitchen.

Then there was my love life. Well, actually, there wasn't.

"He's probably just busy," I said.

"We were supposed to go to the grand opening of EU last weekend."

I shook my head, not understanding.

"Electronic Universe," she explained. "State-of-the-art-electronics store. The only one in the country, I guess."

"You can go next weekend. It'll probably still be open."

She glanced down at her hands. "I don't care that we missed it, of course. I mean, if you've seen one gray piece of plastic, you've pretty much seen them all, but . . . he was really looking forward to it and . . ." She shrugged as if to dismiss the whole situation. "He's been gone almost three weeks."

"Well . . ." I began, then, "Three weeks?" It hadn't seemed

like nearly that long since I'd seen the little Woody Allen look-alike. "Really?"

"Seventeen and a half days," she said.

I winced. She'd been counting. A girl has to be pretty loopy to count.

"You said it was a really big deal," I reminded her. "He's probably just tying up loose ends. That sort of thing."

"He said he'd call every day."

"And you haven't heard from him?"

"I did at first. He phoned every few hours. And e-mailed. Sometimes he'd fax me." She gave me a watery smile. "Left text messages with little hearts."

Yuck. "Uh-huh," I said.

"And then...nothing." She shrugged, glanced at the desk, and shuffled a few papers around. "I don't even know if he won the Lightbulb."

"The what?"

"It's an industry award. He was really jazzed about being nominated when he left, but now..." She cleared her throat. "I think he met someone else."

I blinked. "Solberg?"

"He was in Las Vegas," she said, as if that explained everything. It didn't. She continued as if she were lecturing a retarded duckling. "There are more beautiful women per capita in Vegas than in any other city in the world."

"Uh-huh."

She scowled a little. Somehow it didn't create a single wrinkle in her rice-paper complexion. I would hate her if I didn't love her to distraction. "It's tough to compete with a hundred topless girls juggling armadillos and breathing fire."

"Armadillos?" I asked. I couldn't help but be impressed. Those armadillos are tough.

"He's got a lot going for him, Mac," she said.

I kept my face perfectly expressionless, waiting for the punch line. It didn't come. "Have you heard him laugh?" I asked.

She gave me a sloppy little grin. "He sounds like a donkey on speed."

"Whew," I said. "Then we are talking about the same guy."

She tilted her head in a kind of unspoken censor. "I've dated a lot since moving out here, you know."

I couldn't argue with that. Laney got marriage proposals from guys who hadn't yet exited the womb.

"But Jeen . . ." She paused. I didn't like the dreamy look in her eye. "He never once bragged about how many push-ups he can do or how fast he can run a mile."

"Well, that's probably because he can't do—"

She stopped me with a glance, which was probably just as well. Sometimes tact isn't my number one attribute. I'll let you know when I figure out what is.

"I don't even know his astronomical sign," she said.

"He's a Scorpio."

"You know?"

Sadly, I did.

"Laney," I said, taking her hand and trying to think of a nice way to inform her that her boyfriend was a doofus, "I know you like him and everything. But really—"

"He's never tried to get me into bed."

My mouth opened. Solberg had propositioned *me* approximately two and a half seconds after I'd first met him.

I would like to think that's because I'm sexier than Elaine, but apparently I'm *not* brain-dead, despite the five days and twenty hours since my last cigarette.

"You're kidding," I said.

"No."

"Does he call you Babe-a-buns?"

"No."

"Stare at your chest till his eyes water?"

"No."

"Pretend he stumbled and grab your boobs?"

"No!"

"Wow."

She nodded. "I thought he really cared about me. But . . ." She laughed a little, seemingly at her own foolishness. "I guess he just wasn't interested. You know . . . *that* way."

I raised a brow. Just one. I reserve two for purple extra-terrestrials with wildly groping appendages. "We're still talking about Solberg, right?"

She scowled.

"Geeky little guy? Has a nose like an albatross?"

Now she just looked sad, which made me kind of ashamed of myself, but really, the whole situation was ridiculous. Solberg would sell his soul for a quick glimpse of an anemic flasher. He'd probably auction off his personal computer to hold hands with a woman of Elaine's caliber. And she actually *liked* him. What were the odds?

"Listen, Laney, I'm sorry. But really, you don't have to worry. Just call him. Tell him you . . ." I took a deep breath and tried to be selfless. "Tell him you miss him."

"I did call him. In Vegas."

It was my turn to scowl. Laney generally doesn't call

guys. All she has to do is play the eeney-meany-miny-mo game and snatch a suitor off her roof. "No answer?" I asked.

She cleared her throat. Emotion clouded her eyes.

"Laney?" I said.

"A woman answered."

"A woman? Like . . ." It was inconceivable. "Someone like one of us?" I motioned between us. "Human?"

She wasn't amused.

"Well . . ." I chortled. "It was probably housekeeping."

"Housekeeping?"

"Or . . ." I was floundering badly, but my faith in Elaine was undaunted. "Maybe it was . . . his great-aunt come to visit her favorite . . . nerd nephew."

She looked away. Were there tears in her eyes? Oh, crap! If there were tears in her eyes I was going to have to find Solberg and kill him.

"Did you ask who you were speaking to?" I asked.

"No. I . . ." She shook her head. "I was so surprised. You know. I just asked if he was there."

"And?"

"She said no."

"That's it?"

"I was . . . I don't know." She shrugged, looking unsettled as she chased a few more papers across the desk. "I called back later."

"Yeah?"

"No answer."

"Did you leave a message?"

"On his cell and his home phone." She glanced at the desktop again. "A couple of times."

"I'm sorry," I said, reeking sincerity. "But I'm afraid the

answer is obvious." She raised her gaze to mine. "Our dear little geek friend is dead."

"Mac!"

I couldn't help but laugh. "Listen, Laney," I said, squeezing her hand, "you're being ridiculous. Solberg is wild about you. He probably just got delayed in Vegas."

"He probably got *laid* in Vegas."

I stared. Elaine Butterfield never uses such trashy language.

"Maybe I should have . . ." She paused. "Do you think I should have slept with him?"

I refrained from telling her that would have been a sin of biblical proportions. There's a little thing called bestiality. I was sure even Jerry Falwell would think it made homosexuality look like petty theft by comparison.

"Elaine, relax," I said. "I'm sure he'll be back in a couple days. He'll bring you tulips and call you Snuggle Bumpkins and Sugar Socks and all those other disgusting names he comes up with."

"Angel Eyes," she said.

"What?"

"He calls me Angel Eyes." She raised the aforementioned orbs toward me. "Because I saved him."

"From what?" I hated to ask.

"From being a jerk."

Holy crap. If I had never met this guy I might actually like him. "He'll be back, Laney," I said.

She drew a careful breath. "I don't think so, Mac. I really don't."

I laughed. "You're Brainy Laney Butterfield."

"I'm trying to be practical about this."

"Elaine Sugarcane. No Pain Elaine. The Sane Lane."

She gave me a look.

"Butterfeel?" I suggested. "Nutterbutter?"

"I hated the last one most," she said.

"Yeah." Middle school had been a challenge. "Simons was a creep of major proportions."

She nodded distractedly. "He *could* rhyme, though. Which is about all you can ask of—"

"A WASP whose brain is bigger than his balls," I finished for her. It was a direct quote from my brother Pete. I've always been afraid he meant it as an insult.

Elaine only managed a weak smile.

"Listen, Laney." I sighed. Twelve years at Holy Name Catholic School had taught me a lot of things. Mostly how to sneak boys into the rectory for a little uninterrupted heavy breathing. But I hadn't known until that moment that I'd learned to be a martyr. "I'm going to find Solberg for you."

She shook her head, but I hurried on.

"Because I know . . . I'm *positive* he's just been delayed."

"Mac, I appreciate your faith in my appeal. Really." She squeezed my hand. "But not every man thinks I'm God's answer—"

"Don't say it," I warned, and backed away. "I don't want to hear any self-effacing crap coming out of your mouth."

"I'm not—"

"Quit it," I warned again. "If you say one negative thing about yourself, I'm going to blame it on Solberg. And then . . ." I dipped into my office and grabbed my purse from beneath the table by the Ansel Adams print. "When I find him, I'm going to kick his skinny little ass into the next solar system."

"Mac, you can't blame him just because he doesn't find me attractive."

"You shut your dirty little mouth."

"He dumped me."

I turned toward her with a snap. "He did not dump you!"

"What are you talking about?"

"Listen!" I pulled open the front door. "He might be a stunted little wart, but there's no reason to think he's gone totally insane. Well . . ." I corrected, "there's not conclusive evidence that he's gone totally insane."

"Chrissy—"

"I'm going to go find him," I said.

And when I did, I was either going to whack him upside the head . . . or give him a nice Irish wake.

2

If money don't buy happiness, what the hell does?

—*Glen McMullen,*
father, husband, and
homespun philosopher

SOLBERG LIVED IN La Canada in a sterile, New Age kind of mansion that overlooked San Gabriel's grandeur to the north and Pasadena's flashy wealth to the south. I knew, because I had driven him home not three months earlier. He'd been drunk and gropey. I'd dumped him on his bed, kicked him in the shins, and borrowed his Porsche to get myself home. Well, maybe "borrowed" isn't quite the right term, but my point is, I knew how to get to his place. I can't cook worth refried beans, but I have a kick-ass sense of direction.

According to the digital clock on my dashboard, I arrived at his house at 10:17. I was working on the maxim that there's no time like the present. Maybe there isn't, but the present was damned dark and kind of stormy. If I was one of those girls who had watched horror flicks as a kid, I would have been spooked. Unfortunately, I was. I'd seen *A Nightmare on Elm Street* three times and ralphed four.

But I was all grown up now, with a Ph.D. and enough panting credit cards to prove it, so I parked in front of Solberg's three-car garage and got out. My little Saturn *dinged* at my exit. It's kind of paranoid about having its keys left in its ignition, but I figured it wasn't in much danger of being jacked in a neighborhood where residents pay more for their cars than I had for my education. Besides, the LAPD likes to hide out in that part of town. There was probably a cop in every donut shop between Montrose and Glendale.

Still, I felt a little breathless as I strode up the inclined concrete and glanced to my right. The sprinklers were sprinkling, sweeping an arc across the smooth expanse of Solberg's immaculate lawn. Illumined by his security lights, it looked to me like it had been mowed recently, but I suspected that was no clue to its owner's present whereabouts. He probably had a posse of twelve come every Wednesday and Friday to prevent crabgrass from making a move on his pedigreed turf. Over in Sunland, where I call home, I would have welcomed crabgrass with open arms and three-in-one fertilizer. Almost anything is preferable to thistle and dust.

I rang the doorbell. It played a tinny techno song inside the bowels of his house. I waited. No one answered. I tried again. The same tune played. Glancing around once more, I placed the edge of my hand against my brow and peered through the window beside the door. The foyer was lit by a gigantic chandelier made of dangling bits of rectangular pieces of glass. The entrance marched off in monochromatic sterility in every direction. There was not a wall within thirty feet. Neither was there a scrawny little geek nerd.

Wading through his prickly shrubbery, I checked the next window. The view was pretty much the same, but darker. Traipsing along the side of the house while trying to avoid his overzealous sprinklers, I checked every possible architectural orifice. Not a door had been left open or a window unlatched. Hmmf.

By the time I'd reached the far side of his house I was perplexed. Where was the little weasel? It seemed to me he'd been breathlessly waiting his entire pathetic life for a woman who didn't want to exterminate him, and when such a girl comes along—voilà! All of a sudden, he's gone.

Of course, Elaine's father *is* a minister, I mused. Maybe he'd heard all about Solberg and had been praying on his daughter's behalf. Maybe Solberg had been sent straight to purgatory without passing Go. Maybe the Methodists had more pull than the Catholics. According to my mother, she'd prayed for her offspring every single night since our conception. Judging by the current state of her progeny, I figured Mom better stay on her knees, because my nicotine habit was one of the lesser evils in a clan that accumulates DUI citations like other folks collect coins.

I'd reached the front door again and I was out of ideas.

Scowling through the darkness, I spotted Solberg's mailbox at the end of the drive and eyed my surroundings. All remained quiet, and I figured, *Why not.*

It was a ridiculously long walk. At my house, I can reach

out my window and fetch my morning paper. Holding my breath, lest Krueger be lurking in the bougainvillea and hear me wheezing like a fat guy on a stress test, I glanced down the street again. No one appeared to be lurking, so I opened the box with slow uncertainty. It was crammed to overflowing. I took out the contents, closed the lid, and marched nonchalantly up the drive.

I quickstepped into my Saturn and power-locked the doors. Snapping on the interior light, I creaked my neck to the rear and checked the backseat. Krueger wasn't there, either. I took a few fortifying breaths and rummaged through Solberg's mail.

There was a bill from the electric company, three notes from credit card people, and several letters from environmental organizations asking him to help save everything from amoebas to sea lions.

But not a lot of clues. And regardless how concerned I am about the plight of the sea lions—I mean, God knows we don't want to lose a species that makes me look svelte— I was a little too curious about the whereabouts of the little geekster to give them much thought at that precise moment.

So I flipped through the rest of his mail. There were two periodicals that looked like they came to his house whether or not he wanted them to and a postcard from his dentist, saying he was due for his semiannual checkup. Nothing too intriguing there. But the final circulator did catch my interest.

It was a magazine called *Nerd Word*. I pulled it out from the bottom of the pile and stared at it agog. J. D. Solberg, hitherto and rightfully known as "the Geek," hadn't picked up his preferred techno mag. I knew it was his favorite because Elaine had told me he'd been featured in it on more than one occasion, and if I knew anything about J.D., which, sadly, I did, he would adore any publication that didn't make him look like a half-witted jackass on—

A rap sounded at my window. I shrieked like a startled spider monkey and jerked toward the noise.

A woman stood beside the Saturn, slightly bent, just drawing her hand away. I eased my heart into a sedate gallop and wondered if it was too late to hide the mail. Stealing from the USPS is a federal offense. Isn't it? Or maybe—

The stranger was still standing there, but her smile was starting to droop a little and her brow beginning to furrow.

I took a steadying breath. She was about my age, slim, and neatly dressed, and as far as I could tell, there wasn't a single razorlike implement attached to her fingers. So far so good. Then again, she *was* wearing gardening gloves.

She brightened her smile a hopeful notch and motioned for me to roll down my window.

Polite Catholic upbringing insisted that I do so. But for all I knew, she might be hiding a bloody trowel behind her khaki-colored capris. Then again, it seemed unlikely in this neighborhood. Anyone who could afford the house payments probably had the wherewithal to hire someone to slice unsuspecting psychologists to death for them.

And she was still staring at me.

After some deliberation, I pressed the window button. Nothing happened, as is always true when the car isn't running. So I hit "Unlock" and opened the driver's door. The Saturn *dinged*, its usual insecurities still intact. I pulled out the key. "Can I help you?" I asked, and managed, I thought, to imbue my tone with a nice blend of arrogance and courtesy. As if I had a God-given right to be rifling through Solberg's mail like some weird-ass stalker.

"Hi." She gave me a dazzling smile. Her teeth were aligned like so many perfect little pearls. I decided then and there to try one of those over-the-counter whiteners.

"Hello," I said. Psychologists are paid to listen. Sparkling repartee is not my stock-in-trade.

Her capris, I noticed, were almost big enough to fit Barbie's best friend, Midge, and her cropped, salmon-colored top didn't quite reach her waistband. I noticed, too, that there wasn't an ounce of cellulite to save her from the loathing of the rest of the female populace.

"I was working in my backyard." She motioned vaguely toward the east. "When I saw your car in the drive."

"Oh." It was the best I could come up with on such short notice. I'd only stared through the window at her for about eighteen minutes. It looks like navigating social situations might not be my forte, either.

"Are you a friend of Jeen's?"

"Who? Oh! Yes. Jeen's. Yes. I'm a friend of Jeen . . . Solberg . . . J.D. I'm a friend of his."

Holy crap!

Her smile had dimmed a couple watts. "Oh, sure. I figured as much. Was he delayed?"

I blinked at her. I was still working on the "I figured as much" statement. Was she trying to insult me? Did I look like someone who would fraternize with a stunted little techno geek with more stupid come-ons than common sense? I was still wearing my Chanel suit, for God's sake. And . . . "Delayed?" I repeated.

"He went to Vegas, right?"

"Oh. Yes."

"Is he back? I mean, I was expecting him last week, but he hasn't been answering his phone."

"You were expecting him?" I didn't mean to sound shocked, but she was an attractive woman—with hair and everything. Why would she care when Solberg returned? Unless she wanted to know when to loose her rottweiler and padlock her front door.

"I'm sorry." She laughed, pulled off a glove, and extended her hand. One of her fingernails was broken. I gave a mental sigh of relief. Not that I'm insecure about the state of my cuticles. "I'm Tiffany Georges. Jeen's next-door neighbor." We shook hands. Her skin was soft, but her palm was firm and slightly calloused. Could be she lifted weights. Maybe a little Nautilus. Or she might have a personal trainer. I've always wanted a personal trainer. One of those buff guys who makes you sweat with one glance at his pecs. But personal trainers charge about a hundred bucks an hour. For that kind of money, I figure I should be able to lounge around with a bag of Doritos while they do one-armed chin-ups for my amusement. Naked. Buck naked and—

"And you are . . . ?"

I realized that we were still shaking hands. Her upper arm didn't jiggle at all. I pressed mine up against my side and released her fingers.

"Christina McMullen," I said, and just managed to refrain from adding "Ph.D." I'm a secure, independent woman. No need for pissing contests.

She cleared her throat. "So you're a friend of Jeen's."

"Ummm . . ." It seemed kind of vindictive of her to make me say it twice. "Yes. In a manner of speaking."

"Do you two work together?"

"No."

"Oh, then maybe you don't know when to expect him back, either."

"Are you sure he hasn't returned?"

She scowled a little. Maybe she was wondering why some strange woman who didn't know squat was confiscating Solberg's mail. I kind of wondered the same thing myself.

"I don't think so," she said. "I haven't seen his Porsche in the drive." She looked worried. "I was going to invite him over for dinner, but, like I said, he hasn't answered his phone."

I must have been gaping at her, but the idea that this woman would invite Solberg to anything other than a lynching boggled my mind.

"Are you . . . ?" She looked suddenly embarrassed. "Are you his girlfriend?"

"No!" God, no. "Just a friend of a friend." It hurt to say the words. "Barely that, really. A friend of an acquaintance."

"Oh." Did she care? Did she look relieved? Had the world gone mad? "Well . . ." She smiled. "He must have . . . asked you to pick up his mail for him?"

I looked down at my lap. Yep, his mail was right there, and I'd been taught since infancy that lying was a sin. "Yes," I said. "Yes, he did."

She nodded. "Well, when you hear from him, tell him to give me a call, will you?"

"Sure. I'll do that."

"Well . . . good-bye, then."

"Bye."

She backed away. I closed the door and started my car. She was still waving from the middle of Solberg's driveway when I pulled onto Amsonia Lane and rumbled toward home, where we frown on interspecies propagation.

3

Excuses are like butt holes. Everyone has 'em and they all stink.

—Connie McMullen,
challenging yet another
of her daughter's well-
rehearsed lies

THE PRECINCT HOUSE was about the same as I remembered it.

I hadn't been there since I'd tried to convince Lieutenant Jack Rivera to allow me to help him unravel the mystery of Andrew Bomstad's death. He'd been a star tight end for the L.A. Lions.

It hadn't been an entirely altruistic offer on my part, as Bomstad had died on the floor of my office and the LAPD had thought I was somehow responsible. As I saw it, I had something of a vested interest in the case, but Rivera had turned me down flat.

And not just about the investigation, either.

But I didn't think about the time we'd spent sprawled together on the floor of my vestibule anymore, except during a few embarrassingly vivid nightmares.

Maybe I was a fool to trespass on his turf again, but I'd called NeoTech and learned that Solberg hadn't returned to work. In fact, no one had seen him since the end of October, when his associates had boarded the plane back to L.A. and bid him adieu. NeoTech hadn't been forthcoming with much more info, except to say they were certain he would return before the end of the month.

Much hair pulling and several calls netted the information that Solberg had been scheduled to depart Las Vegas on flight 357 with America West Airlines. But they had no way of knowing if he'd actually boarded the plane.

My crack about our little geek friend being dead didn't seem quite so amusing anymore. Maybe it was guilt that had driven me to Rivera's lair. Maybe it was something else. I was pretty sure it wasn't hormones.

"Can I help you?" The woman who stood behind the front desk was broad and dark-skinned, with earlobes that looked as if she might have, at one point, hung paint cans from them. They reached nearly to the point of her jaw and were currently sporting three-inch peacock feathers adorned with multicolored beads. The name plaque on her desk said SADIE.

"I'd like to file a missing persons report," I said.

"Aw right," she agreed, and slid a yellow legal pad across the counter so that it lay directly in front of her. She had boobs big enough to make a mountaineer swoon and her expression was absolutely deadpan. There was no, "Oh my God, who's missing?" or even an "I'm so sorry for your [quite literal] loss." She looked bored and a little peeved. She might as well have asked if I wanted fries with my report. Apparently, Solberg wasn't the first person to disappear from sight in L.A. In fact, maybe that's why this town called to the huddled masses. Maybe that's why it had called to me. "What's his or her name?"

"J. D. Solberg."

"J.D.?" She lifted her murky gaze toward mine with accusatory slowness.

"Jeen, I guess."

She shifted her weight. It took a while. "You guess?"

"It's Jeen," I said, challenging her to challenge me. It was Saturday morning, for God's sake, and I was doing my civic duty.

She scribbled on her notepad. "When did she disappear?"

"He's a man." Sort of. I shuffled my feet a little. "And he hasn't disappeared . . . exactly. He just hasn't *reappeared*."

She scowled up from under her brows. The woman had attitude to spare. At that precise moment, I would have traded a minor body part for a teaspoon of that juice. My stomach felt queasy.

"What?" She almost made it sound like two syllables. Intimidation was her stock-in-trade. They should have given her a badge and put her out on the street with nothing more than a scowl and a head bobble. She would have been fine.

I cleared my throat, straightened my back, and resisted glancing behind me. I had every right to be there, and the chances of Rivera appearing to remind me I'd acted like an overzealous porn star in the past were astronomical. I had nothing to be nervous about. "He went to a convention and hasn't returned," I explained.

"How long ago he leave?"

"Eighteen days."

Her expression hadn't brightened any. "How you related to him?"

"I beg your pardon?" I said, firing up my licensed therapist tone.

Her mouth quirked and her eyes narrowed. Her brows had been plucked to near extinction, but her hair made up for the loss. It was stacked like a braided beehive atop her head. "You his sister? His mother? What?"

His *mother*! Yeah, she had attitude and she probably swatted down gangsters like houseflies, but I'm Irish, and I was pretty sure I could take her if I had to. "I am an acquaintance," I said.

"An acquaintance!"

"That is correct." I stiffened my spine. "I am a friend, and he—"

"I can't file no report from no friend," she said, and waggled her head for emphasis.

"What are you talking about?"

"You gotta be a relative or somethin'. Where'd he go anyways?"

"What?"

Judging by her expression and the cock of her hip, I had to guess that her patience was running low, and I'm a trained professional. "Where was this convention he never come back from?"

"Oh. The convention. I believe it took place in Las Vegas."

She raised a brow and propped an open fist on one meaty side. "Las Vegas?"

"Yes."

"Girl, you know anything 'bout Las Vegas?"

"Listen—" I might have been losing a little of my professional edge.

"They got things shakin' there that ain't even legal in most the country."

"I'm well aware—"

"Your J.D., he like the ladies?"

My mouth opened.

" 'Cuz they got 'em in feathered flocks over there. More dancing girls than I got bills. And stacked!" She shook her head, in admiration or disbelief. It was hard to say. "They got a Russian gal at the Czar that can spin hula hoops on her—"

"Just file the damned report," I snapped.

She looked patently offended and snorted through her nostrils. "Aw right, but you ask me, your man is gone permanent."

I might have sputtered a little. "He is not my man."

She shrugged, gave me a lazy glance, and waggled her head again. "Hey. You're probably better off without 'im."

"He is *not* my man," I repeated.

"Well, then your"—she smirked and etched quotations in the air—"*acquaintance* is gone. Them dancing girls has butts tight as apricots and—"

I thumped the counter with my fist. "I don't give a damn how tight their butts are or—"

"Is there a problem here?"

I recognized the voice immediately. It permeated my

consciousness like a double shot of Absolut. I froze, hoping I was wrong and wishing I could ooze into the gray, industrial carpet beneath my feet. I waited a moment, but no oozing occurred, so I turned slowly.

"Lieutenant," I said, and there he was. Jack Rivera, in all his officious glory, his dark eyes deadly and his expression as hard as his ass.

"Ms. McMullen," he said.

We stared at each other. It hadn't been too many weeks ago that we had done more.

I cleared my throat. He scowled.

"What are you doing here?"

I pursed my lips and refused to fidget, but it was hard looking at him without remembering the sound of tearing clothing. His, not mine. They don't make men's shirts like they used to. "I'm filing a missing persons report," I said.

"Yeah?" His gaze never shifted from mine. "Who you missing?"

I gave him a tight smile, letting him know that everything was going peachy and that I neither appreciated nor needed his help. "I was just giving that information to your secretary here."

"Oh?" He slowly shifted his midnight gaze to the aforementioned secretary. Maybe he thought that if he turned away I was going to pull out my Taser and zap him between the eyes. Maybe it wasn't a bad idea.

"One Jeen Solberg," Sadie said, and gave a breathy hmmfing noise and a head bobble. "She ain't even a relative."

His scowl deepened. Rivera doesn't have a wide range of expressions. "J. D. Solberg?" he said, still not looking at me.

"That's what she says."

"She say where he went?"

"She says—"

"She's right here," I said, just managing to unlock my gritted teeth.

He turned toward me as if less than thrilled to remember my existence, then seemed to sigh internally. "I'll take care of this, Sadie," he said.

"Fine by me," she snorted, and shuffled off.

The station room was cluttered with desks and dividers, but staff members were few and far between. Apparently, they didn't let little things like murder and mayhem interfere with their weekends.

Rivera stared at me. His brows lowered a little. His lips twitched. A nick of a scar sliced the right corner of his mouth. I'd noticed it the first time I met him. Even before I noticed that he had the behind of an underwear model and the attitude of a Neanderthal.

"Come into my office," he said, and turned away.

I considered refusing. But Elaine's forlorn expression popped into my head and I followed him dutifully.

A moment later he was closing the door behind me and seating himself on the far side of his desk. He motioned toward the opposite chair. His sleeves were folded back from his hands. His wrists were wide-boned, his skin the color of hazelnut coffee.

I sat down on the edge of my chair and tried not to remember the last time we'd been together. He'd been wearing old blue jeans and a long-sleeved T-shirt stretched tight over his nonexistent belly. He'd smelled almost as good as the egg foo young he'd brought in those sexy little Chinese take-out boxes. "So you can't find your techno friend?" he asked.

I considered telling him for the umpteenth time that Solberg was *not* my friend. In fact, I considered telling him a lot of things, like I didn't care how good he smelled, he was still a knob-headed cretin from the depths of hell.

"I wouldn't be here," I said instead, "but Elaine is worried about him."

"Elaine?" he asked as if he didn't remember her.

I scowled. Everyone with a teaspoon of testosterone and a single functioning brain cell remembers Elaine. "My secretary," I explained. I was nothing if not patient.

"Oh, yes," he said, and leaning back slightly, folded his hands over his belt buckle. He was wearing dark dress pants and a navy blue button-up shirt with no tie. His face was lean, his neck dark, with no chest hair showing beneath the scooped hollow of his throat. I swallowed. "Your loyal employee."

I refused to drop my gaze, even though I knew exactly what he was referring to. Elaine had lied for me once or twice. He had found it neither believable nor amusing.

"She's been . . ." I drew a deep breath and jumped in. The water was icy. "She's been dating him."

"Elaine," he said, then paused, "and Solberg." His lips twitched a little.

"Yes."

He gave the slightest shrug as if to say it wasn't his place to question the mystical ways of the cosmos. "And he's gone missing?"

"Yes."

Seconds stretched and frayed. "You didn't kill him, did you?"

For just a moment I let myself fantasize about dropping an anvil on his head. But I wouldn't really do it. That would be wrong. And I didn't know anyone with an anvil. "You're just as funny as I remember," I said.

"Some things never change."

His grin, for instance. It couldn't really be called a smile, since it barely quirked the corners of his mouth. Instead, it just shone with satanic mischief in his eyes.

"Where does he live?" he asked.

"What?" Despite everything, the anvil scenario was distracting.

"Solberg," he said, and slid a notebook across his nearly empty desk as he straightened. "What's his address?"

I gave it to him.

He paused in the middle of writing. "That's not our district."

"What?"

"La Crescenta would have jurisdiction there."

"What are you talking about? His house isn't thirty minutes from here."

He shrugged. The movement was slow and barely discernible. "Cops are territorial. I thought you'd learned that by now."

Something sparked in his eyes. I didn't know what it was, and I didn't care. I'd learned my lesson last go-round. Jack Rivera, with his dark chocolate eyes and wood-smoke voice, was strictly off-limits, like cigarettes, and desserts with fat grams that ran into the triple digits.

"Very well . . ." I rose to my feet and swept my purse dramatically onto my shoulder. Glenn Close should have looked so good. "Where is La Crescenta?"

"Sit down," he said.

"I would love to converse, Lieutenant," I said, "but I'm afraid I don't have a great deal of time to—"

"Sit down," he repeated.

I did so, though I don't know why. Maybe it was because he was a cop, but God knows, I haven't been exactly meek with authority figures in the past. I believe Father Pat, the patriarch of Holy Name Catholic School, had once called me the spawn of Satan, but that whole episode is a little blurry, as I was in a lust-induced haze with a boy named Jimmy at the time. He could spew Jell-O out of his nose on command. It's hard to resist a guy with that kind of nasal capacity.

"I'll take the information," he said.

I wished I were still standing so I could look down at him. "Don't do me any favors."

A muscle jumped in his jaw, then he dropped the pen on the notepad and spread his hands. "Listen, about the other night."

I raised a superior brow. "The other night?"

"When we . . ." He drew a deep breath. His eyes narrowed a little. They were sharp and lethal, softened only by the lush fringe of his lashes, which could make him look mischievous one moment and sexy as hell the next. It was a wonder he didn't chop them off just to hone his hard-ass look. "The other night," he repeated. "At your house."

I blinked as if I were confused. But I wasn't. He was an

ass and I knew it. "I'm afraid I have no idea what you're talking about, Lieutenant," I said.

The muscle in his cheek contracted again. "I know it's been a long time."

I stared.

"I should have called you."

I was determined to remain calm, but suddenly I found myself on my feet and headed toward the door. Elaine could fight her own damn battles. "Thanks for your time, Rivera."

"God damn it, just listen," he said.

I glanced over my shoulder, going for haughty.

He was on his feet, too. "I've been busy."

"Busy!"

"Things have been crazy. Work—"

I stopped him right there. "It's perfectly okay. I understand completely," I said, and reached for the doorknob. Somehow, he got there first.

"Just wait a minute."

But I'd *been* waiting. And there are only a couple of things I liked less. Exercise was the first thing that came to mind.

I glared at him. "What do you want, Rivera?"

"Something came up," he said, "with my ex-wife. I had to take care of it."

I remembered his ex-wife. We'd met in a dog park under rather unorthodox circumstances. She was as cute as a button and as sweet as a lollipop. I could pretty well imagine what had come up.

"Nothing big, I'm sure," I said.

"Well, it was . . ." He scowled, not seeming to appreciate

my pointed entendre. "We had a problem, but we got it worked out."

Worked out? I could feel my stomach do a three-foot free fall. "Well . . . I'm glad for both of you," I said, and nodded to emphasize my euphoria. "Really."

His scowl deepened before apparent realization dawned. "No. Shit." He thumped his palm on the door not twelve inches from my head and glanced impatiently out the window. "I didn't mean we're back together."

"Oh," I said. My heart did some complicated maneuver in my chest. I don't know why. It's not as if I cared. Couldn't have cared less. He may smell like sun-warmed lust, but he isn't my type. My type has an Ivy League education and doesn't carry handcuffs like most guys sport hair-combs.

"Well . . . I'm sorry to hear that," I said.

He glared. "Are you?"

I gave him a fabulously casual shrug. "She seemed very nice. Sweet even."

"She's . . ." He drew a deep breath through his nostrils and straightened slightly. "The point is—it was her . . . who called when I was at your house."

"She," I said. He quirked his brows in question or irritation or a twisted combination of the two. "It was *she* who called," I corrected.

I think he gritted his teeth. "It sounded urgent. I thought I'd better take care of it right away.

"The point is . . ." He paused, probably trying to remember the point. "I should have contacted you afterward. Told you I couldn't make it the next day."

"Or the next," I added congenially.

He glanced out the window again. The muscle worked in his jaw. "I know it's been a long time."

"I'm sorry," I said, and reached for the door again. "I have to go. I think I left my toaster on."

He grabbed my arm. "Damn it, McMullen, I'm trying to apologize."

I gave him my sweetest expression. "Having any luck?"

"You could make this easier."

"Easier!" My voice had risen a little. Casual was beginning to fray toward maniacal. "We had a date," I reminded him. "You're a month late."

"So you settled for Solberg?"

My mouth dropped open. "What?"

"He's got the cash. I'll admit that."

"You think I'm dating Solberg?"

He tilted back his head and laughed. "You could have thought up a better story."

"What the hell are you talking about?"

"Elaine!" he said. "And Solberg?"

I straightened my back. "So. You think Solberg and I are a match, do you?"

He shrugged. "He was spending a lot of time at your house, as I recall. Seven o'clock in the morning. Five o'clock in the afternoon. I mean, shit . . ." He glanced to the side again, tension tight across his jaw and throat. "I know you're lonely, but . . . Solberg?"

It was difficult to resist kneeing him in the groin. But self-discipline saved the day. That and the idea of sharing a jail cell with a tobacco-spitting woman named Slammer. "Get your hand off me," I said. "Or I swear to God, I'll file charges that'll make your eyes cross."

"Listen, McMullen—"

"Move it or lose it!" I snarled, and jerked out of his grasp. He glowered down at me, but I was already leaving.

Sadie lurched away from the door just as I stepped out. Sidling her gaze to the left, she shuffled some papers on a nearby desk as if she couldn't have cared less if we'd just been going at it like Energizer bunnies.

"He'll be back!" I growled.

She glanced up, no eyebrows to be seen. "What you talkin' 'bout, girl?"

"Solberg, he'll be back," I snarled, and stalked out the door.

I'm pretty sure Freud himself couldn't possibly have handled the situation with more panache.

4

If at first you don't succeed, stretch out on your La-Z-Boy with a six-pack and a porn flick. Y' still won't succeed, but you sure as hell won't give a shit.

—*Victor Dickenson,*
better known as
Vic the Dick

I T TOOK THE rest of that morning and three maple-frosted long johns to stem the tide of curses I laid on Rivera.

But by noon I was back on track. By three I had filed a report with the sheriff's station on Briggs Avenue. No one there accused me of dating outside my genus or tempted me to knee him in the gonads.

When I returned home, my phone was ringing.

I answered before my machine picked up, but there was no one there.

It rang again five seconds after I hung up.

"Hello?"

"Chrissy."

"Mom." Perfect. That'd teach me to check caller ID. It's not as if I don't love my mother. It's just easier with a little distance between us. Say, two thousand miles and an inhospitable desert or two.

"I'm so glad I got ahold of you." Her voice was tense. "Have you heard from Peter John?"

"Pete?" My stomach immediately cranked up a notch. Pete's my middle brother and probably the reason for four years of teenage acne. I'd like to blame him for other things, too. Say, the depletion of the ozone layer and the disappointing number of calories in a cup of peanut butter—but that might be unfair. "No. I haven't heard from him. Why?" I asked, and immediately started rummaging through my cupboards, stretching the tangling telephone cord past the corner of my aged refrigerator. Familial contact tends to make me want to eat my weight in saturated fats.

"He's gone."

"Gone?" I repeated, momentarily abandoning my search. "What do you mean, gone?"

"Just gone. Holly's worried sick."

Holly is Pete's girlfriend. She hadn't been foolish enough to become Mrs. McMullen yet, but it didn't look good for her continued mental health. She'd allowed him to move in with her last February as a kind of trial to see if they could cohabitate peaceably together. If Holly had the brains of a tea biscuit, she'd hie herself to a nunnery before the fatal words were spoken. History has shown that the McMullen brothers do not good husbands make. They're not that fabulous at being human, either.

"So he hasn't called you? Or stopped in?"

"Stopped in!" I gripped the cupboard door with white-knuckled fingers. "Here?"

"He's always wanted to see L.A., you know."

"No! No, I didn't know." I felt inexplicably panicked. Maybe it's the fact that Pete had, in our younger years, enjoyed dispensing dead rodents like confetti and making me eat unpleasant items disguised as food. I don't want to put too fine a point on the subject, but Pete's an idiot.

"Well, he has, and Holly thinks he might be heading your way."

I started rummaging in the cupboards again. Faster now. Where the hell was that peanut butter? I needed fat grams, stat.

"Chrissy?"

"Yes. I'm here."

"So you'll call me if you hear from him, won't you?"

"Yes." Right after I contacted 911.

"Maybe if he shows up the two of you could drive home together."

My head snapped up. "What?"

"It's almost Thanksgiving."

"I know, but I—"

"We haven't seen you in months."

"Well, I can't really leave—"

"I bet Elaine is going to see her parents." There was a grating whine in her voice, followed by dead silence. I stiffened my back.

"I'm afraid my practice—"

"Is she?"

I cleared my throat. "What's that?"

"Is she coming home for the holidays?"

"I don't really know." It was an out-and-out lie. Elaine had bought plane tickets more than three weeks ago. I felt perspiration pop out on my forehead like dandelions on Dad's front lawn.

"She's always been such a nice girl. I bet she is."

"Well, maybe. I'm not—"

"Never caused her mother a moment's worry. Remember when she was in grade school? Remember? She'd bring her mom flowers every time—"

I could feel a pimple erupting as she spoke. "Hey, Mom," I said. "I think someone's at my door."

"At your door?" Her tone was breathless. It's not easy making Mom breathless. "Is it Peter John?"

Maybe, but more likely it was just my fiendish attempt to get her off the phone before my head exploded like Chinese firecrackers. "I don't know," I said. "I'd better check."

"Call me if it is."

"Sure," I said, and hung up like the chickenshit I am.

After that, I went through my kitchen like a threshing crew, eating everything but the door handles.

Guilt, and the fact that I felt like an overinflated water balloon, convinced me to go running. I laced up my shoes and chugged up Grapevine Avenue, then across on Orange. By the time I returned home I smelled like fermented skunk juice, but felt marginally better. Sometimes I run to keep the fat from squeezing the air out of my lungs. But sometimes it's just because I don't have a camel-hair shirt.

I checked caller ID instead of the answering machine since it was several inches closer. Nothing. So I showered, then, limp from the exhilaration of exercise, I sat in my kitchen and carefully didn't think about things . . . such as

Pete and his fondness for dead rodents cleverly positioned between my blankets...or my mother and her fondness for other people's daughters. Or Rivera.

His memory sparked hot, dark feelings inside me. But thinking about him wouldn't do me any good, since I'd never perfected the art of voodoo, so I might as well consider something else, like where the Geekmaster had gone.

He was still nowhere to be found, despite my stellar sleuthing. In fact, I didn't even know where he *wasn't,* although I was pretty sure I could rule out the immediate vicinity, namely my kitchen.

But maybe I was being hasty. Perhaps I'd better look in my freezer again. I did. He wasn't there. But there was a bag of green beans, some fish sticks, and a box of individually packaged cheesecake slices.

I was hungry again, maybe from running, maybe from talking to my mother, so I took out a piece and sampled it while I ruminated. It wasn't bad, even frozen.

I sat down at my battered kitchen table and called Elaine, but she didn't answer. She was probably at her audition. But maybe she was home, moping and refusing to answer the phone.

The idea made me a little sick to my stomach. I ate some more cheesecake as a sort of gastric balm.

After an adequate influx of sugar, I realized that if I had so much as a pair of brain cells ricocheting around in my cranium, I would forget this whole Solberg fiasco. It wasn't as if Laney couldn't find herself a new and better man... one with hair that hadn't been harvested from south of his belt line. So why was I knocking myself out trying to find the little twit?

The truth was painfully obvious and came hard on the heels of the first wave of my glycogen high. I wanted to know there was hope . . . for me . . . for happily ever after . . . for Mars and Venus in the same orbit. And I knew, I was certain, that if someone like Solberg couldn't be faithful to someone like Laney, girls like me—everyday kind of girls, girls with fat cells and hair disasters—were dead out of luck.

I mean, she was Zany Elainy, voted girl most likely to . . . do whatever the hell she wanted . . . with whomsoever she damned well pleased.

Why she chose to hang out with a freakazoid like Solberg was beyond my comprehension. I'd met him more than ten years ago at the Warthog in Schaumburg, Illinois, where I used to serve drinks. His come-on line had had something to do with his hard drive getting it on with my motherboard. Not the kind of suggestion that makes a girl go weak in the knees.

I mean, I know good men are hard to come by. In fact, judging by my own rather checkered past, the species might have become extinct shortly following the demise of the Tyrannosaurus rex. Still, no woman with all her ducks in a row should settle for a Solberg. In fact, no woman who had any fowl of any sort should associate with a guy like Solberg.

Then again, his neighbor had seemed strangely interested. And she looked like she had some poultry. What was that all about? One hip cocked against my cracked vinyl counter, I finished off the slice of cheesecake, returned to my frozen Mecca, and rummaged for something toward the ground level of the food pyramid. But the nutrition fairy had yet to arrive, so I settled for another cream cheese treat and was immediately rewarded with an insight: Why had Solberg's classy neighbor been gardening in the dark?

I'm not sure why I hadn't come around to that question earlier. Maybe my own misplaced guilt regarding the confiscated mail had retarded my suspicions, but now the entire episode seemed ultimately surreal to me. Most people don't go rummaging around in their backyards in the middle of the night.

Well, all right, technically ten o'clock isn't the middle of the night. But it was well after dark. What had Tiffany Georges been doing out there in her Barbie doll capris and gardening gloves?

Curious enough to abandon dessert, I wandered into the adjoining room. Its size suggested that it might once have served as a closet for an adolescent midget. I used it for my office. I squeezed inside. Turns out my cheesecake had accompanied me. Huh. Loyalty. I like that in a dessert.

Sitting down at my desk, I pulled the greater L.A. phone book from the bottom drawer and dragged it open.

Georges isn't an uncommon name. But it just so happened I knew Tiffany's address—or at least her next-door neighbor's.

Her number was listed under "Jacob Georges." Which probably meant that either little Tiffany was still living with her parents or she was married. Remembering her deplorable lack of fat molecules, I was betting on the latter.

So where was her husband, and how did he feel about his wife inviting the Geekster over for supper? Not that he'd have anything to worry about. After all, Solberg wasn't exactly Pierce Brosnan . . . or human. But still, he might be

considered competition if . . . *Nope,* I thought. He was an irritating little worm from every possible angle. Surely there
wasn't a husband alive who would approve of his presence.
So where *was* the husband?

Firing up my PC, I did a Google search, but it soon became apparent that if Tiffany had buried her spouse in the
backyard, it hadn't hit the *Times* yet.

And what the hell was I doing? I dropped my forehead
onto my desk and groaned. What was I doing? Protecting
Laney? Maybe. But the question remained—what should I
do next? Logic suggested that if I was idiotic enough to
continue my foray into Solberg's missing person status, I
should ask Elaine for some pertinent information about her
little geek beau. But truth be told, I wasn't absolutely positive Solberg wasn't doing the horizontal bop with some
bimbo in Vegas, and I had no desire to upset Laney further
until I had all the facts. So I'd have to garner information by
some other clever means.

I ruminated on that for a moment, wondering who
might know his whereabouts. No great brainstorms brewed
in my mind. In fact, other than Solberg's parents, I couldn't
think of anyone who might take an active interest in his
life.

So I dialed 411 and asked for the number of any Solbergs in Schaumburg, Illinois, where I'd first met him. The
woman on the other end of the line sounded less than ecstatic that I didn't have a first name, but she looked it up,
then duly informed me there were more than twenty such
listings in the surrounding area. She could give me the first
three. I wrote down the names and phone numbers. Amy,
Brad and Joyce, and Brianna. I called all of them. On the

first two tries, I got answering machines. I left messages, asking to have Jeen contact me, and tried Brianna. She hung up before I even got done with my spiel. Brianna was kind of rude.

Not knowing what else to do, I called Directory Assistance back and repeated the entire process. Whoever said third time's the charm must have had more Irish luck than I do, because it wasn't until my sixth trio of names that I hit the jackpot.

"Solberg residence, Teri speaking."

I sat bolt upright in my chair. The woman's voice sounded exactly like J.D.'s. If she had brayed like an ass, I would have been sure she was lying about her identity and was the Geekster himself. As it was, I cleared my throat and launched into "Hello. I'm looking for Jeen Solberg."

There was a pause on the other end of the line. I held my breath and scrambled to figure out how to handle the situation. Maybe I should simply tell the truth.

But the truth had rarely garnered me more than a grinding headache and a pack-a-day smoking habit. And I had no idea what to expect from this conversation. Maybe the geekster had taken out a second mortgage and bribed a Vegas dancer into spending the week with him. Maybe his parents thought fraternizing with a professional fornicator was a dandy idea and wouldn't appreciate me sticking my nose in their baby boy's business.

"I'm sorry. He doesn't live here anymore," Teri said. "Can I take a message?"

My plans fell into place with a snick of insanity. "Oh, well . . . hope so. This is Frances Plant." Mail theft having its advantages, I'd seen the name in the byline of a *Nerd Word* article. It wasn't until that moment that I realized Frances might be a man's name, but it was a little late to change the timbre of my voice, so I charged on like a demented rhino. "I do a column for a kickin' techno mag."

I tightened my fist on the receiver. Mom had once told me that liars go straight to hell. I had lied immediately thereafter and nothing had happened. I hadn't felt a lick of flames. I hadn't even gotten a glimpse of purgatory—unless you count my senior prom. I've been a doubter ever since.

"Which magazine is that?" she asked.

Nerd Word," I said. "You heard of it?"

"Oh." She sounded breathless at the mere mention of the magazine. Maybe geekiness is genetic, passed down through the maternal line like hemophilia or male-pattern baldness. Or, more to the point, like impetuous stupidity in the McMullen clan. "Well, I most certainly have," she said. "You did that lovely article about Jeen last summer."

"Absolutetomoto," I said. "That article was screamin'." I had no idea what I was saying, but it suddenly seemed to me that being branded with a name like "Frances" would have caused some lasting emotional damage to my character. "Anyways, we were just 'bout ready to put the January issue beddy-bye. I'd done a bang-up piece about a guy making robotic mousetraps, but turns out he was a droid, so I need a new line quick. Thought maybe I could do a follow-up on J.D."

I let my lunacy soak in for a moment.

"Another article?" Teri said. "That'd be swell. But, like I said, Jeen doesn't live here anymore. He's got a nice big house in L.A. now."

"At 13240 Amsonia Lane," I said. Clever, see, because

that would make her think the Geekster and I were buds and she could trust me with anything from his Social Security number to his ring size. "I called him at his pad this A.M., but it was a no go, and I need some info ASAP. You don't know his present loci, do you?"

She was silent for a moment. I wasn't sure if she was trying to decipher my gibberish or decide if she could trust me with her little angel's whereabouts. "Well, no," she said finally.

I felt my shoulders droop.

"But...wait a minute." I heard her cup the phone. "Steven, when was Jeen going to that big convention?"

"I don't know," came the answer.

I assumed the voice was Solberg's father's, because, by the sound of it, he couldn't have cared less if J.D. had been conferring on Ursa Minor. The tone reminded me of the first twenty-odd years of my life. Schaumburg men are solid citizens: They have fifty-hour workweeks, high cholesterol, and belly fat. Give them three solid meals and a remote and they don't complain. But mess with their evenings in front of the tube and there would be hell to pay.

"Yes, you do." Teri's voice suggested that she might already be contemplating a battle for the revered remote. "He told us about it."

There was a mumbled response.

"Remember, he was doing that presentation. He and that Hilary girl were working on it together."

My ears perked up. Hilary? A woman? Solberg had found a woman who was willing to work with him? Was every female in L.A. on the skids? And could it possibly be that Elaine had been right? Might Solberg have actually fallen for someone else? Someone female? Someone with an opposable thumb?

I shook my head.

Teri came back on the phone. "I think he may be at that big convention. The one in Las Vegas."

"Oh, yeah!" I said it like it was an epiphany, and didn't bother to tell her that the convention had been caput for several days now and Jeeno still hadn't turned up. It was, after all, entirely possible that maternal instinct was stronger than the instinctual desire to stamp out mutants, and that she would, therefore, worry about Solberg's absence. "The con. He and Hilary are doing that gig together, huh?"

"Yes. I believe they are."

"She seemed like a cool chick. Maybe I can do a piece on her sometime, too. What was her last name again? Meine, wasn't it? Or—"

"No, no," she said. "It started with a *P*. Patnode. No, that's . . . Sheila's married name. Pierce. Pershing! It's Pershing."

"Righto," I said. "Pershing. Good job." I scribbled the name in the margin of *Nerd Word*. "Hey, you don't happen to know where they bedded down while in the big V, do you?"

There was another pause as she considered my odd verbiage. What the hell was wrong with me? "I think they were staying right at the hotel where the event was held."

They. Not *he.* Damn him to purgatory! "Spectacular," I said. "I'll try him at those digs. Oh, but . . . hey, when was he expected back in L.A.? Phone interviews are okey-doke, but face-to-face with the Geekster himself . . ." I let the sentence hang as if the idea gave me goose bumps. In a way it did.

"I'm not exactly certain."

"Sure hope he doesn't get caught up in the slots there," I said, trolling madly for some kind of feedback.

"Jeen? Oh, no, he wouldn't. He's very responsible. They love him at NeoTech."

Uh-huh. Well, life was just damned weird, wasn't it? Had I not known better, I would have expected a guy like Solberg to be flipping burgers at the Dew Drop Inn, not buzzing his way up the technological ladder of success while the rest of us scraped by, cursing and sweating. The idea made me feel cranky and mean. Sometimes I can feel good about other people's triumphs, but sometimes generosity's not in my fifty best attributes.

"And he loves them," she added. "Or at least . . ." She laughed. "He loves all that crazy new technology. When he was home here he couldn't stay off the computer for more than an hour at a time. I used to get kind of angry with him. I swear, the boy forgot to take out the garbage every single night of the week. But now I'm glad he took such an interest, because it's really given him a leg up at NeoTech. His colleagues think the world of him."

"I'm certain they worship the ground he walks on," I said. There might have been just a tinge of sarcasm in my tone. "When was the last time you heard from him exactly?"

The phone went silent, then, "What did you say your name was?"

Shit! I'd lost my fictionalized persona. In fact, I seemed to have spoken in what Elaine calls my nose voice. And now I couldn't remember my imaginary name.

I glanced frantically at *Nerd Word*, and realized with electrifying abruptness that I had closed it. A chubby-faced geek holding a silver sphere I couldn't hope to identify smiled at me from the cover. I flipped through the magazine frantically, but the appropriate byline failed to pop up before my idiotic eyes.

I croaked a laugh. "My apologies, Mrs. S., you probably think I'm J.D.'s stalker or something."

She didn't seem to find such lunacy amusing, which made me wonder if the whole world had gone mad. Who would stalk J. D. Solberg? Certainly not a woman who had a Ph.D. and . . . walks erect.

And, oh, crap, she was still waiting for an answer.

I skimmed the table of contents and finally spotted the name.

"Frances Plant," I spouted, then cleared my throat and slowed my tone. "I'm super sorry to bother you, but my editor's a first-class papilloma sometimes." I made my voice go whiny. It wasn't that hard. "I'm crunchin' deadlines. You know? Sweatin' twenty-four-seven. And I gotta get ahold of the Geekster, stat. You know of any friends he might be hangin' with?"

"Well . . ." Her voice trailed off. "I'm not certain. Jeen was always popular. Even in high school. Especially with the girls."

I blinked stupidly. Could it be that I had contacted the wrong Solbergs? I removed the receiver from my ear and stared at it, then placed it tentatively back against my lobe, lest it explode into a thousand plastic shards. "Uh-huh," I said.

"Seems like he was calling a different young woman every night of the week."

I relaxed a little, wondering if she had noticed that their names were in alphabetical order and that he was working his way down the columns of the phone book.

"You know if there's one particular chick he's diggin' on?" I asked.

She paused. I laughed with embarrassment. It wasn't completely manufactured. It was entirely possible that a sane person would have just called the woman up, said her son was missing, and asked for information.

"I wouldn't ask," I said, "but the Mag Mag Awards is coming up and this edition is humungo important."

"The what?"

I tightened my fingers in the telephone cord and tested my mother's hell theory once again. "The Mag Mag Awards," I lied. "It's a big whoop in the techno magazine industry, and I thought, if I could get another explosive interview with J.D. . . ." I let the statement hang in the air.

"Well . . ." She sighed. "I'm sorry I can't be more helpful, but I don't think Jeenie's seeing anyone special."

My jaw dropped. Not seeing anyone? No one special! What the hell was she talking about? Maybe in her eyes Oprah was no one special. Maybe Cher was of no particular interest. But Elaine, Elaine was goddamn special!

That conversation haunted me for the rest of the day.

Where was the Geekster? Why hadn't he called? And who the hell was Hilary Pershing?

Devoid of better ideas, I checked the Internet again.

After a few slow starts, a photo of Hilary popped up on my screen. She was by no means a raving beauty, but when I saw the shot of her and Solberg accepting an award together at a banquet in San Francisco, I had to admit they looked comfortable together. Were they an item? *Had* they been an item? Had she been dreaming of rings and roses and gallumping down the aisle with Geek Boy?

Maybe. Anything was possible. Someone had agreed to marry Michael Jackson. *Several* someones, if I remembered correctly.

I searched on, and eventually found a small article about Hilary and cats. Show cats. Abyssinians, to be precise. They looked exactly like the litter of kittens I had found snuggled between the hay bales on my uncle's farm. Cousin Kevin and I had stood for hours at the livestock auction in Edgeley, North Dakota, giving them away for free. Pershing's kittens weren't quite such a stellar value. They started at nine hundred dollars a pop.

You know what I really needed? A cat. And information about Solberg.

*H*ilary Pershing lived in a developing development in Mission Hills, where they were carving space out of the scrubby, inhospitable hills for a dozen or so new upper-income homes. I stood dressed for success on her front stoop. Nothing says "I can afford a nine-hundred-dollar farm cat" like a buttercream angora sweater, herringbone tweed slacks, and chocolate leather wedge heels.

"Hello," I said when the door opened a crack and one eyeball peered through at me. It didn't strike me as unusual behavior. Not for L.A. Most Angelites won't invite you in unless you're blood kin and come with a signed affidavit from your mother.

But a moment later the door was thrust wide and I was motioned in. I stepped inside with broad misgivings. A woman I assumed was Hilary Pershing locked the door behind me. I clasped my chic handbag to my chest and examined her. There was a ballpoint pen nestled into mousy-colored hair that had been permed to frizzle. A roundish nose overlooked a doughy face and multiplying chins, and a cable-knit cardigan was buttoned up tight from good-sized bosom to charitable hips. In short, she was perfect for Solberg.

"You must be Ms. Harmony," she said.

"Yes." I know my conversation with Teri Solberg should have taught me I'm not bright enough to remember an alias, but sometimes the most hard-learned lessons are the ones most easily forgotten. "I'm sorry to bother you on such short notice. I was just so excited when I found your website and realized you were right here in town," I said.

"Do you show Abbies?" she asked, peering over her shoulder at me as she led the way inside. She was a good four inches shorter than me, but she had a commanding air about her. If Solberg liked strong women, he should have been in weenie heaven. On the other hand, if he liked heterosexual women . . .

"Show? Oh, no," I said, as if breathless at the thought that I, too, could be among the honored few. "I mean, I'd love to, but for right now I'm just looking for a pet. And maybe, you know, to have a few kittens eventually."

"Kittens?" She stopped dead in her tracks.

"Umm . . . yes?" I ventured.

She turned slowly toward me, her lips pursed and her voice absolutely monotone. "Raising kittens is not for amateurs, Ms. Harmony." In retrospect, I have no idea why I chose that name. I was not feeling particularly harmonious. And she didn't look exactly peaceable, either. Her face had gone cold. "These cats are the direct descendants of the sacred companions to the pharaohs."

"Oh, well . . ."

"I don't sell my cats for indiscriminate breeding purposes. You can't simply toss 'em together and let 'em mate willy-nilly like animals."

But . . . they were animals. "No." I shook my head. Holy shit. "Of course not."

"If you were to adopt one of my feline friends I would have to insist that you sign a waiver giving up all breeding rights."

"Certainly." I nodded, not wanting to send her into cardiac arrest at the thought of unauthorized mating. Geez, what kind of pedigreed stud muffin did *she* take to bed? "I can understand that."

She stared at me. Apparently, I passed the litmus test. "Good, then," she said, and gave me a smile that suggested the storm had passed. "Would you like to meet the little ones?" She said it like she was about to introduce me to a magical coven of fairies.

"I can't wait."

She led me past a kitchen that boasted a handsome bay window but no curtains. By NeoTech standards, her house was fairly modest. Maybe she spent her money feeding filet mignon to Pharaoh's cats, or maybe, for inexplicable reasons, Solberg made twice her salary and she was pissed about it. Pissed enough to forgo buying curtains for her untreated living room windows and take out a contract on the Geekster's pathetic life. Or—

"Here they are."

Four kittens lay snuggled together in a basket on the couch in front of a gas fireplace. They blinked and stretched, equally as cute as the litter I'd given away at the livestock auction when I was a kid.

"Ohh . . ." I made the sounds I thought were appropriate, although honestly, if a pet can't fetch your slippers and refuses to bring you a beer after work, he's never been very welcome in the McMullen clan. "They're beautiful."

"Yes, they are," she said, and picked them up, one after the other, spouting mumbo jumbo about lineage and colors.

I uh-huhed like I cared and wondered when to launch into my reason for being there. I hoped it would be before my allergies kicked in. My eyes were already beginning to itch. I could only assume the pharaohs weren't sensitive to feline dander.

"Would you like to see the sire?" she asked.

"Well—"

"You can't legitimately judge a kitten without assessing his heritage," she said, and hurried toward what seemed to be a bedroom. She opened the door a hair, shimmied in, and reappeared carrying a tom, who flipped his tail and looked generally pissed at the world.

"This is Silver Ra Jamael. Best of Color three years running at the Mid-Pacific."

I stared at him. His color was gray. I swear it was. "Amazing."

"Yes, and the mother—" she began, but suddenly the bedroom door creaked ominously open behind me. I swung toward it, breath held, but there was nothing more sinister than a cat slinking through.

I gave a sigh of relief, but Hilary was already lurching toward the door and pulling it shut tight.

She turned back, giving me a sticky smile. "That's Cinnamon Obanya," she said, indicating the escapee. "Seventh-best shorthair in 2004."

"Beautiful." My throat was starting to close up. And Pershing was weirder than shit. What was in the bedroom? More cats. That much was obvious. But what else?

"Maybe I should get an adult," I said, mind spinning. "Could I see your grown-ups?"

She scowled at me. "I've only got a couple," she said, "and they're not for sale."

"Oh. I guess I misunderstood. I thought J.D. said you had more."

The house went absolutely silent.

"J. D. Solberg?" she asked.

"Yes." I kept my expression casual, but frantically searched hers for clues. "He said you're the one to come to for Abyssinians."

Her mouth was tight. "I thought you said you found me on the Internet."

"Well, J.D. mentioned you first, then I hopped on the Net and learned more about you. Your site was very impressive."

"Where did you say you were from?" she asked.

"Just south of here. In Baldwin," I lied.

"And Solberg told you to stop by?"

"Well, no. Not exactly. I mean, I haven't spoken to him in weeks. I think he had . . . didn't he have a big convention in Reno or something?"

"I wouldn't know. Listen . . ." She suddenly paced toward the front door, her short strides determined. "I just remembered a previous engagement. I'm afraid I'll have to ask you to leave."

"Now?" I asked.

"Immediately."

I blinked at her. "But what about the kittens?" And Solberg. Where the hell was Solberg? And why was she so eager to get me out of her house? A minute ago, she'd been quoting cat lineage back to King Tut.

"These cats are my family, Ms. Harmony. I don't let any of 'em go without references."

"References?" I echoed.

"And a cashier's check."

"You don't take cash?"

Her face froze. "I think you'd better leave," she said, and whipping open the front door, all but tossed me onto the sidewalk.

I gathered the shreds of my dignity around me and strolled off to my Saturn. Once there, I drove around Hilary's block, parked down the street, and watched her house for half an hour. No one came or left.

My mind spun in ever-widening circles. Why was she suddenly in such a rush to get rid of me? Had she and Solberg been an item at one time? Was she the jealous ex?

Or was she his current fling? Maybe that's why he hadn't

called Elaine. Maybe he had a thing for freaky cat ladies with faces like hot cross buns. I had to admit it was possible. There are, after all, boy bands and sea anemones to remind us that weird shit happens.

But maybe I was on the wrong track entirely. Maybe she had Solberg bound and gagged in her cat room.

I scowled. It was almost dark, so I drove around the block again, slowly, casing the neighborhood. As is the L.A. way, the houses were packed together like copulating pickles on the dusty hill. I parked on Dayside Avenue and waited another fifteen minutes. The sun sank with lethargic slowness. I exited the car, took a deep breath, and cut across the first lawn like a golfer surveying the eighteenth hole.

Nobody's dog ran out to chew off my leg. No one zapped me with a stun gun.

All was well. Still, by the time I had reached Pershing's house I was experiencing chest pains and blurred vision.

In the end, though, neither my medical problems nor my brave expedition did me a bit of good. Unlike her kitchen and living room, the window to her cat room was completely shuttered, except for a narrow track well above my head.

I drove home with a thousand errant thoughts floating like confetti in my mind, but the prevailing one was that I was either mentally ill—or a really kick-ass best friend.

5

A friend is someone who'll bike to the ice cream shop
with you, even when you don't look so great.

*—Brainy Laney Butterfield,
shortly after getting her
orthodontic headgear*

BY SUNDAY NIGHT I felt like my brain had been
squeezed through a ringer washer.

My phone was on the fritz. I'd gained one and a half
pounds, and my bathroom was beginning to smell like it
was organizing a rebellion. So I called the phone company,
ate a carrot stick, and prayed, since there was no way I
could afford a new septic system.

Frustrated and nervous, I graduated to eating Doritos by
the handful and considered everything I knew about Solberg: He was short, he was irritating, and he laughed like a
jackass.

I slowed down on the Doritos and dug a little deeper; oh,

all right, he was smart, he was rich, and he was obsessed with computers. That seemed to be a recurring theme. So where was he getting his techno fix if not at his own domicile? Maybe he was hiding out at a friend's house, lying low until whatever troubles were blowing blew over. But, according to everyone who knew him, that friend had better have a computer powerful enough to blast Solberg into the next millennium, or the Geek God would never be happy. And what were the chances of Solberg having a friend anyway?

Feeling crazy and alone, I finally phoned Elaine and invited her to a movie. She agreed. Apparently, she didn't have more than a couple other offers to turn down since Solberg had become her main squeeze. I shuddered at the thought and eyed her across the table.

We were in Fosselman's, my post-theater feeding grounds, and my favorite ice cream parlor in the universe. The little brick structure had been built in 1919 when Alhambra was probably a cow town instead of a squished annex of West Coast insanity. I'd like to think it's the stained-glass lights and historic ambience that draws me to it, but it might just be the butterfat content of its desserts.

"So what'd you think of the movie?" I asked. Hugh Jackman had been the box office draw. He'd taken off his shirt on more than one occasion. It had been something of a spiritual experience for me.

"I don't know." Elaine shrugged and fiddled with her lemon sorbet. Its calorie content probably ran into the negatives. "I thought the supporting characters were a little lackluster."

"Yeah," I agreed, and wondered what the hell supporting characters had to do with Hugh Jackman's naked chest.

"And some of Hugh's lines were a little flat. For a hundred and ten million, you'd think he could have given a more inspired performance."

"A hundred and ten mil," I said, masticating thoughtfully. "For that kind of money he should have been able to take off his pants, too."

She gave me a smile. I almost winced at the pathetic effort—talk about a lackluster performance.

I didn't want to broach the topic, but I couldn't avoid it any longer. "About Solberg, Elaine, I—"

She glanced up suddenly. "Hey. Did I tell you I'm going out with the ice cream guy?"

I shifted gears rustily. "The ice cream guy?" I echoed.

She bobbed her head. A young man stood behind the glass counter. He couldn't have yet reached his twenty-third birthday, but he wore the expression typical of every male who wanders across Laney Butterfield's path—a twisted meld of wistful hope and goofy adoration.

"You know the ice cream guy?" I asked.

"I think his name is Andy." She didn't bother to glance his way. He shuffled from foot to foot, studiously ignoring his patrons. I'd seen the syndrome a hundred times, but it never failed to fascinate me.

"And you met Andy . . . ?"

"Couple minutes ago," she said, "while you were ordering."

"Uh-huh." I shoveled in the last of the whipped cream and reminded myself I did not hate her, even though I was pretty sure young Andy would have the kind of stamina that would put Secretariat to shame. "Approximately how old do you think Andy is?"

She shrugged. "Age only matters if you're a perishable food product."

"Are you sure?"

"It was a line in a play I auditioned for once."

"Uh-huh. 'Cuz sometimes I feel like a banana."

She gave me another smile. I felt my heart sink. I had asked her out in an attempt to convince myself that she wasn't all that fond of Solberg—probably didn't even really like him. Maybe she was just attached to his car. He had a hell of a car.

She took a minuscule bite of sorbet, then pushed it aside. "You ready to go?"

"You didn't finish your . . ." I glanced at it. "Ice."

"I'm full."

"Sure. You probably had lots of air today," I said, and rose to my feet before I asked if I could finish her dessert. I didn't like sorbet. But I had once eaten a full bag of Cheetos in a single sitting. I hate Cheetos.

Seconds later, I was sliding onto the passenger seat of Laney's vintage Mustang. It was primo, but it took a buttload of upkeep, or so said my idiot brothers. As it turns out, though, upkeep is no problem for Elaine. She has a herd of seventy-two grease monkeys who would give their spleens to do the work for free.

We jumped onto the San Bernardino Freeway, headed west, then zipped onto the 5. It was nine-thirty on a Sunday night, so there weren't more than a million cars doing the highway bump and grind. At rush hour, it'd be more like a lap dance. Nearly devoid of actual movement, but heavy on perspiration.

Laney lives in a block-shaped apartment building in Sun

Valley. It's not a great section of town, but her landlord will periodically refuse to accept her rent. He's about ninety years old, and it's probably the sight of her that keeps him breathing.

"How'd the soap audition go?" I asked, and settled cautiously into a cane-back chair. She had decorated her apartment with lovingly selected primitive pieces, which meant the furniture might collapse beneath one's weight at any given moment, especially after one has eaten her weight in high-caloric treats.

She waggled her head in a so-so motion as she poured two fluted glasses full of something that looked like pulverized seaweed. Elaine doesn't drink alcoholic beverages . . . or eat, a nasty habit that goes back to our teens but has become exacerbated since our move to Movie Star Land.

"I haven't gotten a callback. Kale and aloe," she said, and handed me a glass. I had tasted her concoctions before—all reputed to be wondrously beneficial . . . by civilizations that thought bloodletting was medicinal gold. "But there's another part I'm going to try for. I'd play opposite Brady Corbet."

"That's great." I didn't know who Brady Corbet was. But I'd be thrilled to see her opposite Pippit the three-legged wonder dog if that would make her forget about Solberg. "Do you need help running lines?"

"Sure." She disappeared for a moment, then emerged from her bedroom with a few sheaves of paper.

I eyed the truncated pile. "Short movie?" I asked.

She gave me a copy. "Just a side," she said. "They didn't give me the whole script."

"Ahhh." I actually understood the lingo. It's virtually impossible to live in L.A. without a little entertainment retardation rubbing off on you. "What's the title?"

"Bronx Moonlight," she said, skimming the first page.

Wow. "So who am I?"

"You're a crook."

I thought about my actions over the past couple days. Mail theft, false identities... Seemed about right. "Okay."

"Your name's Hawke."

"Great. Who are you?"

"I'm Sugar, your accomplice. It takes place during the Depression."

"All right, Sweet Cakes," I said, employing my best lisp. I'm not sure who I was trying to imitate. Cagney maybe, or a cockatiel with hearing loss.

"It would be best if you didn't make me want to slap you," Laney said.

"I'll make a note," I said, and read silently through my part. Now, I'm no expert, but I'm pretty sure the script would make *Gigli* look like a box office smash.

"So I was just apprehended," she said, glancing at her papers. "By the coppers."

"The coppers," I repeated, using my Cagney voice again. "I like the sound of that. If this shrink gig don't work out, maybe I'll try acting."

"Please don't," she said with feeling, then, "Anyway, I've been caught and they've knocked me around a little."

"Bastards! Can't trust no stinkin' coppers."

She gave me a flat stare. I thought my dialect was getting better. "Now they've caught you."

"They'll never take me alive."

"They already did. So here we go: 'Hawke,' " she said, her voice faint, as if she were short of oxygen and maybe a couple of brain cells. "No. Not you, too. Why did you come? You shouldn't have come."

I found my part with my finger on the line. "I couldn't hardly stay away, could I, Sugar?"

"You can do anything you want, Hawke," she murmured. "Always could."

I chuckled where it said to do so. Whoa. Sounded bad, but the show must go on. "Just so happens I wanted to see yer mug," I intoned. "How you doin', doll?"

She tilted her head. "I been better. But just hearin' yer voice..." She smiled wistfully and reached out as if to touch me. "I missed you."

"I guess I sorta missed you, too."

"Then blah blah blah. The cop says to take me away, then..." She paused and winced. "No!" she wailed. "Take me, too. I'm as much to blame as he is."

"You stay, Sugar," I said.

She stared into my eyes. "I guess we had a good run while it lasted, huh?" she mused, seeping drama from every perfect pore.

"All good things gotta come to an end."

"All right," Elaine said, her voice casual again. "So then we exchange a meaningful glance and whip into action."

I looked up. "We do?"

"Yeah. We're hardened gangstas."

"Do we get away?"

"Of course," she said, and took a sip of juice without even wincing. "Sugar was raised on the mean streets of New York."

"Well, good for her." I followed her example with the juice. It wasn't going to replace champagne, but the Ipecac people were in for a horse race. "Would you do your own fight scene?"

"I don't know. Maybe." She shrugged. "Wyatt showed me how to throw a punch."

"Wyatt?"

She plopped down on the couch, tucking her feet up under her nonexistent thighs. "You remember, the self-defense guy."

"Oh, yeah." Wyatt had been a first-class hotty, and crazy about her. "Are you still seeing him?"

"No. Not since..." She stopped abruptly and fiddled with her script. "Not for a while."

Not since Solberg, I interpreted. Shit.

I refused to fidget, and raised my so-called beverage. "Well, Sugar and I don't need no stinkin' Wyatt in our lives. I grew up with brothers."

"Of course," she said, and tried a smile. It was unsteady near the corners. Shit and damn. "The McMullen version of survival of the fittest."

"Do unto others before they sober up," I said.

That damned smile again. It made me want to cry... or hit someone. A million years of college and a Ph.D. couldn't change my Irish ancestry.

She cleared her throat. I knew the question was coming long before she spoke the words. "By the way, you didn't find out anything about... um... Jeen, did you?"

I didn't know where the hell to begin. "Listen, Laney, I'm sure—"

"It's okay," she interrupted, and stood abruptly. "Really."

She brightened her smile a couple watts. "I've decided to move on."

"Move on?" I asked.

She shrugged. "It's not that big a deal, Mac."

"What's that?"

"The fact that Jeen dumped me."

I felt my bicuspids grinding, but she smiled again. The expression didn't reach her eyes. Hell, it didn't get all the way to her nostrils.

"He probably met someone else." She shrugged. "I can live with that."

Maybe, I thought. *But he can't. Not if I find him.*

"Still . . ." She finished off her drink. "I've been thinking."

Dark premonition settled into my stomach. Or maybe it was the kale.

"Maybe I should go to Vegas."

"What? Why?"

"Just because he . . ." She paused and set her glass aside. "Just because we're not an item doesn't mean I don't care about him. I mean, what if he's hurt?"

"Then my job's done," I said.

"What?"

"His job's probably not done." Clever cover, if Elaine was a concussed guinea hen. Unfortunately, she was a drop-dead gorgeous girl with a stratospheric IQ and a strangely fragile heart. A heart I couldn't bear to see broken. What if she went to Vegas? What if she found Solberg? What if he really had lost his last marbles and was shacking up with some bimbo whose cup size was found at the latter end of the alphabet? What then? "Listen," I said. "Don't do anything rash, huh? I'm sure everything's fine."

She shrugged.

"Just give it a few more days. He'll turn up."

"You think so?" Her eyes looked misty.

"I'm positive," I said, and swore on my brothers' future graves to redouble my efforts to find the knobby little nerd.

6

Let us talk about oxymorons. Common sense, for instance.

—*Sister Celeste,*
first-hour English

I T WAS WELL past midnight when I arrived at Solberg's house. Or, more correctly, when I arrived half a block down the street from Solberg's house. I'd called him a couple dozen times on my cell phone on the way there, just to make sure he really wasn't home.

Either he wasn't or rigor mortis had already set in. No one could resist the phone that long and still be breathing.

My heart was pounding and my mouth felt dry when I turned off the Saturn, but damn it, no one dumped Brainy Laney Butterfield.

I was going to get to the bottom of this. In other words,

I was going to find Solberg, and if he was still alive, I was going to kill him.

I sat in the dark and ruminated. *What the hell am I doing?* was the first thought that zipped through my head. But I was fueled with twelve thousand fat grams and girlfriend rage, so finally I pulled the keys from the ignition, shut off the dome light, and stepped silently into the night. Okay, "silently" might be something of a misnomer, since I dropped my keys on the street and they rattled like a fifty gun salute. But I did step into the night. Streetlights lined the curving boulevard, but it was still relatively dark.

I hadn't returned home after Elaine's. Instead, I had driven straight to La Canada after her horrific "I don't give a damn" performance.

Luckily, I wear black as a matter of course. Not because it's slimming. When you're as naturally svelte as I am, you don't have to worry about such mundane considerations. I just wear it because it's chic. And God knows I'm nothing if not chic. I glanced down at my footwear. Reeboks. Can't get classier than Reeboks. At least if you're a prowler.

Little bits of gravel crunched under my shoes. I paused, listening, then continued on. I would have liked to cut across the lawn, but the sprinklers were at it again, so I stopped at the end of Solberg's drive and glanced casually up and down Amsonia Lane. My heart didn't jump out of my chest. Casual. Not a creature was stirring. Which meant the children must be nestled all snug in their beds.

The climb up Solberg's drive felt like the ascent to Everest. Not that I've ever scaled Everest. In fact, I didn't even like StairMasters, but still . . .

My heart was beating like a mixer on high speed by the

time I reached his front door, but I put on my devil-may-care face and leaned on the bell. Inside the house, his chandelier was still blazing and his odd techno bell chimed.

There was no other noise. I tried again, holding down the button and counting to ten. Still nothing. The tinny song faded into oblivion. Maybe I was just trying to delay the inevitable when I pushed it a third time. But the results were the same.

I glanced around again. I'm pretty sure I wouldn't have survived the shock if I had actually seen someone, but I was absolutely alone. All evidence indicated that I might also be insane.

I'd called the sheriff's department and been coolly informed that the La Crescenta precinct was doing everything it could—which, I determined after about thirty seconds of conversation, was just short of nothing.

So, cranking up my courage, I stepped carefully into the bushes. From the half shadows, I studied the surrounding neighborhood again. The sprinklers whirred. A dog barked somewhere toward the rugged darkness of the San Gabriel Mountains. Besides that, nothing.

I swallowed my bile and went to work. I had read somewhere that over seventy-five percent of Americans keep a key hidden near their front door, but I wasn't relying on that general assurance. Instead, I had spent a nauseating amount of time recalling everything I could about Solberg—every bray-infested conversation, every idiotic come-on—and sometime before retching I had remembered a sloppily delivered invitation.

He'd been drunk off his ass and precariously seated on a

bar stool at the Warthog, where I had worked for a couple lifetimes.

"Anytime you need a little geek lovin', babykins, I'll leave the front door open."

"Not worried about some cocktail waitress murdering you in your sleep, Solberg?" I had asked.

He'd given me his donkey imitation. It was always good, but when combined with six Jack Daniel's and a Sex on the Beach, it was damned near perfect. I'd refrained from drowning him in his whiskey. *"I'm a techno genius, Chrissy babe. Got me a security system could rule the world. Don't matter how many keys I leave inside fake rocks, nobody gets past my HomeSafe."*

Okay. I stood sweating like a bucking bull on his front walk. True, that conversation had taken place a lifetime and half a continent ago, but according to old wives' tales, leopards don't change their spots. I was willing to bet vertically challenged techno dweebs didn't either.

One more glance around assured me I was alone. But I still scanned the shadows as I dropped to my knees.

Despite the security lights, it was pretty dark in the shrubbery. And prickly. I tugged a barberry thorn impatiently out of my bra and patted around the lava rocks that surrounded his bushes. Nothing.

Shuffling forward on hands and knees, I continued my search, starting near the house and working my way out. I squeezed between two indistinguishable mounds of foliage, making my way toward the street, and there, tucked beneath a tenaciously blossoming camellia, was a rock the size of my fist.

Breath held, I picked it up, and sure enough...it was

hollow. I hunkered back on my heels and tried to control my breathing.

I wasn't doing anything wrong, I reminded myself. Hell, I was doing a friend a favor. In fact, I was doing the police a favor—doing their work. If I was discovered, I'd let them know they didn't have to thank me.

But apparently my respiratory system didn't agree with my philanthropic state of mind, because I was panting like a fat man at a pie-eating contest.

I waited a moment. My hands almost quit shaking. Chrissy McMullen, bold adventurer.

The rubber stopper at the bottom of the faux rock popped out easily. A key lay inside. I dumped it onto my palm and felt a flush of victory. But it passed quickly, followed by a cold sweat.

There was still the much-lauded security system to bypass. But it hadn't been that long ago that I had hauled the little geek out of his azaleas, where he'd just deposited a half gallon of predigested alcohol. His voice had been slurred when he'd given me his security code. But it had been memorable. Thirty-six, twenty-four, thirty-six.

I pushed the key into the lock and tried not to think what it meant that I still remembered the numbers. Freud would have had a field day—but then, Freud had coined the phrase "penis envy." Freud was a nut job—like I wanted one more droopy body part to worry about.

The door creaked open. It sounded like the prelude to a horror flick, and even though the interior lights were bright enough to illuminate Dodger Stadium, I couldn't help glancing nervously around again. Still no lecherous murderers or adulterous geeks waiting to do me in. I took a deep breath, closed the door, and punched in the inappropriate numbers.

I found I was chanting Jesus' name under my breath. He didn't appear to save me, but after an interminable second or two, a green light blinked on. Coincidence? I don't think so. I wilted against the wall, muttering thanks until I felt strong enough to wander into the bowels of the manse.

I considered switching the lights off, but the idea of tottering around in the dark made my teeth go numb. So I turned unsteadily and pattered farther inside.

I crept through the house as if it were land-mined. The kitchen lay off to my left, tiled in something that looked like Italian marble, though I'm not very well educated in the nationalities of rocks. A great room lay dead-ahead. The far end of the yawning chamber was occupied by a television the approximate size of my garage. Wow. If I were a burglar . . . and had brought a crane . . . that would be the first thing I'd lift.

But I wasn't a burglar. I repeated that three times in my mind, hoping to make it sound convincing in case the police showed up.

Through a hallway the size of a semi, I saw another room. It seemed, at first glance, to be the only chamber with actual doors. I tiptoed in that direction and stepped inside. It was like entering a techno geek's wet dream. Every gadget known to mankind was in there. And several that I was pretty sure were unknown to everyone, extraterrestrials included.

A silver disk that looked like a miniature spaceship blinked a blue light from the ceiling. A multiarmed thing made of neon green plastic groped from the desk, and a keyboard imprinted with strange symbols was propped against the wall. But it was the photos that snagged my attention.

There were dozens of them. Outside the office, the walls had sported modern art, neatly framed in sparkling chrome. But in here it was different. Devoid of any decorator's glacial touch, there were pictures everywhere. Unframed and raw, they were stuck to the walls, leaned against electronic devices, and taped to furniture.

And every one of them was of Elaine.

On the one hand, it made me feel better. After all, it seemed highly unlikely that Solberg had fallen for someone else when Elaine was staring at him from every possible surface. On the other hand, some of the pictures were of the two of them together. And that was just unnerving. It was like seeing a shark and a puppy cuddled up on the couch. It just wasn't right.

Snapping my mind from the jarring wrongness of the photos, I began searching his desktop for God knew what. All the clutter that had eluded the rest of his house had congregated in his office. I searched one paper at a time.

Under an unusually tidy pile, I found a stainless-steel answering machine that looked like it might have aspirations of being a spaceship. The top was a dome of polished silver. I fiddled with it for a minute and it popped open, revealing enough buttons to operate Sputnik. Several of them seemed to deal with different languages. I pressed "English" and was miraculously rewarded with his messages. There were two from Elaine asking if he had been delayed, one from a guy offering to clean his carpets, one from his mother, and one from Hilary.

I froze as she announced herself. "Yeah, Solberg, this is Pershing. I just wanted to tell you that this ain't over. You got that? This is going to turn around and bite you on the ass."

I played it again. Not surprisingly, it was the same message. But what did it mean? And when was it recorded? The tinny voice that announced time and date said it had been received on April twenty-ninth, which was approximately six months ago. But then, it had said that Elaine had called about the same time. Which probably meant that even Solberg wasn't geeky enough to figure out an answering machine.

I searched on. Unfortunately for me, there was no little black book in which to search. Neither was there a daily planner. Whatever notes Solberg had jotted down concerning his schedule were gone.

Unless he kept them on his computer.

Once I thought of it, all other possibilities seemed as outdated as last year's yogurt. So after a quick search of his desk, I sat down in his chair and clicked on his PC. It hummed to intelligent life—the Lamborghini of the electronics world. A picture of Elaine popped onto the screen. She was sitting on a porch swing. The sunlight hit her hair at an oblique angle and her smile was little-girl perfect. I sighed and proceeded.

But as it turned out, switching on the system was about all I could manage. Psychological analysis doesn't exactly thrive in the techno world. I'd learned very little since the computer craze struck a couple decades earlier. But I did find what looked like a calendar and clicked over to that screen. October popped up. There were several notations, lunches, appointments, and flights, all of them seeming perfectly innocent—and boring.

I traveled over to November. It wasn't much more intriguing than last month had been, except for the message written on the thirtieth. It said "Combot" and was bracketed with two dollar signs on each side.

I sat and stared at the screen. What the hell did that mean? And where had the little rat gone? *Maybe his e-mails will give me insight,* I thought, so I concentrated on finding them. But once I got to the password thing, my bag of tricks was pretty much empty.

I did some more staring. The screen told me it was 2:44 in the morning on November fourteenth. I couldn't remember how long it had been since I'd had a cigarette. Did that mean I had gone over to the dark side of sanity? Or maybe . . .

Apparently, I sat there longer than I realized, because the screen switched over to a running display of photos. Once again, each featured Elaine.

I controlled my gag reflex. True, it might be nice to have someone adore me with such stomach-turning intensity, but only if he were human and . . .

That was it! His password. It had to have something to do with Elaine.

I touched a key. The screen zoomed back to business. I typed in "Elaine." It was rejected. As was "Butterfield," Laney's birthday, and "babekins." I tried sickeningly gooshy words like "love" and "amore" and "forever." Still nothing.

And then, on the blinding edge of a brainstorm, I typed

in "Angel," and suddenly I was welcomed into the inner sanctum.

There were forty-seven messages. I scowled at the number. If I left my computer unattended for a couple weeks I would have had approximately nine thousand. Of course, someone was obsessed with sending me ads about penile enlargement, and since, contrary to Freud's assertions, I don't want a penis, I consider them spam. Still, even if Solberg had a top-flight spam blocker, he would have more than forty-seven messages. Wouldn't he? He was the Geek God. He probably ordered his Big Macs online.

I didn't know what all this meant, but it seemed likely that he had read his e-mails fairly recently. I checked the right-hand column and found that the oldest message was dated October thirtieth—the day he had been scheduled to return to L.A. I read each and every e-mail. Two of them were from Elaine. I skimmed the contents, feeling itchy about invading her privacy, but there was nothing that could be misconstrued as a clue. The other messages were beyond boring. Nevertheless, I made a list of all the addresses and the authors' names. Then I tucked it into my purse, did a cursory search of the rest of the room, and exited into the hall.

The majority of the lower level didn't seem worth searching, but I gave it a once-over anyway.

Not surprisingly, the kitchen was the most interesting, but only because I discovered a package of Oreos in the cupboard. Poor Elaine. There wasn't a bottle of aloe gunk to be found. In fact, there wasn't anything to suggest Laney had actually been here. Not a grain of health food, not a leftover movie script.

I stood back and gave the situation some sagacious consideration. Could it be that she'd never even been to Solberg's house? And if so, why not?

I sampled another Oreo and pondered.

Maybe Solberg didn't trust himself enough to bring Elaine to his domicile. I mean, according to Laney, he'd never propositioned her, and what were the chances he could be in his lair with a woman like Elaine and not fire up one of his dumb-ass come-ons?

I checked the fridge for some milk, but there was only Coke and a couple cans of Red Bull. I'd rather drink battery acid, so I took another cookie and munched as I continued my search.

A few minutes later, I headed up the stairs. They creaked under my weight, but the Oreos had amped up my courage and I no longer imagined boogeymen around every corner.

The layout of the house was pretty much as I remembered it. The bottom floor was ginormous, but the upper level was somewhat truncated and perched at the top of the stairs to survey the remainder of the house from a bird's-eye view.

I started with the room closest to me. As big as a vegetable garden, it boasted a whirlpool, a shower, and a heated floor—in case that doomsday prediction came true and hell really did freeze over, I suppose. The towel drawer didn't reveal much . . . except towels and a deplorable lack of color creativity. The gray tones were beginning to put me in a catatonic state.

The medicine cabinet, however, woke me up by suggesting Solberg had several problems other than the obvious ones.

In an effort to live out my Nancy Drew fantasies, I

snagged two of the prescription bottles from the shelf and shoved them into my purse. Who knew? Maybe I would end up questioning his pharmacist. Or maybe I'd someday change my mind about that penis thing and want a really gigantic erection.

Freaked out by my own thoughts, I shook my head and wandered on.

Perhaps I shouldn't have been surprised to find an exercise room. I mean, of course a guy like Solberg would want to be attractive to the ladies.

I wandered past the sleek equipment. I'm no Richard Simmons, but it looked pretty state-of-the-art to me. The bench press was set at fifty pounds. I almost felt sorry for the little gnome as I moved on to the bedroom.

It was as tidy as Granny's silver chest. The white silk coverlet was stretched so tight you could have bounced a penny on it. I resisted trying, not wanting to lose a penny . . . or touch his blankets.

His closet was in perfect order. He had eight pairs of shoes, aligned just so against the back wall. It seemed like a lot for a guy—but then, Solberg wasn't really a guy, was he? His drawers were orderly. I shuffled garments aside until I got to his underwear. It would take a court order and the promise of a steamy night with Russell Crowe to convince me to touch those.

Finally, I stood in the middle of the room and surveyed it with my best Agatha Christie eye. If this had been a television series, I was pretty sure that by now I would have found a safe hidden behind a picture. Inside there would be a note that told me Solberg's whereabouts and why the hell he hadn't returned home.

There was only one picture in the room. I checked, but the wall behind was notably devoid of safes ... and notes.

I pushed the drapes aside. They were floor-length, and if I was any judge, they, too, were made of worsted silk. But there was no safe behind them, either. Instead, there was a deck. I peered outside, through the French doors, and what a deck it was. It ran off toward the side of the house, with stairs that spiraled toward another deck, then down again to the endless lawn. Unfortunately, I saw no clues whatsoever as to Solberg's whereabouts. Of course, there was no reason to think there would be. If I couldn't find anything in his office, where he obviously spent the majority of his geekmaster time ...

But wait a minute, if his ideas were so precious, why hadn't he locked his office? Most Americans are paranoid by nature, and Los Angelites habitually border on the psychotic. Surely a man with a couple mil in the bank had to have something to hide. But where would a truncated little über dweeb be sure no one would look if he wanted to hide that something?

My gaze fell automatically to his underwear drawer. I winced, but I was already trudging through the ankle-deep carpet to his dresser.

He wore whitey tighties. I grimaced, pushed a pile aside, then another, and there, hidden against the back of the drawer, was a CD.

I pulled it slowly into the light and stared at it. Scrawled in bloodred on the silvery disk was the word "Combot."

Well, the tricky little—

My thoughts crashed to a halt in mid-insult.

Had I heard a noise?

I froze like a startled bunny. Fumbling the disk into my purse, I cut my eyes toward the hallway.

Had I locked the front door?

Of course I had. Only a moron would break into someone's house and forget to lock the door.

Damn it! I'd forgotten to lock the door.

Down on the first floor, something creaked.

I almost screamed as I jerked toward the hall. I could see the opposite wall of the lower level, but not much more.

I heard an object click against something solid. A gun barrel against a wall? A knife blade against a banister? A grenade against . . . ?

My imaginings shrieked to a halt. I didn't have to analyze the situation. I had to hide. But where? I looked around, taking in the possible options. Behind the curtains. Beside the door. Under the bed!

I bolted across the floor and dove beneath the mattress. It didn't occur to me until that moment that I was absolutely, certifiably insane. Under the bed? Why under the bed? The closet was bigger. And if the intruder turned out to be Solberg, returning home from a fortnight of debauchery, I could simply pop out and scare him to death instead of beating him senseless as I had planned. Or—

I heard what sounded like footsteps squishing quietly on tile. Was he in the kitchen? That would mean he was nearly at the staircase.

I glanced wildly toward the door, hit my head on the mattress boards, then wriggled madly out from under the bed, dragging my purse behind me.

I goose-stepped across the floor. I had left the folding closet doors partway open. I dove inside. The strap of my purse caught on the door handle and my heart thumped like a gavel against my ribs. I jerked my gaze to the doorway. Nothing. One yank. My handbag fell into the closet with enough commotion to wake the dead. I held my breath. *Don't think about death. Don't think about . . .*

I knew the moment he entered the room. Some people say they feel things in their bones. I feel them in my feet. A tingling along the arch. I curled my toes and held my breath. There was a rustle of noise, like fabric against an immobile object.

Time hung like a scythe over my head.

And then I heard the sounds of domestic satisfaction. A sigh. A shuffle. The jingle of keys being tossed onto the nightstand.

Holy crap. It *was* Solberg. I felt myself go limp, too limp to even consider the trouncing I had planned. Shimmying sideways, I prepared to reveal myself, but when my gaze skimmed the edge of the door, the first thing I noticed was a pair of endless shoulders. The second was the back of a full head of dark hair.

I jerked into the closet. That wasn't Solberg. Solberg didn't have shoulders, *or* hair.

I held my breath, waiting to be discovered. Nothing happened, except I think I might have wet my pants a little.

I covered my mouth with my hand, took a careful breath, and tried to think.

Okay, what did I know? Not much. The man with whom I shared the room was a big guy with . . . Salvaging every bit of courage I could muster, I leaned forward a scant inch and peeked through the space between the folding doors.

The only thing I saw was a gun.

Sweet Jesus.

Surely there was a logical explanation for this. After all, this was real life. *My* life. Christina McMullen, Ph.D. Four months ago, the most exciting thing that had ever happened to me had taken place in the back of Jimmy Magda's Corvette. He'd been a world-class kisser, and . . .

A loud click brought me back to my new reality with a snap. Through the narrow opening in the closet door, I could see the intruder standing near the deck. Looking out. Why the hell hadn't I gone onto the deck? Did he know he wasn't alone? Had he seen me come in?

No. He couldn't have.

This was all ridiculous. Some sort of unfortunate misunderstanding.

He was probably a friend of Solberg's. It probably wasn't a real gun.

Of course. That's it, Chrissy. The Geek God had a six-foot-two friend with shoulders like a running back, who, on occasion, crept into his house in the middle of the night carrying a gigantic water pistol and searching the rooms for inhabitants. It was just something he did when he was bored.

What the hell had I gotten myself into?

I remembered how to pray then, with sincerity and piety, promising to floss after each meal and throw out the cigarettes I'd stashed in my purse and . . .

The mace! Did I still have a can of mace in my purse?

Much as I believed in prayer, I thought there might be a more direct means of intervention. I snapped my handbag to my chest.

My hands were shaking. Lip balm, checkbook, notepad, a half-eaten Snickers. Nothing. Unless I wanted to bribe him with a check and stick him in the eye with a pen, I was out of—

My cell phone!

It winked at me from the bottom of my purse. My mind scrabbled for possibilities.

I could throw it at him. Or . . . even better, I could call the police.

But he would hear me if I spoke, haul me out by the hair, and—I'd just gotten it colored, a rich mahogany that enhanced my eyes and—

He muttered something. I swallowed, mind scrambling as I tried to think of plan B.

The phone was in my hand. And then it came to me. I could call Solberg's home phone. Wouldn't the hairy gunman be curious who was calling at 3:07 in the morning? Wouldn't he, ergo, trot downstairs to check the answering machine in the office?

Wouldn't I die if I guessed wrong? Literally.

I opened the phone. What if my call didn't go through? Sometimes they didn't. The digits glowed blue. I jerked my gaze up, certain the numbers were shining through the open door like a newly discovered star. Maybe I could blind him with it.

I heard his shoes rapping against tile. He was in the bathroom. I could imagine him glancing about and prayed he would go inside. A shower might be nice. Maybe a Jacuzzi. But his steps didn't click farther across the tiled floor. There were no clothes sighing as they wafted to the heated floor.

No sound of running water or delighted splashing as he prepared to bathe.

In fact, I could almost hear him turn his attention toward the closet. It was now or never. I tightened my grip on the phone until my knuckles ached.

Solberg's was the last number I had called. I poised my finger over the SEND button and froze. Did my phone beep when it dialed? Was I sure I hadn't called someone else since trying Solberg? Could Hairy hear me hyperventilating in the closet?

Shoving the phone back inside my purse, I hunched over it to muffle the noise, jabbed SEND, then jerked my head up to the door crack and held my breath.

All I could see was the corner of the mammoth bed and a stretch of eggshell wall.

But I heard something, some indefinable noise. Had he spoken? Did he curse? Had he heard me? Was he . . . ?

The phone blared in the bedroom. I think I screamed, but maybe I was too terrified to actually make a noise. It took me a couple of lifetimes to realize I was still alive and was cupping my mouth with my hand.

An eternity scraped past, and then I heard Hairy turn. I cringed against the wall, but he didn't reach in to drag me out by the hair, or even by the ankle. Instead, he strode out the door and down the stairs. A full twenty seconds creaked by before I realized the enormity of the fact that he was gone. Another ten seconds before my bladder was under control. But once I was on my feet, I knew what I had to do. One glance toward the doorway, and then I was off, racing across the bedroom, ripping the drapes aside, yanking open the—

The door to the deck was locked. I jerked around, muscles frozen, sure Hairy was already behind me, but the room was empty.

Noise sounded on the stairs. In my mind, I imagined him bounding up them, three at a time, gun in hand.

My fingers bumbled on metal. I think I was crying. The lock turned. I yanked the door open. I could hear footsteps on the landing in front of the bedroom, but I was already outside, flying across the deck, half falling, half flying down the stairs.

Don't look back! Don't look back. I looked back and shrieked.

He was following me.

I hit the ground running, stumbled to my knees, scrambled to my feet, and sprinted across the dark lawn. A gun exploded. Pain struck me square in the face. I screamed, but my legs were still working and I didn't dare stop. Veering wildly to the left, I raced toward the Georges' fence. It loomed above my head. I don't know how I got over it. One minute I was panting in Solberg's yard and the next I was over the top and running flat-out.

I heard a grunt behind me and twisted toward the sound. I thought I saw a figure perched atop the fence I'd just cleared. Were there two of them? Was...? But suddenly the earth pitched away beneath me. I fell with a gasp, legs collapsing under my weight.

I was in a hole. A grave! Wild imaginings scrambled through my head. I tried to claw my way out of the abyss. My ankle screamed with pain. And then I heard footsteps thundering over the lawn above my head.

I cowered against the dirt. The footsteps kept running.

Except for the sound of my own breath rattling in and out of my lungs, the world went quiet. I crept up a half an inch.

No one pounced on me from the darkness.

I waited, breath held, trying to peer over the top of the hole. Liquid ran warm and steady into my right eye. I blinked. My vision blurred.

I could see no one, could hear nothing. Weak in the hazy aftermath of fear, I closed my eyes and sunk like a boneless chicken to the bottom of the pit.

7

Sometimes the truth'll set you free, maybe. But sometimes it'll get you six months to a year at juvie hall.

—*Blair Kase*
(Chrissy's sixth-grade crush),
explaining truth, justice, and
the American way to Sister
Celeste

I WAS STILL shaking when I reached my Saturn.

I had remained in the hole for what seemed like forever, and the journey across the Georges' yard had felt like a death sentence, but I had remained unmolested. Still, unlocking the car was almost more than my wobbly fingers could manage. Once inside, however, I power-locked the doors and sped for home, too scared to take a moment to assess my wounds.

My key bounced erratically in my front door, but I finally managed to shove it into the slot, then pushed inside and locked the door behind me. In a fresh wave of panic, I almost forgot to disarm my security system. It was relatively new, installed after the last attempt on my life. It's nice to keep things fresh.

The memory made my stomach twist. I switched on the lights. They flared around me like fireworks. I pressed my back against the door and told myself I wasn't going to cry.

Okay, I wasn't going to cry *anymore*.

Stumbling into the bathroom, I turned on the light and stared breathlessly at myself in the mirror.

There was no blood. No gushing wounds. Not even a scratch. All my parts seemed to be in place, not misaligned like an inexplicably high-priced Picasso as I'd feared.

I touched my fingertips to my cheek. It was streaked with dust, and in that instant I realized the truth. I hadn't been shot by some unseen sniper. I'd been struck in the face by a stream of water from Solberg's sprinkler.

I stroked my face with reverent thanksgiving. Turns out I liked it better than I had realized.

Reality settled in by slow degrees. I was safe. I was home. I took a deep, shuddering breath and considered trying to do something mundane to shore up the feeling of normalcy. I could brush my teeth or clean my toilet. I could take a bath or wash my clothes. I glanced down at them. The mud was starting to dry in sharp clusters. Laundry might be a good idea. But it was almost four o'clock in the morning.

And there's only one thing that's truly normal at four o'clock in the morning.

Two minutes later I was fast asleep, the house lit up like Dodger Stadium.

*   *   *

You okay? You're acting kinda funny."

I snapped my attention back to my client. His name was Henry Granger. One did not want to be told one was "acting funny" by Henry Granger.

He'd told me during his first session that his friends called him Willy, and since then had regaled me with tales of the tea parties he'd enjoyed while wearing his wife's garters and little else. I studiously refused to think about why I should call him Willy.

"I'm fine," I said. "Have you decided whether or not you want to tell Phyllis?"

He cleared his throat and scowled at me. He was a big man, well over two hundred pounds, and seventy years of age. But maybe it's never easy to tell one's spouse you've been playing dress up in her undies.

" 'Bout the parties?" he asked.

I wondered vaguely what else he had to confess. Then wondered if I would be ready to hear it anytime soon. I was still a little shaky from the previous night, but I tried not to wince as I broached the next question.

"Are there other details about your past that are bothering you?" I asked.

He cleared his throat again and glanced out the window. "Not really."

That meant "yes" in psychology terms.

I braced myself. I hadn't awakened until nine-fifteen. My first appointment was at ten. It was a half-hour drive to work if there weren't more than three cars involved in the 210's current fender-bender. I'd once tried taking the 5 down to Eagle Rock, but subsequently decided I'd rather make myself a cardboard sign and join the other panhandlers on the off-ramp downtown than brave that kind of insanity again.

My hair, when I'd finally glanced at it in the rearview mirror, looked as if I had undergone some sort of medieval shock therapy, and though I'd doused myself in enough Jivago to drown a killer whale, I was afraid my particular meld of body odor and terror might be wafting up from under the gallon of cologne.

Life didn't look good on a fast five hours of sleep and the jouncing memory of a guy running me to ground like a grizzly after a field mouse. Was he simply a burglar or had he seen me enter Solberg's house?

But wait a minute. He hadn't been searching for some*thing*. He'd been searching for some*one*. I was sure of it suddenly. The gun was burning a hole in my mind.

"I don't see how telling her's gonna help things any," said Mr. Granger.

"Well . . . ," I said, and glanced at the clock. It was twelve-fifty. "That's something for you to think about this week, But I'm afraid our time is done for today."

He stood up. I bid him adieu.

The Hunts came next. Their weekend had gone better than mine. She'd made him waffles on Sunday morning, and he'd reciprocated by cleaning the bathroom.

She sounded fairly shocked when she told me about it, and gave him a smile for his efforts.

Maybe I wasn't a total screwup, I thought later as they hustled out the door. From my tiny reception area down the hall, I heard murmured voices. I sighed, cupped my hand over my eyes, and tried to refrain from wilting under my desk like yesterday's spinach.

"You look tired."

I jerked up my head with a squeal of surprise.

Lieutenant Rivera stood in the doorway. He raised one dark brow, the cynic's version of a smile. "You're awfully jumpy," he said, stepping inside and closing the door behind him. "You getting enough sleep, McMullen?"

Memories of the previous night came filtering back to me. I'd been chased by a guy with a gun and a lot of hair, which might be a good thing to tell the police. Then again, the LAPD might still be holding a grudge about one of L.A.'s favorite football stars dropping dead in my office three months earlier. And certain members of law enforcement might consider my foray into Solberg's house to be less than legal, especially since a few items may have fallen into my purse before my departure—including Solberg's secret computer disk, which I still hadn't had a chance to look at.

I glanced longingly toward the door, but I was pretty sure Rivera would notice if I tried to dash past him, so I tidied the papers on my desk and gave him a dignified glance.

"What can I do for you, Lieutenant?" I asked.

A hint of amusement frolicked around his eyes. He wore a soft burgundy sweater tucked into black pants. They were cuffed at the ankle and rode low on his hips. He looked good—a forbidden cross between Antonio Banderas's smoldering sensuality and Colin Farrell's lawless magnetism. But I didn't care. I had dignity. Screw magnetism. Please.

"Shall I assume you look so tired because your little geek has finally returned?" he asked.

I straightened my back and entwined my fingers on the top of my desk. "By my little geek, I assume you mean Solberg?" I said.

He sat down across from me and stretched his legs out in front of him. His eyes were half-masked and his mouth lifted slightly at the scarred corner.

"Kind of an impersonal form of address for the love of your life, isn't it?" he asked.

I gave him a gritted smile, letting him guess whether I wanted to kill him or laugh at him. "No," I said.

"No, it's not impersonal, or no he hasn't returned?"

"You're the investigator," I said. "Doesn't that make it your job to investigate?"

He shrugged. The movement was slow and languid. His eyes were the color of Scotch whiskey. I'd discovered early in life that I could get smashed on about two tablespoons of Scotch whiskey. I felt a little dizzy already. "So you haven't been looking for him?" he asked.

I shifted my gaze back to my desk and shuffled a few more papers into companionable piles. I had reports to file. Clients to see. A heart attack to schedule. Busy me. "I'm sorry, Lieutenant," I said. "But unlike some people . . ." I paused and gave him a Sweet'n Low kind of smile. "I have real work to do here. Unless you've come to accuse me of murder . . . again, I would appreciate it if you would allow me to do my job."

He lifted one hand as if to indicate peace. "I don't think you murdered anyone."

"Whew." I made a delicate swiping motion with my

knuckles across my brow. "What a relief. Now, if you'll excuse me—"

"Just breaking and entering this time. Maybe burglary."

My heart jolted to a stop. "And what far-flung fantasy are you living out now, Rivera?"

Something dark and perilous sparked in his eyes. Temper flexed his jaw. He straightened abruptly, leaning over my desk. "Someone broke into Solberg's house last night."

"Really?" I felt my heart bump to life like a Chinese gong. "That's terrible. He wasn't home, I hope."

"You tell me."

I forced myself to stay in my chair and meet his eyes. "I know you have some strange delusions about Solberg and myself," I said, "but believe me, he's not my type."

"Really?" His eyes were like lasers. Scotch whiskey lasers. "Last time I checked, he was still breathing."

I jerked to my feet. "You f—" I snarled, but I lowered my hackles and tried again. "Excuse me," I said. My tone was stunningly gracious. My teeth ached with the Herculean effort. "I have clients to see."

Rivera rose, too, slowly, holding my gaze the whole time. "What the hell were you doing in Solberg's house, McMullen?"

I pressed my hands against the desk to keep the world from tipping me onto the floor like rotting sushi. "I wasn't in Solberg's house."

"My sources say you were."

Jesus God! Sources! He had sources? I wanted sources. "Well then . . ." I gave him a smile. Could be only half of my mouth still functioned. Maybe the heart attack would have to wait until I was done having a stroke. "Your sources are as deluded as you are, Lieutenant."

"My sources are his next-door neighbors, who got a close-up view of you scrambling over their fence at three-fifteen in the morning."

I held my breath. In my mind I was blubbering apologies and confessions like a white guy on the soul train. But the truth dawned on me like a flash of glorious light. No one could have identified me. It had been as dark as hell in the Georges' backyard, despite the stupid security lights. I'd been sprinting like a Kentucky Thoroughbred, and my car was parked well out of sight.

Rivera was just yanking my chain. Even if Tiffany Georges had pressed night goggles up to her patio door, she couldn't possibly have known it was me. Could she?

"I'm sorry, Mr. Rivera." I gave him a prim smile. "But you must be mistaken, because I'm not the scrambling type."

He stepped closer and leaned across my desk again. He smelled like bedroom. "I hate to disagree," he said, "but I distinctly remember you scrambling."

Memories of a night not so long past trilled along my frazzled nerve endings.

"I had to put my hand on your ass to . . . assist you," he said.

The memory came tumbling back at me. We'd been in Bomstad's backyard and Rivera had boosted me over the security fence. It had taken all my considerable fortitude to slide down on the opposite side instead of falling on him like a love-starved retriever.

And despite the fact that he irritated the hell out of me, I was having a smidgeon of the same trouble now.

"I could have gotten over the fence by myself," I said. My voice was not the least bit breathless.

His eyes never shifted from mine. "What fence?" he asked. "I was talking about the night at your place."

I felt my throat grow dry and my tongue wooden.

"You remember it," he said. "The time you tore my shirt all to hell. You were scrambling like a wild—"

"I wasn't in anybody's stupid yard!" I snapped.

He raised a slow eyebrow. "Then, where were you last night?"

"In bed." I swallowed, wishing to hell I were there now. Or anywhere. Anywhere but here, with him reading my mind like a black-eyed gypsy. "My bed. All night."

His eyes smoldered. Honest to God, like a fire that wouldn't be doused no matter how much Kool-Aid you pour on it. "So you weren't dressed like a cat burglar and slinking through Solberg's sprinkler system?"

Jesus. Oh Jesus, save me from myself.

"You have a rich fantasy life, Lieutenant," I said.

His gaze burned into mine. "You've no idea, McMullen."

My lips felt parched. Really. That's why I licked them. Rivera dropped his gaze to watch the movement.

Silence screamed around us. He leaned toward me a little farther.

"Ms. McMullen?"

I almost shrieked at the sound of Elaine's voice. I jerked away from Rivera, heart thumping and hands sweating.

"Yes!" My voice cracked. I cleared my throat and tried for a more restrained tone. "Yes? What is it, Elaine?"

"Susan Abrams is here for her one o'clock appointment,"

she said, but all the while she was giving me her "Is everything all right or should I squirt him in the eye with my mace" look.

"Thank you, Elaine." My voice was now coolly melodious. I found that I wanted quite badly to swoon like a Southern belle, but I've never perfected the art, and Rivera was staring into my shuddering soul like the devil come to retrieve the damned. "You can send her in in a few minutes. The lieutenant will be leaving momentarily."

"Very well," she said, and paused, giving me one more chance to go for the mace. I declined. She left, closing the door behind her.

"So you were home last night?" Rivera asked.

"All night," I repeated, and found that my hands had gone inexplicably numb. If I was lucky, my tongue would follow suit.

"Got anyone to collaborate your story?"

I gritted my teeth. "It is not a *story*."

His eyes crinkled a little at the corners, as if amused that I had skirted the issue. "What time did you go to bed?"

"You concerned with my sleeping habits, Lieutenant?"

His nostrils flared slightly. "What time?" he asked again.

I gave him a shrug and rose to my feet. My knees worked like magic, but the door seemed like a thousand light years away. "Ten o'clock."

"And you didn't have an appointment until ten this morning? That gives you, what? Eleven hours of sleep?"

I gave him a carefully honed smile, like he was oh-so-amusing. Like I wasn't going to drop to the floor and quiver like a palsy victim. "A girl needs a little time to brush her teeth in the morning, Lieutenant."

"Uh-huh. So what time did you roll out of bed, McMullen?"

I concentrated on staying vertical and gave him a lazy glance, as if I didn't have time for such foolishly mundane questions. "Please, Lieutenant—"

"When?" he asked, but his voice had lost some jocularity.

"Eight o'clock." My own tone was on the fast track to pissy.

"So you probably had time to do more than brush your teeth. Maybe even a few minutes to mess with your hair."

Jesus God, my hair, I thought, but managed to keep from trying to pat it into place. It would have taken a battalion of hairdressers armed with gardening tools and shellac to make it look as if it weren't inhabited by bats. "You plan to arrest me for having a bad hair day, Lieutenant?"

"Not at all," he said, reaching up and brushing a strand away from my face. His fingers skimmed my ear. I put a steadying hand on the wall. His lips twisted up a fraction of a millimeter. "I was just wondering about your ablutions."

"Ablutions?"

His fingers brushed my cheek. I held the orgasm at bay. "Are you going to night school, Lieutenant? English Vocab 101?"

His eyes laughed. "Well..." He drew back slightly. "I'll let you get back to work."

I nodded. Casual as hell. Hardly panting at all.

He turned toward the door and reached for the knob, but at the last moment he glanced back at me. "I like your hair like that, McMullen. It's kind of sexy," he said. "But you've got a little mud. Right below your left ear."

*   *   *

I don't remember returning to my desk, but sometime later I found myself sprawled across it.

"Mac."

I squawked at the sound and jerked to an upright position. "Laney!"

"What's wrong?" She entered the room and closed the door behind her.

"Nothing. Nothing's wrong."

She started to shake her head, then froze. "It's about Jeen, isn't it?"

"What?"

"What happened?"

Excellent question. I had no idea what had happened. Except that Rivera wanted to fry my ass. Except for the fact that someone had been sneaking around Solberg's house with a gun the size of a blow dryer.

But I had my suspicions, and they made my blood run cold. Solberg had done something stupid. Maybe it was the illegal kind of stupid. Maybe it wasn't. But the fact remained that he was in deep shit, and if I wasn't careful, Laney was going to be there with him, up the proverbial creek with no proverbial paddle in sight.

I stifled a shiver. "Listen, Laney..." I paused, having no idea what I wanted her to listen to. I couldn't tell her the truth. She wouldn't believe it. And if she thought the Geek Nerd was in trouble... The idea froze my heart. If Laney Butterfield had a fault, it was her unrelenting loyalty toward those she loved.

I'd learned that firsthand when she'd picked me up after

my one and only date with a guy named Frankie Gallager. He'd had a reputation for being a fast mover. I had a reputation for finding that irresistible. She'd begged me not to go out with him, but good sense had not been my strong suit in my younger years.

Three hours after leaving my house, I'd had to knee Mr. Gallager in the groin to make him see reason. He'd left me stranded in a part of town my mother refused to drive through.

Laney was the only one I dared call. She'd stolen her dad's keys to the Chevy and snuck out to rescue me. For the only daughter of a Methodist minister, that was tantamount to mass murder.

"What?" she said again, face pale.

I was shaking my head. I didn't know why. "You can't go to Vegas."

"Why not? What happened?"

I flickered my eyes toward the door, mind spinning. "I don't know how to tell you this." Or what to tell her.

Her eyes were as big as dinner plates. "Is he hurt? Tell me if he's hurt, Mac. I can—"

"No. No. He's not hurt, Laney—"

"He's dead." Her face was absolutely colorless. Even her lips had gone white.

"No! No." I reached across my desk and grabbed her hand. "He just . . . He . . . You can't go to Vegas."

She stared at me.

"Because . . . he did meet someone else." The words hissed out on the wind of insanity. I swear my brain was in no way connected to them.

She blinked.

"I didn't want to tell you." Ah, a breath of truth.

She stepped back a pace and eased into a chair. A dab of color had returned to her cheeks. "How do you know?"

"I . . ." . . . was going to hell. Straight to hell. And for what? For trying to help a friend. The irony of it hurt a little. "I talked to him," I said.

"You called him?"

"He called me." I nodded, hating myself with increasing and surprising measures. "Said . . . He said he was sorry. Said I should tell you."

She sat absolutely still for a minute, then drew a careful breath. "That was nice of him."

"What?" I tilted my head toward her, 'cuz I was pretty damn sure I'd heard wrong.

"He doesn't want me to worry," she said. "Even though he's with . . ." Her voice trailed off. She rose to her feet.

"Laney?"

"No. It's okay. I'll just . . . I think I'll go home for a little while. If you don't mind," she said, then turned away and left.

I let my head fall onto my desk. I was a liar and a thief and an ass. What I wouldn't do for a friend.

8

Love makes the world go around, but so does a gallon of vodka and a box of Cuban cigars.

—*Pete McMullen,*
shortly after his second
divorce

I KNEW BEYOND a shadow of a doubt that I should not continue to investigate Solberg's disappearance. I was in over my head. I didn't have a clue what I was doing, and I didn't even like Solberg. In fact, I detested Solberg. Elaine would get over him, just like she'd gotten over the measles in second grade.

"Ms. McMullen?" Emery Black, executive supervisor, rose to his feet as I entered his office. Reaching across his desk, he offered his hand. We shook once. Solberg's boss had a handshake like the Terminator.

"Yes. Thank you for seeing me," I said, and sounded, I thought, perfectly sane. But then, I was wearing taupe.

Taupe blouse, taupe skirt, taupe shoes. You can't get more sane than taupe, even if you're wearing strappy little sandals with three-inch heels and spend your time panting across people's lawns for no good reason.

Emery Black's office was large and bright, awash in natural light. But then, it would be. NeoTech, Inc., was basically a glass pyramid, noted by architects from L.A. to Boston for its innovative design. Or so said the receptionist, with whom I had spent an informative five minutes.

Unfortunately, she had known more about architecture than she had about Solberg's absence.

I glanced around the palatial office. Expensively framed posters, most dealing with climbing the proverbial ladder of success, adorned Black's walls. By the look of things, he was pretty securely perched on the top rung. Money, power, family et al., if one were to judge by his surroundings. Twin photos, professionally matted and framed, showed two young men wearing tasseled mortarboards and capes. I could only assume they were his progeny.

But there was no sign of a wife, girlfriend, or concubine. And no ring on his left hand. Hmmm. Successful, good handshake, and single. What more could a girl want?

It was Wednesday, two days after Rivera's preemptive visit. Which means I had spent forty-eight hours trying to convince myself to forget about this stupid problem. But Solberg still hadn't made an appearance. I'd popped the purloined disk into my home computer, but the gibberish that sprang onto my screen might just as well have been hieroglyphics. So I'd hidden the CD under my kitchen sink, where only the bold dare tread, and made an appointment with Emery Black, certain there was someone at

NeoTech who could shed light in the darkness of my ignorance.

I glanced about the office again, maybe analyzing his personality, maybe snooping. Sometimes it's hard to tell the difference.

A dracaena grew lustily in front of his east bank of windows. Adjunct to the trio of chairs that surrounded a Persian rug near the back forty of the room, a small teak table boasted an inverted gold pear on a porcelain pedestal that had an inscription I couldn't make out. Or maybe it just looked like a pear. Maybe it was a golden water balloon, or—

Black cleared his throat. "So you're a friend of our J.D.?"

"No." I jerked my attention back to him, realizing my answer was too quick and might have been considered rude in certain circles. Say, those circles that didn't think Solberg was an irritating little wart dweeb. "I mean . . ." I gave him a smile, set my purse on the floor, and sat down in the chair he indicated with a jab of his hand. "He's more a friend of a friend."

"I see." He seated himself behind his desk. It was big enough to roller-skate on. "And what is your concern?" He steepled his arms, interlocked his fingers, and scowled at me over his knuckles. His hair was dark brown and receding somewhat, giving way to half a century of life.

"Well, my friend was expecting him home, and he hasn't returned. I thought perhaps you knew why."

"What's your friend's name?" he asked.

"Chester," I said, 'cuz, what the hell, the truth and I weren't exactly on intimate terms these days anyway. "He hasn't heard from him in more than two weeks."

"And what of you, Ms. McMullen?" he asked, giving me a schooled smile. "Have you heard from him?"

If I had, would I be sitting there in his boss's office admitting a relationship, however remote, to Solberg? "No, but like I said, we aren't . . ." . . . both human. "Close," I said.

He stared at me, unspeaking. He had eyebrows like dark caterpillars that threatened copulation. I waited in silence for several seconds, then prodded.

"Have you?"

He rose to pace to the window. He was tall, over six feet, but he carried a few extra pounds, making him look shorter but maybe more capable. I've always thought it was one of God's cruelest jokes that men are considered mature when they go to fat. While women are considered . . . well, fat.

"And Chester is his . . . significant other?" he asked.

I went from surprised to baffled. "What?"

"Don't get me wrong," he said, glancing my way. "J.D.'s preferences are no concern of mine. I just like to make certain my employees are . . . content."

He thought Solberg was gay, I realized hazily, and that was just weird. Hadn't he seen Will of *Will & Grace* fame? Gay guys are intelligent, well dressed, and sophisticated.

"Frankly," he said, "J.D. is a great asset to NeoTech."

"An asset who has called you recently?"

He gave me a cat-at-the-canary-cage kind of smile. "I'm afraid not," he said, "but you needn't worry. He told me before I left Vegas that something came up that needed his immediate attention."

"What was it?" I asked.

He shrugged his beefy shoulders. And there you go! "Beefy"! Like having shoulders like a corn-fed steer is a good thing or something. If a guy has beefy shoulders he's manly. If a woman has beefy shoulders she's . . . a cow. "He didn't say exactly."

I twisted my mind away from what's for dinner and focused. "But you must have some idea."

"Listen, Ms. McMullen . . ." His tone was a little patronizing, a little apologetic. "A man at the helm of an empire such as NeoTech must decide who to trust and when to trust him. I'd trust J.D. with my life."

Really? 'Cuz I wouldn't trust Solberg with my phone number. In fact, I hadn't, but one infamous evening not too long ago, he'd oozed into my vestibule just the same. "Then aren't you worried about losing him?"

"Not at all. Why would I be?"

"I just thought maybe you were concerned about him taking his knowledge elsewhere."

"What knowledge?" he asked. His tone insisted he was relaxed, but was there the slightest bit of tension around his eyes?

"Nothing specific. I just thought . . ." What had I thought? Why was I there? For all I knew, Emery Black was the reason for Solberg's disappearance. "I just thought you might be concerned about his absence if he hasn't kept you apprised."

"I can assure you, Ms. McMullen, J.D. is extremely happy at NeoTech. We have given him endless opportunities."

"What kind of opportunities?"

"He makes a good deal of money here and will make a

good deal more. I'm certain he'll be back before the end of the month." He said the words as a dismissal. I'd never liked to be dismissed.

"Why?" I asked.

For a moment he looked as if he was envisioning me with a volleyball stuffed in my mouth, but he managed a smile. "For people like J.D.—geniuses, perhaps I should say—friends come and go. But computers..." He spread his pudgy hands. "He can't live without them. Technology's his mistress."

"So you're saying he'll come back because he's having an affair with his motherboard?"

He laughed. "Well, he'll be back within the next couple of weeks. I'm certain of that."

"Have you considered the possibility of some sort of accident?" Like a hirsute guy with a gun the size of a tank mowing him down in his sleep. I felt sweat break out on my brow at the memory. Had the guy tried to shoot me as I scampered across Solberg's lawn, or had I imagined the gunshot?

Black stepped toward the door. "It is certainly good to know our J.D. has concerned friends such as you and Chester, but I can assure you, he's perfectly fine."

"Why is that?" I asked.

"What?" He turned toward me, struggling for patience and almost winning.

"How can you be so certain he's okay if you don't know where he is?"

He studied me for a moment, as if I were an interesting form of lower life—the middle-income species. "The truth is, Ms. McMullen, J.D. has been working very hard for a long while. He deserves a vacation. If he feels it necessary to take that vacation now, I'm more than happy to give him some leeway."

"That's very generous of you."

He smiled. "Generous, I am not. But I am highly intelligent, and I know what my employees need. J.D. and I have worked extremely well together in the past and will again in the future. So if he wants a couple more days on the strip, that's perfectly acceptable."

I let his words sink in. They permeated my skin like toxins, pushing up new suspicions in their wake. "Is he with someone?" I asked. Was he gay? Was *Will & Grace* all a lie?

He shook his head, looking almost regretful. "I'm afraid I can't tell you that."

Anger shot through me. "Who is it?" I asked.

"It's been nice meeting you," he said, and opened the door. "I'm sorry I can't be more helpful, but I assure you, our J.D. is perfectly safe."

I jerked to my feet. "Is it someone he met in Vegas?"

Impatience ticked in his jaw. "I take my employees' privacy very seriously, Ms. McMullen. I hope you will respect that," he said, and practically pushing me out, closed the door behind me.

I saw the world through a red haze. Damn Solberg's worthless hide! He was cheating on Laney. What the hell was wrong with men? Four months ago he couldn't get a date with an organ grinder's monkey, and now . . . Well, now it looked like he could, didn't it?

I glanced around, wanting to hit something.

Glass cubicles marched away in every direction. On the far side of the floor were more offices. Maybe one of them was Solberg's. Maybe, if I happened inside, I might learn the organ grinder's monkey's name and address.

I eased across the floor toward the offices on the far side of the building. Nonchalantly, like I had some sort of business that was neither illegal nor unethical.

A little guy with wire-rims glanced up as I walked by. I gave him my "I'm supposed to be here" smile. A woman wearing red pants two inches too short said hi, but other than that I was pretty much ignored.

I wondered vaguely about Hilary Pershing. Was she here somewhere? Maybe grooming a cat and plotting my demise? Maybe thinking of past nights of bliss with the Geekster?

I could see that each door on the far side of the room had a name etched into the glass, and wandered in that direction. "Jeffrey Dunn" was engraved into the first one. The second said "Kimberly Evans."

I hit paydirt on the third. It said "J. D. Solberg" in the same utilitarian font as the first two. Maybe I should have felt guilty about trespassing. I didn't. The glass handle felt cool against my palm.

"Can I help you?"

I jerked toward the speaker while simultaneously trying to keep my heart in my chest. "Yes!" I snapped, then eased my tone toward something short of panic and tried again. "Yes. I hope so." I cleared my throat. I had no idea where to go from there. "I had an appointment with J.D." I said his name like we were old pals, chums from nerd school.

The man who stood in front of me was only a few inches taller than myself, but they were nice inches. He stared at me for a moment. I did my best not to shuffle my feet. Feet should not be shuffled when crammed into leather sandals that cost more than your monthly house payment. Even if they do pinch like hell.

"J.D. always did have the luck," he said.

I realized I had been holding my breath. "What?"

He thrust out his hand. "Ross Bennet," he said. "What can I do for you?"

"Oh, ummm . . ." I took his hand, then glanced guiltily toward Solberg's office. "Isn't J.D. in?"

He leaned sideways to look past me. "Not unless he's worked out that invisibility formula," he said, and grinned.

I literally stepped back. Turns out he had a smile bright enough to drop a Lakers Girl at fifty yards. Whoa. Be still my rampaging heart. I shut Solberg's door.

"Was this a professional visit or . . . ?" He paused, waiting for me to fill in the blank.

"No. Well . . ." I laughed a little. Silly ol' me, causing no trouble for no one, certainly not perpetrating a misdemeanor. "Yes, sort of. We're friends, I suppose you could say."

"Yeah?"

"We've . . . ummm . . . known each other for years." I flipped my hand. "And sometimes we like to . . ." I wobbled my head. "Toss ideas around. You know."

He waited for me to go on.

"Like the invisibility problem," I said. "That's a stickler."

He watched me for a moment longer, then laughed. "I'll

make sure to tell him his accomplice was here to see him. What's your name?"

I gave him the real deal.

"Well, it's his loss, then, isn't it, Christina?"

"What is?"

"That he wasn't here to see you." He smiled again. Down girl.

"Oh. Huh-huh." That was a laugh. It sounded like I was about to barf. Maybe I was. I glanced toward Black's glass-fronted office. He was nowhere to be seen. "Do you happen to know where he might be?"

"J.D.?" Reaching up, Ross rubbed the back of his neck. He wore a rolled leather bracelet and no other jewelry—such as a band of gold on his left ring finger. "Now that you mention it, I haven't seen him for a couple weeks. Not since the convention."

"Oh?" Black's door opened. He stepped out. I shifted my gaze back to Bennet. "What convention was that?"

"Big do in Las Vegas," he said, and shook his head as if weary of the whole thing.

I studiously ignored Black, though he was making his way between the workstations toward me, like a beefy spider on the move. Casual. Casual. He probably hadn't called security yet.

"You don't like Las Vegas?" I asked.

"J.D.'s better at that sort of thing than I am."

Had they been there together? "Really?"

"Yeah. You seen one gorgeous topless dancing girl, you seen them all," he said, and smiled again.

I forced a laugh.

"Ms. McMullen." Emery Black had arrived with his scowl.

I considered bolting, sure he was going to fling me from his building by my hair, but he just lifted a hand. My purse dangled from it.

"You forgot this," he said.

Bennet shifted his gaze from me to Black. "You two met?"

"Oh, well . . . thank you," I said, and slipped my purse from his fingers. "It was nice meeting you, Mr. Bennet." He gave me a boyish smile. "You, too, Mr. Black." The CEO scowled. I coolly examined them both for an instant, but meanwhile my internal cocktail waitress was duking it out with my psychologist in residence.

"Don't be obtuse," warned the shrink. *"Bennet's too pretty to be as innocent as he looks."*

The barmaid snorted. *"And I suppose you'd trust Black, seeing's how he uses dumb-ass terms like 'significant other' and has an office the size of a Neptune."*

"Well, the size of a man's office is a far better calibrator of his character than the size of his—"

"Come again," interrupted Bennet.

"Thank you," said the shrink and the barmaid in unison, and turned away with quiet dignity. But inside, we were both pretty much wondering if our hips looked wide in taupe.

I wrestled with a hundred questions during the next twenty-four hours. Why had Black been so eager to get rid of me? Who was the guy in Solberg's house? Why did Tiffany Georges have a three-foot hole in the back of her manicured lawn? And was Bennet's smile as tantalizing as it had seemed?

I researched each question thoroughly and came to the conclusion that Black had a multimillion-dollar conglomeration to protect. I had no idea who the guy in Solberg's house might have been. And Tiffany Georges's odd digging habits were her own secret.

I leaned back in my home office chair and stared out my pea-sized window. Papers cluttered my battered desk, but I was comfortable with clutter. It was unanswered questions that made my skin itch.

I'd struck out on all counts regarding my ongoing investigation. Except the Bennet question. I was pretty sure his smile was the real deal.

But maybe I'd better check into that. I mean . . . Not his smile. I didn't care about that, of course, but it would make sense to talk to him again. After all, he'd seemed willing to converse. In fact, compared to Black, he won Mr. Congeniality hands-down. And they were nice hands. Good shoulders, too.

Not that I would have cared if his neck was directly attached to his nipples, but I had to find Solberg before Elaine did something stupid and . . . Well, what the hell, I already had the receiver in my hand.

I stared at it in some surprise and dialed.

"NeoTech." The woman on the other end of the line had a voice that would make Minnie Mouse giggle.

"Hi," I said. "I'd like to speak to Mr. Bennet."

"Mr. Bennet. Of course," she squeaked. "Can I tell him what this is concerning?"

"Umm. Sure. Tell him it's about a secret formula."

There was a blip of silence, but then she found her Minnie perkiness. "And who shall I say is calling?"

"The invisible woman." Don't ask me what was wrong with me. It could have been anything. Lack of sleep. Insanity. Nicotine deprivation. Okay, I admit I'd lit up a couple Slims on the way home from NeoTech, but I was pretty sure they didn't count for at least forty-eight hours after scampering across the lawn in front of a hairy guy with a gun the size of New Mexico.

"Very well," said Ms. Mouse. "Can you hold for a minute?"

"Christina." Ross's tone was smooth when he answered the line.

"How'd you know it was me?"

He laughed. "Most women I know are fully visible. I was hoping you'd call."

"You were?" I tried to hide my surprise, but my luck hadn't been exactly phenomenal for the past, oh, thirty years or so.

"Yeah, I . . ." He paused, sounding flustered. "I was just chastising myself for failing to get your phone number."

I stopped myself from saying, "Really?" in that squeaky tone I remember from adolescence. "Well . . ." I said. "Chastise no more. I can give it to you now."

He laughed. "Maybe I'll just ask you out while I've got you on the phone."

"Really?" My voice squeaked. Damn.

"Are you busy Saturday night?"

I'm afraid my mouth may actually have dropped open. Generally, if a guy asks me out, he's legally prevented from traveling more than five hundred yards from his trailer house.

"Saturday night?" I resisted shouting "Yes!" and noisily thumbed the pages of the romance novel I was reading. The beautiful thing about romantic fiction is the girl always gets her guy. And what a guy. He's handsome, intelligent, and neat, and never ever owns a trailer house. "I'll have to check my schedule." More shuffling as I counted to fifteen. "Saturday the nineteenth?"

"Yeah."

I happened to know that Saturday stood out like a glaring rectangle of nothingness on the planner I'd shoved into my purse. "I'm sorry. I'm afraid I'm busy that day." It was the memory of a man named Keith Hatcher that made me lie. I'd dated Hatcher for almost five months. He'd been a real estate agent and an amateur photographer. I thought we might be able to cohabitate quite congenially together until I saw pictures of myself on his office bulletin board. I'd been asleep. My mouth was open. My hair was smashed up against the left side of my face. And I was naked. Naked as a jaybird.

"All day?" Bennet asked.

Seeing oneself naked between photos of condominiums and fixer-uppers tends to make a woman kind of jumpy. "Yes. It looks like it."

"How about Sunday?"

"Ummm . . ." I closed my eyes. The photo was still stuck pretty firmly in my mind. My thighs had looked pudgy. But then, it had been taken at a bad angle. Like within fifty feet. "I'm sorry," I said. If someone's going to be photographing me, I like to have six months' notice, and clothes. A boat-load of clothes.

"Listen, Christina, I know us techno types come off pretty nerdy, but I'm a decent guy." He paused. "Really."

A sliver of guilt sliced through me. It was wrong to judge men by others' mistakes, but I'd been so absolutely, incredibly naked. "It's not—"

"I trim my nose hairs," he said.

"I really am—"

"And I hardly ever watch anime anymore." He paused. "Unless it's Sakuru. She's smoking."

I couldn't help but laugh.

"Friday night," he said. "If you don't have fun, you can Taser me and dropkick me into East L.A."

I tried to resist, but the man seemed spectacularly . . . normal. A rush of pleasure pulsed through me. I mean, I had to try to find Solberg—for Elaine's sake. And Ross, Mr. Bennet, might be able to give me some clues. Or mouth-to-mouth resuscitation.

Still, memories of my past boyfriends trickled through my mind like so much rotting sewage.

"You're thinking too hard," he said.

"Well . . . I have plans," I countered, then closed my eyes and took the plunge, knowing with every fiber in my being that the impact was going to hurt like the devil. "Oh, what the hell. I suppose I can have dinner with Clooney another time."

He laughed. It sounded nice. "Good point. Six o'clock okay?"

"Okay."

"Want me to pick you up?"

"No thanks, I'll meet you somewhere."

"Uh-oh."

"Uh-oh what?"

"That's the sign of a woman who's been wounded."

Well . . . I had been, and on more than one occasion. But he probably meant emotionally. That was true, too.

9

There are lots of fish in the sea. Some are sharks,
some are angels, and some are bottom-feeders.

—*Elaine Butterfield*
on dating

YOU DOING OKAY, Laney?" I asked. It was four o'clock
on Thursday afternoon. I'd just escorted my last client out
of the office. Collette Sommerset was the mother of two
toddlers. Personally, I think any woman who's the mother
of two toddlers should seek help, but Collette needed it
more than most. Her husband was a nasty drunk . . . and he
was short. My first thought was that she should can Mr.
Sommerset's ass and sue for alimony, but I was trying really
hard to nod and ummm-hummm and help her connect
with her own wishes.

Elaine flopped down in the chair behind the reception
desk and gave me a shrug. "Sure. I've got a date tonight."

Alleluia! "You do?"

She nodded. "Guy I met at an audition."

"An actor?" Okay, *most* guys should be subjected to polygraph tests and multigenerational probes into their heredity before being allowed to date Elaine, but actors . . .

"Producer," she said.

I tried to put the Geekster out of my head, but I couldn't quite manage it. He stuck like an eye booger. "So . . . you're over Solberg?"

She shrugged again and leaned back in her chair. Oh-so-casual. "If he wants to get ahold of me, he knows where I live."

"Yeah, that thought keeps me awake nights, too."

She laughed. Her eyes were too bright. Guilt crept along my nerve endings. Maybe I should have told her about my trip to Solberg's sterile mansion. Maybe I should have told her about the guy with the gun. And maybe that would make her march off to Vegas, armed with nothing more than stunning good looks and the foolish idea that Solberg was worth a skinny minute of her time.

Creepy images darkened my thoughts. When she and I had first escaped Schaumburg, I'd promised Laney's dad I'd take care of her. I know it sounds kind of funny, since we're the same age, and supposedly the same gender, though one couldn't be too certain if one compared our cup sizes. Still, it had seemed like the right thing to do at the time.

"So you're all right?" I asked.

"Sure." Digging her keys from the bottom of her purse, she stood up and headed toward the door. "I guess I'm not the first girl to get dumped."

I ground my teeth and reminded myself that this was

what I deserved for lying my ass off, so I simply retrieved my handbag and followed her outside. "When I'm reincarnated as a gorgeous, nubile blonde with big boobs and a stratospheric IQ, I'm not going to be so humble," I said.

"Promise?" she asked.

"Count on it," I told her, and left the building.

Thirty minutes later I was at Tiffany Georges's house. Well, actually, thirty minutes later I was stuck in traffic and conversing, via sign language, with a guy who'd missed my rear bumper by a curse and a hair. Twelve minutes after that I was parked in the Georges' driveway.

I took a deep breath and steadied myself. Okay, maybe Tiffany really had identified me as the prowler in her backyard. Maybe she would take one look out her window and call the cops. Maybe Rivera would come charging through her front door and haul me off by the hair. But I was willing to bet that none of those things would happen. In fact, I was willing to bet Rivera had been lying through his teeth. For while I was certain Tiffany had reported seeing someone perched on her fence, I was pretty sure she couldn't have seen my face.

Which meant that Rivera had jumped to that outrageous conclusion on his own. Why the hell would I be scampering across Solberg's lawn in the middle of the night?

Anyway, it was now or never. Carting up all my moxie and lifting my chin like a Marine on a mission, I stepped out of the Saturn and marched up to Tiffany's front door. I could hear the bell chiming in the interior, then nothing. I tried again. Waited again. Still nothing.

I took an abbreviated step to the left. Maybe she wasn't home. In which case I could probably take a little stroll through her backyard and . . .

"Can I help you?"

I actually squealed as I jerked toward her. The little sneak was standing behind me. I clasped my hand to my chest and considered having my heart attack right there on her cobbled walkway.

"Oh! I just . . . Oh," I said again. Clever. I might as well have said, "I didn't break into Solberg's house. It wasn't me falling over your fence. And I'm pretty sure you're not digging a grave in which to bury your latest victim."

"Do I know . . . Oh," she said, and looked almost relieved. "You're, ummm . . . Christina, isn't it?"

"Yes. Yes." I realized rather belatedly that she was carrying one of those four-pronged garden thingies, but so far she had neither stabbed me with it nor called the cops.

This is what I call a good day.

"Haven't you heard from Jeen yet?" she asked.

"No," I said, still trying to catch my breath, and maybe a few fluttering brain cells. "I haven't, and I was just wondering if maybe you had learned anything."

"No, but there's been some weird goings-on over there," she said, nodding toward Solberg's yard.

I was tempted to blink, press my fingertips to my chest, and say, "Whatever do you mean?" in my best Scarlett O'Hara imitation, but I managed to control myself. "Really?" I said.

"There was someone in his house the other night."

I felt as stiff as uncooked linguine. "Maybe it was Solberg."

"Well, if it was, he came shimmying over my fence and racing across my yard."

"Across your yard?" I actually gasped when I said it. Move over Julia Roberts.

"In fact, I think there might have been two of them."

"Two of what?"

She scowled a little. I think. There wasn't a wrinkle to be seen. Either she'd been introduced to Botox or her face was made of wood. "People," she said.

"You're kidding."

"I wish I were."

"Well..." And here is where my real genius shone through. "I hope your husband was home."

She paused for just an instant, shifting the garden implement to her other hand. "He's, ummmm...out of town."

"You mean you were alone when all of this was going on?"

She nodded and glanced restlessly down the street. "What did you say you needed?"

"Oh." I shook my head. "I was just concerned about Solberg, but now I'm worried about you. Your husband's home now, isn't he?"

"Yes. Of course. He came home last night."

"Oh, good. I mean..." I laughed. Ha ha ha. "Men. They're the next best thing to a guard dog and a loaded bazooka, huh?"

She didn't say anything.

"And I'm told they're good for yard work," I rambled. "But mine never has been."

I waited for her to chime in. She didn't.

"It looks like you have to do your own, too, huh?"

She glanced down at her pronged thingy. "Well, Jake's awfully busy with work."

"Oh? What does he do?"

"He's a corporate attorney . . . with Everest and Everest."

"Probably works evenings and weekends."

"Sometimes." She shifted her gaze away again. "Well, I'm sorry I can't help you with Jeen. Tell me if you learn anything, will you?"

"Of course," I said, and knowing that was my cue to leave, I headed for my car. I drove away waving merrily, rounded the block, and headed up a windy road into the foothills. It wasn't five minutes later that I parked on a scruffy little knoll that overlooked Solberg's neighborhood. Los Angeles has a thousand such places. The city covers about a zillion square miles of desert, but half of that is perched on inaccessible crags that even Angelites avoid.

On this particular mountaintop, paths marched away through the scrub in several directions, but I was only interested in the houses below. If I'd had binoculars I could have looked straight into Tiffany's toilet bowl.

But why would I want to?

Three hours later, I'd had ample time to consider that question. I was also hungry and my left butt cheek had been numb so long, it felt like it had been amputated.

No one had entered or exited the Georges' abode, which, of course, didn't tell me much, but as I traversed the 210 toward Sunland, I was sure Tiffany had lied her little ass off.

Her husband hadn't come home. And she knew more than she was saying.

Which was a hell of a lot more than could be said about some of us.

One glance at Elaine's face on Friday morning reminded me why I was continuing the search.

She'd been crying. Her eyes were red and her nose was runny, but she still looked gorgeous.

No one ever said life was fair. At least no one in the McMullen clan. But then, we come from a long line of depressed Irishmen who tend to drink when they're down, or happy, or otherwise emoted.

"Angie." I greeted my final client of the day. She'd just turned seventeen a couple weeks ago and had celebrated by getting a tiny clutter of stars tattooed below her left ear.

Angela Grapier had been my client for over a year. She was small and cute and would have been adorable even if you dressed her in burlap and cut her hair with a buzz saw.

"How are you doing?" I asked.

"Good." She shrugged, and grinned a little. "Well... pretty good. I suppose if I were too good, I wouldn't get to skip Algebra and come here, huh?" She tossed her backpack onto the floor, slipped out of her untied sneakers, and curled her legs under her on the couch.

If I ever have a daughter, I'd like her to be like Angie. Only without the drug addiction and the boyfriends I wanted to exterminate.

Or rather, ex-boyfriends. I gave myself a mental high-five. I took some credit for getting rid of Kelly. He'd been a loser of profound proportions. She'd known it even before coming to me, but I liked to think I helped her muster up the nerve to kick his ass out of her life.

"So . . . how's it going with Sean?" Sean Kippling was her latest beau. He liked classical music and wore pants that didn't fall off his hips and show his underwear, which was what the cool guys wore, but Angie seemed able to forgive him his fashion faux pas.

"He's good."

"Have you made him see the glory of rap music yet?"

"I'm working on it." She grinned again. I'd seen her smile more in the last three weeks than in all the previous months put together. "You ever heard of Enya?"

"Just polkas for me. Remember?"

"Oh, yeah." She laughed. "Anyway, she's not too bad."

"I'm sure she'd be thrilled to have your endorsement."

"Sean gave me her CD," she said, and fell silent.

I waited. She chewed her lip. "Other day he left an African violet on my desk in Chem class."

"You like violets?"

"Yeah." She looked thoughtful. "I guess I must have told him. But I can't remember when."

I stifled a sigh. A guy who listened and actually responded appropriately. Maybe if she dumped him I could get him on the rebound. So what if I was his girlfriend's therapist . . . and sixteen years his senior. There's not much point to living in La La Land if you can't do something idiotic, and maybe felonious, once in a while.

"He likes to give me stuff," she said.

"Sometimes guys are like that when they're in love," I said. Not that I'd know. I'd once dated a guy who gave me panties at every possible opportunity. Size 2. I couldn't fit a size 2 on my head.

But again, why would I want to?

"You think he loves me?" she asked.

The age-old question. I shrugged, hoping to look enigmatic but secretly thinking that plucking a daisy might give her more insight.

She scowled. I waited. It had taken her a few weeks to open up to me, but since then it had pretty much been nonstop chatter.

"Is something wrong?" I asked.

She looked at me. She had eyes like a beagle puppy. She shifted them toward the floor and back.

"He doesn't want to do it," she said finally.

Uh-oh. I leaned back in my chair, looking casual. "Do what?" I asked, but I was pretty sure I knew what she meant—the ubiquitous "it."

"You know. Sex," she said, confirming my suspicion. The topic usually comes up at therapy sessions. And if it doesn't, it probably should. My personal theory is that hormones rule the world. But who rules the hormones?

"Oh." I nodded, trying to look wise. But in my experience no one looks very wise where sex is concerned. It's simply an illogical act. There's no making sense of it. I mean, if you try to think of it in practical terms, it'll boggle your mind. It's been around since man exited his first cave, and yet it's still a number-one box-office draw. The Rubik's cube came and went, but it looks like sex is here to stay. "What makes you think that?" I asked.

"Well . . ." She chewed her lip some more. "He says we should wait."

I folded my hands in my lap, patient and deeply philosophical. "Maybe there's a difference between not wanting to and believing you shouldn't," I suggested.

She glanced up, eyes bright. "Yeah?"

"Could be."

"You believe in waiting?"

I refrained from snorting. What the hell would I wait for? Judging by some pretty accurate physical evidence, I wasn't getting any younger. "Sometimes it's a really good idea," I said.

"How come?"

"You've got a lot on your mind. School, family problems. Are you still hoping to get into Berkeley?"

"I'm going to fill out the application this week."

"You're going to have to keep up your GPA."

"That's what Dad says."

She and her father had come to an understanding of sorts recently. I liked to think I'd had a hand in that, too.

"Sex can really mess with your head," I added.

"Yeah."

"Maybe Sean knows that."

She looked thoughtful. "So you think maybe he wants to do it, only he doesn't think it's a good idea?"

Uh-huh. "Unless he's a homosexual, I think it's pretty likely."

She scowled. "I don't think he's gay."

I let her go at her own pace.

She scrunched up her face. "When we kiss I can feel his . . . you know."

I thought I did, if memory served.

"So you think he finds you attractive?"

She shrugged. "Jenny Caron walked by the other day when we were talking and he didn't even glance at her."

"Jenny's good-looking?" I guessed.

She rolled her eyes. "Jenny's got boobs like torpedoes. Everybody looks at Jenny. Hell, *I* look at Jenny."

I tried not to laugh, in honor of her serious expression.

"He says when I'm around he can't think of anything else, and that he's afraid if we had sex he might walk in front of a bus or something. Get spattered all over the street." She crinkled her nose. "He's a weird guy."

I thought for a minute that I might be in love. Weird guys often affect me that way. My very first crush had had six toes on his left foot. He'd shown me on the playground on the first day of school—proud as a patriot.

"It does kind of sound like he's attracted to you," I said.

"Yeah." She grinned again, impishly, then sobered slowly. "So you think . . ." She paused, thinking herself. "Do you think good guys, you know, the guys who really care about you, do you think they maybe think they should wait?"

"Could be," I said, inscrutable to the end, but later I sat alone in my office and swore a blue streak.

I hate it when I learn stuff from clients. Especially when they're half my age and recovering drug addicts.

But the truth couldn't be avoided and went something like this:

A: I hadn't had a mature relationship with a man in all of my thirty-three years; and B: I owed it to Elaine to find the long-celibate Solberg.

10

Men have two outstanding features—their brains and their genitalia. Unfortunately, both rarely function simultaneously.

> —Professor Eva Nord,
> who may have had some
> dating issues of her own

MY TOILET BACKED up after work. I plied my plunger like a jackhammer and prayed for divine intervention. God is good, and apparently didn't want me to waste my money on a new septic system any more than I did.

I was only five minutes late and pretty sure my hands didn't smell like raw sewage when I walked into the Safari.

"Hi." Ross stood as soon as he saw me.

The restaurant was decorated in an African motif, with reed mats on the floor and wooden masks leering from the walls.

Leaning forward, Ross touched my arm and kissed my cheek. Nice. "Thanks for coming."

My nerve endings were still buzzing from the unexpected skin-to-skin contact, which interfered with my talking apparatus, so I said, "Thanks for inviting me," which wasn't original, but at least it didn't contain any syllables that made me spit.

The hostess's name was Amy. She was the approximate width of a chopstick. She beamed at us as if we'd been sent by God. Or maybe Allah. She might have been Muslim. Her eyes were the size of twin Cinnabon. The analogy made me realize I hadn't eaten since . . . well, since lunch. But lunch had been small and more than two hours ago. No wonder I was starving. I had quit smoking again—after finishing off a pack while I sat in my Saturn down the street from Hilary Pershing's house.

I'd learned nothing, except that I truly loved to smoke, and that I didn't have the attention span to become a private eye.

Assuring us that our waitress would be with us shortly, Amy handed off the menus and sprinted away. I checked to see if my date watched her backside. He didn't. Instead, he smiled across the table at me. Hmmm. Off to a promising . . . and surprising . . . start. Maybe she wasn't Jenny Caron, but she wasn't compost, either.

"You didn't have any trouble finding the place?" Ross asked.

We sat on a little raised dais near the window. An exotic hide that I couldn't identify hung on the wall beside our table. "No," I said. "No trouble." I didn't bother telling him that I could find a sugar donut in a snowstorm. "I called ahead for directions."

"Good. I hate getting lost. And this place is hard to find.

Once . . ." He stopped himself, lips parted, then laughed. "I'm sorry. I'm chattering like a chipmunk."

He was also as cute as a chipmunk.

"I do that when I'm nervous."

I tried not to look stunned. But why the hell would he be nervous? As for me, I was afraid I was going to sweat right through my swanky blue jacket. It was cut short, as the fashion gurus insisted. Apparently, the fashion gurus don't worry about the width of my ass, which I had covered in cobalt slacks that matched the little jacket to perfection.

"Can I get you some drinks?"

Wouldn't you know it, the one time when I'm not salivating for a waitress, she shows up, Johnny on the spot, like a damned meter maid.

Ross motioned toward me.

I ordered a strawberry daiquiri. Usually I stick to iced tea, but I wanted to encourage Ross to imbibe. Not that I was trying to get him drunk or anything. It's just that he would probably be more inclined to tell me everything he knew if he'd had a few. And besides, daiquiris are pretty tasty. Like liquid dessert.

He ordered a lager.

The waitress hurried away to fulfill our every desire. I was fairly comfortable with the width of her hips and didn't bother to notice if Ross watched her departure.

"Nervous?" I said instead, picking up the frayed thread of our conversation.

"Yeah, well . . ." He rubbed the back of his neck. As nervous habits go, it wasn't a bad one. I'd once dated a guy who would break out in hives. In retrospect, I think he might have been allergic to me. "I don't date much. I mean . . ." He lowered his arm and shrugged. He was wearing a tan button-down shirt with a black tee underneath. He had nice shoulders. "I just broke up with someone."

Warning bells chimed like fire alarms in my head. I had to drown them with a drink of water. Could be I'd need something more potent. Like a case of vodka. "Oh?" And the tone—oh-so-nonchalant.

"Well..." He grinned. "I guess 'just' is a relative term. I haven't seen Tami in over a year."

I tried to muffle my sigh, but I felt my shoulders droop with relief. "How long did you date her?"

"Six months maybe. But..." He shook his head. "I'm sorry. Old news. What about you?"

"I'm not dating Tami, either."

He laughed. It might not have been entirely out of pity. "Have you heard anything from J.D.?"

"No." I shook my head. Our drinks arrived. I took a sip. Good stuff. "How about you?"

"Sorry. But I really don't think you have to worry."

"Oh?"

"J.D...." He shrugged. "He likes the girls. And there are a few of them in Vegas."

I would have liked to explain that the Geekster couldn't possibly be interested in someone else after Elaine, but there's something about that missing X chromosome that makes men... Well, men are stupid. I know it sounds sexist. But I'm a trained professional and I've done thirty-odd years of research. Which meant what? That the Geekster had gotten involved with the Vegas mob scene?

When I ran the idea through my mind, it didn't sound as ridiculous as it should have.

"So you think Solberg stayed in Vegas for . . . entertainment purposes?" I asked.

Ross took a sip of his beer and shrugged. "Could be."

I studied him. It wasn't much of a chore. "Did he meet someone there?"

He squirmed a little. "We all met someone there. I mean, it's a bunch of us nerds at a Vegas convention."

I wanted to ask who he had met but I stuck to the topic like bubblegum. "Do you know who Solberg met?"

He shrugged. "Sorry."

"Does that mean no?"

He gave me a palms-up gesture. "J.D. seems like a decent guy. But I don't know him very well."

"We're not all that lucky."

"What?"

"Listen," I said, leaning into the conversation, "I know it seems weird. I mean . . ." I shook my head. "I can hardly believe it myself, but my friend is in love with him."

"With J.D.?"

It was hard to admit. But sometimes you just have to suck it up and tell the truth. "Yes."

"Oh." He nodded, as if thinking. "Well, that's good news for me, then."

"What?"

He laughed, looking relieved. "I thought you were the one who was interested in him."

I felt the blood drain from my face, but I held his gaze. "You don't have to be cruel," I said.

He paused a moment then laughed out loud. "What's your friend's name?"

"Elaine."

"And she's . . . three-dimensional, right?"

"On the other hand . . ." I raised my drink to him. "Cruelty suits you."

The waitress with the acceptable hips returned and flipped open a notepad. The name "Grace" was written on the cover in neon orange and circled with childish, lopsided hearts. Grace wasn't wearing a wedding ring, and she looked tired but stoic under the fire of the evening crowd. Ross ordered swordfish with saffron rice. I got a shrimp salad. I always feel virtuous when I order a salad, even if I douse it in enough dressing to lubricate a thrashing machine.

Ross's greens arrived. He ate very precisely, cutting his lettuce into bite-sized pieces. But "bite-sized" is really kind of a relative term, isn't it? He had nice hands. I know I've mentioned them before, but he really did. They were lightly tanned, long-fingered. Hands that would . . .

I put the kibosh on those thoughts and reminded myself why I had met him in the first place.

"So . . ." I dragged my gaze from his hands. He had plucked a cherry tomato from amongst the greenery and was eating it like a tiny apple. A seed stuck to his bottom lip.

"So . . ." I said again. My breath was perfectly steady, despite the damned seed. "When was the last time you saw him?"

He glanced up. "J.D.?"

"Yes."

He canted his head and gave me half a grin. The expression was boyish and charming. Which made me pretty sure he was either gay or married. Or maybe both. They can be both. Don't ask how I know.

"You sure you're not the one interested in him?" he asked.

I considered saying, "Cross my heart and hope to die," which made me wonder if I was already getting tanked. To say I'm a cheap drunk would be an understatement of dangerous proportions. Two more ounces and I'd be under the table—or on top of Ross.

"I mean . . . no offense." He gave an abbreviated shrug. "J.D.'s got some good qualities."

I elevated one brow in his direction. "Such as . . . ?"

"You seen his car?"

As a matter of fact, I had. The Porsche and I had once bonded on a zippy little stretch of road between Studio City and Glendale.

"Yeah, well . . ." I put the thought of his car firmly behind me. "Laney's been my best friend ever since she warned me I had toilet paper stuck to the bottom of my patent leather shoe."

"Laney?"

"His . . ." I suppressed a shudder. "Girlfriend."

"So you're asking around on her behalf?"

"She thinks he dumped her. I told her even Solberg couldn't be that dense, but now . . ." I shrugged.

Ross scowled, saying nothing.

"No comment?"

"Like I said, I just don't know him that well."

"How well don't you know him?"

He exhaled heavily and let his shoulders slump. "I'm

sorry, I don't ... I mean ..." He glanced away, then caught my gaze in a steady hold. "I really like you."

I stared at him, shocked. It seemed sort of early for the breakup speech. I mean, so far there was nothing to break up. But I could hear his next words. *You're a great gal, but we don't quite click ... mesh, hit it off.* Pick your euphemism for "you're ugly."

I waited, looking dignified. I'd been working on that look for the past seventy-four guys.

He sighed. "I didn't want to tell you, but—"

"You're gay." The words sprinted out on their own.

"What?" He laughed, sounding shocked.

I almost closed my eyes to block out my own liquor-intensified stupidity. "Nothing. I didn't say anything. Go on."

"You think I'm gay?"

"I just meant I thought you were ..." As far as I know there isn't a straight guy in the universe who appreciates being mistaken for a homosexual, no matter how well they coordinate their shoes with their sweater vests. "Jolly. Happy. You know ..." God help me. "To be alive."

"I'm not gay."

"No. Of course not." There was truly something wrong with me. "What were you going to say?"

I waited. At the very least he must have a thing about his mother. Who doesn't have a thing about his mother?

"I saw J.D. with a blonde."

I blinked as my brain cells flopped around like so many beached fishes. "A blond what?"

"A woman."

I let the news soak into my saturated brain. Anger was

slowly boiling in my gut. "Solberg?" I asked, just to make sure. "With a woman?"

"I'm sorry."

I drew a careful breath. "Who was she?"

"I don't—"

"Was she a dancer?"

He leaned back a little, as if to put some distance between himself and the woman who might, at any moment, morph into a fire-breathing feminist.

I eased up. Maybe it was the alcohol that made me a little intense. Maybe it was the fact that I'd grown up with brothers who had never once knocked before entering the bathroom. Yeah, I think I'll blame it on them. "I'm sorry," I said. "It's not your fault. I just don't want Elaine to get hurt." I gave him a cultivated smile. "Where did J.D. meet the blonde?"

He seemed to relax a little. "We took in a magic show."

I sipped my drink, looked casual, and refrained from pouncing.

"We?" I said.

"Bunch of us. J.D., Jeff, Hilary—"

"Hilary Pershing?"

"Yeah. You know her?"

"Not really. Were she and Solberg . . ." I fiddled with my napkin, reminding myself not to tear it to shreds and pretend it was the Geekster's hair. "Were they an item?"

He shrugged. "Like I said, I don't know him that well, but I did see them together at the convention one night."

"Do you remember when that was?"

"No. I just assumed they were talking shop. They've

helped each other out with some projects from time to time, you know."

"What projects?" The word "Combot" flashed in blood-red through my mind.

"Have you ever heard of Insty List?"

I shook my head. No. But I'd heard of Combot. What the hell was Combot?

"Well, it's going to be big when it hits the public. And it's their baby."

"Do you think that's what they were talking about?"

He scrunched his face as if thinking. "Could be. But the conversation looked kind of heated."

"Heated?" Curiosity shifted toward suspicion.

"Well, maybe not heated. Maybe . . . animated."

I didn't have time for political correctness. "Did you hear what they were fighting about?"

"Not a syllable."

"But they were fighting."

He shrugged.

I cursed inside. "Were there any other projects they were working on together?"

"Probably."

"Anything special?"

He gave me a funny look. "Why do you ask?"

Past experience suggested that I should never trust any-one with a Y chromosome, but I was in need of a confidant. Could I trust him with the truth? Could I ask straight-out about the disk I'd found in Solberg's underwear drawer? But sanity prevailed. Men were hardly trustworthy by virtue of attractiveness. In fact, the opposite might very well be true.

"No reason. How about Black?" I asked, remembering back to my conversation in his office. "Did he and Solberg have any projects together?"

Ross shook his head. "As far as I know, Black's strictly administrative."

But Black said that he and Solberg had worked well together. Maybe he'd meant it in a vague sense, but it had sounded more personal than that.

"Do you know of any friends Solberg might be staying with?"

"Friends?" He looked pensive. "No. Not offhand. He works a lot. Probably doesn't have time for relationships."

"He had time for the blonde, though."

"What?"

"The magician's . . ." I almost said a word that would have gotten my mouth a fresh washing not so many years back. "Uh . . . what exactly did she do in the show?"

"Oh. I think she might have been the lady he sawed in half."

"Really?" I tightened my grip on the daiquiri glass. "Which half did he leave with?"

Ross laughed, but the sound was a tad jittery. "I admit I'm a little jealous of J.D. I mean, the man's a frickin' genius. Took home the Lightbulb Award three years in a row, but I don't want to cause him any—"

"What's her name?"

"Pardon—"

"The magician's half-a-bimbo," I said, wonderfully controlled. "What's her name?"

He shook his head. "I didn't actually meet her. And there

were four of them. Besides, it might have been completely innocent."

I gritted my teeth. "They were probably discussing the theory of relativity."

He looked sheepish. "J.D. is more into time expansion."

I had no idea what he was talking about, but I saw the irony of the situation very clearly, despite the two ounces of rum sloshing around in my system. Here I was with a great-looking guy who wasn't even gay and we were discussing the Geek God. The idea hurt me somewhere deep inside. Real deep. "How about the magician?"

He looked baffled for a moment, but he had a quick mind and knew where I was heading. He blew out his breath and settled back in the booth. "Something foreign."

"Like François, or more like Juan?"

"No. Egyptian maybe, or Arabic. I think he wore a turban."

"You think?"

"I may have been a little drunk when I saw the show."

I waited.

"The Magical . . ." He shook his head, thinking. "Martini?"

"The Magical Martini?" I repeated, dubious.

He laughed, pushed his salad plate aside, and reached for my hand. His skin felt warm as he clasped my fingers.

"Listen, I didn't intend to tell you all that. I just . . . I wanted to see you and . . ." He shrugged. "I'm really sorry."

I looked into his eyes. They were Caribbean blue and honeysuckle earnest.

"It's not your fault," I said, finally realizing the truth of it.

He was definitely male, but maybe he wasn't responsible for the faults of the entire gender.

"No," he said, and rubbed my palm with his thumb, "but I'm afraid it's going to come around and bite me on the ass. You know what I mean?"

I did. I'd been thinking of doing that very thing only minutes before.

Ross stroked the back of my hand with the tip of his ring finger—which was, by the by, still noticeably bereft of jewelry. "Maybe we could just forget about him for tonight. You know, get to know each other better."

My hormones sizzled to attention. He was right. There wasn't anything I could do for Elaine tonight. In fact, if Solberg had screwed up as badly as I thought he had, there wasn't much I could do for her at all. Except maybe hire a hit man, unless someone had already taken care of that little detail. The thought made me feel a little squeamish inside.

"I have a confession to make." The corner of Ross's mouth shifted up a notch, and for a moment, possibly for the first time in my life, I considered skipping dinner and dragging him out to my car. "As soon as I saw you walk into Neo, I told myself I was going to ask you out."

"You didn't see me walk in," I said. "You just caught me when I was about to break into Solberg's office."

He laughed and leaned back slightly. The sound was low and lovely and rumbled through my system, revving up rusty hormones as it went. "You were going to break in?"

"Laney's a good friend."

"I saw you walk in," he corrected. "You were wearing a

sleeveless blouse and shoes that made your legs..." He paused. "Well, I thought ol' Greg was going to drop his teeth when you smiled at him. I loitered around while you talked to Black, trying to figure out a way to introduce myself."

He turned my hand over and stroked my knuckles.

"I'm glad I didn't have to staple my tie to my forehead or anything to get your attention," he said.

His fingers had moved up my wrist. I swallowed hard and kept my feet firmly planted on the floor. The last time my hormones had been shaken from slumber, I'd found myself straddling a bad-tempered cop like a pit bull on an estrogen drip.

"Is that how you usually go about it?" I asked.

"Sometimes I knock over the wastebasket."

I gave him a look. He grinned. I felt the effects down to my bone marrow. "I'm a nerd. I'm lucky I can breathe and operate a joystick at the same time," he said, and grinned so that the corners of his eyes crinkled endearingly.

I was beginning to salivate. "You sure you're a nerd?"

"Want to see my pocket penholder?"

"Is that some kind of metaphor?"

"Would I seem too obvious if I said I kept it in my bedroom?"

It was the closest he had come to an out-and-out proposition. I opened my mouth to respond, but just managed to stop the lascivious suggestion that curled my tongue.

Instead, I cleared my throat and straightened a little. "So...Emery Black," I said, knees clamped like a librarian at an auto sales convention. "What's his story?"

"He's a zillionaire. Divorced. Runs a tight ship."

"What does NeoTech produce exactly?"

"You have a long lifeline," he said, tracing the crease in my palm. I kept myself erect, despite the shivery feelings that threatened to knock me flat on my back. "So maybe I have time to tell you."

"You guys didn't create the solar system or anything, did you?"

He grinned. "Everything but. Neo . . ." He shook his head again. "We produce everything. We improve on even more. The little chips for car engines. The material that makes up contact lenses. Products for Homeland Security."

"Stuff for the government?"

"Yeah."

"Like . . . weapons?" Maybe Solberg was a gunrunner, I thought wildly, but the idea of him wearing camouflage and delivering AK-47s to grim-faced desperados kind of scrambled my mind.

"More like stealth listening devices, that sort of thing, I think. But that's really not my area of expertise."

"Is it Black's?"

"Black oversees everything. I'm sure he has his hand in that, too."

I nodded, thinking back to my conversation with him. "Do you know of anything that's going on at the end of the month?"

"Not specifically. Why?"

"No reason really. It's just that Black said he was sure Solberg would be back by then."

"It was probably just an arbitrary date."

Or some sort of babbled platitude to get me out of his office without involving fisticuffs.

"Are Black and Solberg close?"

"Close?" he repeated.

I shrugged, not quite sure what I was getting at. "Do they like each other?"

He took a sip of his drink. "Solberg makes a lot of money for Neo. Black likes that. But interoffice relationships aren't my area of expertise, either."

"What is?"

He winced. "Mice."

"I beg your pardon?"

He shrugged. "Some guys try to make a better mouse-trap. I try to make a better mouse."

I blinked at him.

"The kind that directs your cursor."

"Ohhhh," I said, and he laughed.

"You don't have to try to make it sound interesting."

"I'm not."

He tilted his head. "I really couldn't be more boring, could I?"

His eyes twinkled at me. "I'm still awake," I said.

"Yeah?" He leaned in a little closer and trailed his fingers up my arm. "Would now be a good time to tell you how beautiful you are?"

"No time like the present," I managed.

He gave me an almost smile. "You're polished," he said. "But not cold."

Nope. In fact, I was feeling downright flushed.

"Almost perfect . . ." He caressed my cheek. "But still touchable."

Holy crap! I opened my mouth, maybe to say just those words, but at that moment my cell phone rang.

It sounded very distant but finally managed to permeate my lust-induced haze. I rolled my lolling tongue back into my mouth and tugged my hand gently from his. "Ummm, excuse me." If it was my mother telling me Pete was parked in my front yard, I was going to slit my wrists with a butter knife.

I fumbled around in my purse and came up with my trophy. Giving Ross a smile I hoped wasn't cannibalistic, I flipped it open.

"Hello?"

"Don't say anything." The voice was hissed and desperate.

I almost objected.

"Just listen. You gotta help me."

"Who—"

"The Oaks. Half an hour. Don't tell anyone. 'Specially not the cops. And don't trust nobody. It's life or death, babe. Life or death."

The phone went dead. I closed it in numb silence.

"Is something wrong?"

I glanced up. I had actually forgotten Ross existed.

"No. Well . . ." The voice had been Solberg's. Hadn't it? Yes. I was sure it was. Maybe. "Actually, yes, there is," I said.

He frowned. "Can I help?"

"Thank you," I said, "but it's . . ." Holy shit! What had just happened? "Elaine."

"What's wrong with her?"

"She's just . . ." I found myself scooting toward the edge

of the booth before I could form any kind of rational thought or override the rum messing with my plodding thinking apparatus. "She's really down."

"You're leaving?" he asked, grabbing my hand.

I managed, after some soul searching and a few self-imposed threats, to tug my fingers regretfully from his. "I'm sorry," I said. And I really was. But some parts of me were sorrier than others.

11

I don't trust nobody that don't have my name tattooed on her ass, and then it's iffy.

—Roger Reed,
Chrissy's most lucid uncle on
her mother's side

*T*HE OAKS. HALF an hour."

I knew what he'd meant. The Four Oaks was a restaurant where I'd once squeezed information out of Solberg.

I drove fast, my mind racing along with the Saturn's little tires in the darkness. What was going on? Had that really been Solberg?

I thought so. Who else could be that melodramatic? *"It's life or death."*

On the other hand, maybe it really was life or death.

My stomach twisted tight. I swallowed and opened my glove compartment. A can of mace huddled between an under wire bra and a Snickers bar. Good to know my emergency kit was still in place.

Pulling out the mace, I shoved it into my jacket pocket and concentrated on the conversation just past.

"Don't talk."

Those had been his first words. Obviously, he didn't want anyone to know he had called, but why?

Life or death. Whose life? Whose death? If it had to be anyone's, I rather fervently hoped it wasn't mine. Lately things hadn't been working out so well for me in the danger department. But at least the Oaks was in a ritzy part of town. I'd be safe there.

I reached the restaurant in record time. Wouldn't you know it, just when I really didn't want to get somewhere, L.A. traffic disappears like a streaker at baccalaureate.

I pulled into the parking lot and found an available spot a couple dozen yards from the door.

My hands were unsteady and my throat felt dry. I turned off the engine and checked my purse again. My phone was still there. Maybe I should call someone. But what would I say? *"Look, I'm meeting someone I don't know for reasons I can't explain."*

My limbs felt strangely detached as I pushed my door open and made my way into the restaurant. I passed a couple on my left. They were laughing. I felt sick. I hurried inside, searching. Solberg was nowhere to be seen. The lobby was busy. A woman with a little girl in braids waited by the door. Three men in blazers were sharing a conversation about cumulus clouds.

"Can I help you?" I jerked as if shot. The hostess looked at me with some curiosity. Apparently, I hadn't been shot.

"Yes." I tried to calm my breathing. It didn't go as planned. "I was supposed to meet someone here, but I can't find him."

"Can you describe him?"

I did. Worry made me unusually kind.

"I'm sorry. I don't believe he's been here, but if you want to have a seat, I'll let you know as soon as he arrives," she said, but I was already opening my phone.

I pressed "Redial." The tone sounded sketchy. I stepped outside to try again, walking as I did so, searching for better reception.

Where was he? Had it even been him? Was—

My thoughts were interrupted by a noise to the left. I jerked toward it. Someone grabbed me.

I tried to scream, but his hand closed over my mouth and suddenly I was being pushed into a car. Another man appeared on my right and slammed the door shut behind him.

I did scream then, but the sound was muffled by a hand slapping across my mouth again.

We squealed out of the parking lot and onto the street.

"What happened?" asked the driver.

"Little bastard got away." The guy to my right was breathing hard. There was a gun-shaped bulge in the pocket of his windbreaker and his breath smelled like garlic.

I wondered if I was going to faint.

"God damn it! Can't you do anything right?"

I darted my eyes from one to the other and prayed wildly.

"What we gonna do with her?"

"I don't know yet." The driver leaned toward me. I

crouched away, recognizing him suddenly—the guy in Solberg's house. "You gonna be good?"

I nodded woodenly.

"Damn right," he said, and nodded at his partner.

The hand slipped away.

"Where are you taking me?" They were the first words out of my mouth. I'm not sure why. In retrospect, it probably didn't matter much. I doubt they were planning an evening at the petting zoo.

"Look through her purse."

Garlic Breath tugged my handbag from my shoulder and pawed through it.

"Find anything?" asked the driver. I was mesmerized by the memory of the gun in his hand as he chased me over the Georges' fence.

"Got this."

I turned stiffly toward the second guy. He was loose-jointed and skinny. Maybe from drugs, maybe just genetics. He was holding up a tampon and chuckling.

My stomach pitched.

"Jesus, you're a moron. Put that away."

He did so, still chuckling.

"Where will he go?"

I turned toward the driver again. "What?" My voice sounded funny, sort of thick and wobbly.

"The geek. Where will he run to?"

My breath caught in my throat. "Solberg?"

"Listen to her," said the driver. "She's a fuckin' genius, ain't she? Musta had some big-ass education. Yeah, Solberg."

I shook my head. I felt faint and breathless. "I don't know. How would I know?"

"You'd know 'cuz he just called you."

"How—"

"We got our ways." The scent of garlic washed over me. I didn't turn toward the speaker. Instead, I swallowed and did my best not to barf. They'd probably get mad if I barfed in their car. It was an early-model Cadillac. My brother James would have called it "vintage" and told me the horse-power and a dozen things regarding its engine, but just about then I wouldn't have cared much, because my chest felt suddenly empty, like my heart had shriveled and my lungs had collapsed. Some unidentified mewling sound crept from between my lips.

"What's wrong with you?" Garlic asked.

I couldn't speak. Couldn't breathe. I clawed at my jacket.

"What's wrong with her?"

The car was crumpling in on me.

"Jed!" said Garlic. "What's the matter with her?"

In some vague corner of my mind, I felt the car lurch to a halt. It was as dark as hell, or maybe it was just my system shutting down, but I sensed the driver turning toward me. And then my head snapped against the seat behind me.

My cheek stung like hell where he'd struck me. My lungs broke free. My hands fell to my lap like limp noodles.

"That's better," said Jed.

"What happened?" Garlic asked. Somewhere in the back of my stuttering mind, a dry-voiced pragmatist informed me that he was the weak link. But just then I didn't care much more about weak links than I did about car engines.

"Nothing a couple a good slaps won't fix. Now . . ." The driver sneered at me. His shoulders were beefy. No, wait.

They were fat, just damned fat. "You're gonna tell us a little story."

I tried to formulate a question, but no words would come.

He slapped me again, and somehow my hand managed to find my jacket.

The can of mace felt cool against my palm. My attention never drifted from that meaty face. I lifted my hand. My finger moved. There was a hissing sound.

Jed shrieked like a hyena and clawed at his face.

I saw it all through a slow-motion haze.

"What's going on?" Garlic's voice was panicky, but his friend didn't seem to notice. He had yanked the door open and was concentrating on breathing.

"What happened?" Garlic screeched.

I turned toward him and blasted him in the face.

There was a shriek. He clawed at his door handle. Fresh air rushed in like a cold tide. He retched, hanging on to the door and leaning outside.

Maybe it was the influx of air. Maybe it was the hint of freedom, but whatever the case, my mind finally clipped into gear.

"You bitch!" Jed's voice was slurred, but he was already turning toward me. His nose was running, and his teeth were bared.

Adrenaline and fear washed through me like water in a flume. I cowered away.

He reached for me. I yanked my knees up to my chest and kicked him in the ribs with both feet.

He toppled sideways, hit the ground cursing, and went down on all fours.

I slammed myself behind the wheel and yanked the car into reverse. Jed levered himself onto his knees and grabbed the steering wheel.

I screamed and thumped the accelerator with power born of terror. The door plowed him under.

"Damn you!" Garlic swore, and turned toward me.

I yanked the lever into drive, punched the accelerator, and cranked the wheel to the left. Tires spun on gravel.

We lurched forward. Garlic teetered sideways and was sucked out of the car like a moth from a windshield.

There was a *ping*ing noise. The rear window shattered. I screamed and ducked.

The Cadillac hit the ditch then bucked like a beluga beneath me, but suddenly I was on the highway. I dragged the wheel to the right, careened across the road, hit the gravel, and righted the vehicle.

It was a good ten minutes before I had any idea where I was or where I was headed. But I was pretty sure I was still alive, 'cuz my nose was running and I'd wet my pants.

12

Sometimes stupid is crime enough.

—*Lieutenant Jack Rivera*

WHEN I AWOKE in the morning, reality seemed a little fuzzy around the edges. I lay on my back in bed. The overhead light was on, as was the one in the hall. I could tell that much without moving my head.

Memories streamed in on me like the austere sunlight pouring through my bedroom window. "Austere," good word. Apparently, my mind was still functioning at primate level.

I realize some people might think it strange that I could sleep after the previous night, but I'm a world-class snoozer and I like to keep my God-given talents well oiled. Use it or lose it.

I closed my eyes and wished I were still unconscious, but the memories were getting a little raucous.

What had happened exactly?

Solberg had called. Maybe. Or someone had called. Then two guys had jumped me and shoved me into a car. I had somehow made it back to the restaurant, snatched my purse out of the Caddy, and stumbled into my Saturn.

With quivery fingers I'd tried calling Solberg several times, but there was no answer.

I don't remember the drive home. Maybe I had cried. Chances were pretty good. My eyes felt like tennis balls, oversized and scruffy.

A noise exploded beside my bed. I jerked upright with a shriek, yanking the unsuspecting sheet to my chin.

It took me a minute to realize the sound was nothing more deadly than my telephone.

My hand wobbled when I reached for the receiver. My voice sounded foreign. "Hello?"

"McMullen."

I snatched in a breath. It was Rivera, like a shadow in the darkness.

"You still in bed?"

"Ummm." My nerves were jumping like bacon over a campfire. I steadied my hand on the receiver. "No. I'm up. Been up for hours." I'm not sure why I lied. Habit maybe.

"Yeah?" His voice was dark and smoky, as if he expected a conspiracy around every turn. "Thought you might have had a late date last night."

"Late date?" My voice squeaked a little. *Tell him the truth,* I thought. *Just tell him. What's the worst that could happen?*

Possibilities swarmed like vampire bats. Suspended psychology license, my mother flying in to "straighten things out," Rivera grinning at me through iron bars. I cleared my throat. "No. Why would you think that?"

"No reason. I'm going to be by in about half an hour. Something I need to talk to you about. Stay put," he said, and hung up.

I stared at the receiver for a full five seconds, then launched out of bed like a programmed missile. Holy crap, holy crap, holy crap. What did he want to talk to me about? Had he found out I'd broken into Solberg's house? Did he know I'd stolen the little geek's disk?

Or was it something more serious. I froze. Jesus Christ, maybe I had killed one of the guys last night. Maybe . . .

There was no time for maybes, no time for terror. I had to get out, to think things through before I talked to Rivera. He could squeeze a confession out of a turnip. I wasn't as tough as a turnip. More like a tomato.

Luckily, I'd slept in my clothes again. I grabbed my purse off the counter where I had dropped it, lurched through the door, and ran into Rivera full steam ahead.

I shrieked like a Hitchcock starlet.

He steadied me with his hands on my arms. "Where you going?" His voice was deadpan steady.

Mine teetered dweebishly on the edge of hysteria. "What are you doing here?"

He raised a brow. "I told you I was coming by."

"In half an hour! Half an hour! You said half an hour."

His lips hitched up a quarter of an inch. His left brow did the same. "Does it matter?"

I was breathing hard. I could see myself in his sunglasses. Or maybe it was a tornado victim. My hair looked like I'd been hooked up to a car battery. I had mascara down to my collarbones, and bloodred veins ran through my eyeballs like teeming estuaries.

"I . . ." I may have tried to pat down my hair. I think it patted me back. "No. Of course not. I mean . . . I have to go." I nodded sensibly. "Out. Elaine. Ummm . . . Laney needs me." I'd tried the same lie the night before with Ross Bennet— the first viable date I'd had since potty training. Look how nifty that had turned out.

I couldn't see behind Rivera's sunglasses. Dear God, what was he thinking behind his glasses?

From the far side of his chain-link fence, my neighbor, Mr. Al-Sadr, watered his lawn and stared across the wreckage of my yard at us.

Rivera glanced toward him, then at me. "Maybe we better step inside for a minute."

My stomach hit my knees. "I . . . I can't. . . . Really. I'd like to, of course, but Laney . . ." I kept babbling, but he was already steering me into my house.

The door closed with a *snick* behind me. Maybe it was more of a *thud,* like the lid of a coffin slamming shut.

He took off his shades. Turns out, he didn't look particularly jovial.

"What . . . ?" I swallowed the frog in my throat and tried again. "What are you doing here?"

"Me?" He shrugged. He was wearing a black T-shirt with a V-neck. It lay smooth across his chest. "I just thought I'd stop by, give you an update," he said, wandering into my living room.

I glanced toward the door and considered making a dash for it. He turned his gaze toward me. There might have been a challenge there.

I swallowed my cowardly impulse to bolt and followed him into the interior of my peanut-sized home. "An update?" I said.

He raised one brow a minuscule distance. "About the case."

I shook my head, then, "Oh yeah." I chuckled. I felt like I was going to vomit. "Solberg."

"Uh-huh."

He waited. I shuffled from foot to foot. "What about him?"

"He's still missing, right? You haven't heard from him?"

My hair was starting to sweat. I shook my head. It wobbled unsteadily.

"Why don't you sit down?" he asked.

I glanced rather manically toward the door again. "Laney—"

"I'm sure she'll understand. You can give her a call."

I blinked. "Why?"

He raised that one eyebrow again. Maybe the other one was disabled. "Tell her you're going to be late."

"Oh . . ." I laughed. "Oh. Well . . ." I plopped down on the couch. He'd taken the La-Z-Boy. Bastard. "She's probably still sleeping anyway."

He was watching me like a fox at a rabbit hole. I'd seen it once on the Discovery Channel. The fox had just lain there, waiting, watching. The poor little bunny hadn't had a chance. I like bunnies.

The house was as silent as a tomb. *Don't think about tombs. Don't think about tombs.*

"I've been worried about you."

I stared at him. I had my palms pressed together and clamped between my knees, trying to keep everything from bobbling off. "Worried? About me?"

"That whole thing with Bomstad." He shook his head. The tendons in his throat shifted. There had been a time when I'd had a thing about guys' throats. "Then the Geek disappearing..." He shrugged. "What was his name?"

"Solberg."

"Yeah. You said you haven't heard from him?"

I shook my head again. Lying was wrong. It was wrong. I was on the fast track to hell. Not a damned handbasket in sight. What is a handbasket anyway? "You, either?"

"We're looking," he said. "But..." Another shrug. "We're short on manpower."

"Uh-huh."

"You okay?" He narrowed his eyes at me. "You look kind of..." Electrocuted? "Nervous."

"No." I chuckled. My voice rasped like sandpaper. "I'm fine. Just tired. You know... didn't get much sleep."

"Late night?"

"No!" Too quick. I'd answered too quick. And about five decibels too loud. I cleared my throat and tried again. Smooth this time and dulcet as a songbird. "No. Why? Why do you ask?"

The house went quiet again. I was pretty sure I could hear the adrenaline pumping through my veins.

He gave me a smile. "Because you look tired."

I tried a laugh. "Oh, yeah. Of course."

"Good, though," he said. He eyed me steadily. "Fit. You been running?"

"Yes." I nodded. "Yes. All the time. Well . . . you know, few times a week."

"I can tell." He skimmed my body with his sin-dark eyes, then exhaled softly. "Truth is . . ." He rose to his feet. I had to crank my head back to follow his movement. "I wanted to stop by and apologize again."

"Apologize?" I searched his eyes for a lie, but he looked absolutely sincere. Then again, he's Hispanic. There's no one who can look as earnest as a Hispanic guy. They can lie through their teeth and still look twice as sincere as an Irish priest. Swear to God.

"I'm sorry I had to leave so abruptly that night at your place."

"Well . . ." I reminded myself to breathe. "Your wife—"

"Ex-wife," he corrected.

I cleared my throat and refused to let my mouth drop open at his choice of words. "Yes. Ex-wife. She needed you."

The tic of a grin lifted the enigmatic scar at the corner of his mouth. "Actually, it was Rockette that needed me."

I gave him a look.

"My dog was sick." The grin lifted another millimeter. "You remember Rockette," he said. "I believe you interrogated her under false pretenses."

I pursed my lips and fiddled with a fold in my slacks. "I did not interrogate your dog," I said.

"It must have been my ex-wife you were interested in, then."

I gave him a prissy look. So what if I had confiscated a

friend's pet, showed up at the dog park at the precise moment his ex-wife arrived, given her a fictional name, and drilled her about her ex-husband. Any number of people might have done the exact same thing.

"Anyway, I should have called you," he said. "Later... when I had to cancel our date. I'm sorry I didn't. Especially after I saw you at the precinct house." Was there a compliment in his tone?

I rose to my feet. I had looked pretty good at the precinct house. I smoothed down a pant leg. It remained as wrinkled as a fourth-grader's love note.

But the look he gave me suggested he didn't give a rat's ass about the condition of my pants. I couldn't help but remember the night we'd gone at it like pirates in my vestibule.

My hormones were starting to hum again. They'd been fired up when Bennet had caressed my hand the night before, then left to simmer. Well... maybe "simmer" isn't the right word. After all, a couple of thugs had abducted me. So my system had probably had other things to worry about, but those ol' chemicals are hard to keep down. Real scrappers.

"I'm sorry about Solberg, too," he said. "I mean, he's probably fine. I'm just sorry you have to worry. I checked the airlines. He was scheduled to fly home on the thirtieth."

I nodded. I'd checked, too.

He grinned a little. "Maybe I was wrong."

"Probably," I said, and swallowed. He did not have the sexiest smile in the universe. It was just the celibacy talking. "About what?"

"About you going into forensics. You'd make a hell of a detective. I suppose you called his hotel in Vegas, too."

I had. "They said he hadn't checked out, but that doesn't mean much." I scowled. "He could have left days ago. They wouldn't necessarily know."

"Or tell you," he added. Silence lengthened.

I tensed. "What *do* you know?"

He shrugged, looking nonchalant. "Not much more than you do. You leave a message at the hotel?"

I nodded.

He did the same. "Me, too. No news."

"And no one's reported seeing him?"

"No."

"I . . ." I scowled, surprised to be saying it. "I appreciate your help, Rivera."

"I figure I owe you. After . . ." He shrugged. The movement was slow and liquid. "Well . . ." He brushed a strand of hair from my face. I didn't swoon. "Some people get kind of pissed when I accuse them of murdering the guy who tried to rape them."

I shrugged. I was beginning to relax a little. "I like to be different."

"You're succeeding. Well, I'd better let you go," he said, and moved toward the door.

"Ummm, yeah," I said, stomping out the estrogen that was smoldering like a forest fire. "Thanks for letting me know—"

"Oh, I almost forgot." He stopped and turned, then reached behind him and pulled something out of his back pocket. I glanced at his hand. He was holding my wallet.

It took a full three seconds for reality to thump me up-side the head. I yanked my gaze to his. I could feel my heart banging against my ribs, probably trying to wake up my brain.

"What's that?" I don't know why I said it. But they were the first words that popped into my cranium.

His eyes had gone deadly dark. Not a muscle twitched. "You don't recognize it?"

Jesus God, what was he doing with my wallet?

"McMullen?" he said, as if he'd found me at the bottom of a deep well and was wondering if I was still lucid. "You okay?"

"Well, I . . . Well, I . . . Sure," I said, rather unsteadily. "I'm fine. Why wouldn't I be?"

13

It is far better to know the painful truth than to live with a kindly falsehood.

—*Father Pat*

RIVERA STARED AT me. Nothing moved in the entire world. Not a sound was made, not a soul whispered.

"So this isn't yours?" he asked.

"Mine? *Mine?*" In that moment I sincerely hoped that big, hairy Jed would come around the corner and shoot me dead.

"It's got your driver's license in it," he said.

"My license?" I laughed. I sounded like Fran Drescher on speed. "That's... preposterous." I was shaking my head like a dog fresh from the pond. "No. I... My wallet's in my purse."

"Go get it," he said.

"What?"

"Get your purse."

I motioned spastically toward the couch, where I'd left my handbag only minutes before. "It's . . ." My hand was waving wildly. I caught sight of my wristwatch and yanked my arm toward my face as if it were entirely disconnected from the rest of my body. "Oh, wow! Look at the time. I've got to go." I jerked toward the door. But he reeled me in by the back of my shirt before I'd taken the first step.

"Get your wallet," he ordered.

I swallowed hard. There was nothing I could do. I knew he held my wallet in his hand. And I knew where he had gotten it.

I raised my chin a dignified inch, tugged my elbow from his grasp, and flowed gracefully toward the couch. Or maybe I tottered.

I picked up my purse, slowly. My mind was spinning out of control. Maybe I could hit him in the head with it. Maybe I could fake a seizure. Maybe I could offer to sleep with him in exchange for the privilege of my continuing freedom. Maybe—

Wait a minute. Seducing Rivera would be a heinous experience, of course. But perhaps for the sake of sweet freedom I could manage it.

I glanced toward Rivera. He remained where he was. No incoming 911s, no shoot-outs at the OK Corral. Damn. Just about then even an emergency call from his ex-wife looked pretty good.

"Are you going to check if it's there?" he asked.

I realized in that instant that I'd been staring at him for a good seven seconds. He stared back, but *he* wasn't drooling, so I lifted my chin with haughty nonchalance and propped my purse on the couch's armrest to better rummage through its contents.

He watched in silence. I scowled and bent studiously over the thing. Still nothing. Go figure. Taking the few steps to my staircase, I sat primly on the third one, plopped my purse on my lap and gave it my all, practically crawling inside the bag in an effort to prove my certainty that I had not lost my wallet to two thugs in a Cadillac while they plied me with threats.

The silence stretched on, accented by the click of my lipstick against my compact.

"Anything you want to tell me, McMullen?" Rivera asked.

I glanced up. A full confession was on the tip of my tongue, but he looked so damned smug, I couldn't seem to force the words past my lips.

And anyway, Solberg, damn his anemic hide, had said that secrecy was a matter of life or death.

"I can't believe it," I said. "I didn't even know it was gone."

His expression remained absolutely bland.

"Last night . . ." I shook my head and made an exasperated *tsk*ing noise. "I . . . went out, but I only left my purse unattended for a couple seconds." I was shaking my head and hoping it wouldn't flop right off. "What's the world coming to?"

"You're saying your wallet was stolen?"

I was still shaking my head. I don't know why. I'm pretty sure I was trying to convince him of the affirmative. "It must have been. Wherever did you find it?" *"Wherever?"* Jesus, McMullen. *"Wherever?"*

"Funny story," he said. But his expression suggested it might not be ha-ha funny, but the other kind. The kind that gets you five to ten in San Quentin. "It was in an old Cadillac that was found parked in front of the Four Oaks."

"Really!"

"The back window had been shot out."

"No!"

He said nothing.

"You mean my wallet was just lying in someone's car and no one..." I swallowed, wondering if I was going to hurl, or be struck dead. "No one took the car...or the wallet. That's...lucky."

"You don't know anything about it?"

Oh, yeah, I was going to be sick. "How could I?"

A muscle jumped in his jaw. "We haven't found the owner of the car yet."

"Well..." I shrugged and smiled. "It's a big city."

"Found his friend, though. His late friend."

As the reality of his words seeped in, I felt myself go sickly green. I swallowed. "Late, as in...tardy?"

His smile was carnivorous. "Late as in dead."

"Jesus."

"Want to tell me about it, Chrissy?" he asked, taking a step toward me.

I retreated, though I don't know how my knees managed it. They felt about as sturdy as dental floss. "I don't know what you're talking about."

"All right, let me refresh your memory. There were two

guys. One was scrawny. The other one was big, going to fat. The scrawny one was called Lopez. You know him?"

I tried not to remember the clawing terror. "Any relation to J. Lo?"

A muscle jerked in his jaw. "He was a known felon. Kid found him this morning on his way home from a sleepover at his buddy's house on Zinnia Way."

Oh God. Oh God. "Found him where?" My voice sounded hollow.

"Couple miles from the restaurant. He'd been shot in the back of the head. Brains were spattered across fifty feet of asphalt and—"

"Are you . . . ?" I stopped him, breath hitched in hopeful anticipation. If Lopez was shot, I hadn't killed him. It's amazing what will lift your spirits sometimes. "Are you sure he was shot?"

"Close range. Nine-millimeter Sig. Any idea what a bullet will do to a man's cranium at four yards? We were lucky we could get an ID. Half his face—"

But I never heard the rest. I was stumbling toward the bathroom, covering my mouth and gagging.

Five minutes later I felt a little better. At some point in my not too distant past I had stashed a pack of cigarettes under my sink. It had been unopened. There was a God. I only hoped he was forgiving, or had a kick-ass sense of humor.

I was sitting on the bathroom floor. I'd slammed the door shut after entering. Rivera hadn't tried to follow me. Maybe he was a gentleman after all. Then again, maybe it was the retching sounds that had made him so atypically considerate.

I sat some more, then drowned my third cigarette in the toilet bowl, closed my eyes, and dropped my head against the wall behind me.

I could hear Rivera moving around in the kitchen. Maybe he'd make himself a sandwich and go home.

But finally I heard him stride across the floor and rap on the door.

I didn't respond. He pushed the door open, scanned the bathroom, and dropped his gaze to my position near the toilet.

Our eyes met.

"Have you been smoking?" he asked.

I shook my head. "Quit," I said. "Years ago."

"There are butts in your toilet."

"Damned plumbing."

He made a snorting sound. "You feeling better?"

I nodded.

"Well, you look like hell. Have you had breakfast?"

I shook my head. I had my back propped against the scant stretch of wall between the vanity and the toilet. The room didn't smell that bad, even from my position. Mom would have been proud.

"I'll make you something," he said, "while you shower."

I blinked at him. "I didn't shoot anyone," I said.

He made some kind of noise that defied description and closed the door.

I didn't know what that meant. I didn't know what anything meant, and I didn't know what to do. So I might as well shower, even if it had been his suggestion.

I started the water running and stripped down, but not

before I locked the bathroom door. I'm not a complete idiot.

The water felt good against my back. The tension eased a notch, but my mind was still spinning. I didn't know what the hell Rivera was going to do, but I was pretty sure he wouldn't be accusing me of employing vast quantities of common sense.

A knock sounded at the door. "Breakfast's ready."

I considered making him suffer by letting the meal go cold. But there's some saying about not cutting off your nose to spite your face. I shut the water off, toweled dry, and realized I hadn't brought any clean clothes into the bathroom with me.

Rethinking the complete idiot idea was kind of painful. I rummaged around in the cabinet, dragged out a Little Mermaid beach towel, and wrapped it around my body. Twice, 'cuz I'm so skinny. Or because it was the approximate size of a parachute. Then I towel-dried my hair, added a little product, did the finger-trilling thing, and turned toward the door. I stopped, turned back.

A little makeup wouldn't hurt. I didn't want to be one of those women with a bad mug shot. Or, on the upside, maybe if I looked really hot, my indiscretions would entirely slip Rivera's mind.

So I dabbed on a little mascara. And some eyeliner. A swipe of lip shimmer. Not lipstick. I wasn't trying to drive the guy mad with lust, just convince him to keep me out of the pokey.

I studied my reflection in the mirror. My hair was droopy and my face looked as pale as soy milk. I was pretty sure his sanity was safe.

Sighing, I unlocked the door and stepped into the hall.

Rivera was just raising his hand to knock again. I shrieked, scuttled backward, and clasped my towel against my chest like a shield.

He lifted a brow as if trying to judge my level of rationality. "You ready?"

My bottom was pressed against the vanity. "For what?"

The scar at the right corner of his mouth twitched. But his eyes remained steady. "I was thinking breakfast?" He left the statement kind of open-ended, like a question.

All the air had been sucked out of the bathroom. We stared at each other.

"Oh." When I found my voice, it didn't sound like my own. "Sure. Yeah. Just let me . . ." I took a tentative step, trying to skirt around him. He stepped aside just as I did the same thing. Unfortunately, we headed in the same direction. Despite my attempt to cover as much flesh as humanly possible, the towel had slipped a little. I was squeezing my arm tight against my torso. His gaze dropped. Mine did the same. My boobs were pressed together like Pillsbury's finest and spilling over the top of the towel.

I raised my gaze. He raised his, slowly.

"Bribing an officer of the law comes with a sizable penalty, McMullen," he said.

My mouth dropped open. I tried to step around him. He tried to step out of the way. Maybe. Anyway, we bumped again. I bumbled against him, squeezed my arms harder against my chest, and glanced at his face.

His lips curved up with dark amusement. It was about as close as he ever came to giddy giggles.

I glared, shoved him out of the way, and stormed past.

It only took me a couple of minutes to dress. It wasn't as if I was trying to impress him. The man was Satan's hand . . . child . . . hand. . . . The man was Satan.

He turned from the stove as I entered the kitchen. His eyes roved over me. They're Spanish dark, but there was a funky light behind them. I resisted tugging my sweater up. Not that it was low-cut or anything. Okay, it was kind of low-cut . . . and clingy. But it was one of the few sweaters that had survived my exodus from Schaumburg, and it was chilly outside. November in L.A. Brrrr. Couldn't have been more than seventy-five degrees. On Sunset Boulevard the nouveau riche would be donning their furs.

"You look better," he said.

I didn't know if I should thank him or stab him in the eye. I settled for taking the plate he handed me.

A trio of something that looked like crepes sat in the middle of the dish. A slice of orange was twisted into a spiral and stood upright beside them.

I blinked stupidly as I sat down at the table. He took a wineglass out of the freezer, filled it with grape juice, and set it beside my plate.

I stared at him, dumbfounded. He shrugged. "Mamá always wanted a girl."

As he turned away I couldn't help but notice she hadn't even gotten close. His hips were narrow, his ass as tight as a California plum.

"It would be more appetizing if you had some cilantro," he said.

I doubted it. His ass was pretty much perfect. But I jerked my gaze to my meal just as he turned toward me. My fork was already in my hand. Like a Boy Scout. Always prepared. "What are these?"

"I call them tortillas locas."

"Seriously?"

"If I wanted to kill you I'd think of a more expedient method."

"Huh?" I couldn't get past the fact that Rivera could cook. It defied all kinds of logic. I didn't even know he could eat.

"I'm not trying to poison you," he said.

"Oh." I nodded, then dizzily cut off the end of a tortilla and tasted. I felt my salivary glands buzz to life and my brows shoot skyward. Suddenly, I was glad Jed hadn't shown up to shoot me dead. Luckily, Rivera had already turned back toward the stove and didn't witness my unadorned adoration.

He settled into the chair on the far side of the table with his own plate, and took a sip of his grape juice. Chilled . . . in a wineglass.

"I met a cop once," I said, my voice monotone. "Name was Jack Rivera. Any idea what might have happened to him?"

He didn't bother to glance up. "Good-looking guy? Charismatic as hell?"

"You got the hell part right."

The corner of a grin tugged at his lips. "I'm just trying to keep you off balance until you decide to tell me the truth."

My stomach quirked a little. "About what?"

He sipped his juice. "Right now I'll settle for just about anything." His gaze shifted to mine again, devil dark and unwavering.

"Okay." I gave him a nod and tried not to melt under his gaze. Latin men should either be married or locked up. Possibly both. Both are good. "The tortilla thingies are excellent."

"The trick's in the sauce."

"What?"

"I added some Chablis."

"Oh." I wrenched my eyes from his, took another bite, remembered I had missed supper, and considered inhaling the rest. It might have seemed uncouth. I took a third minuscule amount. "So your mother taught you to cook?"

"Give her a tomato and a stick of celery, she can make you a three-course meal."

There was pride in his voice and a soft sort of reverence. Lieutenant Jack Rivera, momma's boy. Life was weirder than shit. "So . . ." I cleared my throat. "You don't have any sisters?"

"No brothers, either."

Even the grape juice tasted better than normal. Holy crap. How do you improve grape juice? "Why is that?"

He shrugged. "Could be I was as much trouble as a whole houseful of kids."

I could imagine him as a little boy. I don't particularly like kids. They tend to drip from every possible orifice and smell like things gone bad. But he would have been a cute little bugger.

"So you haven't changed," I said.

He'd already finished his meal and leaned back to study me. "Some parts have."

I caught his gaze, then skittered my eyes back to my

meal. I couldn't get a bead on this guy. Was he trying to seduce me or get me hanged? Or both? Possibly both. Holy
crap.

"I was told..." I stopped, remembered my source had
been his ex-wife, whom I had met under rather false pretenses, and tried again. "I heard your father was in politics."

He nodded. "A senator."

"Is that good?"

"If you're a special interest group or have funds in a
Swiss bank account."

"Am I to understand that you don't like him very—"

"Listen!" He leaned abruptly across the table toward me.
Uh-oh. Good cop gone.

"Much as I enjoy reminiscing about my familial roots, I
think it's time we get down to business. Don't you?"

I hadn't finished my tortillas yet. Surely I deserved a last
meal. "What business?"

"What the hell were you doing last night?"

I shook my head. "Whatever are you...?" Oh, crap. I
sounded like Penelope Pitstop. "I don't know what you're
talking about."

"I'm talking about a dead guy, a shot-up car, and your
damned wallet." He raised the thing like a smoking gun.

"I told you, I don't have any idea how it got there. Is it
my fault it was stolen?"

"Damn—" he began, then gritted his teeth, leaned back
in his chair again, and folded his arms across his chest.
"Okay, tell me your story. But if you lie to me..." He shook
his head. "Swear to God, McMullen, I won't be this pleas-
ant when you're in front of a judge."

I felt my hand shake. I set the fork carefully on my plate,

linked my fingers across my lap, and licked my lips. I really wanted to eat the tortillas. But I'd kind of lost my appetite. And that made me mad. So I fluffed my dignity and gave him a hard look in the eye. "I really don't think it's any of your concern how I spent—"

"God damn it!" The table jumped like a trampoline when he slapped it with his palm. I jerked in tandem.

"Okay! Okay! You don't have to take it out on the furniture." My head was spinning. What now? Run like the wind? Lie through my teeth? Tell the truth? Stall? Yep.

I stroked the unoffending table. "I bought it at that little flea market in Culver City. And it wasn't cheap. I'm not on a government salary, you know. Can't afford to buy new furniture whenever some hard-nosed—"

"McMullen." His voice was low and deep and promised unpleasantries to come.

I swallowed, lifted my chin, and honed haughty to a fine point. "I was out with a friend last night."

"A friend."

"Yes." Dad would have called my tone prissy and threatened to warm my bottom with his belt. Elaine might have used the word "constipated." "I didn't want to tell you . . . knowing how you feel about me."

Judging by his expression, he felt like throttling me. But apparently he wasn't the kind who wanted to discuss his deepest emotions.

"Go on," he said—and rather coldly, I thought.

"I dined with an acquaintance."

"What time?"

"Six o'clock."

"With who?"

"Whom," I corrected.

He showed his teeth.

I fiddled with my fork and gave him a snooty glance. "I don't care to get him involved."

"That's unfortunate."

I sharpened snooty into downright mean. It might not have been up to snuff, considering my knees were knocking on the legs of my flea market table.

"What's his name, Chrissy?"

I pursed my lips and glanced into my living room as if I were trying to decide whether or not to tell him the truth. But I was pretty busy holding my bladder. "I know how you get, Rivera. I don't want you bothering him."

"Bothering him?" His eyes glowed like a werewolf's, although I have to admit I'm using some imagination here. I mean, I've dated some weird-ass men, but most of them only had the usual amount of hair. And hardly any of them howled at the moon. "When have I ever bothered anyone?"

"You're bothering me right now," I said placidly.

He smiled. To say there was no warmth in it would have been a gross understatement. But "glacial" might have come close.

"And remember Solberg?" I asked. "You nearly gave him a coronary." I tugged the peel off my orange slice for something to do. "Perhaps that's why he's missing. Because he—"

"Who was the lucky guy, McMullen?" he asked.

"Listen, I don't—"

He leaned across the table. I leaned back.

"Okay, his name is Ross. You satisfied?"

"Ross who?"

What now? What now? What now? "It doesn't matter. If

you don't believe me, you can contact the restaurant we patronized. I'm sure they'll remember us."

"You dance nude on the table or something?"

I tried another glare. It was getting there. "Ross happens to be a very attractive man."

"Is he?"

"And successful."

"You sleep with him?"

I jerked to my feet. "I think we're done here, Lieutenant."

He remained where he was. What the hell was I supposed to do now? Call the cops? It seemed a little redundant.

"What'd you do after dinner?"

I licked my lips and glanced longingly toward the door. I was a fast eater and a whiz at short division. But I wasn't all that speedy at hoofing it.

"We went to the Four Oaks for a drink," I said.

"They don't serve drinks at the restaurant you . . . patronized?"

"I like the atmosphere of the Oaks. Elegant but comfortable."

"And that's where you left your purse . . . unattended."

I nodded. The movement was surprisingly difficult to perform while continuing to breathe. "I forgot all about it."

"Who can blame you, with a hunk like Ross."

I spread my hands and gave him a "Well, there you go" expression.

"So how long were you absorbing the rarified ambience of the Oaks?"

"Not long. As I said, only a few minutes."

"You and ol' Ross think of better things to do, did you?"

I gritted my teeth. "As matter of fact, we did."

He stared at me, his eyes lazy and mocking. "So the dearth has finally ended?"

The sexual reference was not lost on me.

"Get out," I said.

"You have to carry him into your bedroom like Solberg, or was he able to make it under his own steam?"

I felt my nostrils flare. Maybe I hadn't had sex for half a decade, but that didn't give him the right to take cheap shots. "He could beat your ass to a pulp," I said. I may have lost a little hauteur.

One eyebrow rose. "Easy, girl," he soothed. "I didn't mean to disparage the love of your life."

"I'll disparage your—"

He laughed. "How long did he stay?"

Anger is all well and good, but when terror starts pouring in like acid rain, anger tends to run for cover. I glanced toward my front door.

"He's not one of those fellows who kiss and run, is he?"

I zapped my gaze back to his. "He stayed plenty long."

His lips twitched, but I was far past reading the meaning. "Kind of out of practice, weren't you?"

I snarled at him.

"No wonder you looked like hell this morning. Maybe you better give me Ross's last name. I'll tell him to go easy on you next time."

"I'm sorry you're jealous, Rivera," I said. "But you're just going to have to accept the fact that I'm spoken for."

"Spoken for?" He rose to his feet. The movement was

slow, like a sleek, hard-muscled predator sizing up an unsuspecting bunny. I don't like being the bunny. Even if they are cute.

He came around the table just as slowly, his gaze never leaving mine. I followed him with my eyes, frozen in place. Poor, poor bunny.

"You know what I think, McMullen?" He was standing directly in front of me, his eyes deadly. "I think you're lying. I don't think there is a Ross."

I filled my lungs with air. "Oh, there's a Ross," I said.

"Yeah?" He stepped a little closer.

"He's taller than you."

He quirked up his lips. "I heard it's girth that counts."

"Makes twice your salary. He'll probably pull in more than Solberg in another couple of years, and he's not even a nerd."

He laughed. I fumed.

"Well," he said, tossing my wallet onto the table and turning toward the door. "I've heard gigolos can make a hell of an income these days."

14

I'd rather be pissed off than pissed on.

—*Chrissy's version*
of Father Pat's
truth maxim

ONCE I QUIT slavering and my blood pressure simmered back down to the triple digits, I put Rivera firmly out of my mind and called Directory Assistance.

It was simple enough to get a phone number for Electronic Universe. Having no better options, I dialed the number immediately.

The man on the other end had a slight Asian accent. The kind that immediately makes me feel stupid.

"Yes, hello," I said, using my nose voice in self-defense. "I'd like to speak to J. D. Solberg."

There was a pause. "I am sorry. Is he an employee here at E.U.?"

"No. He just comes in from time to time to try out your fabulous equipment."

"Can you describe him?"

I did. "It's an emergency. Please put him on the line."

"I am sorry," he said. "But your Mr. Solberg does not seem to be here at this time."

My heart rate sped up. "But he has been in the past?"

"I can't say for certain."

"Was he there today?"

"I do not know."

"Yesterday? Was he there yesterday? You'd know him if you saw him. He has a nose like a—"

He hung up. I promptly drove to Santa Ana, where E.U. is located just off Mesa Freeway. It's an imposing building the approximate size of Montana. Once inside its black glass doors, I searched every face and listened to every voice. Solberg was nowhere to be found. But there was enough electronic gadgetry to send a man to the moon. Which meant, I believed, there was also enough gadgetry to entice Solberg from his hiding place. If he was hiding. And if he was hiding, he must have some kind of plan to extract himself from his current troubles. He might be a cross-eyed little drip, but he wasn't stupid.

Still, even smart cross-eyed little drips need accomplices to save their drippy hides.

I glanced around the store. The staff was dressed all in black. They weren't your usual techno-geek employees. For one thing, they were all over the age of seventeen. They were sharp, predominantly male, and somber.

But I have yet to meet a man who can remain coherent in

the smiling face of cleavage, so I popped open the top button of my sweater, gave my arms a squeeze, and approached the nearest employee.

"Hello."

I gave him a smile. "This is amazing." I looked around the store, wide-eyed. "I've heard nothing but good about E.U."

"Thank you." He gave me a little bow and dipped his gaze momentarily toward my chest. "Is there something I can help you with?"

"I'm not sure. I was just wondering...if I brought in a disk that has...well...some pretty high-tech schematics, would I be able to open it on your computers?"

He gave me a sagacious glance. Or maybe he was looking down my sweater again. "Well, that depends. How familiar are you with E.U. technology?"

"Not very, I'm afraid."

"Then you might be a little lost. We're pretty innovative."

"But your equipment would be able to handle it?"

He looked affronted on behalf of his machines, E.U., and technology in general. "Absolutely."

"No matter what it is?"

"If it can be done, we can do it here."

I thanked him and sauntered away. After that, I spoke to every employee I could find, asking about Solberg, but none of them admitted to seeing the little geek, although I thought a youngish fellow named Rex seemed somewhat nervous when I gave him J.D.'s description.

"Call me," I said, giving him my phone numbers and a glimpse of cleavage. "As soon as you see him. Please. I'd be eternally grateful."

He nodded numbly and flushed, proving that even gadgets can't compete with boobs when they're up close and personnel.

I returned home in unsurprised defeat and spent the rest of the day on the Internet, searching for the magician Ross had mentioned.

But there was no one on the Net called the Magical Martini. Go figure. After exhausting all my possible avenues, however, I did find a show called The Mystical Magic of Menkaura, which played at a hotel called La Pyramide.

It sounded foreign to me, and sure enough, when I popped onto his site, the man was wearing a turban and a long black cape, which flowed out behind him—like magic.

I learned a buttload of stuff. For instance, the Magical Menkaura descended from an ancient Bedouin tribe known for its mystical ways. He looked damned good with his tasseled cape flying in the air-conditioned breeze. And all of his assistants were gorgeous, curvaceous . . . and topless.

I blinked at my monitor. Perhaps it should have occurred to me that Las Vegas magicians would have topless assistants, but the thought had never crossed my mind. And even though I was staring at a photo of several of his nubile bimbos, I found the idea somewhat unbelievable. Obviously, they couldn't shove things up their sleeves.

Which made me rather concerned about where they would stow them.

But when I saw the picture of the horse, I realized their props were a little large for concealing in clothing . . . or other places.

A kohl black stallion, as the photo advertised, was one of the act's main attractions, and much "admired" by Menkaura's lovely ladies.

I made a face at the bevy of barely clad assistants draped suggestively around the poor animal, then searched the screen for the names of said assistants. None were listed, but maybe they didn't need names. Maybe Menke just called them by color, because it sure as hell seemed that bimbos came in every shade. One bronze, one ebony, one brown, one redhead, one blonde. Maybe he was trying to make a statement, or maybe he just liked variety.

I stared at the blonde. I would have liked to believe that no man could have found her more attractive than Elaine, but men are unpredictable . . . and stupid.

Stymied, I ate a carrot and tried to think. But carrots aren't very conducive to deep ponderings, so I wandered back into the kitchen and tried a Snickers bar. Sure enough, a thought struck me within seconds.

I went back to the website and gazed disgustedly at the photos. Five scantily clad bimbos gazed back. Five. Ross said there had been only four. Of course, he'd also said he was drunk, but I had a feeling a guy would notice how many 36D topless girls were on the stage, unless there were a thousand or something. Then he might be one or two off.

Which meant . . . the Magical Menkaura was short one bimbo.

I ate another Snickers bar and ruminated, but in the end, despite my deep thinking, I resorted to picking up the phone.

"La Pyramide Hotel and Casino. How may I assist you?"

The woman on the other end of the line sounded genuinely thrilled that I had called, not at all like she was promoting virtual bestiality and plain dumb-ass porn on a stage probably not a hundred yards from where she sat in air-conditioned comfort.

"I sure hope so," I said. "I'm trying to get ahold of Menke."

There was a pause. "Menke?"

"Yeah, the Mystical Menke."

"Oh." Her voice had gotten a little frosty around the edges. It's probably near impossible to act high-class in Las Vegas, but she was giving it the old college try. "Menkaura Qufti, the magician here at La Pyramide?"

"Yeah. That's 'im."

"I'm sorry, he's not here at the moment, but you could leave a message if you like."

"Not there?" I said, as though baffled that the man might be mystical *and* mobile.

"No. I'm afraid not."

"Oh, crapski. Well, tell 'im to call Pinky, will ya?"

Another pause. "Certainly Ms. . . . Pinky. Can I get a phone number?"

"Sure." I gave her my number. "And tell 'im I'm looking for a job, will ya?"

"Of course."

"And tell 'im, too, that I'm built like a cello, but I can fit into a medicine cabinet if I gotta."

She didn't have much to say to that. I hung up.

By then it was time for supper. I looked in my fridge. Even the cheese was gone. Damn Rivera.

It was a ten-minute drive to Vons, where I buy my groceries. Elaine won't shop anywhere but Whole Foods, where there's a circus atmosphere on sample day and lines queue up a week in advance.

As for me, I used to make sure my milk came from cows not treated with rbST. I'd later learned that one of the suspected side effects of hormones was increased breast size. I'm not quite so fussy anymore.

It didn't take me long to unpack my groceries. It wasn't as if I intended to cook—or was able to. But if the SWAT team muscled its way into my kitchen, they'd have enough staples to make us all a nice omelet or something.

Sometime around nine o'clock, still not certain which direction would actually lead to Solberg, I checked into Hilary Pershing's professional life again on the Internet. I didn't learn much. I hopped around from site to site, and although there were a few mentions of her work at NeoTech, her life in the cat show circuit seemed to be her obsession. She had five adult felines listed. None of them had names like Oscar or Scruffy. Hilary tended to lean toward the dramatic—Fyrelight's Silver Onyx, that sort of thing.

She should probably get together with the Mystical Menkaura, I thought, and wondered groggily if she had Solberg locked up in a cat cage in her basement.

Despite my world-class abilities, I didn't sleep well that night. I had dark dreams involving men with severe halitosis and nasty-looking weaponry.

On Sunday, I considered going for a run, but the nightmares—and the waking reality—convinced me it was too risky. Always nice to find the silver lining.

In the afternoon I took my place on the ridge above Solberg's neighborhood. It would probably have been smarter to try to track down information on the men who had abducted me, as Rivera hadn't been very forthcoming about information regarding them. But I returned to the one place I was certain Solberg would eventually return.

Unfortunately, he didn't show up. But at two-thirteen, the Georges' garage door opened and a BMW backed out. I snapped up my binoculars, focused quickly, and discovered that Tiffany was alone in the car. The garage was empty. Which meant that either the Georges only had one vehicle, which seemed unlikely in a neighborhood where gasoline consumption outshone the national debt, or Mr. Georges was gone . . . again.

I drove down the hill, parked in their driveway, and hardly felt at all nervous about knocking on their door. No one answered. I tried their doorbell. Nothing. I leaned on their doorbell. Still nothing. Either Mr. Georges was deaf or the house was empty.

Glancing around, I skirted their garage and headed into their backyard. My heart was pounding. Despite my actions of the past week, I still found it intimidating to be trespassing.

But the sight of the pit halted all other thoughts. It was six feet long, a good four feet deep, and lay directly beside a filled-in area that looked like it had boasted the same dimensions.

A noise sounded from Amsonia Lane, jump-starting me back into motion.

I was breathing hard by the time I reached the Saturn. My imagination was running rampant.

She'd dug graves in her backyard. Tiffany Georges had dug graves. For her husband? For Solberg? For both?

Fueled with the certainty that I was on to something, I climbed back up to my perch above her house.

By five o'clock I was bored out of my mind. By midnight I was certifiable.

Mr. Georges still hadn't arrived and Tiffany hadn't returned.

I had sat there long enough to think about the crazy things that happen. I knew from a million years of school, and a millennium of waitressing, that people sometimes just flip out and kill people. Hell, I'd considered killing Rivera just yesterday, and I wasn't even married to the guy.

Wasn't it possible that little Tiffany had wigged out and murdered her husband? Wasn't it also possible that Solberg had found out about the crime and met the same fate? Although, that didn't really account for the strange phone call and the guy with the gun who had chased me across the turf.

Life, I reflected when I was safe at home once again, was just as messy as hell.

I saw three clients before noon on Monday. The first two seemed considerably more lucid than myself. I did a lot of ummm-humming and sent them on their way.

My third client was Howard Lepinski.

I'd been seeing him for obsessive-compulsive disorder and a shitload of other problems for almost six months. He mostly talked about nothing more consequential than his luncheon options. My own sanity looked pretty solid in comparison.

"Do you think I should use whole grain bread?" he asked. "I mean, studies show that fiber can be advantageous for your colon, but white bread is lower in calories. And—"

"Mr. Lepinski..." I interrupted ever so gently, though my nerves were tapping like castanets. "You do realize you're discussing your lunch menu again, don't you?"

He stared at me from behind thick, round glasses. He was a small, thin man with an excellent ability to look offended.

I gave him my professional smile. "I had hoped we were beyond that at this point."

His mustache twitched. There had been a time when I had compared him rather unfavorably to the client whose session followed his. That client's name was Andrew Bomstad. Andy was a certified hotty . . . and rich. Mr. Lepinski hadn't stacked up very well, until Andrew had revealed his true nature and his engorged penis all in one fell swoop. A few weeks and a murder investigation later, I had learned to reserve judgment.

I'm trying to be more tolerant these days.

"Diet is important," he said. His tone was disapproving. "You are what you eat. Haven't you ever heard that?"

I nodded. I had. But so far I didn't much resemble a caramel-coated peanut. Call me a doubter.

"I've been considering the Atkins diet," he said.

I have to say I was surprised. I mean, I knew Atkins was the latest nutritional craze, but Mr. Lepinski was only marginally wider than my spleen.

"Not to lose weight," he explained. "To bulk up." He lifted a scrawny arm and made a muscle. Maybe. "High protein. You know." He flicked his eyes toward my door and back. "You think I'd be more attractive if I were buff?"

The idea of putting "Mr. Lepinski" and "buff" in the same sentence made my brain rattle inside my skull, but I held tight to my game face. "Do you feel a need to be more attractive, Mr. Lepinski?"

"Well . . ." He shrugged and looked defensive. Some people are like that about self-improvement. I think it's the fact that we're fed, from infancy, the line that we are, each of us, spectacular, and shouldn't change a thing. Which is a bunch of hooey as far as I'm concerned. Most of us are as loopy as corkscrews and any kind of self-improvement is worth a shot.

But despite the fact that Lepinski often irritated the hell out of me, deep down I thought he was a pretty good egg.

"No," he said, then "I don't know." He paused, looking worried. "It couldn't hurt, I suppose."

There was something in his tone—a wistfulness, maybe, that intrigued me. I tilted my head and poked gently. "How does your wife feel about your interest in fitness?"

"Sheila?"

I nodded. He didn't look like the polygamist type, thus the question seemed supercilious, but I managed to keep my musings to myself.

He glanced toward the door and back again. Toward the door and back. I waited. He shifted restlessly, but his knees remained perfectly locked and his shoes, brown leather wing-tips, were aligned with martial precision.

His knobby knuckles were white against his skinny thighs.

I waited some more.

"I think she's having an affair," he rasped finally.

I felt drained and beaten by the time he left my office. Drained, beaten, and useless. The poor guy's wife was stepping out on him and all I could come up with was, "How do you feel about that?"

I slumped behind my desk. The past couple weeks had been hell. First Solberg's disappearance, then being attacked by thugs, then Rivera. I'd almost preferred the thugs.

At least they hadn't doubted that I'd had a date. At least they hadn't made me say stupid-ass things like "He's taller than you." Or "He'll probably make more than Solberg in a couple years," or...

My mind stuttered to a halt. Good God. I'd mentioned Solberg and Ross in the same breath. What if Rivera put two and two together? What if he called NeoTech and found out Ross worked there? What if I was a total moron?

My hands shook as I dialed the number for NeoTech. Someone with a nasal twang patched me through to Ross's office without delay.

"Bennet here."

I swallowed a lump the size of a Schaumburg cockroach. "Ross?"

"Yes?"

"This is..." I took a deep breath. "This is...umm..." Now was not the time to forget my name.

"Chris." His voice was warm. "Hi. How are you?"

"Fine. I'm...umm...fine." I had a stranglehold on the telephone cord.

"And your friend? Elaine, wasn't it? How's she?"

It took me a moment to remember my fabricated reason for leaving him high and dry at the Safari. "Oh, yes." I cleared my throat, fighting my conscience. I had bigger problems. My waning sanity, for instance. "She's fine."

"Good."

The phone went silent.

"Listen, ummm, Ross, I'm calling to ask for a favor."

"Shoot."

I winced. I'd never been such a stickler about phrase-ology. "I'm in a little bit of trouble. With the police. Nothing big," I hurried to add. "Just, you know..." I tried a laugh. Yikes. "A misunderstanding. Unpaid parking tickets, that sort of thing." Stupid, stupid, stupid. "Well, not..." I laughed again. It sounded worse than the first time. There was a little squeaky noise at the end of it, like a dog that had gotten hold of a chew toy. I was going to have to quit that. "Not parking tickets exactly." If Rivera contacted Ross, how much would he tell him? Probably not much. He was the crown prince of antisocial behavior. I was banking on the dark lieutenant's aversion to communication. "There was a little vehicular incident Friday night. Someone crashed into someone and someone thought it was my car. But it wasn't. In fact—"

"Does this have anything to do with a..." He paused as if checking his notes. "Lieutenant Rivera?"

My mouth dropped open and stayed open. My mind spun to a halt, like a Maytag on spin dry.

"Hello?"

I blinked. "You've already spoken to him?"

"Well, no." He paused. "But he called. A couple times. I was out, though, and this morning's been crazy. I haven't had a chance to get back to him."

"Ohhh . . ." I felt like I'd been overcooked and left in the strainer too long. "Well, I . . ." I inhaled carefully, lest my lungs explode. "I was wondering if you could do me a favor."

"I'll try."

"I'd, ummm . . . I'd, ummm . . ." Just say it, God damn it! "I'd like you to tell Rivera we were together all night," I spurted, then bit my lip and squeezed my eyes shut. "At my house."

He was silent for what seemed forever, then, "Was it as good for you as it was for me?"

The air escaped my lungs in a hiss. My shoulders drooped like yesterday's lettuce. "I didn't do anything wrong, Ross. I swear to God. I swear it on my grandfather's grave."

He was silent again.

"I loved my grandfather," I said into the abyss.

He laughed. "All right."

"You'll do it?" I whispered.

"Yes. But you'll owe me."

"What?"

He delayed a moment. "Dinner? Your place?"

Damn it, I'd rather give him my firstborn. Or sex. What was wrong with sex? Didn't anyone blackmail people with sex anymore?

"Okay."

"All right, then. How about Friday night?"

We settled on a time, after which point I filled him in on how we'd spent our time together. He sounded surprised, but not disappointed.

I took it as a sign of better things to come.

15

Celibacy sucks, no pun intended.

—*Eddie Friar,*
shortly after coming
out of the closet

THE WHOLE WEEK was a disaster.

Devoid of any better ideas, I had trotted Solberg's confiscated disk over to Eddie Friar's house. Eddie's an ex-boyfriend. He's also gay. I'm sorry to say that hardly qualifies our relationship as weird—in comparison to a few dozen others. In fact, Eddie's one of the few guys with whom I still communicate. He's articulate, good-looking, and kind. Unfortunately, his guess regarding the CD was no more educated than mine—it seemed to contain blueprints and schematics for some kind of new invention.

I thanked him for his time and he asked if I'd like to join him for Thanksgiving dinner. The idea seemed a little pathetic—a gay guy and a raging hetero spending turkey day together—but not so pathetic as me alone with a can of Spam, so I thanked him again and went on my not-so-merry way.

With no idea where to go or who else to trust, I let the situation simmer as I worried about more immediate problems—such as my continued survival.

Some months ago, I had purchased a minimal security system for my modest abode. But in light of recent circumstances, I thought it might be time for an upgrade.

The installation guys came by on Tuesday to do the work, then stood in the vestibule and looked at me as if wondering what the hell there was to steal. True, you could fit the entirety of my house in a double-wide trailer and I didn't have so much as a single pair of matching spoons, but I thought my life was worth the cost.

Maybe I was wrong. Their fee was tantamount to extortion. I'd have to counsel two more Peeping Toms and a schizophrenic for a year and a half to pay it.

On Wednesday, the Vegas magician returned my call. I recognized his area code on my caller ID. Apparently I had played the dumb blonde pretty convincingly when I left my message.

I tried to find that same platinum frame of mind as I picked up the phone.

"Yeah?" I said.

"Good afternoon," he responded. His voice was lush and theatrical. I think I may actually have shifted the receiver from my ear to stare at it. "Might there be a Ms. Pinky at these premises?"

"Yeah. This is Pinky. Who's this?" If I had been chewing gum, my world would have been complete.

"This is the Mystical Menkaura."

I delayed a moment, then, "Menke, hey, thanks for returning my call." There was a good deal of noise in the background—people chattering, something being scraped across the floor. At one point I thought I heard an elephant trumpet, but that might have been my imagination. "I'm between gigs and I heard you're short a girl." I held my breath.

"From whom did you hear this news?"

"From whom?" Was this guy for real, or was there the hint of a Brooklyn accent in his sheikish voice?

"Guy named Orlando Gonzalez." I had seen his name on the Internet and hoped to hell Menke didn't know him personally. "Maybe you heard of him. He's making some splash in Dallas. Anyways, I was his box jumper for a while after one of his girls got knocked up, and he says you might be needing someone, so I took in your show last Sunday."

"Did you indeed?"

"Yeah. You got yourself a winner there, Menke. And the horse . . . oooh, talk about your sexy beast."

"Is he not beautiful? He is Bedouin bred, the eagle of the desert sands."

Uh-huh. "Anyways, I thought maybe you and me could help each other out," I said.

He paused. I chewed my lip. Maybe I'd overplayed my hand.

Or maybe I hadn't played it enough. "Even though your other girls ain't as buxom as me."

I might have been mistaken, but I think he was holding his breath.

"As it happens," he said finally, "I am in need of a new assistant."

"Yeah?" Him and Hugh Hefner. "That's great. How's 'bout I pop in and see you first part of next week?"

"I believe I may be able to arrange that."

He suggested a time.

I apologized and told him that was my full day with my personal trainer. "If your buns ain't tight, nothing's right," I said, and gave him a hee-hawing laugh.

He tried again, and we agreed.

"Fabuloso," I said, then, cleverly, as if it were an afterthought, "Hey, your gal, the blonde one, what's her name? I think I may have been her double in Dallas a couple years back."

"My fair-haired assistant?"

"Yeah."

"She is called Athena."

Athena! *Got it,* I thought, but his tone tripped a little bell in my mind. He said it as if he were speaking to an audience of zillions instead of to a bubble-brained bimbo with a cerebellum the size of a lintel.

"Athena, yeah, that was her stage name," I said. "But wasn't her real name something kinda plain-Jane, like Louise or Hazel or—"

"Gertrude," he said, and I noticed that even he couldn't say the name with much panache. "Gertrude Nelson."

I hung up moments later and tried Directory Assistance for Las Vegas, but Gertrude's phone was unlisted, so I trotted off to work and let the information stew, along with a thousand other tumbling details.

My caseload was light that day. Thanksgiving was fast

approaching, and most of my clients were probably visiting relatives. My mother had called again and asked me to come home, then suggested she could invite Ernie Catrelli. I'd known Ernie in high school. He was the quarterback for Holy Name's football team. Now he's on his third divorce and living with his parents.

I'd opted for the gay guy.

Elaine entered my office.

"So . . ." I tried to sound cheery because, God knows, if she looked sad I'd probably blubber the truth all over the place and send her marching off to Vegas in a blind attempt to save Solberg's skinny ass. "You're leaving for Schaumburg tonight, huh?"

She sunk into the chair on the far side of my desk. "I've decided not to go."

"What?" Going home had been a great idea. She needed time away. I needed to find Solberg. Alone. "Your folks will be heartbroken."

She shook her head. "They're busy anyway. I decided I'll spend more time with them during Christmas."

"Oh." I couldn't think of anything to say to that. But "I didn't break into Solberg's house and no one chased *me* through his backyard with a gun the size of Milwaukee" was my first impulse.

"So what are you doing?" she asked.

We hadn't had much time to talk lately, what with me pretending to be a cello and her dating the ice cream guy.

"Eddie Friar asked me over," I said. If she was going to stay in L.A., it would be best if she stayed close. "You want to come?"

"You don't think he'd mind?"

I gave her a look. "Has a guy ever minded when you show up, Laney?"

Her eyes got a little misty. "I don't know what I'd do without you, Mac," she said.

I gave her some clever rejoinder, but guilt was riding me pretty hard, 'cuz I knew what she'd do without me. She'd date guys who would give up their kidneys to spend a half hour with her, instead of mourning some emaciated little twit who'd run off to Las Vegas and maybe had the bad manners to get himself killed, or worse. Worse being having an affair so that I had to hire the mob to have him killed.

My mood was pretty low when I drove home that afternoon, but it was nothing compared to how I felt when I saw there was a car parked in my driveway.

It was an early-model Thunderbird. I stared at it narrowly as I made my way to the front door.

"Christopher!"

I shrieked and jumped sideways as a man popped up from beneath the bumper of the car. He doubled over laughing like a hyena and I swore I could feel the stress-induced acne erupting like popcorn on my face.

"Peter," I said.

"Holy shit, sis, you're as jumpy as a virgin."

I managed to make my way up my single step to my front door and shove in my key. "What are you doing here?"

He sauntered after me. "I just needed a little downtime. Thought I'd come see my baby sister."

"Why?" I asked, and pushed my way into the house.

He laughed as he stepped inside and gave me a bear hug. "I'm happy to see you, too."

My ribs groaned. "Where's Holly?"

He glanced into the living room, then wandered away, like a toddler looking for trouble. "Hey, you get new furniture?"

"No." I put my purse on the counter and followed him in. "Where's Holly?"

He plopped down in my recliner and gazed up at me. There had been a time I had thought him the best-looking boy in the universe. That was before he gave me sheep droppings and told me they were raisins. It's hard to think charitable thoughts when you've got your head in your cousin's toilet.

"She's home," he said.

I sat down across from him and tucked the smooth silk of my skirt under my thighs, as if I were in a session. But no such luck. Peter McMullen and mental stability would never share so much as a passing glance.

"What happened this time?" I asked.

He fidgeted, tapping the chair's arms and glancing out the window. "What are you talking about?"

"You're not even married yet." He usually managed to remain faithful until the wedding. I think.

He stared at me a moment, then dropped his head back against the seat cushion and closed his eyes. "Sometimes I think I'm not the marrying type."

"You can't be the divorcing type unless you're the marrying type, Pete," I said.

He brought his head up to stare at me again. "Jesus, when did you get so damned prissy?"

I rose to my feet. Familial visits make me want to scratch my skin off. There's something about remembering who I once was. Or maybe it's about remembering who I still am. My mood was deteriorating from bad to dangerous.

"I think it was when you told Greg Grossman that I was a lesbian," I said.

He laughed. "Hell, I thought you was a lesbian. You never dated no one."

I didn't tell him that no one ever dated me. Instead, I went to the fridge and started pulling out calories. I had the acne, might as well have the fat.

"So are you dumping her, too?" I asked.

"No." He followed me into the kitchen, glanced into the freezer, then moved on to the cupboard. In a moment, he'd pulled out a jar of peanut butter. "I'm not dumping her. I just . . ." He unscrewed the top, lost interest, and set it aside—which just proves his lack of sanity. What kind of sane person loses interest in peanut butter? "Shit, I don't know what to think."

So nothing new in Chi-town.

"She's . . ." He shook his head. A few strands of dark hair had fallen over his forehead. His eyes were the color of polished amber, as soulful as a saint's. Girls had been falling for his soulful amber eyes since the day I wriggled out of my first diaper. Men might be a pain in the ass, but sometimes women are just downright moronic.

"Too fat?" I guessed, opening the bread bag.

"Fat?" He scowled at me. "No. Why would—"

"Too old? Too smart? Too ugly? Too bitchy?" I had heard them all.

He was silent. That wasn't usually the case with my

brothers. Unless they had passed out. I glanced up, ready to roll him onto his stomach to keep him from drowning in his own drool. My mother had taught me well.

His face looked stricken. "Jesus, Chrissy," he said, "have I been that big of an ass?"

I straightened, guilt already nibbling at my edges. "I'm not the woman to ask, Pete," I said.

He nodded slowly. "I was going to say she was too sweet," he said.

I stopped buttering the bread. "They were all sweet, Peter," I said.

He glanced toward my front door and stuck his hands in his back pockets. The man still had no belly. Damn him.

"Yeah." His voice was quiet. "And I don't wanna...I mean...Maybe I'm not good—"

My doorbell rang. I stared at him. "Not what?" I was stunned by his seriousness. Amongst my charming, Irish brethren, nothing was serious except a beer shortage. That was paramount to the seven plagues.

"Someone's at your door," he said.

I glanced toward it.

"You better see who it is."

I wasn't sure he was right. Good news hadn't often come knocking of late, but I wandered in that direction, my mind swirling. Maybe brother Pete was growing up. Maybe there really was a Santa Claus.

I opened the door. It wasn't Claus. It was Rivera, standing on my stoop wearing chinos and a dark sweater and looking as sexy as sin. His charisma hit me like a sock in the gut.

"Hi," he said.

I opened my mouth. Nothing came out.

"You busy?"

Sexy and civil. Holy crap. Maybe this *was* Santa's doing.

"Did you need something?" I asked, my tone cautious. He'd been civil before. Generally it ended up with us spitting at each other like scalded cats.

He glanced toward the Al-Sadrs' nauseatingly perfect yard. "I'd like to talk to you."

My stomach corkscrewed. "What happened?"

"Nothing."

"Are you arresting me?"

"Christ, McMullen. I . . ." He paused. "Should I be?"

I ignored that question. Something about the Seventh Amendment tickled my mind. "I don't know how my wallet got into the Cadillac, Rivera. Really."

He scowled.

"Besides." I felt breathless and fractured. "It's almost Thanksgiving."

"I realize that, McMullen." He already sounded peeved, but so was I. He had no right to show up on my stoop smelling like a sex slave in heat when all he intended to do was prolong my inadvertent celibacy.

"Hey, Christopher . . ." Pete appeared beside me like a bad dream, nudging the door wide and glancing at Rivera. "Hi. I'm Pete." He thrust out a hand. Rivera took it, his expression darkening. "I'm just gonna . . ." He motioned toward the interior of my house. "Go to bed. I'm dead on my feet."

He was gone in an instant. The house went silent.

Rivera was staring at me, no expression discernible on his chiseled features. "That Ross?"

A crossroads. I realized in that instant that a normal, mentally balanced human being might very well tell him the truth. But normal, well-balanced human beings rarely have brothers like Pete, who would be more than happy to wax eloquent about the time I glued a beer can to his left cheek after a particularly irritating bender.

"No," I said.

"Making up for lost time, McMullen?"

A flood of emotions washed through me and I think I might have snarled. "Listen, you—"

"Well..." He stepped back, dark eyes masked as he smiled grimly. "I'll leave you to him. Happy Thanksgiving."

*H*appy Thanksgiving!

I was still seething the following morning. But I'd dutifully called Eddie and asked if two more could come for the feast. He'd assured me the more that came the merrier it would be—but then, he hadn't met my brothers.

I'd also called my mother to inform her of Pete's whereabouts, but I'd done so from my cell phone, 'cuz it has a tendency to cut out. It hadn't disappointed me.

"Christina," Eddie said in his lovely baritone, and gave me a hug when he opened the door. I hugged him back. I genuinely like Eddie. In fact, I had the whole time I dated him. My gaydar is usually pretty accurate, but he'd fooled me right down to my short hairs. "And you must be Peter."

"Yeah." My brother stepped forward. They grasped hands in a moment of time-honored male bonding. Some things even sexual preferences can't override. "Thanks for having me. It smells great in here." Pete grinned and turned toward the kitchen. "I think I died and went to heaven."

"Yeah." Eddie nodded and skimmed his gaze down my brother's backside. "Me, too."

I gave him a look. He looked back, sober as a monk. He lives a couple light-years ahead of me in a pretty little bungalow in Santa Monica. The beach scene there is a little weird for me, but I had to admit, Eddie had a kick-ass tan, and pecs that prompted poetry. If it weren't horribly embarrassing, I'd admit I'd once penned a little sonnet about them.

"So Laney hasn't arrived yet?" I said.

"N—" he began, then stopped as the doorbell rang and went to look through the peephole. "Does she look like an anime character?"

"Let her in," I said.

"Wow." He turned toward me. Peter had wandered into the kitchen. Eddie glanced in that direction. "Where do you find these people?"

"Chicago," I said, shouldering him aside and opening the door.

Eddie's greyhound lay on the couch, one ankle crossed elegantly over the other and seeming to reserve judgment as Elaine gave me a hug.

"How are you?"

"Great," she lied, but with more flair than usual. I made the introductions.

"You are the most beautiful woman I've ever seen," Eddie said.

I think she blushed. As if she hadn't heard that a million times.

"Laney?" Peter said from the dining room.

"Peter." She hurried through the house and gave him a hug, too. "I haven't seen you for years."

"Years!" He pushed her out to arm's length to ogle her better. "I've never seen you."

Oh, crap! If I didn't love her like a sister, I would have been ready to slice my wrists with the carving knife.

"Christina, help me in the kitchen, will you?" Eddie said.

I followed him toward the source of the smells. I hadn't died and gone to heaven yet, but I did feel a little preorgasmic.

"What the hell!" he said, turning toward me.

"Still gay?" I asked, peering into the oven and jump-starting my salivary glands. Little crab canapés were roasting happily beside a lovely prime roast and tiny candied carrots. Atop the stove, garlic mashed potatoes smiled merrily. The man could even make vegetables look sexy.

"I can't decide." He peeked out toward the living room. "You're brother's not—"

"He's been divorced four times." I checked the fridge. A strawberry cream-cheese pie reposed unchallenged on the center rack. My mouth actually hurt at the sight of it.

"I'm feeling straighter every minute," he said, and nudged my shoulder on his way to the oven. "Get the wine, will you?"

"Hey." Peter showed up in a matter of seconds. "What can I do? I don't want to be a freeloader."

Since when? I glanced up, saw that Elaine was right behind him, and had my answer.

Men get weird around Laney. I'd once seen a guy dump his gin and tonic down his pants when she smiled at him. I truly don't know why. But by comparison, Pete was doing okay—for Pete, although he still irritated me.

The meal was as good as the scents had promised, and while I have no firsthand knowledge of gay guys' performance in the bedroom, I have to say, the hype about them being good in the kitchen is no exaggeration.

I ate until my stomach threatened me with expulsion and impending embarrassment. Pete dished out the appropriate and justifiable compliments, cleared his place, and offered to help clean up.

"Isn't football on?" Laney asked, busing her dishes.

"Yeah, but I like to help out."

I gave him a look that should have curled his hair. He grinned back, chipper as a toddler.

"Watch the game," I commanded. "Laney and I will take care of the kitchen."

"But—"

"Watch it," I repeated, and Eddie smiled as he settled onto the couch beside his greyhound. She rested her head on his crotch and looked up at him with adoring eyes.

I had to get me a dog. Apparently, they have the ability to pull men away from impending fornication—not that I was rehashing old problems with almost boyfriends, or becoming morose at the thought of the looming holidays.

"So what's Pete doing here?" Elaine asked.

I ran hot water in the sink. "Staring at you?" Maybe there was a little vitriol in the statement.

"He looks good."

"Laney!" I said, turning on her with venom. "Don't you—"

She laughed. "In that make-you-eat-sheep-droppings kind of way."

I relaxed. Elaine may be eccentric, but she knew a Neanderthal when one dragged her around by the hair.

I turned back to the sink with a harrumph.

"You okay?" she asked.

"Sure." I shrugged. "It's just that stupid Rivera."

The words slipped out in my postconsumptive haze before I could suck them back in.

She stared at me. "You saw the lieutenant?"

Crap. If I was any dumber I'd spit out my own kidneys. "Yeah, he . . . stopped by."

"What did he want?"

"I don't know." I shrugged, wanting to dunk my head in the sink. "Something about talking to me."

"About what?"

Shit. "About . . ." I'd almost scrubbed the color off a serving bowl. "That whole Bomstad fiasco, I suppose."

"You're kidding. Again? Did he say that?"

"Well, no, but it was implied."

"It's Thanksgiving."

"Uh-huh."

"That's crazy."

"He's male."

"I noticed. What did he say exactly?"

"Geez, Laney, I—"

She put her hands on her hips. "What did he say?"

I scowled at her and thought back. I was getting mad just thinking about it.

"He asked if I was busy and said he wanted to talk to me. I asked what was wrong and he said 'Nothing.' I said it was almost Thanksgiving and he said he was aware of the fact and then—"

"He wanted to ask you out."

The kitchen fell into silence. My mind went as numb as a moon rock. I stared at her. "What?"

"Geez, Mac, he came by to invite you to Thanksgiving dinner."

I was shaking my head. "That's crazy."

"He's male."

"I noticed." I blinked, then shook my head again. "You're wrong."

"I'm never wrong about men. Well, almost never. Does he cook?"

I nodded stupidly. She gave me her "There you go" shrug. I felt a little sick to my stomach, though I couldn't have said why exactly. It might have been that fifteenth crab canapé.

16

Lust and love. They both put a fire in your damned shorts. How you supposed to tell 'em apart?

—*Pete McMullen,*
after every divorce

I SAW MY USUAL clients on that post-Thanksgiving Friday. Most of them seemed thankful to get the family get-together behind them.

The Hunts arrived. I asked them about their holiday. Their son had come home for the traditional meal, then rushed off to be with his girlfriend. Their teenage daughters were spending the weekend with their cousins in San Diego.

Some parents feel the empty-nest syndrome most intensely during the holidays. But that didn't seem to be the case here.

I pried gently. 'Cuz that's what I do. I don't so much shrink as peck.

"Larry made the meal," said Mrs. Hunt. She was sitting very straight and proper, but there was something a little different about her, a little less rigid.

"Oh?" I have to admit being impressed. In Mom's house a man was taking his life in his hands if he so much as glanced into the icebox. "Is that a first?"

"I'll say," said Mrs. Hunt.

"And how did that turn out?"

She glanced at her husband from the corner of her eye. There was a bit of color in her cheeks. "Good," she said.

"Yeah," he agreed. Their gazes locked. "But the candied yams was the best part."

I thought there was some sexual innuendo in the exchange.

By the time I limped out of my office fifty minutes later, I felt like I'd been subjected to audio porn.

My last session of the day canceled. I gave Laney the short version of the weirdness, wished her luck on her date with a plumber, and hurried home.

It was almost dark when I arrived there. I glanced up and down Opus Street. There was an unknown blue Toyota parked a couple hundred yards down the street, but there didn't seem to be any boogeymen or guys with smirks and tampons lurking about. Still, I knew from the edification of horror flicks that it's the ones you don't see that you have to worry about, so I hurried inside, locked the door behind me, and punched in my security code.

Pete had left sometime after I'd hustled off to work some

eight hours earlier. I glanced warily from side to side, wondering where he'd put the dead rat, but it was nowhere to be found. Not even in the kitchen sink.

Either he was growing up, or he was ill. Either way, I was grateful, because Ross was due in an hour and a half.

Being the culinary genius that I am, I had purchased a pan of prefab lasagna, which I popped into the oven without even having to read the owner's manual. Look out, Julia Child.

I'd planned to have French bread and a tasty yet nutritious salad, but I forgot to buy fresh lettuce and the stuff in my fridge looked kind of brown and sloppy, so I dumped the bag in the garbage and pulled out the Spumante. It had been chilling since morning—on its side, of course. I can't cook worth a damn, but I'm not a barbarian.

Choosing an outfit was the most painful part of the entire ordeal. I dragged off my slacks, stood in front of the mirror in my underwear, and flipped through my wardrobe.

Five skirts and a mound of blouses later, I exited the bedroom in the same pants I'd worn to work. They were black. I accented them with a black blouse . . . my usual first-date attire. Elaine calls it my premourning ensemble.

It was 6:57. I still had makeup to artfully apply and my hair to arrange in a casual but fashionable coiffure. No problem, if I were gorgeous and talented. Or bald and male.

I happen to be neither.

I hit my hip on the doorjamb as I rushed into the bathroom, but I had no time to rub away the pain. It was now 6:58. If he arrived early, I had every intention of jumping out the window and heading for Seattle.

I tried to apply my mascara while curling my hair. But the hot rollers kept ending up in the sink and I stabbed myself in the eye twice.

When the doorbell rang, my hair was stacked atop my head in purple Styrofoam and I was trying to blink mascara out of my right eye.

I think I may have been cursing.

The doorbell rang again. I winced, yelled, "Just a minute," and whipped the curlers out of my hair while simultaneously applying a cloud of hair spray. I ended up with most of it congealing over the layer of mascara in my right eye, and hustled back into the bedroom, hitting my opposite hip on the way through.

There was a mound of clothing three feet high on my orange-and-green sculpted carpet. The doorbell screamed again. I kicked the garments under the bed, fluffed the coverlet, and jammed my feet into a pair of strappy but understated heels.

By the time I answered the door, Ross had aged a little bit, but he didn't look any worse for wear.

"Hi," he said.

"Sorry about the wait," I said.

His smile etched twin grooves into his cheeks. I found that I was inordinately happy that I'd had the clever foresight to kick my clothes out of sight.

I may have to add housekeeping to my list of less-than-stellar attributes.

"I was sure I had the wrong house," he said, leaning forward and kissing my cheek.

"But you waited anyway."

His smile shifted up another notch. Guys oughta be

more careful with smiles like that. I've gotten fresh for less—say, a wisp of cologne and a "How do you do." "I was hoping whoever lived here would have mercy on me and give me a meal."

I pulled the door open wider and he stepped inside. "You're in luck," I said, and led him into the kitchen.

I had him open the wine while I fished the lasagna from the oven and sliced up the bread. I'd forgotten to heat it up.

The lasagna stuck to the pan and dripped across the tablecloth when I served it, but it didn't taste half-bad.

He said as much. "So I talked to your Lieutenant Rivera," he added, changing the subject with mind-numbing suddenness.

I choked a little, then cleared my throat and shook my head. "He isn't my lieutenant."

"Whose, then?"

"I think he's a stray," I said, and took a sip of wine. Casual me. And elegant. Once I'd taken a breather I'd decided I didn't look half-bad, but I'd been gazing at myself through a sheer of mascara. "What did he have to say?"

He shrugged and cut off a corner of his lasagna. "Not much. Where was I on the night of the eighteenth, that sort of thing."

My throat felt suddenly dry, my bones strangely fragile. "And . . . ?"

"I told him I had a big game with my squash buddies."

I could feel the life drain out of me.

He stared a moment, then laughed. "I'm kidding," he said. "I told him I was here."

I considered thumping myself on the chest to recharge my heart.

"I'm sorry. You okay?" he asked, and chuckled as he reached forward to squeeze my hand. "I lied my ass off, just like you asked." He leaned back, drawing his fingers from mine. I chanced a careful breath. "I didn't think I had much choice after you gave me all those details about our evening together."

"Well . . ." I cleared my throat, realizing I was still alive. "I just wanted to be thorough."

He took a sip of wine and let the glass dangle from his fingers. "I was especially impressed that you told me the color of your bedsheets."

I felt flushed, but I wasn't sure if it was the wine or the talk of sheets that sent the blood to my head. "I hope he didn't give you too much trouble."

He shrugged. "Don't worry about it." His eyes were the color of the Caribbean at high tide. Okay, I've never actually seen the Caribbean, high tide or otherwise, but anyway, his eyes . . . well, they were blue. "I was hoping to find a way to get back into your good graces," he said.

I blinked foolishly and fiddled with my fork. "My good graces? What are you talking about?"

"Oh, come on," he said, and gave me an oblique glance across the table as he swirled his wine. "I've used that line a dozen times."

"What line?"

"Getting an emergency call in the middle of a date."

Somehow, I'd never even considered the fact that he'd think I'd wanted to escape. I mean, he had high-tide eyes. "It really was an emergency," I said.

"Uh-huh."

"Really."

He watched me for a moment. "Honest?"

"Of course." Did I look crazy? More crazy than desperate? "I'm sorry I ran out on you. It was a . . . It couldn't be avoided."

"Was it really your girlfriend?" He leaned forward on his elbows, adroitly avoiding his lasagna.

Ummm . . . Okay, now things got tricky. "Yes."

"I think you're lying," he said.

"I don't . . ." I began.

He raised his brows.

"Well, okay, I do lie sometimes."

He laughed. Maybe he liked liars. Excellent. A match made in heaven.

"But it really was an emergency."

"Well, that's a relief," he said. "I thought I'd offended you with my body odor or something."

I watched him. The lights were low, I was on my second glass of Spumante, and he had . . . some sort of eyes.

"Believe me, there's nothing about your body that offends me," I said, and he gave me that smile that made my toes curl in my strappy, understated sandals.

Fifteen minutes later we were sitting side by side on the couch with our wine. Music played softly in the background. Classy.

"A psychologist," he said.

I shrugged. "For about a year and a half."

"So what brought you to California?"

I took a sip of wine. "If one intends to make one's living dealing with psychological disorders . . ." I let the sentence dawdle.

He laughed. "Head to La La Land. Good thinking."

"How about you?"

He shrugged. "Got a job offer at Neo. Couldn't turn it down."

"They have quite a reputation, I take it."

"Other than E.U., there's nothing can touch us."

"E.U.?" I asked, but I remembered the place. It was the high-tech store where none of the employees had seen the Geekster.

"Electric Universe," he said, eyes alight with enthusiasm. "They're coming on like gangbusters. They're really a Japanese company. Just opened their first store in the United States. Apparently, if you know their secret hand- shake, they'll let you play with their stuff."

"You know the handshake?"

"I don't even know the address. But tell me more about your job. Is this really the place to be if you're a psycholo- gist?"

"Oh, I don't know." I swirled my wine and looked lan- guidly intelligent. "I think psychological difficulties are pretty universal." I was waxing philosophic and rather en- joying the sound of my own voice. Christina McMullen, sounding smart, or drunk. "I mean, if the caveman hadn't been so busy fighting off saber-toothed tigers, he probably would have been obsessing about his relationships with—" But in that instant Ross leaned in and kissed me.

Our teeth bumped.

"Sorry," he murmured, and pulled back half an inch. "I'm not very good at this."

My heart rate had escalated to hummingbird status.

"You're not?" My voice sounded breathy.

"Once a nerd, always a nerd."

"Yeah?"

"Yeah," he said, and kissed me again.

There were no teeth this time. And he was lying about his abilities.

He shifted sideways, half reclined. I did the same. He stroked my arm. His lips slanted across mine. He smelled like... I don't know what he smelled like—something I could eat in one bite. But he drew back. Maybe he was aware of my carnivorous tendencies.

We stared into each other's eyes. Here comes the big question, I thought. And it was wrong to have sex on the first date. Wrong. So wrong. But in another light, this wasn't really my first date. It was about my thousandth. Just not with the same guy.

"Do you need to answer that?" he asked.

I blinked, dreamily rising from a fog. "What?"

He tilted his head slightly, eyes smiling. "Your bell's ringing."

"Bell," I agreed.

"Someone's here," he said.

I heard it then. The chime of the doorbell, followed by a pounding fist.

I don't know how I missed the noise. It surely wasn't my heavy breathing. Heavy breathing is strictly for sexually frustrated women who don't know how to keep their knees together.

"Oh."

He sat up. I didn't have much choice but to do the same. I would have felt like a doofus lying there alone.

"Yeah, I... Yeah," I said, and rose to my feet. My knees

were a little wobbly . . . and not completely together. Guy could suck face like a kissing gourami.

I wandered hazily toward my vestibule. If this was some door-to-door salesman, he was going to get his ass kicked. Unless he was selling Girl Scout cookies. I mean, kissing's all well and good, but it's hard to hold a candle to a box of Caramel deLites and a half gallon of milk.

I glanced hopefully through the window, and every blissful thought frizzled to oblivion.

Rivera stood on my stoop, and he didn't look happy.

What should I do? My mind had stormed into high gear, but didn't seem to be generating a lot of fabulous results.

Maybe, I thought, on the blinding edge of inspiration, if I was quiet, he wouldn't know I was home.

"Open up, McMullen," he said. "I know you're there."

I gritted my teeth against a curse and swiveled to smile at Ross.

He was watching me with unblinking curiosity.

"This isn't a good time, Rivera," I said, turning back toward the door and speaking quietly.

"Good time, my ass," he growled. "Let me in."

I gave Ross another smile, debated all my marvelous options for about three seconds, and snatched the door open.

"Damn it, Rivera," I hissed. "I've got company."

"Congratulations," he said, and pushed his way inside. He scanned my house like an exterminator checking for roaches, then nodded toward the living room. "Who's that?"

"Get the hell outta my—" I began, but just then I heard Ross rise from the couch and make his way toward us.

I swallowed another curse and turned a beatific gaze on

my guest. "Ross," I said, but it was damn hard speaking between my teeth, "this is Lieutenant Rivera. Rivera"—I hardly growled at all when I said his name—"this is Ross."

The lieutenant was silent for about a third of a second, then, "Bennet?" he said.

I was struggling to think of a way to deny it, but Ross was already stepping up and reaching for Rivera's hand. For a moment I thought the cocky bastard would actually refuse that most honored of male rituals. But he didn't. Their fingers met and clasped. Their eyes did the same. They might just as well have sniffed butts and circled each other snarling.

"What can we do for you, Lieutenant?" Ross asked, and drawing his hand from Rivera's, he dropped his arm with proprietary ease across my shoulders. I tried not to jerk like a startled bunny as he skimmed his fingers down my arm.

Rivera watched the caress. His mouth twitched a little.

"I hate to bother you," he said. I'd heard better lies from my parish priest. "But I have to speak to McMullen here."

"Chrissy?" Ross asked, and turned his gaze down toward mine. Our eyes met. He smiled, warm and slow. My bones felt soft. "We were kind of busy, Lieutenant," he said, and drew me marginally closer to his chest.

I stifled a shiver. Oh, yeah, I knew he was playacting for Rivera's benefit. But I know Cruise is acting up on the big screen, too, yet memories of him in *Top Gun* keep me awake nights.

"I'm sure you were," Rivera said. His tone was as murky as his eyes. "But this won't take long."

Ross pulled his attention from me. "Couldn't this wait until morning?" He turned his attention to me again, and for a moment I thought he was going to kiss me right in front of God and the dark lieutenant. "I'll drive her to the police station myself. First thing in the morning, if you like. Then . . ." he said, and dropping his hand, ran his fingernails gently down my spine, ". . . we could have breakfast at Russell's."

"Russell's?" I said, dry-mouthed.

"It's a great little place I know. Not fancy, but comfy, you know? Belgian waffles as big as an office building and—"

"No," Rivera interrupted.

We turned toward him in tandem. Me breathless, Ross's smile just starting to fade.

"This can't wait."

Their eyes met.

"Listen," Ross said, and his tone wasn't so congenial anymore. In fact, he straightened slightly, as if to add height. And damned if I hadn't been right. He *was* taller than Rivera. "It's just a couple traffic tickets. No reason to get all bent—"

It was then that my sex-deprived brain snapped to attention.

"Ross!" I'm afraid I may have shouted his name.

He turned toward me, brows raised toward his hairline.

"I, ummm . . ." I calmed my voice and gave him an angelic smile as I raised my hand to his chest. "I'm sorry . . . darling." I refused to glance at Rivera, though he pulled at me like a snake charmer to a cobra. "But I suppose I should speak to the lieutenant."

Ross scowled, but simultaneously reached up to grasp my fingers. "I can wait in the other room, if you like."

What other room? There weren't very many. The bedroom, the bathroom, and my office. The office looked like a tornado had touched down, it would seem wrong to make him sit on the toilet while he waited, and my boudoir boasted an Everest-sized pile of clothing. What if he had time to look around . . . say, under the bed! My mind was panting along somewhere behind my hormones, trying to catch up.

"I can't ask you to do that," I said. "And I have to get up early tomorrow morning anyway."

"Are you sure?" he asked, and looked directly into my eyes. If I was mistaken about the longing in his, I ought to return my shrink license and go back to schlepping drinks.

My knees buckled. I forced them upright.

"Yes," I said.

A minute later, he was gone. My wet dreams went with him.

Rivera watched him leave, then turned toward me.

"So close," he said.

17

You don't need to be smarter. You just need dumber friends.

—Michael McMullen,
when his sister compared her
grades to Brainy Laney's

WE FACED OFF in my vestibule, estrogen and dread swimming around like intoxicated fish in my overtaxed system.

"Aren't you going to ask me in?" Rivera said.

"No." I didn't mention the fact that he was already in. It seemed obvious to those of us whose brains hadn't been dehydrated and stored in our testicles. "What do you want?"

He glanced around, then walked into the living room. There were two wineglasses on the coffee table. Both were empty.

"Taking a break from your tireless search for your geek friend?" he asked.

"They let you off the leash for the whole night, Rivera, or should I expect the dogcatcher soon?"

He tilted his head at me. He was dressed in blue jeans and a black sweater. The corner of his mouth jerked up half a millimeter.

"You always get snappy when you're deprived? Oh, but wait," he said, "you've been bad-tempered since the first time I saw you, looking flushed and disheveled over Bomstad's dead body."

I thought of a half-dozen really nasty and fairly creative retorts, but I lifted my chin and made my way to the couch. It was still warm where Ross had sat. Sigh.

"What can I do for you, Rivera?"

His eyes narrowed slightly. "You look a little flushed now, too."

I gave him a smile, the one I reserve for the mentally handicapped and hopelessly perverted. "I'm fantasizing about dropping an anvil on your head."

He stared at me, then chuckled as he settled into my recliner. "Sorry to break up the party," he said.

"I'm sure."

"Really." His eyes snapped amber fire. "Believe me, McMullen, there's no one I'd rather see get laid."

I tried to come up with a saucy rejoinder, but I didn't know if there was a double meaning there, and if there was, I didn't know what it meant, and even if I could decipher . . .

Oh, hell. I dragged my attention from his and stared

at my hands. They were locked in a death grip on my knees.

"Did you learn something about Solberg?" I asked.

There was a pause. It might have been pregnant, but it was for damned sure late. "You haven't heard from him, then?"

I shook my head, and was fairly impressed to see that my body still functioned on a rudimentary level. He leaned back and crossed his right ankle over his left knee, watching me the whole time.

"How well do you know him?" he asked.

"Who? Solberg?"

He scowled. "How much have you had to drink this time, McMullen?"

I glared at him.

"Of course Solberg," he said.

I would have liked to have lied to him, to tell him Solberg and I had been slavering lovers, but my lips wouldn't touch anything that distasteful.

"Not well," I said instead.

"You sleep with him?"

I popped to my feet. It didn't matter that I had just contemplated telling him that very lie. Hearing him suggest it irked the hell out of me. "Do you have a purpose for barging into my home?"

He rose, the long line of his body all muscular angles and hard planes. "You're up to your ass in trouble, McMullen. I'm just trying to get you out."

I glanced toward the door and back. "I don't know what you're talking about."

"I'm talking about the guys at the Four Oaks. Kind of ugly bastards. One of 'em's dead. Ring any bells?"

"I don't know what you're talking about." My voice had gone weak.

"You already said that."

"Well . . ." At that moment I wished quite fervently that I had not had that second glass of wine. "Well . . . I mean it."

"Lopez was wanted for manslaughter."

I felt the blood drain out of my brain and into my feet. I knew immediately who he meant, but I shook my head, either to clear it or to deny his words or both. "Who?"

He grinned. The expression showed not a glimmer of humor. "The guy you shot in the back of the head."

I felt faint. "I didn't shoot anyone in the back of the head," I whispered.

"Closer to a forty-degree angle," he agreed.

"I don't know—"

He gritted his teeth. "I suppose you don't know anything about the money, either."

I blinked, trying to keep up. But here's the deal: I have hormones and I have brains. They don't function at the same time. And if you throw in a couple murder accusations, I'm lucky if my bladder remains in working order.

He was glaring at me. "Chrissy?"

"What money?"

"We got an anonymous call. Turns out NeoTech's missing a buttload of cash."

"NeoTech?"

"You remember. Your boyfriend's company."

I couldn't even come up with a denial.

" 'Bout half a million dollars."

"Half—" I began, then stopped in mid-sentence in an attempt to draw a breath. "That's—" It hadn't worked. I still couldn't breathe worth shit.

"What, Chrissy?" he asked, as if genuinely interested. "What is it exactly?"

"That's impossible."

"Because Solberg's too honest?"

"Because he's too . . ." I searched hopelessly for a lick of sense. Nothing. "Whipped."

He leaned back a scant couple inches. "You got him wound that tight, do you?"

I laughed. It sounded breathy and idiotic. "Don't be stupid." I couldn't help but remember the photos in Solberg's office. The way he had looked at Elaine. The way he had spoken of Elaine. I shook my head. He couldn't have faked that. "He worships Laney. Adores her." Or at least he did until about four weeks ago. Who knew what the hell had happened since then? "He hasn't had time for embezzlement."

Rivera narrowed his eyes at me. "How'd you know it was embezzlement?"

I felt my stomach pitch, but I forced out a laugh. "What was I supposed to think, Rivera? That he held up Emery Black at gunpoint?"

He didn't argue.

I shook my head again and paced into the kitchen. My mind was starting to function. My stomach was bound to be next. "He's a nerdy little frog, but he wouldn't do that to Elaine."

"Do what?"

I opened my freezer. A dead rat lay smack-dab on top of the ice cream carton. In the freezer. Genius. I closed the door.

Rivera gave me a look, marched over, and mimicked my motions.

"McMullen . . ." He didn't even glance at me. "Why is there a dead rat in your freezer?"

"Warning to the other rats," I said, then, "Solberg wouldn't chance losing Laney."

He closed the freezer.

"Maybe it was her idea."

I narrowed my eyes. "And maybe you're an ass."

"Much as I like having you fantasize about my body parts, McMullen, maybe we should stick to the subject. Could be she's into something you don't know anything about," he said.

"She's into tofu, gluten-free baking flour, and size five jeans."

"Size six," he said.

I stared at him. He stared back.

My mind ran willy-nilly in a thousand directions, like a kite in a gale-force wind.

"You knew all along that he was dating her," I surmised.

"I was pretty sure when I saw the five thousand photos in his home office."

But Black had thought Solberg was gay. And Ross hadn't even heard of Elaine. Unless he was lying. Unless they were both lying.

"You knew about Solberg and Laney," I said, "but you still accused me of being with him."

"Two-timing's not a federal offense, McMullen. I thought he might have been seeing you on the side."

"We're talking about Elaine."

His eyes were midnight bold. "And you."

What the hell did that mean? I tried desperately to think of some snazzy comeback, but my snazzy was pretty much all sapped out. "She didn't have anything to do with this."

"Tell me about Jed, Chrissy."

"I . . ." I was drowning in his damn eyes. What did he mean, "and you"? "I don't know anyone by that name."

"I believe you went for a little evening ride with him and his friend."

"I don't know what you're talking about."

"Try to focus, McMullen. You were at the Safari, dining with the charming Mr. Bennet. You got a phone call."

I opened my mouth to speak, narrowed my eyes, and stopped. "How do you know that?"

The shark smile again. "I'm a detective, Chrissy. In fact, I'm detecting right now."

We were about two millimeters apart. His arm brushed mine. I shivered. "What are you detecting?"

The corner of his mouth lifted. He touched my cheek with the back of his fingers. "Solberg called you, didn't he?"

"Why would he do that?" My throat felt dry.

He shrugged and brushed a strand of hair behind my ear. "Maybe you're right. Maybe he didn't want to risk his relationship with Elaine. Maybe he wanted to give the money back. Maybe he wanted you to help him."

I felt breathless. It could have been for any number of reasons. "I don't know what you're talking about."

"But he's in a little deep."

"I—"

"Your hair's mussed again," he said, and drew his fingers down my neck. "Looks good."

I planned to back away. Unfortunately, my legs didn't even make an attempt. I was frozen to the floor. "I don't know anything about any missing money. I swear to God I don't."

"But you know about Solberg. Where is he?"

I shook my head. He stepped closer. "I'm on your side, McMullen. I just want to help him. I think he got in over his head. Schwartz is a small-time thug, but he's mean and he's desperate."

He scraped my collarbone with his thumb.

My knees felt weak. I was pretty sure it was the memory of my abductors that did it.

"Could you see their faces?" he asked.

I blinked. "What?"

"Did they wear masks?"

I shook my head. Maybe to deny any knowledge.

"Then they planned to kill you."

I tried to voice a denial, but . . .

"They couldn't afford to let you identify them," he said. "Tell me what you know."

"I didn't shoot anybody." My voice was no more than a croak.

"I know. I think Jed shot his buddy. Maybe by accident." He stroked the hollow at the base of my throat. I shivered down to my bone marrow. "But you were in their car."

I stared at him, mind racing. Maybe I should tell him. Maybe I should confess all. Jail might be relaxing.

But I remembered the raspy plea in Solberg's voice.

I licked my lips and pulled away. "I don't know what you're talking about."

He slammed his palm against my countertop. I jumped as if shot.

"Why the fuck won't you let me help you?"

"Help me?" I rasped. "Half the time you're accusing me of murder. The other half—" I thought he'd just been toying with me, firing up my hormones, confusing me. But his eyes were bright with some emotion I couldn't quite identify, his body tight as a fiddle string.

"What about the other half?" he said, grabbing my arm and nudging me up against the refrigerator. His body felt as hard as the appliance behind me.

I kept myself absolutely stiff, lest I start humping his thigh. "I try not to get involved with men who accuse me of manslaughter on more than one occasion."

He ran his hand down my arm. The air crackled like fireworks around us. "I think we're already involved, McMullen."

I was melting from the inside out. But I braced myself. "Leave me alone, Rivera," I said. "I'm not drunk enough for this."

He smiled, the edge of that wolfish smirk, and then he kissed me.

I felt the starch go out of my knees. I felt my mind go limp.

He drew back. I caught the edge of the counter with the heel of my hand and propped myself upright.

"If I hear you're withholding information, McMullen, I'll throw your pretty ass in jail."

I blinked.

"Lock the door behind me," he said, "and get rid of that damned rat."

18

There is wrong. There is dead wrong. And then there's Miss McMullen.

—*Father Pat,*
who never quite forgave
Christina for her various, but
imaginative, indiscretions

I WAS SOUND ASLEEP when my phone rang on Saturday morning, but my mind kicked into gear with unusual speed. The past few days had been hard on my nerves, but pretty good for my mental clarity.

"Chrissy." It was my mother. As far as I know she never sleeps. Three o'clock in the morning, eleven-thirty at night—it didn't matter when I had been sneaking into . . . or out of . . . the house. She always knew. "You sound funny. You okay?"

"It's . . ." I turned the alarm clock toward me on my bed stand and resisted swearing. Mom wasn't above traveling two thousand miles to wash my mouth out with soap. "Early," I said.

"It's after eight."

"In Chicago," I corrected, and hoped she would remember a little thing called time zones.

"Oh, that's right. Well . . ." Her tone was breezy. "I wanted to tell you Peter John got home safe and sound."

"Great." *My* tone might have lacked a little enthusiasm. But I really *was* glad. If he was in Chicago, he wasn't in L.A.

"Well, it *would* be great, except Holly won't let him in the house."

I sat up in bed, immediately impressed. I didn't remember Holly as being particularly bright or confrontational. "What?"

"She says she's having second thoughts."

"Holly?" I was never sure she'd had a first thought.

"Yes, Holly." There was a momentary pause. "I want you to call her."

"What?"

"You're a psychologist. I want you to call her and tell her to take him back."

I think I breathed a weird sort of laugh. "Mom, this is none of my business. I can't just—"

"Never mind, then." I could imagine her drawing herself up. Like a martyr ready for the flames. "I guess you don't have time to help out your family."

And there it was—the guilt. Right there below the surface, ready to erupt like a festering boil at the least provocation.

"Well . . . I'll let you get back to sleep," she said.

I gritted my teeth, but the words came out anyway. "Okay. I'll call her."

"No. Don't bother. I'll—"

"I'll call her," I repeated.

We hung up not twenty seconds later. I went to the bathroom, drank a glass of water, and tried to go back to sleep, but I couldn't. Cursing a blue streak, I pattered barefoot across my kitchen floor, dragged my address book out of my top drawer, and called Pete's latest phone number.

Holly answered on the third ring. Needless to say, she was surprised to hear from me. I don't exactly have my brothers on speed dial as I'm rarely in a huge rush to have someone force-feed me sheep droppings.

"Chrissy." Her voice was as little-girl sweet as I remembered.

"Yes, hi." I cleared my throat, having no idea whatsoever where to go from there. "Ummm . . . how are you?"

"I'm fine. How are you?"

"Good. I'm good. Say, I just wanted to make sure Pete got home okay."

"Yes." There was a pause. "He's back."

"Good." I nodded. "Excellent. He seemed upset, you know, and I wanted—"

"Did your mother tell you to call?"

"Well, actually . . ." I was hoping she'd interrupt before I completed the sentence, but she didn't. "She was worried . . . about you . . . and Peter."

"He's not a child, you know," she said.

"What's that?"

She drew a heavy breath. "Listen, Chrissy, it's nice of you to call and all, but . . . Peter's not as perfect as you think."

"Perfect . . ."

"He's . . . Sometimes I think he's just in it for the sex."

Jesus! "I—"

"Not that the sex is bad. I mean, really, it's amazing. He can make me—"

"Holly!" I think I might have shouted her name, but if there was one thing I didn't want to hear about at 6:33 in the morning, it was my brother's phenomenal sex life. "I don't think Pete is perfect."

"You don't?"

For God's sake, had the world gone mad? "No. I think . . . I think he might have a few flaws."

She sighed. "He's just . . . Sometimes he's kind of immature."

Kind of? I had a dead rat that suggested she was being rather generous here.

"But, I mean . . ." She paused. "I still love him."

And wasn't that just the kicker. The man had the mind of a possessed two-year-old. But she loved him. I leaned back in my slatted wooden chair and let those words sink into my fuzzy brain. "Have you two considered counseling?"

"Counseling?"

"Therapy."

There was a long pause. "I don't think he'd go for that."

Neither did I, but an errant thought struck me. "Where's he staying now?"

"I think he's in his old room."

"At Mom and Dad's?" I think I grinned a little at the thought. If I remembered correctly, Pete liked to have a few beers in the morning and sleep in. Mom had a habit of waking everyone at six-thirty sharp. Like revelry.

"What if you said you'd consider taking him back if he went to couple's therapy?" I asked.

"I don't think he'd do it."

"Then you don't have to take him back, do you?" The words were out of my mouth before I could stop them. I closed my eyes and chastised myself in silence. If Mom heard about this, she'd be on the first plane west.

"But I . . . I love him."

"Then you have to decide whether you're willing to put up with his infantile cr—" I stopped myself judiciously. "You have to decide what you want, Holly. It's up to you."

There was a long pause. I waited. "There's, um . . ." She cleared her throat. "There's something else."

Her tone sounded funny. I felt a premonitory tingle of trouble along the arches of my feet. "What?"

"I'm pregnant."

I remained absolutely mute. Unable to speak. My brothers were morons. My brothers were adolescent. But there was one thing they'd consistently done right—they'd failed to procreate. It had been like a miracle. But now . . .

"So, see?" Her voice was even softer than usual. "That's why I have to just . . . accept him as he is."

Something inside me—good sense maybe—insisted that I keep my mouth shut. But it opened anyway. "Yeah, I suppose you're right," I said. "That's what his ex-wives always did."

The conversation lasted another thirty minutes. I hung up feeling kind of queasy.

I spent the rest of the day waiting for the phone call that would banish me from the family, smoking, and searching for clues about Jed and Lopez.

Mom didn't call. I smoked half a pack of Slims, and I found nothing on either criminal. There simply wasn't enough information.

But I had to find Solberg. If my conversation with Holly had taught me one thing, it was that the little geekster wasn't as bad as he could be. True, he was as irritating as hell and not good enough to breathe Laney's air, but at least he hadn't gotten her pregnant and skipped town. In fact, he hadn't even tried to sleep with her. Maybe he really loved her. And maybe he was really in trouble. And maybe, probably even, that trouble was somehow tied to NeoTech.

I had to find out. That much was obvious. Perhaps it wasn't so obvious that I should drive back to Hilary Pershing's house, slither through her yard like an egg-hungry weasel, and try to sneak a peak through her window again. But I was planning to do just that, because someone had embezzled from NeoTech, probably the same someone who had caused Solberg's disappearance. And wouldn't it make sense if that someone made considerably less money than her fellow employees?

At 11:42 I sat in my car down the street from her house. My palms were sweaty, but I had my flashlight and stool and I was determined.

At 11:47 I made myself leave the sanctuary of my Saturn. The street was dark. My shoes sounded loud against the blacktop. Pershing, like ninety-five percent of L.A.'s paranoid populace, had erected a metal fence around her property, but by this point in my investigative insanity, it was little more than a nuisance. After a minute I was on the inside, carrying my stool and slinking along the side of her house. I could hear my own breathing in the darkness. If I didn't start jogging again soon, I was going to die of cardiac failure long before anyone got the chance to shoot me.

When I had reached the window in question, I stood with my back pressed to the rough stucco of the house. All was quiet. It was now or never.

I positioned the stool, stepped onto it, and switched on my flashlight.

"Turn it off," ordered a voice from behind.

I froze like a Fudgsicle, nerves cranked up tight.

"Did you hear me?"

I switched off the flashlight and tried to look behind me, but something poked me in the back.

"If you turn around I'll shoot you. Swear to God."

"Hilary?" My voice was shaking.

"Who are you?"

It *was* Hilary. I didn't know if that should make me feel better or worse. I guess when someone has a gun pressed to your spine, the assailant's identity isn't of utmost importance.

Ideas were whirling through my head like water down a toilet. I caught one and spun it out.

"I'm a cop, Hilary," I said. "And I know the truth."

"You're not a cop."

"I am." Sweat trickled between my breasts. "Officer Angela Grapier. Precinct twelve. My partner knows I'm here, Hilary. Frank'll be meeting me in a couple minutes."

"Get down from there."

I did so, slowly, joints stiff, not daring to turn. "Don't do anything you'll regret, Hilary. You're in trouble, but I can help you." Or hit her in the face with my flashlight and run like bloody hell. "Put the gun down. We can talk. I know about you and Solberg. I know he . . ."

But there was a thud and a moan behind me.

"Hilary?"

"I love 'em."

"Ummm . . . Can I turn around?"

"I love 'em so much. Don't take 'em away from me."

I turned slowly, the hairs on my arms prickling. She was on her knees. A short-handled broom lay on the grass beside her.

"I know I've done wrong." She was scrunching her fists up against her chest. "But I can't let 'em go to just anyone."

"Ahhh . . . Is he inside?"

"They all are. All of them."

My mind blinked and struggled. "All of . . ."

"My cats. All my cats. I know I have too many. City ordinance and all that. I know. But they're like family. Damn Solberg for turning me in."

"Ummmm." Now, here was a weird turn of events. "Where's Solberg?" I asked.

She looked up. Her face shone with tears in the uncertain light. "How the hell would I know? That snotty little worm. What does he care how many cats I have? He's known about 'em for years. All of a sudden, he's some goody-two-shoes. Says I should get rid of 'em. Like they're trash or something. I coulda killed 'im."

"Did you?"

"What?" She blinked. "Of course I didn't kill 'im. What would happen to my babies if I was in jail? I confronted the nasty little mongrel, but he just walked out."

My mind was buzzing. "Walked out of where?"

"His room in Vegas," she said, and scowled. "It was twice the size of mine. That bastard Black has always favored 'im."

Okay.

So I could cross Hilary off the short list. She was as nutty as a granola bar and as bitter as hell, but she hadn't killed Solberg and stored his rotting body in her spare room. Instead, she had stored forty-seven cats. Apparently, Solberg had known about them and threatened to tell City Hall. She'd retaliated by promising to remove his balls if he did. That's when he thought it prudent to leave his room. It was also when Elaine had called.

Anyway, I took one look at all those cats, told her she had six months before the Los Angeles Police Department came down on her like a ton of farmyard waste, and fled the premises.

"But I live in Irwindale," she said, which was an excellent point, but I was already out the door and halfway to my car.

The next morning I drove up to what I referred to as Wilderness Point again and spent a zillion hours watching the two houses on Amsonia Lane. Tiffany had come and gone and come and gone. Neither Solberg nor Mr. Georges, the esteemed barrister, had shown so much as a wilted tail feather.

Later, I did some digging into Tiffany's past. I didn't even discover a speeding ticket. Which, in the end, only made me more suspicious. I mean, what kind of person doesn't speed? Certainly not anyone who's lived in Los Angeles for more than an hour.

I dropped my head onto my desk and considered committing caloric suicide, but once I'd wandered into my kitchen and surveyed my culinary domain, I realized I was going to have to concoct another means of doing myself in, as there were only a few spears of broccoli and half a bag of spinach leaves with which to terminate myself.

I ate a broccoli bush while I stood in the open door of the refrigerator. Memories rampaged through me. How had Jed and Garlic known I would be at the Safari? Had they been the ones to call me in the first place, or had it really been Solberg? Maybe they had tapped his phone, but I didn't even know if that was possible with a cell. So perhaps someone had overheard my truncated conversation with the Geek.

But who—

The answer popped like bubblegum into my head.

Bennet.

My stomach dropped at the thought.

Had Bennet known it was Solberg on the phone? Had he sent the goon duo to question me? Had he meant to have them kill . . . ?

But no. I was being ridiculous. Bennet was attractive and had eyes that twinkled like . . . some sort of body of water. He couldn't possibly have done such a thing. Besides, he couldn't have heard Solberg's words. So he'd have no way of knowing where I was going. . . .

Unless he'd followed me.

The idea spiked the hairs along my arms and neck.

What if it was Bennet who had embezzled money from NeoTech? What if Solberg found out and called to...warn me?

The idea of the wriggly little Solberg trying to save me instead of attempting to crawl into my pants sent my head spinning, but maybe the time he'd spent with Elaine had changed him. It was possible. Pershing had said he had known about her cats for years, but only now warned her to do the right thing. Maybe it was the same with Bennet. Maybe Solberg knew he was embezzling, and warned him to come clean before it was too late. Maybe Bennet had threatened Solberg. Maybe Solberg had been lying low ever since, but came out of hiding when he found out I was involved.

Then again, there was no way to positively identify the voice on the phone. It may not have been Solberg at all. That fact made me feel a little better. If the truth be told, I wasn't sure which would be worse—owing Solberg or being murdered by Bennet.

Actually, neither option sounded that great, which made learning as much as possible seem prudent.

After several minutes of brain-shattering thought, I called the Safari. A man answered on the second ring.

"Hello," I said, and hoped to hell I had remembered our waitress's name correctly. "May I speak to Grace, please?"

"Grace?" said the voice, then, "Hey, hurry up with the soup. If it's not cucumber, we serve it hot." He was back on in a minute. "Grace Hyat?"

Hyat. I scribbled the name onto a scrap of paper I'd fished out of recycling. "Yes," I said.

"Damn it!" he cursed. "I said sautéed, not charbroiled."

Whoever I was talking to was in serious need of public relations training . . . or a rabies vaccination. "What do you want?" Probably both.

I was feeling more empathy for Grace by the minute. I was also dead sure Cujo was not about to allow me to talk to his browbeaten waitress for anything less than a court order, but I gave it a try anyway. "I'm her cousin, Jules Montgomery . . . from Fresno. I'm only in town for a couple hours, and I was hoping to—"

"She's busy," he said, and hung up without another word. You gotta like a man who doesn't draw out the good-byes.

I didn't bother changing clothes before hopping into my Saturn and driving to the restaurant. It seemed to me there was no time to waste.

The Safari was hopping with the mealtime crowd. Apparently, America had whetted its appetite at Thanksgiving and saw no reason to stop gorging anytime short of Christmas.

Maybe I would have been wiser to wait, but I had no way of knowing when Grace would work next, or if she'd survive the rush.

I caught a glimpse of her serving a table of eight.

The hostess approached me with a notepad and a million-dollar smile. Or maybe about five grand. My parents hadn't given a lot of thought to dental care. I'd first seen an orthodontist about eighteen months ago. He had trotted out a list of necessary procedures as long as a fishing rod and told me the cost of his services. I had opted to continue eating instead.

"Your name?"

"Chrissy," I said, "but I'd like to wait for a table by the

window up there." I pointed to where I'd seen the harried Grace.

She gave me a pitying look. I wasn't sure if it was because she'd glanced at my attire and decided I was homeless, or because I was obviously deranged. "I'm afraid that might be quite a wait."

"That's all right," I said. "I'm dieting anyway."

She gave me a smile with less wattage, scribbled a note in her ledger, and moved on to the couple next to me. They had a fractious toddler with a runny nose and a gleam in his eye that promised to wreak havoc on their dining experiences for the next fourteen years.

Meanwhile, I jockeyed my way toward the fake-leather bench near the door, not wanting to miss my opportunity should someone be called into the inner sanctum.

It took almost half an hour before a stretch of vinyl opened up. I wiggled my butt onto a corner and waited some more. The general populace, I noticed, was considerably better dressed than me. In fact, the toddler had me beat, but at least I didn't have a snotty nose that I habitually wiped on my sleeve.

Forty-five minutes had passed by the time I was led to a table.

I ordered a hot water with lime in concession to my growing waistline and my dwindling finances. They never charge you for hot water. I'd learned that during my pre-graduate days, when I'd considered McDonald's a four-star restaurant.

Grace arrived with her childishly embellished notepad and an apparent headache. Maybe I was wrong about her head, but my own was beginning to throb. I think it was the toddler.

She still wasn't wearing a wedding ring and her expression was weary behind her professional façade. As far as I'm concerned, waitresses should be canonized at the earliest possible opportunity. "What can I get for you?" she asked.

I didn't waste time on preliminaries. Instead, I put a twenty-dollar bill on the table and caught her gaze. "Do you remember me from last Friday night?"

She narrowed her eyes a little as if wondering why the hell she always got the weirdos. "You left early," she said. "I believe you were with a gentleman."

"The scumbag," I said, and made sure I added a nice dash of vitriol.

Her eyebrows were perfectly groomed. They rose in twin arcs.

"He's the first guy in three years I introduced to my son," I said. I'm not a liar by nature. Well, okay, maybe I am, but I was sure Grace didn't care if I gave her the real story. I was also sure, judging by her degree of fatigue, that she'd empathize with my fictional maternal situation. "Little Tony loved him like a father."

She was still staring.

I gave her a scowl as if she was slow on the uptake. "Bastard's cheating on me."

"Ohhh." She nodded, cocked a hip, and let the notebook drop to her side.

"I got a call from a friend while I was here last time. She's been sick every day of her third trimester, but she was really bad this time. Hacking up her lungs. She had to go to the hospital. I didn't know what else to do. I couldn't just let her go alone. Her rotten husband was nowhere to be found."

She nodded again. I felt a spark of something between guilt and pride and sisterly camaraderie.

"So I hop in my Saturn and take her to Huntington. And meanwhile Tony's idol is steppin' out with his ex."

I shook my head and gazed out the window. I would've liked to have been able to conjure up a few fat tears, but it was no use. In lieu of the moisture, I bit my lip and scrunched my face. "I hope I'm wrong. For little Tony's sake." I zapped my attention back to her. "But I owe myself the truth." I took a deep breath and straightened my back bravely. "That's why I came to see you. 'Cuz I gotta know. Did anyone meet him here after I left?"

She thought back for a moment, then shook her head slowly. "No," she said. "He rushed right off after you did."

"Rushed off?"

"Within seconds. When I came back with your orders, he apologized, dropped a hundred on the table, and took off."

"He didn't eat his . . ." I paused. "A hundred . . . dollars?"

She shrugged. "He might be a bastard, but he's not a cheap bastard. It works that way sometimes." She scowled. "Believe me. Anyway, he didn't ask for change or anything, just charged out of here. In fact, I'm surprised you didn't see him in the parking lot."

Why was he in such a hurry? I wondered wildly, but I remembered my little Oscar-winning performance and continued on. "I bet he went to her place, then. Couldn't wait another second. Did you happen to remember which way he headed?"

She exhaled a laugh. "You kidding? Half the time I can't remember my own name."

I got a burger at In-N-Out because I could. Wendy's is better, but you can find them anywhere.

Once home, I checked my answering machine.

Mom's voice filled the room, telling me to call her. I didn't. The next message was from my optometrist. The last was a hang up. I checked caller ID. It had been someone from E.U., whatever that . . .

My brain cells popped into order. Someone had called from Electronic Universe. I dialed the number with spastic fingers.

A man answered on the second ring.

"Yes." I felt breathless and tense. "This is Christina McMullen. Someone called me from this number."

There was a moment of silence, then, "What was it in regards to, ma'am?"

"I'm not certain."

"Do you know who it was?"

"No."

"Then I'm afraid—"

"Rex," I said before he could hang up. "I think it was Rex. Is he there?"

There was a pause before he said he'd check, and did so. In a minute he was back on the phone. "I'm sorry. Rex seems to be gone for the day."

"But he was there earlier?"

"I'm not sure actually, and we're just about ready to close up for the evening. You're certainly welcome to call back tomorrow."

"Can I get a message to him?"

"He might be in tomorrow."

"But what about tonight? It's extremely important."

"I don't have his home phone number."

"But you must be able to get it." My thirty-second boyfriend had once compared me rather unfavorably to a bulldog. It may have been this type of behavior that prompted the comment, or the drooling when I'm stroked. "Can you find it and give him a message?"

"Well, I don't know. I mean—"

"This is a matter of life or death."

"All right." The life or death caveat gets them every time. "Give me the message, I'll try to get ahold of him."

"Tell him Christina McMullen called. Remind him that he tried to contact me and tell him to try again as soon as possible," I said, and left my phone number.

"That's it?" He sounded deflated. Maybe he'd expected a message from the president or something.

"It's urgent."

"Uh-huh," he said, and hung up.

I was wired after that. I mean, I didn't know if Rex had called because he'd spotted Solberg or because he remembered my cleavage kindly, or even if he'd called at all. Maybe it was just E.U. trying to sell me an electronic . . . can opener or something. I paced for a while, but it didn't do me any good, so I settled back into my previous plan.

It didn't take any great detective abilities to find Bennet's address. Any doofus with an L.A. phone book could have done as much. But it took a doofus with some severe mental-health issues to continue with my harebrained plan. I seemed to qualify.

I showered quickly, shaved my legs, cut both knees, stuck tissue to the lacerations, and squeezed into a topaz-colored skirt that stopped mid-thigh and looked like it had been shrink-wrapped to my hips. I then donned an ivory-colored cami. It was beaded at the top and showed every ounce of cleavage I could hoist up under my collarbones.

I curled my hair, overdid my makeup, and checked my mace. But since I didn't know what I was looking for, I decided to believe it was in serviceable condition and shoved it into my purse.

I chose a pair of sandals with heels that could have been registered as lethal weapons and headed for the door.

When I stood on my stoop, I saw that the morning clouds had withered away and the sun shone merrily down from a crystalline blue sky. It was warm for the end of November. Or maybe there were other reasons I was sweating like a linebacker.

I turned on my heel, marched into the bathroom, and slathered on another layer of underarm protection. Then I grabbed a bottle of Bordeaux and marched resolutely out of the house.

Two minutes later, armed with false bravado and suicidal tendencies, I was heading east on the 210 with half of the rest of Los Angeles's populace, assuring myself I was perfectly safe, while smoking like a house on fire.

My hands had almost quit shaking by the time I reached Ross's townhouse. It was a quad. Made of stucco almost the same color as my skirt, it boasted jacarandas and eucalyptus set beside quaint, arched doorways, but I was determined to slither into his serene domain and lie my ass off. Again. I closed my eyes and tried to think of other ways to ferret out the truth, but no brilliant ideas flashed to mind. So I levered myself out of the car and onto my fashionable heels.

The trek across his front yard took my breath away.

I rang the doorbell. Nothing happened. I waited all of five seconds, then let out a puff of relief and turned away, ready to bolt for home.

"Chris?"

I jumped, plastering my back against the rough wall and breathing hard.

Ross Bennet stared at me from five feet away. He was wearing blue running shorts and nothing else. Well, shoes and maybe underwear. I couldn't tell. But his chest was bare. That much I was pretty damn sure of.

His eyes skimmed me, top to toe. "What are you doing here?"

I realized rather belatedly that I was slurped up against his house like forgotten linguini.

He tilted his head at me. "Are you okay?"

I exhaled rapidly.

"Yes. I just . . . Sure. I'm fine. Why wouldn't I be? I just . . ." I lifted my hand and was somewhat surprised to find it wrapped around a relatively expensive bottle of Bordeaux. "I f-felt badly about Friday night." My voice actually stuttered. *Buck up, McMullen. Buck up,* I thought. *You've been through worse.* "I was . . ." *Not in the neighborhood. Don't say you were in the neighborhood.* "In the neighborhood." Damn! "And I thought I'd stop by . . . to apologize."

He approached. I skittered sideways. He gave me a funny

look, shoved his key into the lock, and pushed the door open.

"Do you want to come in?"

I eyed the interior like one might a grizzly's cave, then pitched my gaze back to him.

"Sure," I said, and remained exactly where I was. When in doubt, freeze like a blinded bunny. *Good thinking, McMullen.*

He laughed. "Go ahead, then."

"Oh, yeah." I didn't move. "Thanks." Still nothing.

He raised his brows. I produced a chuckle, peeled myself from his plaster, and slunk inside.

The hairs on the back of my neck were standing upright, but there were no dead corpses in the immediate vicinity. Then again, I hadn't seen his kitchen yet. Martha Stewart says the kitchen's where you really get to know people. I wonder if she was talking about felons. Come to think of it, she might know a good deal about felons these days. Nothing like the inside of a prison to open your horizons. I may yet be in luck.

"So where were you?" he asked.

I snapped my gaze to his. "What?"

"Where in the neighborhood were you?"

Jesus. "Ummm, church."

He smiled and checked out my blouse. "In that?"

I glanced down. There's a reason they called it a push-up bra. My breasts were squeezed together like porn stars in the money shot.

"I went to confession," I said. "For my wardrobe."

He laughed. Dimples popped out in his cheeks. It struck me that a guy with dimples like that couldn't possibly be guilty of anything more serious than fornication, but since my life was on the line, I decided to withhold judgment until I'd seen the kitchen.

"Can you give me a minute to clean up?" he asked.

Blood-spattered walls zapped into my mind. "Clean up what?"

He stared at me. If I remember correctly, he wasn't the first person to look at me as if I'd lost my marbles.

"I've been running," he said. "I need a shower."

"Oh." I laughed. I sounded like an intoxicated clown. "Sure. No problem. I'll just . . . I'll wait in the . . ." I pointed my wine bottle toward the adjacent room. There was a leather couch, a matching recliner, and enough reading material to suggest he was starting a lending library. "In there."

"Okay." Was he looking at me like he was about to decapitate me or like I was nuts? Maybe both. "Sorry about the mess. Make yourself at home. I'll only be a minute."

"Take your time," I said, and tried to look casual as I wandered shakily into his living quarters.

I sat down on his couch. Maybe I was trying to make him think I was harmless. Maybe I felt faint. I glanced at his reading material as I heard the shower start up. From where I sat I could see about a dozen books on financing, two on technology, and one that dealt with the training of puppies. I glanced around. No puppy. Maybe he planned to get a puppy. How bad could a guy be if he had dimples and planned to get a puppy?

I dropped my head into my hands. I was obviously insane, I deduced, but from the corner of my eye I noticed the hallway and an open door that looked as though it might lead into an office.

My Human Sexuality professor had once said I had a keen sense of curiosity. My brothers said I was nosy as hell.

I was never sure if either of those summations was true, since I was pretty sure my professor wanted to get me into bed, and my brothers were morons. But either way, I slipped out of my sandals and headed toward the office as soon as I heard Ross step into the shower.

It would have helped a lot if I'd had any idea what I was doing, but my absolute cluelessness was one of those unfortunate realities of life. As it was, I snuck into his office and glanced around. I had hooked my purse firmly over my shoulder. It wasn't exactly a hip holster, but the mace was there. Like a six-shooter.

Bennet had a rolltop desk. The grooved oak cover was down. Who keeps the cover down? I opened it carefully. It creaked. I held my breath. The water was still running, and the bathroom door was firmly closed. I eased the rolltop up the rest of the way and scanned the contents. There were a lot of them, crammed into the dozen or so little cubicles that lined the back and lying scattered across the surface, but at first glance there were no notes that said "I killed Solberg" or "Your usual luck with men is holding, McMullen. I'm a scumbag." There wasn't even a smoking gun. I rifled through the papers. Nothing.

I tried the top right-hand drawer next. It was marginally neater, but no more helpful. The next two down were filled with catalogs for toy aircraft and video games.

When I opened the upper left drawer I caught my breath. There was a checkbook in a navy blue plastic casing.

I jerked my gaze to the door. The shower droned on. I

fumbled the checkbook open and ran my gaze down to the balance.

There wasn't five hundred thousand there. In fact, there was barely five hundred. I scowled. Bennet was an executive for a highly successful company. He didn't seem to live extravagantly, except for the C note left at the Safari, of course, and he didn't seem jumpy enough for a heroin addiction, so why didn't he have more available funds? I shoved the checkbook back into the drawer and tried the next one, then the next, then the bottom. It was locked.

My breath did a little hitch in my throat.

Why would a man who lived alone lock his drawer? And more to the point, where would he keep the key? I scanned every visible surface in the room. Nothing. Well, lots of stuff, but . . . nothing. I began searching the cubbies, each one, starting at the top and working horizontally, then down. I found the key in a box of blank checks with ocean scenes on them.

I shot my eyes toward the bathroom. The shower was still buzzing away. I snatched up the key and shoved it into the hole in the bottom drawer. It stuck.

The shower hissed to a halt. I jerked my head up. The door was still closed. I jiggled the key, but nothing happened.

I heard Ross step out of the shower. A few seconds. I had just a few seconds while he dried himself off. I tried the key again, but in that instant he stepped into the hall—wet, and naked as a newlywed.

19

Maybe there is a fine line between love and hate, but it makes a hell of a difference what side of the line you're on.

—*Pete McMullen,*
after his third divorce

I JERKED TO MY feet. My eyes threatened to pop out of my head. It wasn't like I'd never seen a naked guy before, but they weren't usually so ... three dimensional.

"What the hell?" he said.

I yanked my gaze to his. Our eyes met through the doorway. His looked dark and not so Caribbean blue as dangerous beneath the dripping fringes of his saturated hair.

"I ... I ..." I fumbled for my purse, disjointedly remembering my mace.

His eyes narrowed and dipped toward his desk. "I know what you're doing." He took a step toward me. I stumbled backward. He grabbed my wrist. My hand froze on my mace.

"You're snooping," he said, and pulled me into the hall-way.

My heart was banging like a jackhammer in my chest.

"So now you know my secret."

I swallowed, wondering if it was too late to scream. Too early to pass out.

"I'm a slob," he admitted, and dropping my arm, shut the door firmly behind me.

He grinned. I blinked, realizing with belated brilliance that he had snagged a towel from somewhere and held it loosely in front of his . . . stuff.

"And I'm not very modest." He cleared his throat. "Sorry. Thought you'd still be in the living room," he said, and backed into what I assumed was his bedroom.

I stood there blinking like a befuddled cheerleader. I heard him shuffle around inside.

Questions bombarded me like rotten eggs. Was he as in-nocent as his dimples suggested? Did he always walk around naked? Why would he ever bother to wear clothes?

And what was in the bottom drawer?

Besides the key. Holy fuck! I'd left the key in the drawer.

I glanced frantically toward his bedroom, then eased the office door open and ducked back inside to yank the key from the lock. But something came over me. Let's just call it curiosity. I turned the key with shaking fingers. The lock clicked open. I looked toward the doorway. Still empty.

The drawer opened silently under my hand. And there, at the top of a heap of papers, was another checkbook. I stared at it, dumb as a paperweight.

In the adjacent room, I heard Bennet patter across the floor.

I snatched the checkbook up without giving myself time to consider the consequences. Something rattled next door.

The checkbook jumped out of my hand, hit the arm of the leather chair, and bounced under the desk.

Shit! I jammed the drawer closed, yanked out the key, and shoved it under a pile of papers.

A floorboard creaked in the bedroom.

I torpedoed out of the office like a launched rocket.

Ross stepped into the hall half a breath later, at which time I was gazing intently at a picture on his wall. To this day I can't remember what it was. Could have been a photo of Brad Pitt naked for all I know . . . but probably not.

When I got the nerve to glance toward Bennet, he was buttoning a lime green shirt over khaki pants. A sprinkling of soft, caramel-colored hair trailed down his midsection and beneath his low-slung pants. His feet were bare. I swallowed.

"Hi," he said, and leaning forward, kissed my cheek, as if we'd just met on a sunny day in Griffith Park—not at all like he planned to decapitate me and bury my body in . . . Griffith Park. "It's good to see you again."

Guilt hit me like a wrecking ball. He was a nice guy and I was treating him like a convict. A nice lean convict with a great smile and really big . . . Well, suffice it to say, maybe a little bit of lust hit me along with the guilt.

"Hi," I managed.

He smiled. "You look great, by the way."

"You . . ." I pulled my gaze resolutely back up to his face. "You have, ummm . . . really misbuttoned your shirt."

"Oh. Thanks," he said, and began anew. For several seconds I had a view of a narrow line of his torso.

I managed to remain vertical. It might have been because of the guilt. I'm fairly familiar with the emotion, infused into my mother's womb during pregnancy.

"I'm glad to see you're still alive," he said.

I blinked.

"After meeting Rivera, I wasn't sure about your chances."

I tried a chuckle. Somebody shoot me.

"I felt bad leaving you with him."

He fell silent. Apparently, it was my turn to say something. "He's, ummm..." I kept my hands steady and my gaze off his chest and the other stuff. "He's not as bad as he seems."

"Really?"

"No," I said. I felt numb and a little nauseous. "I'm lying."

He laughed and headed for the kitchen.

I turned frantically toward the office, but I couldn't see the checkbook.

"You want to crack that open?"

I jerked toward the kitchen. He leaned around the corner. The man had a smile like a damned lighthouse. "The wine," he said. "Want to open it, or are you just teasing me?"

I swallowed. "Umm...no. Yes. Sure..." I stuttered toward the kitchen. "Let's open it."

He pulled a corkscrew out of a top drawer, refrained from stabbing me with it, and turned to rummage in his refrigerator.

I watched him bend, watched the line of his back, the curve of his buttocks, the bulge of his thigh.

"Can you open that or do you want me to—" he began, and turned, cheese dip in hand.

I was bent slightly at the waist, already popping the cork.

He stared at me. The seconds dragged by.

"Wow," he said.

I was just about to blush modestly when I realized it was my abilities with a wine bottle and not my cleavage that had impressed him. I cleared my throat. "Years of practice," I said.

"Yeah?" He reached for a couple of plates from the cupboard. "You a wino or a bartender?"

"A cocktail waitress."

"Really?" He'd found some crackers. Townhouse. Classy. "Where was that?"

"Schaumburg, Illinois," I said.

"A long commute."

I wanted to laugh, but it didn't seem possible, so I just cranked up a smile. "I lived there," I said, "for the first twenty-odd . . ." I paused. "Lifetimes."

He took down two wineglasses and motioned toward a chair.

I eyed it like it was a gator trap, but he was watching me. What could I do but slide onto it? I perched on the edge like an albatross ready to take flight.

He took the wine and poured us equal measures. "You weren't crazy about Schaumburg?"

"No one's that crazy," I said. "But I kind of like L.A. The food's good, and I don't have to spend so much money on parkas."

He smiled and turned toward the counter. I noticed the knives stuck into their wooden block, dark wood handles at an oblique angle.

He selected a couple. I held my breath. Turning, he set them on the plates, one on mine, one on his. If he was a murderer, he seemed to be the kind who was willing to give his victims a fighting chance. You've got to appreciate that.

He dragged out a chair and sat down across from me. I darted my gaze toward the office and back. The thought of the checkbook lying hidden under the desk was driving me mad.

"How about you?" I asked. "What brought you here?"

"The job," he said. "Plain and simple. NeoTech was a good opportunity."

I took the plunge. "I hear they're having some trouble, though."

He jerked his gaze toward me. "Where'd you hear that?"

My heart stopped. "Just . . . around."

Silence echoed through the room, then, "Geez, I'm sorry, Chrissy," he said. "I mean, it's not proven yet or anything."

"What's not proven?"

"That Solberg took that money. For all I know, it might just be an error in bookkeeping. I hope so anyway. It'd kill Black."

"Who would?"

He gave me a look.

"I mean, *what* would?"

"If J.D. had stolen anything. Black thinks he walks on water. He's worried sick about him. I mean, I am, too, but . . ." He took a deep breath. "I hope this won't affect our relationship."

"Umm. No. Of course not."

He smiled. "Tell me what you're really doing here."

I kept my eyes strictly on his, lest they slip back to his office. The checkbook was burning a hole in my mind and blasting alarms in every direction. Surely he heard them.

"You, ummm . . ." I forced myself to pick up a cracker. "You didn't believe the confession story?"

"Confession's rare these days."

"I'm an old-fashioned girl."

"Not in that shirt." He gave me an appreciative eyebrow waggle and in that moment I really hoped he hadn't killed Solberg. Guys that good-looking shouldn't go around killing people.

"Would you believe I was meeting a friend for lunch?" I asked.

He narrowed his eyes. "Male or female?"

"Female."

He shook his head and eyed my chest again. "You wouldn't be that cruel."

That sounded like a compliment. My temperature rose a couple degrees, but when he stood up, my brain froze.

I scrambled to my feet, though I'm not sure what I hoped to accomplish. "I am cruel," I said. "And strong. I'm really . . ." He was drawing closer. I grappled with my purse, but I was still holding a cracker in my right hand and was having trouble with the logistics. "I'm really strong."

"Great, 'cuz I was hoping you came to seduce me," he said, and kissed me.

It was like putting dynamite in my pants.

He drew away.

"Wow," I said.

He smiled. "Or . . ." He brushed his thumb across my jaw. "If that wasn't your plan . . ." He caressed my throat. I swallowed. "That you'd allow me to seduce you."

My hormones were screaming X-rated suggestions, but my brain was reminding me that he might very well be an embezzler, or a murderer. I was pretty sure he wasn't gay.

"I just . . ." I cleared my throat. "I felt bad . . . about last time." He kissed the corner of my mouth. "About the last two times, in fact."

"There *have* been a lot of untimely interruptions," he said, and slipped his hand down my bare arm.

Jesus God, how could that feel so good? It was just my arm. What if he touched some of the good stuff? "Yeah," I said. My voice sounded gravelly. "So I just thought . . ."

He wrapped his arm around my back and pulled me close.

I swallowed. "I just thought I'd drop by to—"

"Good idea," he said, and kissed me again.

By the time he stopped, I needed a resuscitator.

He leaned his forehead against mine. "Maybe we'd be more comfortable in the bedroom."

"The bedroom?" I panted.

"You don't look like a kitchen table kind of girl."

Which just goes to show that even a guy with a smile like a damned beacon doesn't know everything. I was about ready to toss him under the sink and have at him.

"I, umm . . ." I cleared my throat and tried to do the same with my mind. "I don't know you very well yet, Ross."

"What are you talking about?" He was running the edges of his nails up and down my back. "You've already seen me naked. Remember?"

My throat went dry. "As a matter of fact . . ." I said.

"Hardly seems fair." Lifting his hand, he trilled his fingers over the mounds of my breasts. I shivered down to my toenails.

"Maybe we could even up the odds a little?" He lifted a strap from my shoulder. I felt my head fall back slightly.

It was then that his phone rang. I screamed and jerked back.

He stared at me as if I'd just morphed into an anteater. "Are you okay?"

"Yes! Yes! Yes!" I all but shouted the words.

Somehow I failed to convince him. He took a step toward me. I cowered away.

"The phone. The phone." I waved rather wildly toward it. "You'd better get it."

"I'm sure it can wait."

"No!" I was holding a stiff arm out toward him like a quarterback fending off a nose tackle. "I don't want to . . . inconvenience you. I have to . . ." I darted my gaze toward the hallway. "I have to pee anyway."

He blinked, looking confused. "Okay."

He might have looked a little wounded, too, but I couldn't seem to get my breath. "Answer it," I hissed.

He did so, watching me as he said hello. I didn't wait around to hear more. Instead, I darted into the bathroom, where I pressed myself against the wall and tried to breathe. It didn't go well. I could still hear him talking. I scrounged up all my courage and peeked around the corner. I couldn't see into the office from that vantage point, but I swore I could hear the checkbook screaming at me.

I heard Ross laugh and mumble something from the

kitchen. I darted into his office, scrambled under the desk, snatched up the checkbook, and shoved it into my purse. I was just dashing back into the hall when he appeared around the corner.

I stifled a scream.

"Chris." He scowled at me. "What's wrong?"

"Nothing," I said, and realized I was backed against the wall. "Nothing. I just . . . I remembered something I have to do at home."

"You're kidding."

"No!"

"What?"

"Iron."

"You have to iron?"

I was shaking my head and nodding intermittently. "I left the iron on."

"I'm sure it'll be all right," he said, and reached for me.

"No. Can't. Love to. Gotta go," I babbled, and took off like the proverbial bat, but it was hard to tell if I was leaving hell or heading straight toward it.

20

Haste will get you maced.

—J.D. Solberg,
who knows such things

HOW WAS YOUR weekend?" Elaine looked hopelessly determined to be chipper as she fiddled her way through the top file drawer. I assessed her mood with every gram of therapeutic ability I possessed.

It was Monday morning. Solberg still hadn't shown up, and I'd learned approximately nothing. According to Bennet's checkbook, he had fifty-seven thousand dollars at United Equity Bank. I had no idea what that meant. Except that he was fifty-seven thousand dollars richer than I was.

If he was the embezzler, he had either stashed most of the stolen money in another account or he had an accomplice.

Or, I thought raggedly, he *used* to have an accomplice.

"It was okay. Kind of dull," I said, and wished to God that had been true. "How 'bout you?"

"I went out with that plumber."

"Yeah?"

"And a bodybuilder."

"Really?"

"And a guy I met on my way to yoga."

"You were asked out on the interstate?"

"Traffic was stopped on the five."

I nodded. I don't usually get propositioned during rush hour. Unless you count "Screw you," yelled out at forty miles per hour, in which case I'm pretty popular.

Laney dug out the files for my Monday clients and set them on her desk. Howard Lepinski's was as thick as a novella. "Pete leave?"

"Yeah. He was gone when I got home on Friday."

"He seemed different."

"You think?"

"More . . ." She paused for a moment. "Mature."

"It's an illusion."

"He looked good."

I narrowed my eyes at her. "Laney, you're not forgetting the sheep poop, are you?"

She laughed. "It's hard to forget sheep poop."

I relaxed marginally.

"Besides, I met a nice Armenian guy in Glendale yesterday."

God help me. "Oh?"

"He seemed really sweet. We were both standing in line at that new Whole Foods. He bought my aloe vera juice for me. I tried to make him take his money back, but he wouldn't."

"Uh-huh." For a moment I imagined Laney trying to shove a five-dollar bill back into some poor sucker's jeans pocket. He was probably still in an orgasmic haze.

"Were you wearing a skirt?" I asked.

"I was wearing slacks and a cable-knit sweater."

"I've warned you about those sweaters."

She gave me a smile. It was just a shade too bright.

"He's taking me out to dinner Thursday night." She turned back to her files, casual as a cricket. But I saw it coming, could hear the words even before she opened her mouth. "Say, you haven't heard anything else from Jeen, have you?"

A dozen sorry excuses curled my tongue.

"No," I said.

She nodded. "Well, I just hope he's okay."

"Uh-huh."

"I mean . . ." She sat down on her swivel chair and smiled up at me. Her eyes were as green as springtime. There was a reason seven of the fifteen boys in English Lit had chosen them as the subject of their Introduction to Poetry papers. "Not that I'm holding a grudge or anything, but it'd be great if he was around when I go out with Coco."

"Coco?" I asked, and silently evaluated her tone—a little wistful, a little lonely, a lot out of sync.

"The guy at the grocery store."

"Ahhh."

"He's got a horse ranch out near Santa Clarita."

"Of course he does."

"Asked me to go riding sometime. You know how long it's been since I've been on a horse?"

I settled a hip carefully onto the corner of her desk. I was wearing a dusky silk skirt and didn't want to wrinkle it. "So you don't miss Solberg anymore?"

She was absolutely silent for a moment, then, "I've had some time to think about things. And you know . . ." She shrugged. "It never would have worked out. We were completely wrong for each other. It's best it ended now."

"Because you don't share the same number of chromosomes?"

She laughed, then glanced up, lips trembling only slightly. "Hey, there's Mr. Moniker," she said, and handed me the first file.

I walked to my office, thinking I should increase her pay. If she had to make it as an actress, she'd starve to death in a week. Which is the precise reason I like to keep a little fat on my hips.

I saw seven clients that day, including Mr. Lepinski.

"How was your week?" I asked him, but I remembered our last session pretty clearly and was quite sure it hadn't been great. Unless you compared it to mine.

He shrugged and sat down carefully in the chair across from me. "It was all right. I had lunch at the deli near my office last . . . Tuesday. No, it was Monday. I remember because that was the day it rained and I almost got wet walking back. It's been raining a lot this year. I mean . . ." He shook his head in short little bursts, lips pursed, eyes wide behind round glasses. "Not a lot, not for . . . Seattle or somewhere like that. I'm from Seattle. Did you know that? I was born there." He nodded, concurring with himself. "In 1954. I weighed—"

"Is that where you met your wife?"

He stopped in mid-sentence, mouth open, blinking. His mustache twitched. "What?"

Sometimes my job is really satisfying. Sometimes it sucks the big one. This was one of those latter occasions.

His face looked stricken, his narrow body wound tight as a paper clip.

"Your wife," I repeated. I kept my tone firm and casual, as if I didn't know his heart was breaking in his scrawny little chest. As if I didn't know I should be removing my diploma and putting up a certified bitch certificate in its place. "Is that where you met her?"

"No." Another twitch. "I met her here. She was a secretary . . . legal. Legal secretary. She worked for a firm called, ummm . . . I can't remember now what they're called, but they were pretty good, I think. If you ever need legal advice, you could give them a call. The young guy—Sam Ritchie, I think his name was—he seemed quite competent and their fees weren't outrageous. Not like some of those guys. They're just—"

"Have you spoken to her?"

His eyes looked somewhat magnified through the bulky lenses of his glasses. "Who?"

It was getting harder to grill him, bitch certificate or no bitch certificate. "Your wife. Have you told her that you suspect she's having an affair?"

For a second I thought he might bolt for the door. For a second I almost hoped he would. But he remained where he was, knobby knees pressed together. "I don't want to talk about that."

Me either. "What do you want to talk about?"

"What I *was* talking about," he said.

"Okay." I nodded. "But it won't make things better, Mr. Lepinski. It won't make her quit, or make the pain go away, or make you realize you deserve better."

He opened his mouth, closed it, and looked out the window. "Do I?" he asked, and turned slowly back toward me.

He was a myopic little man with thinning hair and a dozen irritating phobias. "Yes," I said, and knew it was true. "You do."

*T*he rest of the day went just about as well.

The memory of Lepinski weeping into his hands seeped into my bones, dragging me down.

At 1:55 my third client left. I was finishing up some notes when I heard the front door open and close. Voices murmured from the reception area, then, sharp and clear, "No."

I was on my feet in an instant, rushing down the hall. Elaine turned toward me, her face pale, her eyes too wide. Emery Black stood on the opposite side of her desk.

"Mac." Elaine's voice trembled, but she drew a careful breath, calming herself. "This is Jeen's employer."

I slowed my pace, trying to assess a dozen different nuances. Elaine looked shocky and hurt. Black looked angry but controlled. "Yes," I said, and reached out. Black's handshake was as hard as iron. "We've met."

"I'll get right to the point," he said. "I'm afraid there's been some trouble."

I felt my gut drop. "Trouble?"

"They think Jeen embezzled from NeoTech." Elaine's tone was strained, her face pale.

I shook my head. "I'm sure they're wrong, Laney."

"I just want to talk to him." Black's gaze was steady on mine. "I know we can clear this up if he just contacts me. Do you know where he is?"

"No."

"You haven't heard from him?"

I shifted my gaze to Elaine and back. If I had ever had any doubts about her feelings for Solberg, her shattered expression would have laid them to rest for an eternity.

"I'm afraid not," I said.

He watched me a second, then shifted his attention to Elaine. "How about you?"

She shook her head. Her eyes were bright with tears. I felt my heart crack. "No. I'm . . ." She swallowed and raised her chin slightly. "I'm sorry. I haven't heard from him for weeks. Not since the day before he was due to return."

He glowered at her. "Where do you think he might be?"

She never shifted her gaze from his, but pressed her fingertips to the desktop, steadying herself. "I don't know. I thought—"

"What?" he asked.

"I thought we were really close." She smiled a little, pulling herself together. "I guess I was wrong. But I'm sure . . ." She straightened. "He wouldn't have stolen anything, Mr. Black. I'm sure of it."

"I'm certain you're right. I just need to hear it from him."

He scowled out my front door, then turned back. "The longer he's gone, the worse it looks for him, though. But I'll do everything I can to clear his name. Everything in my considerable power." He paused. We waited. "You're certain you don't know where he might be?"

Elaine nodded. I did the same.

"Call me," he said, and reaching into his billfold, gave us each a business card. "If you hear anything."

The police came not two full hours later. Rivera was notably missing. The two officers who arrived were direct opposites of each other. One was old and short. The other was tall and young. Neither one of them could take his eyes off Elaine and both looked like they'd rather eat their own badges than see her unhappy. They asked their questions, took some notes, and departed, apologizing for taking up our time—the soft side of the LAPD.

I was feeling jumpy and old by the time I arrived home. I glanced up and down the street, checking the immediate vicinity, but all seemed clear. I hadn't seen the unidentified blue Toyota since that first spotting and no unusual cars were parked on Opus Street near my house. A black SUV passed by and kept going. I waited to see if it returned. It didn't.

Once inside, I checked caller ID, found nothing intriguing, and rang up Electronic Universe, but again Rex wasn't there. So I left a message similar to the last one, then called La Pyramide and asked to speak to Gertrude. They asked who was calling and I spouted some nonsense about her winning the grand prize in a mall drawing. They sounded a little dubious, but finally asked me to hold. I did.

"Hello?"

"Yeah, Gertie, this is Kathy Solberg, J.D.'s wife," I said.

"Who?"

"J.D.'s wife!" I repeated, emphasizing the last word, before launching irrevocably into fresh, new insanity. "Listen, you floozy, don't bother to deny it. I know you're shackin' up with my old man, and I know he's a donkey's hind end, and I know I'm the same for wantin' him back. But here's the deal—either you tell me where to find him or I'll—"

"What did you say your name was?" Her voice didn't sound quite like I expected. Maybe I've seen too many gangster movies, but she was a topless entertainer and I had a Ph.D. and I was pretty sure she should only be marginally smarter than petrified wood.

"I'm the woman who's going to kick your ass," I said, "if you don't tell me where to find my husband."

"When exactly did you lose your beloved?" Her tone suggested minimal interest and slight irritation.

"Listen, I know you were with him on the twenty-ninth. A friend of mine saw you together after your sleazy show and if you don't—"

"Listen, Mrs. Solberg, after my sleazy show I go straight home, study for my O Chem class, sleep five hours, and hope to get to school on time. Do you understand what I'm saying?"

I admit to some confusion. I mean, I was expecting her to rise to the bait, defend her chosen profession, and hurl insults mixed liberally with curse words, not tell me about her study regime.

"You're lying," I said. "I know he's there, and I'll tell you what, this ain't the first time he's done this sort of thing. If I was you I'd get myself on antibiotics straightaway."

"Although I very much appreciate the advice," she said, "you are obviously severely deranged, so I'm sure you'll understand if I terminate this conversation."

"Wait!" I said before she could hang up. "Are you serious? You didn't sleep with my J.D.?"

There was a pause. "Listen," she said. By her tone I guessed she was now profoundly irritated and completely uninterested. "I'm a chemistry major, a flutist, and a lesbian. I wouldn't sleep with your husband if you paid me in bullion."

"A lesbian?" Here was an interesting twist.

"Yes."

"Does the Mystical Menkaura have any other blonde assistants who might, ummmm . . . like men?" I thought about Solberg. "Or something vaguely similar?"

"No."

"And you don't know a guy named J.D.? Or Jeen? He's short and skinny, with a—"

"Jeen?" she said.

My heart stopped. "Yes."

She sighed. Maybe thinking. Maybe wondering if she should have taken nursing classes straight out of high school like her mother had recommended. "I met a guy named Jeen a few weeks ago. He was carrying some weird gold pineapple and showed me pictures of his . . ."

"Of what?" I breathed.

"I'm sorry," she said, her voice soft yet firm. "But he showed me pictures of his girlfriend."

"His girlfriend?"

"Yes."

"Did she look like a brainy Monroe?"

"She looked like the girl in my fantasies, minus the broadsword."

I laughed out loud, maybe with relief. Maybe 'cuz I'd lost my mind.

Gertrude was silent for a second. "Didn't you say you were his wife?"

"Oh, yeah," I said. "But I try to be understanding. What'd he do after you left him?"

There was another audible sigh. "I don't know. Some of the girls went out with his friends, I think. But he . . . I think I might have seen him leave with another guy."

"Another guy? What guy? How'd he look?"

"I only saw him from behind."

"What'd his behind look like?"

"Listen, if they have facial hair, they all look the same to me. You know what I mean?"

No. "Was he short, hunchbacked, roly-poly? What?"

"He was taller than your husband, but then, so am I."

"What color hair?"

"Brown, I think. Medium weight? Listen, I'm sorry, but I really don't know."

I hung in there like a bull terrier. "Did you see where they went?"

"It looked like they were headed for the lounge."

"And you didn't see them afterward?"

"No."

I let the silence drag out, trying to think, but it didn't go well.

"Say," she said finally, "if your husband ever breaks up with his girlfriend, have her give me a call, will you?"

I spent that evening sitting up on my lofty perch, gazing down at Solberg's house and trying to think. Maybe Gertrude had been lying to me. But I didn't think so. She didn't seem the type to care enough to conjure up such a convincing fabrication.

Which meant that Solberg very probably hadn't been cheating on Elaine. But that said nothing about possible criminal activity. Still, why would he take such a risk? It didn't make any sense. He brought in a hell of a salary at NeoTech, and while it is true that millionaires are hardly exempt from greed, it didn't seem likely that he would be dumb enough to jeopardize his relationship with Elaine. Then again, the word "Combot" had been encased in dollar signs on his calendar. Maybe he had some gigantic payoff at the end of the month. Maybe he thought it would be big enough to convince Laney to screw morals and run away to live in dual bliss on some deserted island.

But I didn't think so. If Solberg was smart enough to refrain from propositioning Elaine, he was probably too smart to underestimate her.

*S*ometime after seven o'clock I fell asleep with my neck kinked like a tire iron beside my headrest. I was groggy and drooling when I next glanced down the hill.

It was almost dark. But there seemed to be movement in the Georges' backyard. I sat straighter, snatched up my binoculars, and focused. Sure enough, someone was trudging across the lawn.

My thoughts clunked along like driftwood in my discombobulated brain. This little turn of events was probably nothing important. But as I watched, I became certain the figure was Tiffany and that she was dragging something that looked like a rolled-up carpet.

My brain cranked faster, gathering momentum. My phone was out of my purse before I knew it.

"Sheriff's office—911."

I swallowed my liver and found my voice. "Yes, I'd like to report a murder."

"A murder, ma'am?" The voice was as calm as Sunday.

"At 13440 Amsonia Lane in La Canada. She buried him in her backyard," I said, and shut the phone.

My heart was pounding as I drove down the curving slope and parked up the street from the Georges' house.

It seemed like half a lifetime before the police arrived. And when they did, there were only two officers, cruising along as if they were sipping lattes and playing Parcheesi.

I watched them as they passed. Their lights were turning on their dashboard, but their siren was silent.

They got out of their car and converged on the sidewalk. One was tall with a basset-hound expression. The other was squat and balding. They spoke for a moment, then separated, one going around the back and one to the front door.

I sat in my Saturn, nerves cranked as tight as undies in spin dry.

Glancing up and down the street, I exited my car, trying to look inconspicuous, just a concerned citizen, wondering what was going down in the old neighborhood.

The balding officer on the porch shifted his considerable weight and switched from ringing the doorbell to knocking with his fist. He had just begun to descend the steps when the door opened. Tiffany Georges stood in a lavender bathrobe, framed by the light behind.

Even from my position on the sidewalk I could see her wide-eyed expression.

"Mrs. Georges?"

"Yes?" It was something like a question.

"I'm Officer Crevans. Can I come in?"

I assume she answered in the affirmative, because a moment later they had disappeared inside.

I strolled along toward the west, but when I passed the fence that divided the neighbors' yards, I took a right-hand turn and shot onto Solberg's property. A moment later I was creeping along the length of the fence line. My binoculars bumped against my boobs beneath my windbreaker and I was huffing like a lapdog in heat, but a moment later I was hidden between a fat-leafed succulent and an oleander. I crouched next to the fence and peeped between the unpainted boards.

Thirty feet in front of the Georges' deck were the two graves, now completely filled in and mounded. Why? What was there? It looked like the hunched officer was wondering the same thing. He circled them once, then strode toward the deck just as the door slid open.

"I told you," Tiffany was saying, "I just planted some

bulbs and . . . Who's that?" she asked. The second officer was already ascending the steps.

"This is Officer Stillman."

"What's he doing here?"

"Like I said, we got a call." Crevans's voice was low, but I could make out most of his words. "I'm sure it's a hoax, ma'am, but we're bound by law to check it out. You don't mind if we take a look?"

"At my bulbs?" Her tone was already loud and snippy. Either she was as guilty as sin or she'd spoken to California's finest before. Certain officers can bring out the pit bull in a poodle.

"I like horticulture," Cravens said. " 'Specially daffodils. Plant any daffodils?"

Her face looked pinched as she turned toward him. "I don't know what you're talking about."

"About your daffodils," said the tall guy with the deadpan expression.

"I didn't say they were daffodils."

"Then what did you bury there?" asked Crevans. His shoes rapped across the hardwood deck and down the steps. Tiffany followed, her bare feet seeming to stutter along behind.

"So," he said. His tone was casual, but his hand was on the butt of the gun at his hip. "You said you don't know where your husband is?"

"I told you." She didn't turn toward him as she spoke. "He went to work, like he always does."

They had reached the upturned soil. The two policemen exchanged a glance. Stillman shook his head in silent disagreement, as if the lie cut him to the quick.

"At Everest and Everest?" Crevans turned his gaze toward Tiffany.

"Yes," she said, her voice clipped.

The two exchanged another glance. Maybe it was meaningful. As for me, I was about to shimmy over the fence and scream for them to dig up the damn graves and quit yakking like a couple old ladies over tea. "We checked into that before we came here, ma'am. Secretary was working late. He said he hasn't seen Mr. Georges at work for more than a week. We'd like your permission to excavate this area."

"Excavate." She laughed. The sound was short and breathy, as if she'd been running uphill. She shifted her gaze toward the street and back. "That's ridiculous. My husband would have a fit. He's very particular about his yard."

The officers glanced toward the trampled space in tandem.

"Well . . ." She sounded panicky now and a little breathless. "That's just . . . like I said, I was doing some planting. There's no law against that."

"Depends what you're planting," mourned the tall cop. "Do you have a shovel handy, Mrs. Georges?"

"You've got no right to do this," she said, but Hangdog was already shuffling off to the shed. He was back with the appropriate tools in less than a lifetime. Two more officers appeared around the corner of the house.

The first one was young and fresh-faced. He nodded eagerly at Crevans.

"Got the warrant," he said. "Dig it up."

It was silent for a while except for the sound of the spade and an occasional grunt from the tall officer.

Tiffany Georges clutched the edges of her robe together near her throat.

The shoveling stopped abruptly. The gangly fellow glanced up. "I hit something, Lou."

The balding fellow nodded, pragmatic to the end.

"Looks like clothing."

Tiffany's face was pale, her hands like claws against the santiny fabric of her robe.

Crevans rested his hand on his gun, his gaze on Tiffany as he spoke quietly into a Nextel. In a minute he replaced the communicator on his hip and turned his attention back to Georges. "Want to tell us who it is?"

The newly arrived officers were shuffling eagerly from foot to foot.

"I told you." She was on the edge of hysteria. "I was just planting bulbs."

The gangly fellow squatted, scooped some soil aside, and pulled a shoe from the dirt with dramatic slowness. "Name brand," he said. "Real leather."

"Looks like the tulips will be well dressed this spring."

Tiffany dropped to her knees and pressed her fists to her mouth.

Stillman started digging with his hands. "Got something else." He tugged carefully. I held my breath, my ear pressed to the fence.

"He shouldn't have left me." Tiffany's voice was low, a soft keening moan.

"Who?" asked Crevans, immediately at attention. "Who shouldn't have?"

"Damn slut."

The original officers glanced at each other again, then at her.

"Your husband?" Crevans guessed.

"Lights up his soul, my ass." She snorted and dropped onto her butt, spreading her legs out in front of her like a downed toddler. "Probably just a damned coincidence that she has tits up to her eyeballs."

"He left you for another woman," said Crevans, and nodded with understanding while motioning silence from his partner. "So you killed him."

"Woman!" She laughed. The sound was brittle. "She's not a woman. She's a snot-nosed army brat. Twenty-two! She's twenty-two."

"Bastard," Crevans agreed. "Did you kill her, too?"

"Found something else, Lou."

The bald head nodded distractedly. "What was her name?"

"Three years younger than me." She was nodding rhythmically and swaying a little. "Fucker. I should have let his wife keep him. Money wasn't worth it. You know he slept with his eyes open?" She glanced up, looking lost. "Gave me the willies."

Crevans glanced toward the grave. "Yeah, that's creepy."

The two new officers had joined Stillman and were dragging out something large and cylindrical. It looked like the rolled-up carpet.

"Got him." Basset Hound's tone almost sounded excited.

"How'd you kill him?" Crevans asked her.

She frowned and looked up suddenly as if her mind had

just clicked on. "Kill him?" she snarled. "I did worse than kill him."

They carefully unrolled the carpet. I was holding my breath and gripping the fence with fingers numb with anticipation. Blue fabric appeared first. The back of a suit coat. A head of hair lolled to the side, then tumbled slowly away.

It took me a moment to realize it was no head at all, but a brown sweater, unrolling on the trampled lawn.

Stillman leaned forward, drawing two dress shirts and a pair of pants from the pile. There was not a dismembered body part to be seen.

Tiffany was rocking back and forth. "See how she likes him without his fancy wardrobe."

The area went absolutely silent.

"And his job." She laughed. "I called his boss, told him Jakey was screwing his wife."

The basset-hound officer had gone back to digging rather frantically. Crevans was watching him. Stillman came up with another shoe and a tie. He shook his head.

"Where is your husband, Mrs. Georges?"

She snorted. "Acapulco. Having his soul lit," she said, then cried like a spanked two-year-old.

21

Sometimes the difference between fear and wisdom
is all but indiscernible.

—*Dr. David Hawkins,*
who was a murderer, but
a pretty smart guy

BY THE TIME I reached home Monday night I felt like
I'd been run down by a trolley.

It was already dark and I hadn't eaten anything but a
Butterfinger since noon. Snickers are my favorite, but I was
trying to maintain a well-rounded diet. Toward that end, I
had called in an order to Chin Yung's. My cell phone was
acting weird again, but I had managed to convey my message. Maybe it was the desperation in my voice, but they'd
had my meal ready when I arrived. Kung pao chicken
steamed dreamily from its little wire-handled box. I carried
it and its mate carefully, juggling them and my purse as I
schlepped up my tilted walkway. My security light had

gone out again. Some kind of electrical problem, which I couldn't afford to fix. But maybe—

"What the hell do you think you're doing?" said a voice from the bushes.

I screamed. The kung pao chicken soared through the air like a startled warbler, followed by the rice and mimicked by my purse. But I didn't care. A shadow loomed over me. I cowered away.

"Jesus, McMullen. What the hell's wrong with you?"

It was Rivera. I was shaking like a fig leaf and my bladder felt queasy.

"You don't even have a decent security light." He grabbed my arm. "Are you trying to get yourself killed?"

My meal had burst open on the broken concrete and was seeping between the cracks. I blinked at all that gooey goodness and promptly burst into tears.

Honest to God. I can't tell you why. I just know I was boo-hooing like a soap opera queen.

"McMullen." Rivera gave me a little shake, but if he was trying to buck me up, it didn't work. My shoulders were heaving and my nose was running wild. "Quit that."

I didn't. He shuffled his feet.

I was vaguely aware of a jogger passing by, reflective tape bright in the Al-Sadrs' lights.

"Damn it," Rivera said. "You're going to get me written up. Pull yourself together."

I sniffled spasmodically.

"Okay. All right." He spoke cautiously, as if he were addressing a stray mutt of uncertain temperament. "Let's just go inside."

"But m-my . . ." I dropped to my knees by the mess on the sidewalk.

"Don't worry about it. I'll make you something." He dragged me to my feet.

I tugged my purse under my arm. "But I wanted . . . I wanted . . . kung pao. . . ."

"Everything all right there?" The jogger had stopped. I swiped the back of my hand across my cheek and gave him a blurry stare.

"Fuck," Rivera murmured, then, "Everything's fine, sir. She lost her . . . Doberman."

"Oh." The jogger was prancing in place. He was either trying to keep his heart rate up or he had to whiz something terrible. "That's the shits. Maybe I can help you look."

"That won't be necessary," Rivera said, then to me, "Will you unlock the frickin' door?"

"Hey." The jogger again. "I know this neighborhood like the back of my hand. I could—"

"The dog's dead!" Rivera snapped.

I hiccuped, but managed to shove my key into the lock. "Oh."

"Got run over by a bus," Rivera said, then quieter, "Get the hell inside."

I attempted to do just that, but my hands were busy trying to wipe my nose and juggle my purse.

Rivera pushed me away, turned the key, and prodded me inside. He gave the jogger a glare, stepped in after me, and closed the door behind us.

We stood faced off like angry pugilists. Well, he was angry. I was just kind of soggy.

"Want to tell me what's going on?" he asked.

I sniffled, remembered my security system, and punched in the code. "You didn't have to kill my dog."

"Jesus." Turning me toward him, he reached up, flicked down my lower lid, and stared into my eyeball. "Are you high?"

I jerked away. "No, I'm not high. I'm..." Tears were threatening again. "I'm hungry, and you made me...me..." I motioned toward the sidewalk. I was hiccuping.

"Just..." He held up a placating hand. "Just take it easy, McMullen. I'm going to..." He shook his head and gritted his teeth. "I'm going to run over to Chin Yung."

I blinked. My eyelashes felt fat. "Really?"

"Yeah. What did you have?"

"Kung pao...chicken."

"Uh-huh." He turned away, then stopped. "If you're not here when I come back, I'm going to find you and handcuff you to your sink."

"Really?" I said again, and blinked my fat eyelashes.

He cursed. "Lock the door behind me," he said, and left.

I wasn't sure how long he was gone. But when I awoke, I was on the couch and someone was pounding on my front door. I stumbled groggily to my feet.

"If you're not in there, McMullen, I swear to God..." he growled from the far side.

Memories, all of them embarrassing, rushed in on me. For a moment I actually considered leaving him out there and heading out the back, but I could already smell the peanut sauce. It wafted inside, convincing me there might be a reason to go on living.

I opened the door. Rivera stood there with his fist raised and his expression mean.

"What the hell were you doing?" he snarled.

I shrugged and dropped my gaze to the paper bag in his hand. It was big. The sweet scent of Shangri-la drifted to my twitching nostrils. I could feel the saliva pooling at the back of my mouth. He took one look at my face, shook his head, and pushed his way inside.

I followed like a bloodhound on a hot scent.

"Lock the door," he said, without turning around.

I did so. By the time I reached the kitchen, he was already pulling the lovely little boxes from the bag. I reached for the closest one. He slapped my hand away. "Go wash," he said, and retrieved plates from my cupboard.

I considered arguing but I felt weak and kind of faded.

Seeing myself in the bathroom mirror didn't help. The San Andreas Fault wrinkled my left cheek, and my hair stood up like Pee-wee Herman's.

I tried to pat it down, but it stood its ground. So I washed my face, gave my hands a perfunctory scrub, and made a beeline for the kitchen.

Rivera was just pouring milk into two beer mugs. They said "Beer With Me" on the side and had a picture of an intoxicated grizzly quaffing liquor. I'd gotten them on my solo visit to Milwaukee, and I liked the word "quaffing."

"Sit down," he said.

I sat, but not because he told me to. He was divvying up the meal and the sight of it made my knees week.

He shoved a fork in my hand.

"Eat."

He didn't have to tell me twice. We ate in absolute silence. For me, it was a spiritual experience, and I didn't dare defile the moment. As for Rivera, he might have been too angry to speak, but just then I didn't much care.

By the time I glanced up again, his plate was empty and he had tilted his chair back onto two legs. His expression was inscrutable.

"Where were you that you could see into the Georges' backyard?"

I knew immediately what he meant. I wished I didn't.

"What?" I said, and trying to look casual, took another scoop of rice from his box. He hadn't eaten all of his. What the hell was wrong with him?

"I'm guessing you were up on the ridge to the south of the development."

My throat felt tight but I managed to swallow. I'm a genius that way. "Who's George?"

He shook his head. "I should throw your ass in jail. You know that?"

"For what?"

He shrugged. "Invasion of privacy. Falsifying a police report." He paused. "Murder?"

I was nice and full, and a little too tired to be scared witless. Which probably meant there were other reasons for my witlessness. In fact, I felt a little drugged. It would have been fun to think Rivera had doped my food, but copious amounts of calories often affect me this way. "I didn't kill anyone," I said.

He glared at me. "Probably the only damned law you haven't broken."

"I haven't coveted my neighbor's wife, either," I said.

"I was thinking more civil than biblical."

"Oh," I said, and nibbled on a water chestnut. It was the only thing left on my plate.

"What's going on, Chrissy?"

"Nothing. What do you mean?"

"You're starving. You're jumpy. You look like you haven't slept for a month."

"Been busy." I fished a slice of chicken out of his moo goo gai pan. If I were the pope, Chin Yung would be canonized— along with waitresses—in a big ceremony with lots of food. "Work." I glanced up as I chewed, but there was hardly a need to masticate. The meat melted in my mouth. "You know."

He dropped the front legs of his chair to the floor and propped his elbows on the table. "I know you're a piss-poor liar. Tell me about Solberg."

"He's a nerd?"

"God damn it!"

I jumped but held my ground, and shockingly didn't burst back into tears.

"What's wrong with you? You're in deep shit! What makes you think they're not going to show up at your back door?"

I felt the blood drain from my face. "Who?"

"How the hell would I know who? You don't tell me crap."

"I just . . . I . . ." I almost spilled the truth, almost told him everything. I felt alone and vulnerable and scared. And he was . . . well, he was Rivera. Impenetrable and irritating as hell. But I remembered the strangled sound of Solberg's voice on the other end of the line. Life or death. "I don't know what you're talking about. I'm fine. Everything's fine."

He stared at me. I wiped my sweaty palms on my skirt. It looked like hell anyway. I held his gaze as best I could and in a moment he jerked to his feet.

"Christ," he said, running his hand over his face and turning away to stare out my kitchen window.

His back was rigid, his hips narrow, his legs lean. His dark dress pants were wrinkled, and his shirt had come partly untucked. For some reason the sight of it made me want to blubber like a baby and confess all.

"Not even locked," he said, and shook his head as he turned back toward me. "Would it kill you to lock the window? To be just a little bit aware?"

"I'm aware."

He snorted.

"I check for strange cars all the time."

"Really? Where's my Jeep parked?"

I scowled at him. "I was kind of tired—"

"Good God," he said, and retrieving his plate, turned toward the sink.

"What are you doing?"

"Cleaning up," he snarled. "When you're murdered in your sleep you don't want to have a messy kitchen, do you?"

"I hadn't really thought about it."

"You haven't thought about a lot of things."

His patronizing tone made me feel a little pissy. I snatched my dishes from the table and slapped them down beside his. "I haven't done anything wrong."

"Yeah?" He faced me, eyes snapping. "Maybe I think it's wrong for you to be an idiot."

"I'm not—"

The phone rang on the counter beside me.

He glared at it. "Who's that?"

"Still not psychic."

It blared again.

"Answer it."

"I'll answer it if I want—"

"Oh, for God's sake," he said, and shoved me toward the phone. "Answer it."

I picked up the receiver, glaring as I did so.

"Hello."

"Where is he?" The voice was low and gravelly.

The blood froze in my veins. I snapped my gaze to Rivera. His eyes narrowed immediately and he stepped close.

"I . . . I think you have the wrong number," I said.

"Tell me where he is or you'll wish to hell you had," said the voice. The phone slipped from my hand like pudding.

Rivera caught it and brought it to his ear in one smooth motion. "Who is this?" His brows lowered like dark clouds. "Who the hell is this?"

The click on the far end was audible. He slammed down the phone.

"Sit down," he said.

I remained standing, staring numbly.

"Sit the hell down," he said, and pushed me onto a chair. Twisting me toward him with his hands on my upper arms, he stared into my eyes. "Who was that?"

I shrugged.

"Damn it, McMullen, answer me."

"I don't know who it was."

"What'd he say?"

I blinked. "He asked where he is."

"Where who is?"

"I don't know."

He shook me. My head bobbled loosely. "Who?"

"He didn't say." My eyes stung. I wondered rather vaguely if I was going to cry again, or if I was crying already.

He tugged me to my feet and led me like a lost lamb to my sofa. I sat down without being told, like a big girl.

"Have you had other threatening calls?" He was looming over me.

I shook my head.

"Don't lie to me."

"Okay." I was beaten. Beaten and scared.

"Have you heard his voice before?"

"I don't know."

"It didn't sound familiar?"

"There wasn't enough time."

He cursed and paced. "I shouldn't have spoken. Should of had you keep talking." He cursed and paced again, but in a minute he sat down beside me. I turned toward him.

"Think hard, Chrissy. Did it sound like anyone you know?"

I thought hard. It made my head hurt. I shook it. He inhaled carefully. He looked big and hard and strong. I felt small and soft and weak.

"Tell me about the night you were attacked."

I considered lying, but I was too tired. I told him everything. Well, I might have neglected the part about the disk

I'd stolen from Solberg's house, but I didn't see any reason to slip past the stupid line and into the too-stupid-to-live area.

He asked questions. I told him more.

He nodded, rose to his feet, and paced. I watched him.

"You should get some sleep."

I blinked at him, numb as a newel post.

"Come on." He held out his hand.

I took it. He led me to the bedroom and glanced around. "Where are your pajamas?"

"Pajamas?"

The left corner of his mouth jerked up a hair. "You don't sleep in the nude, do you?"

"Mom says nice girls don't do that," I said, and realized rather belatedly that he was unbuttoning my blouse. I glanced down. "What are you doing?"

"I think I might be undressing you."

"Whaaa—" The sound I made was something between a gas leak and a siren. I jerked away. My buttons were undone almost to my navel. "You can't undress me."

He raised his brows. "Awake now?"

"Get out of here."

He shook his head. "I'm staying with you tonight."

I laughed out loud. It sounded better than the "whaaa," but not by much. I buttoned my blouse with tingly fingers. "You are not."

"Here or in jail," he said.

I gritted my teeth and shoved him.

He rocked back a step, laughed, and lifted his hand to my cheek. "Where the hell have you been all night, McMullen?"

he asked, his voice soft, his eyes like dark, crystal balls, pulling me in. "I sort of missed you."

Feelings skittered through my parched system. I tried to hose them down, but my water pressure was weak. "Go away," I said.

He shook his head. "Hope you're not the kind to hog the covers."

My mouth dropped open. He put a hand beneath my jaw and closed it, then turned with a chuckle and paced into my living room.

I followed him in numb silence. By the time I caught up he had taken off his shoes and was unbuttoning his shirt. It was a moment before I could find my voice.

"What are you doing?"

"Your virtue is safe, Chrissy. I'll sleep on the couch."

"No you won't."

He opened his shirt. During the past three months I had spent a considerable amount of time trying to convince myself that, despite my lurid memories, Jack Rivera was not built like a chiseled Greek god. I hadn't been very successful. One sight of him half-naked and I remembered why. I braced myself against the wall beside me.

"You have to leave," I said.

He tilted his head in disagreement and removed his gun.

I watched the movement—brown hands against smooth-grained wood. A dark metal barrel against the backdrop of his rippled obliques.

Now, I like to think I'm a mature woman, one not inclined to wild, girlish fantasies. I don't like macho men, and I have long since put my obsession with Batman behind me. But my knees felt a little sloppy, and my mind was chanting something like "Gimme, gimme, gimme."

He set the gun on the end table and straightened.

"Something you need, McMullen?" he asked.

My mouth was open again. I nodded. The movement was jerky. "Yeah," I said bravely. "I need..." The world swam by in lurid slow motion. "You to leave."

He laughed. The sound rippled like hot-buttered rum through my battered system.

He reached for his belt. And suddenly, somehow—I don't know how—I found myself gripping his buckle in both hands, holding his pants together as if it were Pandora's infamous box.

He stared down at me.

"Swear to God, Rivera," I said, "if you take off your pants, I'll call the cops."

His mouth twitched. "I am the cops, McMullen." He tilted his head. "And I do."

His abdomen was hard and warm against my knuckles. My throat felt like it was being strangled from the inside. "You do what?" I croaked.

"Sleep naked."

My stomach dropped to floor level. "Not here you don't," I breathed.

His hands moved. Mine tightened on his fingers and the offensive belt buckle.

"You can't expect me to sleep in my pants," he said.

"Your pants, your shirt." I thought I felt a pulse beating in my eyelids. "Maybe a full suit of armor."

He chuckled. I could feel the movement in his abdomen "My last breastplate rusted, McMullen."

"I'll run out and buy you a new one."

"All the armor shops close at nine. I think you should get some sleep."

"Sleep!" I was making funny noises again. Something between a snort and a hiccup. "I can't sleep, with you . . ." I loosened one hand from his belt and waved rather wildly at something between him and the toilet bowl. "I can't sleep with you . . ."

He raised one brow.

"In here . . . without . . ."

"I'm not going to molest you, if that's what you're worried about," he said.

"Well." I laughed. "That's a relief. I mean, whew! 'Cuz that's what . . ." I was wheezing like an exhausted hyena "That's what I was worried about. That you'd . . ." I felt panicky and as high as a kite. Maybe he'd drugged my meal after all. Maybe I had no choice but to sleep with him. And holy shit, last time I'd had a half-naked guy in my house, he'd been fixing the kitchen sink and up to his hairy armpits in sledge. "That you'd—" I began again, but then he kissed me.

Fireworks zipped from my head to my toes and back.

"Jesus, you drive me crazy," he murmured.

I was breathing hard. Not panting, of course. Panting would be uncouth.

"You're not even my type," he said, and kissed me again.

I may have whimpered, just a little. "Rivera. Listen. Sometimes . . ." I licked my lips. "Self-restraint isn't my long suit."

"Yeah?" He kissed my neck. "What is?"

My head fell back. "Tuba?" I suggested.

He drew back slightly, watching me.

"I'm a hell of a tuba player."

He chuckled, and reached for my buttons again. I tried to stop him. Really. But my fingers were too busy. His chest felt like sun-warmed marble beneath my palms as I pushed his shirt aside.

He ran his hands down my arms, peeling my blouse away. I shivered hopelessly and pressed against him.

He moaned. Or maybe it was me. I hope it wasn't me.

"Christ, you're beautiful."

I hope that wasn't me, too.

His hands were on my bra strap. I tried to escape, but only managed to arch into him. Then suddenly, he froze.

"You hear something?" he asked.

I shook my head and hoped it wasn't my panting that had distracted him, but suddenly a gun appeared in his hand.

"What...?" I began, but he motioned for silence and backed carefully against the wall. He stood, bare-chested and beautiful, his gun raised nearly to his shoulder.

"Disarm your system, then lock the door behind me and stay away from the windows."

"Lock the—"

"Hurry," he said.

I punched in the appropriate numbers. He jerked the door open and popped outside.

I locked the door with unsteady fingers This was insanity. Like living with Tarzan. I wasn't sure I was up to being Jane. I was more like a . . . Mildred.

I stood frozen beside the door for a while. When that got unbearable, I paced, jumping at every inexplicable sound.

After a couple of decades, a knock sounded at my door. I froze, darted my eyes toward the offensive portal, and ceased to breathe. "Who is it?"

"Let me in."

My heart rate went through the stratosphere. "Who's there?"

"Jesus, McMullen. It's me. Let me in."

I waited. The voice sounded irritable enough to be Rivera, but maybe it was a trick, and I was supposed to stay away from the window, and maybe they'd gotten Rivera, and were—

"Let me in, McMullen, or I'm gonna break your damned window."

Oh, yeah, it was Rivera.

22

Money talks. Mostly it says, "So long, sucka."

—*Pete McMullen,*
after his fourth divorce

RIVERA DIDN'T FIND anyone lurking about my domicile, but the interruption gave me a chance to hose down my raging endocrine system.

What the hell had I been thinking anyway? I didn't need a man to screw up my life. I was perfectly capable of doing that on my own. Messing around with a guy like Rivera would only set me on the fast track to disaster. He was a barbarian—an old-world warrior with new-world weaponry. And what weaponry.

But I hadn't let him draw his gun. Instead, I'd sentenced myself to solitary confinement in the jail I like to call my boudoir.

We were coolly mature when morning arrived, and even though Rivera looked like a sleepy sex machine with his hair messed and his eyes heavy-lidded, I didn't drag him into my private cell and have my way with him.

Instead, I had a bowl of Raisin Bran while he tied his shoes and informed me I'd have to file an official statement. I nodded and chewed, knuckles white around my spoon as I watched him bend over his other shoe. He made me promise to keep my doors locked, call him if anything suspicious happened, and stay in the house all day.

I thought about that as I sat across from my first Tuesday morning client.

I also thought about the phone call. Whoever it was hadn't asked where "it" was. He'd asked about "him." The him had to be Solberg. But why? They didn't want Combot. They didn't want the embezzled money. They wanted him? So the only explanation was that Solberg hadn't been the one to steal the money. In fact, I was certain he'd been the one to find out about the stolen money.

I barely noticed when my client left, although I should have been listening, because he hadn't yet reached his twentieth birthday and he had two kids, a drug addiction, and a mortgage. He might have made my life look better by comparison.

I know my final clients of the morning almost made me look sane.

"We did it in the theater."

My thoughts screeched to a shuddering halt. I jerked my attention to the Hunts. They had opted to come in twice a week. Tuesdays and Fridays. They both sat on the couch, squashed together like overripe bananas.

Mrs. Hunt was blushing. And if half of what she said was true, she damned well should be. In fact, even if it wasn't true . . .

"What's that?" I asked.

"The AMC near our house, just after the trailers."

She was clutching her husband's arm as she lowered her voice to a giggling whisper. "I think the usher might have spotted us."

"I see." I blinked and found that I *could* almost see them—humping away like wild dingoes while Tristan and Isolde went at it on the big screen. And now I was going to have to poke out my eyes.

"It was so exciting. Like we were teenagers again."

Or felons.

"We appreciate your help, Doc," said Mr. Hunt seriously. I couldn't help but notice that he was blushing, too. That made three of us.

"Yes. You're the best," said Mrs. Hunt, putting her hand on her husband's chest and leaning toward me conspiratorially. "We're thinking of doing it in the lunchroom at his work."

By the time they left I felt like I'd been flagellated with a thousand rubber bands. I dropped my head on my desk and refused to believe I was responsible for the Hunts' temporary insanity. I hadn't told them to mate like hamsters on speed. I had simply suggested that they take each other's desires into consideration, that they step back from the pressures of the world and . . .

Oh, what the hell, I thought. They were adults, they were

married, if they wanted to screw like power tools, who was I to object? I had enough problems of my own.

Who had called me? And why? What did they want? The embezzled money? It was the only conclusion I could come up with. But then what? Did that mean that Solberg really was involved? Did that mean he'd absconded with the cash?

The phone rang. I jumped, then sat in a silent haze. It rang again. It took me a minute to realize Elaine was still out to lunch. Longer still to answer the phone. I picked up the receiver, held it to my ear, turned it around so the cord pointed down, and spouted the appropriate salutation.

But the caller spoke before I had finished. "We got your friend." The voice was low and guttural.

The hair on my arms fluttered upright. "What?"

"Your secretary. We got her."

My skin went cold, my chest tight. "I . . . I don't know what you're talking about."

"We don't wanna hurt her."

I was gripping the receiver hard against my ear. "Elaine? You've got Elaine?"

"We'll exchange her for your geek friend."

"For Solberg?"

"He gives us back what he took and we'll let her go."

"I don't know where he is. I don't even know—"

He laughed. The sound quivered down my spine. "Thought you two girls was pals."

"Don't hurt her." My voice sounded odd. Stripped bare. "Please."

"Get the Geek to San Cobina by two o'clock today and everything'll be all right."

"San Cobina?" I shook my head. As if he could see. As if I could think. "I don't know—"

"Take the Two north toward the mountains. There's a side road runs west just after—"

"Wait! Wait." I scrambled for scrap paper and began to write. My hand wobbled erratically. I began again, carefully, like a first-grader with a crayon.

He laid out the route, then, "Be there at two."

"But it's already . . ." I glanced at the clock on the wall beside the door. "It's almost one. I can't—"

"If he don't show, you'd better find yourself a new friend. If you tell the cops, you better find yourself a coffin."

The phone went dead.

I sat listening to the dull drone. My hand hurt from gripping the receiver. I removed it from my ear and stared at it, as if it were a foreign object, as if everything would be all right if I could just identify it. Thoughts tumbled disjointedly in my head. I had not only failed, I had exacerbated the problem. I had jeopardized Elaine.

Laney.

Her name was an agonized wail in my mind. I felt suddenly sick to my stomach. I teetered to the bathroom and threw up, then leaned back against the toilet and stared numbly at the single lightbulb overhead.

And suddenly I knew. I knew who and I knew why.

Standing shakily, I tottered back to my desk. My hand was oddly steady when I picked up the receiver and dialed.

"Electronic Universe. Rex speaking."

I was completely calm now, as if everything was as it should be. "Rex," I said, "this is Christina McMullen."

"Oh. I—"

"I need you to get a message to J. D. Solberg."

"I don't know if—"

"I do. He's been there in the past few days. He'll be there again. I need to get a message to him immediately. Tell him Emery Black has Elaine." I gave him the address her abductor had given me. "Tell him if anything happens to her, he'd be better off dead."

I hung up, then called Solberg's cell phone and his home phone and left the same message.

I was in my car within minutes. The midday traffic seemed terminal. It began to rain, spitting in from the southwest. I drove like one in a trance, slowly, methodically.

Black had Elaine. I was certain of it. But he wouldn't hurt her. He was too smart for that. He needed her.

I should have known when I saw the golden pear in his office that he was to blame for Solberg's disappearance. I should have known, because it wasn't a pear. It was the Lightbulb Award. Which meant he had been with J.D. the night of the banquet. They hadn't gone out with Vegas bimbos to celebrate, because Solberg had Elaine, and Black had Solberg, or at least he thought he did. Companionable, drunk, and giddy with their mutual success, they'd headed for the lounge, where Black had spilled his secrets, and set this whole chain of events in motion.

I took the 210, then turned north onto the 2, reading my directions I as drove.

The highway wriggled like a rattlesnake into the mountains. The road I turned onto was graveled and steep. The Saturn's tires crunched against the unstable surface as I climbed.

A green Pontiac was parked in a bald circle surrounded by ragged mountains.

A big guy got out of the vehicle. It was Jed. My courage sloughed away like water down a drain, leaving me rigid and nauseous. Opening the car door was all I could manage.

Rain spattered down on me, blurring my eyesight.

There were two people in the backseat of the Pontiac, but I couldn't see them well enough to identify them.

Solberg was nowhere to be seen. I was on my own.

I left my door open. The Saturn *dinged* behind me, sounding pathetic and alone in the hard patter of the rain.

"Where's Elaine?" I asked, but my voice was no more than a feeble croak. Jed kept walking toward me. There was another man standing on a rock at the edge of the parking lot, looking down.

I tried again. "I want to see Elaine."

The lookout turned toward me, but no one answered. Panic swelled like bile in my system. I held up a shaky hand and was somewhat surprised to see that it was clutched around my cell phone. "Stop where you are or I'll call the police. I swear I will."

Jed took another step toward me.

"I've already got it dialed," I said. I didn't. Or at least I don't think I did. But then, I'd actually forgotten about the phone completely, so it's hard to say for sure.

The lookout stepped down from his rock. Both men wore jeans and T-shirts.

"I want to see Laney." My voice warbled, but didn't fail me completely.

"Where's the geek?" Jed asked.

"Get your boss on the phone. I'll tell him."

Jed laughed. The noise rumbled evilly through me. "You got balls, bitch. Too bad that ain't enough to keep your friend alive," he said, and turned toward the car.

"I can get the money!" I rasped.

He turned back, a hungry smirk quirking his lips. "What money?"

"Just tell your boss."

"Listen—"

"Tell him!" I snapped.

He pulled a phone from his pocket and pushed a button, his gaze never leaving mine.

I could only hear slivers of the conversation.

"He wants to talk to you," Jed said.

And I wanted to hurl. "Put the phone down and back away."

He grinned.

"Do it," I ordered, lifting my cell, "or the FBI will be down your throat before you can scratch your ass."

He backed away. I crept forward, knees knocking, and lifted the phone to my ear.

"I know everything, Black," I said.

Silence echoed at the other end, then, "You're lying."

Emery Black sounded as if he hadn't slept for a while. But he had good reason for his insomnia, because Solberg had gone to Electronic Universe, and with the help of their mind-boggling technology, had zipped the embezzled money out of Black's account and into safekeeping, until he could, eventually, explain everything to the cops.

Or so I believed. In fact, I was betting my life on it.

"It's the truth," I said. "I know you embezzled from

NeoTech, I know Solberg knows. I know he stole the money from you, and I know how to get it back."

"I don't believe you."

"Solberg trusts me. I'm the one he called when he realized he was in trouble. But you know that, don't you? That's why you had your goons follow me to the Four Oaks."

The world spun dizzily on its course. I was holding my breath, feeling faint.

"I need to speak to J.D.," Black said.

"Speak to him?" I forced a laugh. The sound echoed crazily in the spitting rain. "You need to get *rid* of him. But I don't give a shit about that. Let Laney go. She doesn't know anything about this. I can get the money. I'm assuming you can plant it in one of Solberg's accounts and convince the cops he's to blame."

"What makes you think I'm willing to do that?"

"Don't be stupid. The money's not going to do you a hell of a lot of good in jail. And you'll be more than compensated when the Combot deal comes through."

"How—"

I chuckled. "Give me fifty percent and I'll tell you."

"Tell me what?"

"How I know . . . and where to find Solberg."

"Where?" His voice was low and gritty suddenly, raising the hair on the back of my neck.

"Let Laney go and we'll talk."

"You're a hell of a friend."

"Yes, I am. To Elaine."

"And J.D.?"

"Not everyone finds him as appealing as you do, Black. She'll be better off with him out of her life."

The desperate honesty in my tone must have convinced him.

"All right," he said. "We'll let the girl go, you take her place. If you deliver, we'll—"

"Fifty-fifty on the Combot deal," I said.

There was a huff of disbelief, then, "Sure. Why not? Put Jed back on."

I laid the phone on the ground and backed away, stomach cramped and every joint stiff.

Their conversation was short. Jed shoved the phone in his pocket, then turned toward the car and waved.

A bald guy in black pants got out of the Pontiac. He reached inside. Elaine stepped out after him.

I felt my knees shudder with relief.

Her face was pale and her eyes wide, but she looked well. She looked whole.

"Laney," I breathed.

Her captor led her toward me.

She stumbled a little. But when she looked up, our gazes met and stuck.

"I missed your mug, doll," I said. "How you doin', Sugar?"

Her lips parted, and her eyes widened marginally, but she caught my meaning with lightning-quick speed, and spoke the words I knew she would. "I've been better. Why'd you come, Hawke?" she asked. "You shouldn't have come."

We were twenty yards apart. Terror made me stiff. Hope made me speak. "I . . . I couldn't hardly stay away, could I?" I intoned.

"You can do anything you want," she murmured. "Always could."

"Just so happened—" I began.

"What's this shit?" asked Jed. "Put her in the bitch's car."

Baldy pulled Elaine toward the Saturn. She turned toward me as they passed.

"I missed you," she said.

Our eyes met across the spattered dirt. "I missed you, too."

She stumbled. Baldy yanked her to her feet, pushing her on. I turned my attention to the men ahead of me. Jed was close now, standing just a few feet from the Pontiac. The lookout was ten yards to my right.

The car's doors were still open.

Laney, I was sure, was almost to the Saturn. I took one more step.

"We had a good run while it lasted," she said suddenly. I turned toward her. She jerked her arm from her abductor's and fell to the ground with the force of her release. My stomach pitched. Baldy reached for her. She rolled over. Her blouse had been ripped open and her boobs, big as cantaloupes, spilled out.

I saw the guy stiffen, but I didn't see her strike. Because at that same second I swung my elbow with all my might. I felt it crash against Jed's nose. And then I was praying and diving. I hit the front seat of the Pontiac like a rocket, fumbled forward, and twisted the key.

Laney's abductor was flat on the ground. She was scrambling to her hands and feet and dove for the Saturn. But Baldy grabbed her ankle. She screamed and kicked him in the face. His head jerked back.

A shot rang out. Someone screamed.

"Stop it! Just stop it!"

I jerked my head to the left, and there was Solberg, gun wobbling in his hands.

The world seemed to grind to a halt. Every eye turned toward him.

And then life exploded. Everything happened in an instant. One minute we were almost free, and the next Solberg was sprawled on the ground with a gun to the back of his neck.

"All right!" The lookout was breathing hard, but his hands were steady on the weapon, his legs spread wide as he stood over Solberg. "Out of the car, lady, or the geek here gets it."

I might have chanced it, but even from that distance I heard Elaine breathe Solberg's name.

I raised my hands and stepped out of the Pontiac. Lookout turned his gun toward me.

I could already feel the impact of the bullet, could taste the blood in my mouth.

How had my life come to this? I wondered foggily. I had a Ph.D. I was a high-class psychologist. Well, maybe not high-class, but—

"Police!" someone yelled.

I jerked toward the sound. Men swarmed out of the brush like shadows amidst shadows.

"Throw down your guns," yelled the closest officer. "SWAT" was written in white across his black jacket. "Throw them!"

I watched in a dream as pistols were tossed onto the pock-marked earth. My legs gave way. I sagged to the ground, propping my back sloppily against the Pontiac to keep from falling face forward into the dirt.

The assailants were handcuffed and hauled away amidst muttered curses and disjointed Mirandas.

Across the scruffy hillside, Solberg rose shakily to his feet. His glasses were askew and his hair was standing on end.

Near the Saturn, a SWAT guy with a five o'clock shadow did a double-take at Elaine. The clouds had cracked open and a ray of sunlight slanted down, catching her in its golden rays. Her blouse was still open. Her hair was messed, and her eyes, wide with the tail end of fear and adrenaline, were as big and bright as turbulent seas.

"Hey," he said, his gun still trained on the departing prisoners, "maybe we could catch a movie or something... when this is all over."

23

Money's nice and all, but you can't beat waking up on your own little plot of land with a gal who'll kiss you even if you smell like pig manure.

—*Cousin Kevin McMullen,*
who likes his wife even
more than his sows

JUST WANTED TO stop by and thank you again," Solberg said.

We were sitting around my kitchen table, drinking all-natural papaya juice, which Elaine had thoughtfully brought from home. It tasted a little like cat pee. I've got brothers—I know.

"Don't worry about it," I said. "The half-million dollars is thanks enough."

He brayed like a donkey. Elaine was sitting next to him. She looked at me and smiled. It was the real deal, no artifice, no tears, actual happiness. I gave a mental sigh.

"You're a snooker, Chrissy," Solberg said, "but I'm afraid the money's already gone back to NeoTech."

"So your boss was embezzling," I said.

"Guess so." He shook his head, looking befuddled. But he usually looked befuddled. "Emery Black. Woulda never guessed it if he hadn't . . ." He paused and glanced at Elaine.

"Hadn't what?" I asked, but I already knew the truth.

"Well . . ." He shook his head again, nervous this time. "He got drunk." He tossed up a hand as if to make the whole thing go away. "When we were in Vegas. Said some things he shouldn't have."

"Like what?" I gave him my innocent look. It was cruel of me to make him confess all, but I'm a cruel woman.

He actually blushed. "Like he was worth more than anyone knew."

"Was that before or after he made a pass at you?" I asked.

Solberg's cheeks brightened to the color of tomato paste. He glanced sheepishly at Elaine. I grinned, 'cuz I was right on the money; flush with their mutual success, Black and J.D. had wandered off to the lounge with Solberg's Lightbulb Award and Black's $500,000 secret.

"He said he had a little egg he'd scooped out of Neo's nest. Said he wanted to share it with me. I don't know what he was thinking. How could he think I was gay?"

I noticed he wasn't surprised that Black thought he'd be more than willing to nab a little ill-gained cash.

"The heart will what it will," I said dramatically, then, "So you left your golden pear with Black and scurried for cover."

"Golden—"

"Your award," Laney said, watching me. She knew I had

been lying my ass off for weeks. She knew I'd, ummm...
fictionalized Solberg's affair. She knew why, and she forgave. Life was all right.

"I still can't believe he thought I..." Solberg's words
shambled to a halt. "He has two kids."

I laughed at his naïveté. Apparently Solberg hasn't dated
seventy-five men and learned a million things about the
seedy side of life. "Life's strange."

"But how did you know he was embezzling?" he asked.

"I didn't have a clue at first. He seemed pretty secure...
said you and he had done well together in the past and
would again in the future. It took me a while, but I finally
realized you two must have been working on something
special. Something with a big enough reward to lure you in
to pick up the dough. He was absolutely sure you'd be back
by the end of the month."

"But he was stealing from NeoTech," Solberg said, still
outraged.

"Which he didn't think you'd have a problem with, but
when you did, he knew he had to get rid of you. So he
called in his goons to find you. I didn't have any way of
knowing whose goons they were, though. Black seemed
perfectly normal...until I saw him with Laney."

Solberg was scowling. "What are you talking about?"

"He came to the office and..." Elaine had cried for Solberg.
Actually cried—right there behind the reception desk.
Holy crap. Someday I might have to buck up and admit
she's crazy about a little dweeb I could strap to my back
and carry around like a tent stake. "Well, he upset her," I
said, "and didn't offer her so much as a handkerchief."

"Angel." Solberg turned toward her, stricken and pale, tightening his bony hand over hers. "What'd he do?"

"Nothing." She shook her head. "It was nothing."

"Anyway," I said, "I knew that if he wasn't kissing her ankles and offering his firstborn, he had to be gay."

"But what did that have to do—"

"I spoke to a gal in Vegas who said you didn't go out with the dancing girls. Said you headed off with another man instead. I knew *your* reasons." I shifted my gaze to Elaine. As far as I knew she was absolutely perfect, and I'd known her a long time. "I could only guess at his. But I couldn't quite put everything together."

Solberg shook his knobby head, still baffled. "How could he think I was gay?"

I refrained from rolling my eyes. "My question is, why didn't you just turn him in to the police?"

"I just . . ." He shifted in his chair, his scrawny body wiggling under my scrutiny. I had been perfecting the evil eye. "Well . . . I didn't know right off that he had embezzled. I mean, it sounded kind of funny, him saying he had a half million squirreled away, but . . . Emery Black! You know . . . he's got a frickin' fortune . . . and sons." It sounded like he didn't know which was more unbelievable, that a millionaire still wanted more money, or that a father of two had been eyeing his ass.

As far as I was concerned, they both qualified for the Twilight Zone.

"Uh-huh. So why didn't you call the police?" I repeated.

"Well . . ." He glanced at Elaine again. "Once I figured out what was goin' on, I knew I could handle it myself." He shrugged and sniffed a little. "It ain't easy breaking into them Swiss banks, 'specially when you can't get to your own gear, but I got my ways."

My mind was working overtime. "So why didn't you just let the FBI, or whoever, take care of it if everything was on the up-and-up."

"Well . . ." He scowled at me. "Like I said—"

"It didn't have anything to do with Combot, did it?" I asked.

His face drained of color. "How do you know 'bout the Bot?"

I couldn't contain my smile. Truth is, I didn't even try. "I've got my ways," I said.

"What's a bot?" Laney asked.

He twisted toward her like a man in a nightmare, slowly, as if he might turn and find her gone. His knuckles looked white against her hand. "Listen, Laney," he said, and exhaled carefully. "I thought we had full legal rights to that thing."

Her expression didn't change an iota, but by the look on his face you would think she had spit in his eye.

"Swear to God, Laney," he said, talking fast. "Emery took care of the legal matters. See, years ago, him and a guy name of Franklin had come up with something called 'Compubot.' It's like an interactive computer, kind of. Anyway, Franklin, he fiddled with it for a while, then got tired of it. So Black took it over. He said he got the rights free and clear. I knew ol' Frankie had helped with the early stages. But no big deal. You know? 'Specially when he got that promotion and moved to Texas. The Bot was nothing then. So Black invited me in. He said I should keep it quiet, 'cuz he didn't want anyone to think he was favoring me. Office politics and all that . . . and I thought, *Hey, this might be in-teresting.*

"I worked on that thing for five years. Five full years. I was just doin' it for fun, you understand. But then things started clickin' and Black suggested that we sell it on the In-ternet. I thought maybe we should market it through Neo, but Black says no, we don't want to give away our baby and we can make more money this way. So we've been sellin' a few. You know, here and there. Then Technoware gives us a call and says they're interested in buying the whole she-bang. So we got a chance at big bucks, and they want to get together at—"

"The end of the month," I said.

He gave me an openmouthed look, then turned back to Laney and hurried on. "So I thought, *Why not.* And I . . ." He ran out of steam suddenly, his face still pudding pale. "I didn't know we were doing anything illegal. Black told me, that night, in Vegas, after he dropped the grenade about the half million, he says that Franklin should still have rights to the Bot. I learned . . ." He winced. "A lot of shit." He swal-lowed, gripped her hand harder. "Stuff," he corrected. "Lots of stuff. I didn't mean to do anything illegal. I was just being . . . creative."

"So creative, you might find your ass in jail?" It was hard not to grin. But I mean, I'd been through hell for this little geek.

"No jail," he said, looking frail and panicked. "No jail. There's nothing that can implicate me."

I raised my brows at him. "Electronic Universe must have some really top-notch equipment."

"No." He flashed his gaze to Laney and back. "I mean,

yeah, I made sure there wasn't nothing could tie me to Black's crimes... just to be on the safe side. And that took some time. But I'm giving my share of the rights to Franklin. And the money we made. All the money if he wants it."

Elaine was absolutely silent.

Solberg's shoulders drooped like a wounded soldier's. "Swear to God, Laney," he croaked. "I wouldn't do nothin' illegal. Not no more. I wouldn't do nothin' to..." On his face was such painful adoration, it was almost hard to look at. Not that Solberg's ever easy to look at. "I wouldn't do nothin' to disappoint you," he whispered.

The silence stretched out, and then she lifted her hand and slowly touched his face. "I know," she said.

He looked as though he were going to melt right into the floor. "You believe me?"

"Yes."

"Oh God." He closed his eyes. "I was so worried, Laney. Terrified. I didn't know what to do. Black threatened to pin the theft of the Bot on me if I told anyone about the embezzlement. And I thought... Jesus... I mean... man, oh, man... what if they sent me to the big house?" He paused. His eyes went blank. "What if I couldn't see you? I had no choice but to hide out until I could get the money back and prove my innocence."

Elaine gave him a wistful smile. "You should have told me," she said. "I would have helped."

He looked like he was going to die. "No." He shook his head. "No way. They didn't know nothing about you at Neo and—"

"Why?" I asked, still baffled about that one point.

He glanced at me before skittering his gaze back to her. "Because I . . . Well, maybe I've told some stories about women before. You know, big stories. They wouldn't believe I had gotten someone as perfect as her, and I didn't wanna jinx it or nothing. And then when this all came down, I was glad I hadn't been bragging, 'cuz I couldn't risk my Angel. But I still didn't dare call her, in case he found out we'd been dating."

"You called me, though," I said.

"I couldn't take it no more. I was worried sick 'bout Laney," he said. "I had to make sure she was all right, and I was having a little trouble straightening out the money. I didn't know you'd be asking around about me, so I couldn't guess Black would tap your phone.

"Or that his goons would follow me to the restaurant."

"I was waiting at the Oaks, sort of out of sight, but I saw them follow you in and took off. One of them came after me, but I got away. I tried to call you . . . to warn you, but it was too late. I 'bout died when I saw them take you. I tried to stop them, but I couldn't get there fast enough."

"Uh-huh."

"I called the police," he said lamely, and gave Laney a sick look. She squeezed his hand. "But they got there a little late."

"You think?" I said, remembering the terror.

He gave me a lopsided grin. "I called the cops about Black, too. Anonymously. Said he had embezzled funds. I hoped they would put him away, but they couldn't prove nothing, and then he tried to pin it on me."

"So you've been hiding out all this time?" I asked.

"Stayin' at cheap motels near E.U. Couldn't use no credit

cards, 'cuz I was afraid Black would find a way to trace them. So I had to pay cash, and all the while tryin' to get everything straight—with Neo's money, with Franklin and Combot. He ain't gonna press charges. And . . ." He was still pale. "There's talk of givin' me Black's job."

"It's nice to know you didn't waste a lot of time worrying about me," I said.

He gave me a sheepish smile. "Truth is, I knew you could handle yourself, babe."

"Uh-huh," I said again, pushing back memories of tampons and garlic. "Well, next time I'd appreciate it if you'd leave me out of your shady deals."

He opened his mouth as if to object, then turned his gooey gaze on Elaine once more. "Everything's a little shady, I guess, 'cept Laney," he said, and gave her a moony stare. I squelched my gag reflex. "She's all sunshine."

I realized then that it was time for him to leave. I hadn't had a cigarette in two days and my nerves were a little frazzled.

Mom had called five times in as many hours. I'd let my answering machine take each one, and although she never explained her reason for contacting me, the tone of her voice was acidic enough to fry the poor machine's circuits. It was a safe bet that she'd heard about my not-so-sisterly advice to Holly.

"Well," I said, and stood up, "all's well that ends well."

"Yeah, hey." Solberg glanced up as if awakening from a dream. "You, me, and Laney should double it sometime."

"Double what?"

"Double date."

"Wouldn't that be more like a triple?" And creepy. I opened my front door.

He brayed like a zebroid. "You could get a date. I was thinking, I got a pal at NeoTech. Name's Bennet, Ross Bennet. You'd like him."

Oh, crap. I felt my stomach loop. I still had Bennet's checkbook. Tucked in between the deposit slips, I'd found a picture of a yacht. I had a bad feeling the account was nothing more scandalous than savings for some big-ass boat.

Since I now knew he hadn't murdered Solberg and didn't have any plans of decapitating me with his steak knives, I'd have to call him...later...or maybe I could somehow drop his checkbook into his car or something.

"No, thanks," I said.

"Come on, doll," Solberg said. "It'd be fun. Laney'd like that, wouldn't you, Angel?"

She looked at me. Her eyes were laughing. She pulled her hand out of his, wrapped her arms around my shoulders, and hugged me. "I love you, Mac," she said.

I teared up immediately. Probably allergies. "You're not bad yourself, Sugar."

She laughed, but when she pulled away, her eyes were misty, too.

"See, that's what I'm talking about," Solberg said, not understanding the joke but glancing from me to Elaine and back like an ugly puppy. "We'd have a smash together."

"It's time to go," Elaine said.

"But—" he began.

She linked her arm through his and drew him onto my cracked front walk.

"Oh, okay," he said, and followed along like a pull toy.

I closed the door and returned to my kitchen. It seemed

a little empty. Which, considering Solberg, could be a good thing. But considering the thugs who had recently tried to kill me, didn't seem so great. In fact—

I heard something in my vestibule and froze.

Footsteps tapped quietly across the linoleum. I reached for the drawer to my right and grabbed a butcher knife.

"McMullen."

I jumped like a tree frog.

Rivera was glaring at me from the doorway, making me droop with relief.

"Is there something fundamentally wrong with you?" he asked. He was wearing blue jeans gone gray with age and a plain brown jersey of the same vintage.

I drew a few careful breaths, just to prove I could. "What are you talking—"

"Why the hell don't you lock your door?" he asked, advancing steadily.

"Elaine just left," I said. I was going for bravado, but my voice might have cracked a little.

"So you're sure some crazy, knife-toting drug addict won't jump you for another half an hour? You think there's a time limit on these things?"

I tried to glare at him while simultaneously shifting a worried gaze to the door. No crazy, knife-toting drug addicts in sight. "What are you doing here?" I asked.

"Just visiting," he said, and reaching into my cupboard for a glass, poured himself some papaya juice. After tasting it, he made a face, glanced at the curdling beverage, and raised his gaze to mine. "What the hell are you doing with that spoon?"

I looked in the direction of my right hand. There was no butcher knife. But there was a good heavy mixing utensil.

I scowled at it, then at him. "I was thinking of baking a cake."

He made some sort of indefinable noise that might have indicated disbelief. "Hope you got some groceries since my last visit, then."

"I did."

"Uh-huh." He paced over to my pantry, bent over, and peered inside. His ass was as tight as a walnut. "What kind of woman doesn't keep flour in her house?"

"One that's too busy trying to stay alive when the local cops can't keep a girl safe in her own backyard."

He turned toward me with a smirk. "You been practicing that line?"

"No."

He raised his brows.

"Well . . . just for a little while."

His lips quirked up devilishly. He moved closer. "How's it going with you and Bennet?"

"I, ummm . . ." How was it that this Neanderthal always smelled so damned good? He should stink like wildebeest dung and rotting meat. "Fine," I said. "We're doing fine."

"Yeah? So you're seeing him again?"

I forced myself to shrug. "Sure. He's a nice guy," I said.

He tilted his head noncommittally. "He says you showed up at his house dressed sexy and acting weird."

I stiffened. Why the hell would a man tell another man that? Was nothing sacred? "I did not dress . . ." I paused, winced, changed course. "I did not act weird."

He half smiled. "I assured him that's normal for you."

"I think you got the wrong idea, Rivera. I was on my way home from . . . church and—"

"He thinks you stole his checkbook."

My mouth remained open. I cut my eyes toward the front door.

"Did you happen to steal his checkbook, Chrissy?"

"Why ever would I . . . ?" My voice sounded creaky, and stupid. I tried again. "Why would I steal his checkbook?"

He shrugged. "Beats the hell out of me why you do half the things you do. So you swear you didn't take it?"

My lips moved. Nothing came out.

"Maybe it accidentally fell into your purse."

I glared at him. "I didn't steal it. Exactly."

"What did you do . . . exactly?"

"Well, Solberg hadn't shown up and—"

"You thought Bennet murdered him. So you dropped in at his house in a sexy getup and pinched his wallet. Makes perfect sense to me."

I could only assume he was being facetious. "I had every intention of returning it."

"I'm sure you did."

"I did. I—"

"I'm not doubting you."

"I swear I didn't—" I began, then gave him a dubious glance. "You believe me?"

He shrugged. "You're not the villainous type, McMullen," he said, and setting his juice aside, settled his butt against my counter. Lucky damn counter.

"I'm not?"

"You're more the type to naïvely get involved with the villainous type." His eyes were all crinkly at the corners. I kind of have a thing for crinkly-cornered eyes. "Although, I have to admit, you have an outstanding ability to piss people off."

"I do not. I can be extremely diplomatic."

"Can you?"

"Yes."

"Like you were with Hilary Pershing?"

"How—" I stopped myself. "I don't know what you're talking about."

He chuckled. The sound did funny things to my insides. "She said she found some nutcase—her words, not mine—peering in her bedroom window."

"Really?"

"Said this alleged nutcase was trying to pass herself off as a police officer."

I refrained from telling him she had bought the lie—line, hook, and sinker.

"How odd."

"Agreed," he said. "Tiffany Georges is threatening to sue the city."

"Oh, crap!"

He laughed at me.

I don't like to be laughed at, and straightened my back. He watched me with a crooked half grin.

"Well," I said, "if the cops would keep a closer eye on things—"

"What then, Chrissy?" he asked. "There wouldn't be so many dreaded show cats in one house and folks burying things in their own backyards?"

I sharpened my glare and kept my mouth firmly shut.

"Everyone has a secret," he said. "You had a shitload of

them. That's why I've had someone watching you for a week or so."

"You were—"

"Todd thought you made him in the Toyota, so we had to keep switching vehicles."

"Was there an SUV?"

"There's always an SUV."

"So you were watching my office, too?"

"Todd knew something was up the minute Elaine was two minutes late from her lunch break. I think he might be hoping she'll bear his children. Anyway, soon as you locked up shop in the middle of the day, he had a hunch and called for backup."

"That's why the SWAT team showed up so fast," I said, but suddenly I heard a strange clicking sound in my vestibule. A moment later a monster came bounding through the doorway to my kitchen. It was the size of a small whale. I lifted the spoon in self-defense.

Rivera bent down and gathered the flop-eared beast into his arms. "There you are."

I lowered the spoon. Apparently the ogre wasn't hungry right now. "What is that thing?" I asked.

"What is it?" He straightened slightly, jeans stretched tight across his hips. Lucky jeans. "It's a dog. What'd you think it was?"

It's back was nearly level with my counter. It had ears like bicolored sails and a mouth big enough to swallow me whole. I'm not very large. "A cross between a bear and a sea cow?" I ventured.

"He's just a puppy."

"I'm sure you're wrong." I watched them frolic together. Rivera frolicking. Weird. And not alluring. Really.

"Guy in Eagle Rock found him trying to eat his olean-der," he said, glancing up. "That stuff's poisonous, you know. So don't plant any in your front yard. Stick with the cactus. It can survive anything. Even you." He tugged at the piebald ears. "I haven't had a puppy since Rockette was little."

Rockette—Rivera's dumb-ass excuse for leaving me high and dry not too many weeks earlier. "Uh-huh," I said cautiously. "What's that thing doing in my kitchen?"

"Poor guy was starving." He gave it a smart slap on its ribs. It wagged its tail and circled ecstatically. The damn thing looked like it was still starving.

"Why's it here?" I asked again.

He straightened. There was a spark of something diabolic in his eyes. "You left your door unlocked."

I shook my head. No comprehension.

"You habitually forget to man your security system."

"What—"

"Your windows aren't properly secured."

"That—"

"You don't have the sense of a butterfly."

"I do, too, have—"

"You need a dog."

My mouth fell open. I blinked at him and breathed a disbelieving laugh. "There are a lot of things I need," I said. "A manicure." I held up a hand as proof. "A new septic system. A smoothie maker. But I don't—"

"You need a dog."

"I do not need a dog."

The thing took off into my living room, loping like a delighted, wind-powered elephant.

"You don't have to arm it."

"I don't even like dogs," I said, temper rising.

He took a step toward me. "And I don't like worrying about you every damned second of the day."

"Well, you . . ." I drew a deep breath and gave in to thought. Some might have said it was about time. "You worry about me?"

He took another step forward. His eyes were fudge-brownie dark today. "You don't have the sense of a toy poodle."

I thought maybe I should be offended, but he was standing awfully close.

"You really worry about me?" I asked.

He took away the spoon, led me to the couch, and pulled me down beside him. The so-called dog took up most of the available space, forcing us to sit hip to hip. Rivera's was hard and lean and attached to other interesting parts. Maybe dogs weren't so bad after all.

"That's why I should stay the night," he said, "to keep you safe from all the knife-wielding crazies."

My jaw dropped. "What?"

He grinned and rubbed his thumb across the hollow of my palm. I didn't drool. "That didn't come out quite like rehearsed," he said. "But let's concentrate on the staying-the-night part. We were interrupted last time. I thought maybe I could make that up to you."

"Well, I just . . ." It was getting difficult to breathe. Men! They tend to do bad things to my equilibrium and my thinking apparatus. "I don't know if that would be—"

He pushed a strand of hair away from my face, grazing my cheek with his fingertips. I felt my brain go soft.

"I could sleep on the couch if you really want me to."

"Well, I don't know." I swallowed hard. "Did you bring your armor?"

"No armor. In fact, I think I may have forgotten my boxers," he said, and kissed me.

About the Author

LOIS GREIMAN lives in Minnesota, where she rides horses, embarrasses her teenage daughter, and forces her multiple personalities into indentured servitude by making them characters in her novels. Write to her at lgreiman@earthlink.net. One of her alter egos will probably write back.

Dear Reader,

I hope you enjoyed getting *Unplugged*, 'cuz next we're getting... **UNSCREWED**.

That's right, poor Chrissy still can't quite get her ducks in a row. In fact, just when things seem to be going swimmingly with Lieutenant Rivera, his sexy ex-girlfriend—who happens to be his estranged father's fiancée—is found dead next to Rivera's unconscious body.

Accusations fly, familial bonds are stretched, and there's no shortage of suspects. Maybe Rivera senior killed the poor girl, as the lieutenant himself is determined to prove. Maybe his hot-blooded Spanish mother had a hand in the act, or maybe Rivera himself did the deed in a fit of passion. But one thing's sure: Chrissy is determined to stay out of the mix... for about thirteen seconds.

Tequila with Rivera's mother, a date with his wealthy father, and steamy conversations with the lieutenant's ex-girlfriends teach Chrissy more than she ever wanted to know. But she can't seem to quit snooping, especially when Rivera threatens to tie her to her bedrail if she doesn't—and her curiosity may have deadly consequences.

So pick up a copy of **UNSCREWED** at your favorite bookstore, won't you? Oh, and get *Unzipped* while you're at it—if you missed Chrissy's first investigation, there's a special sneak peek on the following pages.

Enjoy!

Lois Greiman

Don't miss
Unscrewed
by Lois Greiman,
coming from Dell Books in Spring 2007

A sexy therapist.
A dead patient.
A case that's about to come . . .

*U*nzipped

Don't miss Christina McMullen's
first case, available now from Dell.

Read on for a special sneak peek—
and pick up your copy today at your
favorite bookseller.

A sexy therapist.
A dead patient.
A case that's about to come...
UNZIPPED
LOIS GREIMAN

Unzipped

Lois Greiman

Even choosing the perfect dinner wine loses its earth-shattering importance if your guests happen to be cannibals and you, the unsuspecting entrée.

—*Dr. Candon,*
psych professor

MA'AM. MS. McMULLEN."

I tried to concentrate. The police had arrived with head-spinning haste. Apparently someone had heard my scream and dialed 911. My own call had probably gone to a hang-glider in Tibet.

Everything seemed foggy and unfocused, except for the body lying immobile on my overpriced Berber. That was as clear as vodka. His eyes were open and vividly blue, his hands limp, his fingers slightly curled. He lay on his back, but his jacket had fallen across his crotch with blessed kindness. Still, my stomach threatened to reject both the yogurt and the dehydrated orange.

"Ms. McMullen."

"What?" I dragged my attention shakily away from Bomstad's blank-eyed stare and supported myself with a hand on the top of my desk. The oak grain felt coarse and solid beneath my fingers. But the world still seemed strangely off-kilter. Maybe it was because I was wearing only one shoe. Maybe not.

The man addressing me was dark. Dark hair, dark skin, dark eyes, dark clothes. "Are you Christina McMullen?"

"Yes. I'm . . . Yes." I sounded, I thought, about as bright as a Russian olive.

He stared at me for a good fifteen seconds, then, "I'm Lieutenant Rivera."

I said nothing. My gaze was being dragged mercilessly toward the floor again. Those sky-blue eyes, those large, open hands.

"I'd like to ask you a few questions."

"Uh-huh."

"You're a psychiatrist?"

I pulled my attention doggedly back to the lieutenant's face. It was devoid of expression, except possibly anger. A shade of distrust. Could be he looked cynical. Maybe devoid wasn't exactly the right word.

His brows were set low over coffee-colored eyes that matched the dark hue of his jacket, and his lips were drawn in a straight, hard line.

"Psychologist," I said. "I'm a . . ." My voice wavered a little on the vowels, making me sound like a prepubescent tuba player. "Psychologist."

He didn't seem to notice or care about the distinction. "This your office?"

"Yes."

"You work here alone?"

"Yes. No. I . . ." Three men were examining the body and muttering among themselves. A fat guy in a wrinkled dress shirt that was miraculously too large said something from the corner of his mouth and the other two laughed. My stomach heaved.

"Yes or no. Which is it?" asked the lieutenant. Patience didn't seem to be his virtue. Or empathy. Apparently, the fact that there was a dead guy staring at my ceiling didn't faze him much, but it wasn't doing a hell of a lot for my equilibrium.

"No. I usually have a . . . secretary." For a moment I completely forgot her name, but then she'd only been my best friend since fifth grade, when she'd kissed Richie Mailor and declared him to have lips like the spotted pictus our science teacher kept in his aquarium. "Elaine . . . Butterfield."

He was staring at me again. "Have you been drinking, Ms. McMullen?"

"I . . . No."

"There are two glasses."

"Ahhh . . ." My mind was wandering again. My focus crept in the direction of the corpse.

"Ms. McMullen."

"Mr. Bomstad brought wine," I said.

"How long have you two been lovers?"

My eyes snapped back to Dark Man. "What?"

"You and Bomstad," he said. His tone was as dry as Bond's martini. "How long have you been lovers?"

"We weren't lovers."

I can't actually say he raised his eyebrows. Maybe one. Just a notch.

"We weren't lovers," I repeated, more emphatically. "He attacked me."

"Do your customers always bring . . . refreshments to their sessions?"

I stared at him. I'd worked my damn ass off to become a high-class psychologist and I didn't like his tone. "I can't dictate what my clients do with their time," I said.

"It's your office. I would think you could."

So that's the way it was. My brother Pete and I used to have spitting contests. I had been declared the indisputable winner. But perhaps spitting wouldn't be appropriate here. Just a stare-down, then. "You can think anything you want, Lieutenant . . ."

"Rivera."

"We weren't lovers, Mr. Raver."

Something like a grin appeared on his face, or maybe he was just curling a lip as he sized up his prey. There was a shallow scar at the right corner of his mouth. Maybe that's why his expression looked more like a predatory snarl than a smile. The romance novelists would have called it sardonic. I didn't read romance anymore. Now I was studying Tolstoy and thinking deep thoughts. Mostly I was thinking of giving up reading.

"What was he doing here after hours with no one else in the office?" Rivera asked.

"Elaine had a yoga class."

"Did she?" he asked, and I wondered if he actually saw some significance in my blathering. "There a stain on your blouse, Ms. McMullen. Is it blood?"

"No." I had never had a stain that fascinated people to such an extraordinary extent. "What would you think—"

"What was he doing here?"

I felt breathless. As if I'd run a long way. I don't like to run a long way. I'd tried it on more than one occasion. Every Monday, Wednesday, and Friday, in fact, if you call three miles a long way. I do. "What?" I said, struggling with the fog that threatened to engulf the interior of my cranium.

"Lover boy." He nodded toward Bomstad's body. "Why was he here?"

"For therapy," I replied, "like all my clients."

Two more men and one woman had joined the mob by the corpse. One of the men squatted by the body, suit crumpled, pen and clipboard in hand.

"What were you seeing him for?"

The fellow with the clipboard reached for Bomstad with his pen.

I jerked my attention back to Dark Man and raised my chin. I was pretty sure I looked like Hester Prynne. A first-rate martyr, but I felt a little faint. "Impotence," I said.

"Hey." The suited fellow's voice was loud enough to wake the dead. Almost. "Looky here. He's got a woody."

Rivera's eyes burned. I could almost meet them. "Damn, you're good," he said and my knees buckled.

I woke up in my own bed. I didn't remember much about getting there. My head felt fuzzy and my stomach queasy. It took a minute for the memories to come rolling back into my brain. It was a dream. A bad dream, I told myself. But

I'm nothing if not a realist. Which was what had convinced me to become a therapist in the first place. After years of depraved dating it had become apparent that all men are psychopaths. Therefore half the population needs professional attention. It was bound to be a lucrative field, and easy.

How many times could I be wrong?

I shut my eyes, trying to block out the previous night, but a dead body with a hard-on pretty much etches itself into one's memory. A noise distracted me and I rolled over, listening. My doorbell rang, making me wonder foggily if that was what had awakened me in the first place.

Questions rolled around in my head like BBs in a walnut shell but I fought off my bedsheets and staggered toward the door. It took me a minute to realize I was still wearing one shoe. It was a Ferragamo and matched my skirt. My jacket and blouse, however, were gone. I stopped dead in the middle of the floor. The doorbell rang again, drawing my gaze up from my not quite willowy body.

"Who is it?" I asked.

"Police."

A dozen thoughts garbled through me. Not one could be voiced in polite company.

"Just a minute," I yelled and plucking off my shoe, staggered back to my bedroom for a shirt. But once there I merely gazed around in disjointed uncertainty. I'm tidy enough, but I don't like to be obsessive about it. I'd thrown my robe over the foot rail of my bed and left my horoscope beside it before galloping off to work on Thursday morning. I was an Aquarius and yesterday was predicted to be my lucky day.

I dragged on the robe. Classy, it was not. Nor did it exactly match my rumpled skirt or the irritably discarded shoe that still dangled from my fingertips.

The doorbell screamed at me. I plowed toward it and looked through the peephole. Lieutenant Rivera stood on my porch, looking grim.

I braced myself and opened the door. He shouldered his way in. He wasn't a huge man. Six foot maybe, only a few inches taller than myself, and not particularly broad, but every inch of him seemed to be devoid of fat. And this time I mean devoid.

He wore jeans that had seen some life and a charcoal-colored dress shirt. His hips were lean, his eyes steady, and his wrists dark and broad-boned where his sleeves were folded up from his workingman's hands.

"Do you let just anyone in?"

I think I blinked at him. "What?"

"Your door," he said. "Do you let everybody in who rings your bell?"

"I saw you through the peephole."

"You didn't even ask for my badge."

The man was certifiable. Another candidate for the loony bin. Business was brisk.

"You thought I might forget you overnight?" I asked.

The almost-grin appeared, but Rivera turned, glancing around my foyer. It was really nothing more than a narrow entryway, but I liked to call it a vestibule.

"Nice place."

Was he trying to be civil? I wondered numbly, and decided to take a chance. "Would you like some coffee?"

He turned back toward me as if just remembering my presence. "Did you prescribe the Viagra?"

"What?"

"Bomstad," he said. "He'd taken a large dose of Viagra before visiting you. Did you prescribe it?"

I felt as if I'd lost a water ski and was now skidding across the surface of a lake on my face. "No, I'm—"

"Did you know he had a heart condition?"

"I'm a psychologist. I can't prescribe drugs," I said, still working on the last question.

"Even for a heart condition?"

"Not for anything."

"Then you knew he had a weak heart."

"No. I . . . No."

"So you didn't see any harm in trying to seduce him."

I took a deep breath and counted to five. "I didn't try to seduce anybody," I said.

His gaze drifted down from my face. Mine followed, then I snapped the wayward robe together over the top of my bra. It was black and frayed and had cost me less than twelve dollars brand-new. Why spend $49.99 on a garment no one would ever see?

Rivera's lips lifted.

"Why are you here?" I asked. My voice sounded angry. I hope. Maybe it was just a little bit breathless.

"I wanted to make sure you were all right. You seemed disoriented last night when I brought you home."

"You brought—" The truth dawned a little slowly, but I was running on four hours of sleep and visions of a corpse with a woody. "What did you do with my blouse?"

"I was just trying to get you comfortable."

I stared at him, then lifted my right hand. The single

shoe dangled between us like rotten fruit. "You left the shoe but took the blouse?"

He shrugged and walked into my kitchen. It wasn't a whole lot bigger than my vestibule. "Turns out it was a fruit stain. Cherry," he said.

"You tested the stain?"

He shrugged again. His movements were Spartan, as if each one was calculated. His gaze traveled back to mine. "How long had you and Mr. Bomstad been seeing each other?"

"I told you . . ." His attention made me fidgety. I hated being fidgety. Fidgety is not classy. "I wasn't *seeing* him."

A brow flickered. "I meant professionally."

"Oh. Yes." I cleared my throat. "Three months. Maybe four."

"And during that time how often did you have intercourse with him?"

He had taken a notebook from somewhere and flipped it open. I stared in disbelief. "I told you before, we didn't have intercourse."

"No. You told me before that you weren't lovers."

I opened my mouth, then shut it.

"You were going to say something?"

It's not as though I have a temper, but sometimes, when I'm tired, it's best not to push me. Or when I'm hungry. I can get cranky when I'm hungry. And there are certain times of the month when I'm just better off left alone. "We weren't lovers," I said, keeping my tone admirably even. I *was* tired and hungry, but at least I wasn't menstruating. "Neither . . ."—I pronounced it with an elegant hard *i* sound and felt better for it.—". . . did we have intercourse."

"Oh." He said it casually, as if it didn't matter. I ground my teeth and reconsidered the spitting contest.

"Were you aware of his activities?"

"Activities?" I said.

He shrugged. "What he did. Who he was."

"He was a tight end for the Lions," I said. "If that's what you're referring to."

"Did you know he was a Peeping Tom?"

"What?" The air had been squashed out of my lungs again.

"And an exhibitionist?"

"Andrew?"

"Do you address all your customers by their first names?"

"A Peeping Tom?"

"Howard Lepinski said you called *him* 'Mr. Lepinski.' "

"You talked to Mr. Lepinski?"

"I guess that answers my question."

"What the hell were you doing talking to my clients?" I asked, taking an involuntary step toward him. He didn't exactly cower away. In fact, his lips twitched again. I couldn't help but wonder what kind of an imprint a Ferragamo would make on his damned sardonic expression.

"Did you know he was a flasher?"

"Lepinski?" The shoe dropped in my fingers.

"Bomstad."

"Are you shittin' me?"

His brows did rise that time. I squeezed the edges of my robe together and remembered my professional image. "You must be mistaken," I said and lifted my chin in a haughty expression of pride. Start the bonfires, the martyr was back.

"I'm not mistaken," he said. "And neither..."—He pronounced it with a hard, elongated *i* sound.—"...am I shittin' you."

I wandered into my living room and plopped down in my La-Z-Boy. It had once belonged to a man named Ron. Ron was long gone. The chair remained. Yet another way furniture is superior to men. "Bomstad?" I asked, and glanced up at Rivera. His eyes were deep set, like a sculpture's, and his hair was too long to be stylish. It curled around his ears in dark waves. "Andrew Bomstad?"

"The Bomber," he answered. "You're not the first woman he's charmed the pants off of."

"He didn't—"

"Then why did you send him the wine?"

I just stared this time, numb as a cherry pit.

"The Spumante," he said, and stared back at me. "Did you send it to him?"

I shook my head.

"Did you know he had a girlfriend?"

I nodded.

"That bother you?"

"I told you—"

"There were others, too. He liked them young, mostly. Teenagers. You're not his usual type."

"I didn't—"

"Not that I'm faulting his choice, but how did he happen to hear about you?"

"I'm telling you—"

"I mean, I would think a guy like Andy the Bomber Bomstad might find a psychiatrist with more...notoriety. But then, I guess he didn't pick you for your diploma. And maybe you didn't know much about his background. His handler was top-notch at keeping his indiscretions out of the papers. But you're going to have to come clean now. I'll keep it quiet. Make sure it doesn't affect your business. How long had you been sleeping with Bomstad?"

"I was not—"

"A month? Couple weeks?"

"Listen!" I growled and, shooting out of the "boy," stepped up close enough so I had to lift my chin to glare into his face. "I didn't sleep with him. I never slept with him. I haven't slept with anyone for ye—"

He was standing absolutely still, staring down at me, an expression of near surprise on his face.

Lucidity settled in at a leisurely pace. I took a deep breath and backed off a step.

"I didn't have intercourse with Mr. Bomstad," I said.

If he so much as twitched I was going to spit in his eye.

"Ever?"

"Never."

"Oh." He nodded agreeably. "You have a boyfriend?"

"Not at the present time."

He snapped his notebook shut and headed for the door, where he turned. "Years of celibacy," he mused. "It's bound to make a woman short-tempered."

I considered throwing my shoe at him, but I'm a professional. And he was damned quick in the face of a loaded Ferragamo.